DEATH BY CURIOSITY

By Lisa Matthews

To Liam, for reading and re-reading Armitage's story, for keeping me well-stocked in gin and sherry, and for everything you do.

To Mam & Dad, for all their help and support over the years, and for accepting Armitage as their "third daughter".

And to Billy, Penny and Edie, for being the best niblings a girl could ask for.

ONE.

Alright.

Probably a controversial opinion, but I'm going to say it anyway.

Elodia Knight was interesting as hell, and anyone who says otherwise needs to check their definition of the word 'excitement'.

Before you start thinking that I'm some lunatic who actively supports psychopaths and thinks that murder should be a socially acceptable hobby, let me just take you through it.

A couple of weeks before this all kicked off, some sweet old man had been walking his dog through Habely Woods when he stumbled across a lad's body. I'm sure that would've been disturbing by itself, but this – if the papers were to be believed – was not a normal body. No, this guy had been killed in one hell of a brutal way; the papers hadn't gone into too much detail, but what they *had* said was that he'd been found naked and posed in a strange position, with strange symbols carved into his body, a 'significant injury' to his left arm, and his throat slit from ear to ear. Which, in fairness, is weird enough, but what I couldn't get my head around was the fact that this happened in Habely.

Habely.

I live in Habely with my best friend, Angie Fallows, and I have to be honest, it is far from the most exciting place on earth.

Pretty? Yes.

Interesting? No.

It's about ten miles outside of Exleigh – a decent-sized town roughly halfway between Newcastle and York – and while I like it, particularly the number of cocktail bars it has, it's the kind of place where it makes front page news when Myrtle loses her glasses, or George makes it through a whole day without shitting himself, or Rosemary's cat runs away again. (Spoiler alert: Jingles is *not* Rosemary's cat. In fact, the only reason he keeps staging the feline version of *The Great Escape* is because he's trying to get back to his family.) So the fact that any murder at all, let alone such a bizarre one, could happen there blew my mind a little bit.

But it obviously worked for Knight, because exactly one week later, a couple of dogwalkers – luckily not the same old man this time, that probably would've finished him off – found another body in the exact same part of Habely Woods.

Another guy. He was eighteen-years-old, just like the last one, and he'd been on a night out with his friends when he left whichever club by himself and was never seen alive again, also just like that last one.

He was posed in the same position.

He had the same symbols carved into him.

Same significant injury to his arm.

Same cut to his throat.

And then a week after that, *boom!* Another body. Exactly the same again.

Except this time, the Police found it during one of their nightly stakeouts. And they didn't just find the body; no, no, they found the person *dumping* the body while he was actually doing it. And when they dragged this lad – this James Pettyfer – into Custody, he broke down and told them that he didn't have any memory of dealing with the bodies, and that he'd been made to do it by – you guessed it – Elodia Knight.

That's not even all he said, though.

No, the guy decided to go completely off the rails and tell the Bobbies that Knight was a witch and that she'd got him to do whatever she wanted him to by putting him under this spell, so that he had no control over what he did.

Which... yeah. It's ridiculous. Why he thought that anyone would believe that when witches are clearly not real, I'm not sure; the only thing I could think was that he was being clever and laying the groundwork for pleading insanity.

But here's the thing – he gave such a detailed description of Knight (small, skinny and in her mid-late twenties with long hair that'd been dyed black, heavy-lidded eyes, pale skin and a pentacle tattooed inside her left wrist) that the cops managed to spot her a couple of days later, when they pulled her over for some traffic offense or another while she was trying to get out of Cattringham County.

So.

Yeah.

Given that it was much more interesting than the saga of Rosemary and Jingles, and considering the fact that I'm basically 10% human and 90% nosiness, my curiosity was more than a little bit piqued.

Hence the fact that, when Angie blearily stumbled out of her bedroom in our flat that Monday morning, I was already up and sat on the settee, reading the morning paper and absent-mindedly stroking my Black Labrador, Squidge.

'Morning!' I said cheerfully, beaming at her over the back of the couch as she stopped dead in her bedroom doorway and stared at me in a mixture of grogginess and astonishment. 'How'd you sleep?'

She squinted against the light from the lamp that I had on. 'What're you doing up so early?'

'Reading.' In her defence, it was barely six o'clock. And morning coffee really is a brilliant thing. 'I was bored,' I explained patiently, when she continued to stare at me with a vaguely perplexed look on her face. 'So I thought I'd walk Squidge to the shop for a paper. D'you want some toast?'

She narrowed her eyes at me, looking less perplexed and more suspicious as she moved over to the settee and rested her hands on the back of it. 'You were bored?'

'I was.'

'While you were asleep?'

Admittedly not the most believable of stories for someone who'd happily live the life of a cat and sleep for sixteen hours of the day.

'Sure.'

'And because you bored yourself awake, you actually decided to get up early and leave the flat, rather than glomming yourself to your phone and waiting for me to drag you out of bed?'

'Honestly, Angie, I'm as surprised as you are.'

She pressed her lips tight together for a couple of seconds, looking for all the world like she already knew the answer to her next question, but she was going to ask it anyway just in case. 'Is there any chance at all that you didn't make yourself get up early so that you could catch up on what's happening with Elodia Knight?'

'It's possible,' I told her defensively, 'that I wanted to see if anything's changed. And it has, if you're interested. They let her go without bail on Friday.'

She stared at me for a couple of seconds, looking mildly bewildered. '*Without* bail? Are you sure?'

'Well, having only been able to read since I was four, I can't say for certain. But yeah, I'll take an educated guess that that's what it says.'

She shot me an unamused look before leaning over the back of the settee, trying to read the article for herself. 'That doesn't make any *sense*. She's a complete psychopath, they've got all but solid proof that she's behind all this – why the hell would they let her go without bail?'

While I'm fairly confident that anyone over the age of twelve knows that murder suspects generally don't tend to get released without bail, working as Typists for Cattringham County's finest had taught us exactly how odd that is. In the three years that I'd spent typing up Police interviews, I'd come across:

- A Fairfield woman accused of harassing her neighbour by pulling the heads off their prized flowers at every opportunity (a case that *truly* demonstrated First World Problems and resulted in the woman being bailed);

- A lad who'd been clever enough to do a drugs deal in plain view of two uniformed Bobbies, because apparently it hadn't occurred to him that that might not be the best of ideas (bailed, and for some reason not charged with being a complete moron); and

- A guy from our very own Habely who really believed that he had mutual feelings of "properly romantic love" with his father's horse (bailed, with what I'm hoping was at least a half-serious recommendation to see a psychiatrist).

I hadn't managed to come across any serial killers yet, let alone ones who got *bailed*.

'We could,' I suggested lightly, 'ask Johnny.'

'We are not asking Johnny.'

Johnny Wallace was the Detective Constable based in East District CID that Angie had met on a dating site three months earlier and been seeing ever since. I'd known him in passing since I'd started working at East District eight years earlier, when I was working in East District Admin and he'd been in Response, but it was only once he got with Angie that you could really call us friends. He was mild-mannered and easy-going, and it was ridiculously easy to get on with him – not just because he'd quite happily keep us updated on whichever case he was working on, but also because the man was basically the personification of *nice*.

'Well, then,' I told Angie sweetly, flashing her a bright smile. 'If you still want me give you a lift to work, you're going to have to get a move on, m'dear. I want to make sure I get Knight's interview tape before anyone else even gets a look in.'

In a record speed of forty minutes later, I was collapsing in my desk chair in the Typing Pool office, breathless and excited as I shoved Knight's interview into my computer's disc drive.

It'd been a close call to beat Pamela (my main competition for the title of World's Nosiest Typst) into the office, and I'd only managed it by the skin of my teeth; her car had screeched into the car park not even thirty seconds after mine did, and if I hadn't been able to outsprint her (or trip her up at the office door), then I'd have had no chance of getting the tape, and poor Johnny would've had a bruised ear from how often I was bending it.

From the way the newspapers had been screaming about Knight being a real actual witch with real actual magic in her, part of me had expected the video of her interview to be something spectacular.

As it turned out, there wasn't going to be *time* for it to be spectacular; when the interview tape opened up on my screen, the tape player only showed the whole thing to be five minutes long from beginning to end.

Five minutes.

For someone suspected of *murder*.

The lass responsible for the Fairfield Flower Massacre was interviewed for almost four times longer than that.

I pressed down on the foot pedal under my desk, making the footage of the interview start to play on my screen. A tiny version of Knight was sat at an equally miniscule table, with her back resting against the wall and her legs stretched out across the chair next to her as she stared straight ahead at the other side of the room, instead of looking at the two miniature Bobbies sitting on the other side of the table.

'I am not answering any of your questions.'

Here's what gave me the heebie-jeebies.

The lass had been arrested for murdering three people, and she didn't seem phased by it in the slightest.

Pettyfer had *handed* her the cast-iron get-out card of 'he said I'm a *witch*? Well, clearly, the poor guy's insane, we should be getting him some help instead of wasting time in here', and she didn't seem like she had any intention of using it.

She sounded more like she was having a catch-up with friends instead of being interviewed by the Police, and her whole demeanour was far too standoffish for her to not have done what Pettyfer had accused her of.

'We'll get to that,' the hairier of the tiny officers told her brusquely, too busy shuffling through the papers in front of him to look at her. 'Right, Elodia. Those beeps that you just heard mean that the interview is now being recorded –'

'I am not answering any of your questions.'

'Time by my watch is ten past nine –'

'I am not answering any of your questions.'

'– on the evening of Friday the sixteenth of September.'

'I am not answering any of your questions.'

'We haven't asked you any questions yet, Elodia,' he pointed out, sounding much less irritated than I would've been. 'We're just going through the introductions for now. I'm DC Eric Pace of East District CID, and –'

'I am not answering any of your questions.'

'And this is –'

'DC Keith Lyme,' the second, chubbier officer said in a monotone voice, 'also of East District CID.'

'I am not answering any of your questions.'

'Well, that's your choice,' Pace all but snapped, finally putting his papers down on the table and looking up at her. 'But we still have to go through this.'

He'd barely finished speaking when something bizarre happened to her face.

Pace and Lyme didn't seem to see it – or if they did, they didn't react to it – and I had no idea how it happened, but suddenly all of the bones in her face were jutting out from under her skin; even with her head being the size of an M&M on my screen, I could see her cheekbones, her eye sockets, and her jaw far too clearly.

I jerked my foot off the pedal and blinked in surprise a few times, wondering if my computer had just had a major glitch or if my early start to the day was making me hallucinate. (Really, anything before seven o'clock is just unnecessary.) I quickly rewound the footage a couple of times to check, but nope. Every time the timer hit twenty-three seconds, there it was.

Normal face.

Skeleton face.

Normal face.

Skeleton face.

This girl was more of a freak than I'd anticipated.

'I am not answering any of your questions,' she said again, her voice even calmer and more gentle than it had been so far, 'because you will not *ask* me any questions. Do you understand?'

'You don't get a say in that,' Pace said sharply. 'We need to find out what happened to these lads, and in order to do that, we have to ask you about what's gone on. Now, I'm not sure if you've grasped how serious your situation is, but –'

'I understand exactly how serious my situation is, Mr Pace,' she murmured, tracing strange-looking shapes onto the table with her left hand. 'Eric Michael Pace. Named for your father,' she added, abruptly looking up from the table and staring at him. 'And you loved your father so much, but he didn't care about you, did he? Didn't want a son like you, who only wanted to be with him. Didn't care that your mother couldn't cope. And he left you with her, didn't he? He left because baby Eric was *so naughty*. He had to go into the cupboard, like all the other naughty babies who cry too much. And he was left there, wasn't he, while his mother went to the pub for as long as she liked. All alone in the dark, crying and crying with no-one to hear him… *poor* baby Eric. Is that why you joined the Police, poor baby Eric? To help the other naughty babies?'

I hadn't even typed anything at this point.

I was just sat there, staring at the screen with my mouth hanging open and my face tingling from the WTF-ness of the whole thing.

Even if that stuff was remotely true – and going by how Pace was just looking at her, instead of telling her to shut up or putting her back in her cell, I was going to say that it *was* – how did she know that? How could she *possibly* know what'd happened to him all those years ago? What, had he gone into her cell before the interview and said, 'I'm Eric Michael Pace and I'll be your interviewer today. By the way, I was abandoned by my father and neglected by my mother as a kid, maybe you could mention that while we're talking about all the people you've killed'?

'Eric,' Lyme murmured after a few seconds of tense silence, giving him a little shake by his shoulder. He waved his hand in front of Pace's face a couple of times before obviously realising that he wasn't going to get a reaction, at which point he turned back to Knight and said shortly, 'Right, Elodia, we're going to take a short break. When we come back –'

'And you,' Knight interrupted, still using that calm, patient voice that properly creeped me out, slowly turning her head to look at him. 'Keith Lyme. Poor Keith. His parents never had much time for him, did they? They always thought he should be *stronger*, ready to grow up into a big, strong man. He was *such* a disappointment to them, wasn't he? They couldn't love him when they realised they'd raised a wimp. All of the children at school could see it too, couldn't they? They used to call him names and hit poor Keithy. You didn't like that, did you? But you can show them now. You're a big, strong man now, aren't you? That's why you joined the Police. Tell me, Keithy, how many of your old bullies have you arrested so far? What've you done to your parents since you became a big, *strong* man?'

Seriously. What the hell was going on?

Had I somehow crossed over into a parallel universe where this was *normal* for Police interviews?

'Now that I have your attention,' Knight murmured, swinging her legs down off the chair and leaning across the table, 'you will listen to me. You will terminate this interview.'

'We will.' They said it at the exact same time, and they said it in the exact same tone of voice that Knight had been talking in all the way through.

'You will release me from Custody.'

'We will.'

'You will let me go without any bail conditions.'

'We will.'

'You will make sure that I am not re-arrested over this nonsense.'

'We will.'

'Excellent,' she said briskly, getting out from behind the table and standing in the middle of the room, hands on her hips. 'Well then, Mr Pace, kindly let the Desk Sergeant know that I'm leaving. And I think, Mr Lyme, that you can escort me out. After all,' she added, as Pace practically threw himself out of the room and Lyme scurried to her side, 'we are done here, aren't we?'

And just like that, the tape cut out. Literally, the second she said it, the recording stopped dead, leaving them all frozen in their tiny places.

I felt my head jerked back in surprise as I did some rapid blinking, wondering how the frick that'd happened.

In every other interview I'd typed up, the Bobbies had to press one of the buttons on the recording machine to stop the interview – but not one single person in that room was stood anywhere *near* the machine. And it's not as if Cattringham County Police have voice technology in the interview rooms; we're not a rich enough Force to afford that kind of equipment, and even if we *were*, installing it would mean we'd get however many three-second-long interviews for one crime, all ending with the person being interviewed randomly yelling 'STOP THE INTERVIEW!' (Also, I'm not sure whether that technology actually exists yet. But by-the-by.)

Not, of course, that the way the tape stopped was the only baffling thing about that interview; I had no idea what she'd done to Pace and Lyme to make them act like that. Mind you, at least it explained how she'd managed to get released without bail.

I felt that impatient, tugging sensation in my tummy that I always get when I'm feeling particularly nosey, and I squinted at the screen for a few seconds, chewing so hard on my bottom lip that it's only by some miracle that I didn't bite it off.

This whole Knight situation was even more intriguing than I'd first thought.

And unfortunately for Angie, it looked like I was going to have to ask Johnny more questions after all.

I spent the rest of the day thinking about it.

Most of the things I tend to get intrigued by are quite easy to get to the bottom of; they're things like whether one of my friends had decided that shoplifting is an acceptable hobby (they had), or why there were squeaking noises coming from Angie's bedroom the last time she was out for the night. (Spoiler alert: Angie wasn't out for the night. And by sheer, horrifying coincidence, neither was Johnny.) They're things that you can easily figure out by asking the right questions, or by inviting yourself along on their next shopping trip, or by walking into your flatmate's room at the *worst possible time* and seeing things that can never be unseen, no matter how hard you try or how much sherry you drink.

Finding out how a murderous pseudo-witch was putting people into trances and making them do whatever she wanted them to? That was going to be slightly trickier.

At seven o'clock that night, I was curled up in the same spot on the settee that I'd settled into two hours earlier, staring blankly at the TV as I nibbled on my thumbpad and tried to work out where I was going to start digging. I was so lost in my own thoughts about the whole thing that I didn't even notice Angie wasn't sat on the settee with me anymore until she came out of her bedroom, wearing a white turtleneck jumper tucked into a blue plaid skirt, and walked past me on her way over to the wall-length mirror that we'd stuck up in our living room, just to the left of the TV.

'You look nice,' I told her idly, pulling my teeth out of my thumb as I watched her switch on the fairy lights draped around the mirror. 'Are you seeing Johnny tonight?'

'Yeah,' she said, turning sideways on in the mirror and frowning at her reflection. 'We're just having a couple of drinks at Sherlock's. What're you doing tonight?'

'Not a lot,' I said, frowning slightly as I turned off the TV. 'I wouldn't mind having another look at that interview with Knight, but the building will be locked up by now and I have a feeling that breaking into it might be frowned upon.' I shot her the most innocent look I could manage in the mirror. 'It's times like this that knowing one of the building security guards would come in handy, isn't it?'

She rolled her eyes and her face twisted into a little grimace as she pulled her hair back into a bun far neater than anything I could ever do with my hair. 'I'm not getting my brother to let you into the building.'

Ah, well.

Worth a shot.

'Well,' she carried on after a couple of seconds, as if the conversation had never turned in Knight's direction, 'if you have no plans, why don't you come with us? You won't be a third wheel, one of Johnny's mates is coming too.'

Mmm. I bet they bloody were.

I narrowed my eyes at her, feeling a little pang of frustration in my stomach. 'Any chance at all that this mate is someone other than Hadaway?'

She hesitated, ducking her head down to avoid looking at me, and this time it was my turn to do they eye-roll.

'For God's sake, *Angie.*'

'*What?*' she asked defensively, turning to face me with her face the faint pink that it tends to go whenever she's feeling a bit hot under the collar. 'There's clearly something between you, Tidge! Is it really so bad if I'm trying to help the pair of you realise it?'

I rolled my eyes for a second time and let my head fall against the back of the settee.

Not that there was any point in the *slightest* in arguing with her, but let's just let the record show that there was nothing at all between me and Aidan Hadaway.

Hadaway was Johnny's best mate, who also worked as a DC in East District CID. I'm not going to say that he was the worst person in the world, because in all honesty, he was perfectly tolerable; we just seemed to have developed this habit of rubbing each other up the wrong way if we spent more than ten minutes together.

I don't know what it was. He had the driest sense of humour I'd ever known, and given that I adore that kind of craic, you'd think that we'd be able to have a good laugh – but no. I think part of it for him was that he'd known me when I was the twenty-three year old kid who used to loiter around the CID office, trying to find out about the latest cases. I also think he finds me so nosey that he didn't want to talk to me any more than he really had to; bearing in mind he'd never cut me off or abruptly changed the topic while I was mid-sentence, I could be way off base, but it was an impression that I just couldn't shake. And for my part, I was hardly a massive fan of how serious he was whenever he was around me, and...

Well. I dunno. But the guy was an undeniable manwhore, and for reasons that I couldn't quite put my finger on, it just *needled* me.

Of course, it could also have been because we were both so frustrated at Angie and Johnny's constant attempts to set us up that we took it out on each other.

Who knew.

'I don't know if Hadaway actually is coming,' Angie told me as she went to get her boots from next to the door, and I could tell from her voice that she was telling the truth. 'It's all been left a bit up in the air. But he's working on the case too, you know.'

I blinked at her. 'Is he?'

I shouldn't have been surprised, really. It seemed like me, Angie and Johnny were the only ones in the Force who could say the man's name without following it up with a comment about how good he was at his job.

'Yeah,' she said, wedging one of her feet into her shoe. 'So if you really want to know what's going on, it'd be nice if you could ask someone other than Johnny for a change.'

I thought about that for a couple of seconds.

Hadaway wasn't really likely to tell me anything about Knight; he's firmly of the opinion that Police staff don't need to know the ins and outs of cases, which contrasts quite nicely with my own personal views. But he'd had a birthday since I'd last seen him, and who was to say that he wasn't going soft as he got older?

'Well,' I said as casually as I could, swinging my legs down off the settee, 'there's no harm in coming by to hi, is there?'

Johnny and Hadaway were already there when we walked into Sherlock's half an hour later. They were sat at our usual table, Johnny leaning forward with his elbows on the table and Hadaway slumped back in his seat, and for half a second, I wished I'd got myself as dolled up as Angie instead of just swapping my pyjama bottoms for jeans.

The thing about Hadaway is, for all he irritates me, he is – objectively – fit as fuck.

Like, I wouldn't say that Johnny is a bad looking bloke; he's six foot tall with short, dark blond hair, blue eyes, and a nose that's been crooked every since someone he was arresting landed their fist in it. Perfectly decent-looking in his own right, but next to Hadaway…

Well.

In the nicest way possible, there's no contest.

He's got three inches on Johnny, with grey eyes and dark brown hair that he keeps short enough that it's neat but long enough that it just barely scrapes the top of the collar when he wears a proper shirt. His nose is perfectly straight, he's got the type of jaw that you can only describe as 'chiselled', and his shoulders are – I mean, his shoulders are just...

Alright.

In the spirit of full disclosure, I may have had some dreams about those shoulders.

But not a *word* of that will ever be breathed to Angie.

They both looked fairly grim as we walked over to them, nursing half-drank pints and so deep in conversation that they didn't even see us coming until we stopped on the other side of the table.

'You're here,' Johnny said cheerfully, because who doesn't enjoy a good ol' statement of the obvious? He grinned at us as he stood up, wrapping one arm around Angie's shoulders and dropping a kiss on her. 'We best get you some drinks. Prosecco and a triple sherry?'

They toddled off to the bar without waiting for me to answer – not that it matter, I'd hardly have asked for anything else – and I shot my blandest smile at Hadaway, raising my eyebrows as I dropped into the seat opposite him.

'Now then.'

'Now then,' he said back, shooting me a tight smile and taking a swig of his pint. 'How's it going?'

'Fine,' I told him blithely. 'Nothing much to report, really.' And then, even though I knew – I *knew* – that I should stick to the small talk, because small talk was where me and Hadaway were safe, I heard myself saying slightly too casually, 'So, Angie told me that you've been put on this Knight case. What's happening there?'

His eyebrows immediately snapped into a vaguely pissed off, vaguely frustrated frown as he opened his mouth to say something, but before he could get the words out, I heard Angie say from behind me,

'You did not just ask him that.'

'I did,' I said lightly, twisting around in my seat to look at her. She was standing behind me, holding our drinks and looking mildly appalled. 'And don't you go pretending to be surprised, Angie. You're the one who *told* me to ask him.'

'I did not *tell* you to ask him! I didn't,' she added indignantly to Hadaway as she sat down next to me, slamming my glass down in front of me so hard that some of the sherry sloshed over the rim. 'I told her not to ask Johnny.'

He ignored her and carried on looking at me, with his eyes hard and his jaw slightly more tense than it had been a second earlier. 'Why are you asking?'

'*Everyone's* asking about Knight,' I pointed out, looking from one grim face to the other. Even Johnny was looking slightly more tense, and he couldn't have heard the whole conversation; he was only just easing himself back into the seat next to Hadaway. 'When was the last time we had a murderer running around, pretending that she's a witch? What?' I added eagerly, when Hadaway and Johnny exchanged grimaces. 'Do you know how she's doing it?'

'She's not a witch,' Hadaway said bluntly. 'That's all you need to know.'

'Well, it's not,' I said, feeling the first tingles of frustration as I frowned back at him. 'I'm not allowed to ask Johnny.'

'You're not asking me, either.'

We looked at each other for a couple of seconds, Hadaway looking just as irritated as I felt. For God's sake, did he really have to be so rigid? Could he not just answer *one* little question?

'I typed up the interview today,' I told Johnny, barely even noticing that I'd cut across the conversation he was having with Angie. 'That was interesting. What'd she *do* to them?'

'Fuck's *sake.*'

'We're still trying to work it out,' Johnny said heavily, as we both pretended that Hadaway hadn't said anything. 'Eric went on the sick as soon as they came out of that interview room, and he's not felt up to seeing anyone yet. And Lymey...' He warily flicked his eyes around the pub and lowered his voice, so that we had to lean forward to hear him. 'We're not shouting about it, but we don't know where he is. He never came back from taking Knight out of the station, and his family hasn't seen him since he left for work that morning.'

I felt something icy-cold wash over me, and half a glance at Angie told me that she was just as shocked.

'So, hang on,' she murmured, leaning even closer to him with her eyes wide. 'D'you think he's still *with* her?'

'That's how it's looking,' he nodded grimly, taking a gulp of beer. 'We're doing everything we can to find him, but it's slow-going. There's no trace of him anywhere.'

I opened my mouth to ask him if Pettyfer could shed any light on what she might've done to them, but before I could start talking, Hadaway was slamming his pint glass down on the table and saying harshly,

'Jesus, Armitage, give it a rest. You've asked your bloody question, that's enough.'

'It's not enough,' I shot back coldly, glaring at him. 'This is the weirdest case anyone's ever seen, Hadaway, d'you really think I'm the only one who's asking questions about it? Are you just going to tell everyone to shut up?'

'You're not the same as everyone else,' he bit off, and despite how wound up I felt, despite the fact that I knew he meant it as anything but a compliment, I felt something warm shoot through me. 'Anyone else'll ask their question and move on, you just keep fucking going.' He downed the rest of his pint – the whole quarter quarter of it – in one go and stood up, grabbing his coat off the back of his chair. 'Look, I'm not telling you again. This is nothing to do with you, stay the fuck out of it.'

He strode around his chair and crossed the pub without a single look back at us, apparently oblivious to the appreciative looks he was getting from the group of lasses sat a few tables away from us. He disappeared through the door to the car park with his back ramrod straight, we all stared after him in a kind of baited silence, almost like we were expecting him to come back in.

But he didn't.

Of course he didn't.

Say what you want about him, but Hadaway's hardly the type who does things solely for the dramatic value.

I turned back to Angie and Johnny, one eyebrow raised. 'Well, that's a new record.'

'He's knackered,' Johnny told me warily, his eyes still on the door. 'He's worked three fourteen-hour shifts on the bounce. He would've pulled another one tonight if I hadn't stopped him.'

'Why?'

'You know what he's like,' he said dryly, taking another swig of his beer. 'He doesn't know when to stop at the best of times, let alone when we've got a case like this on our hands. It hardly helps that we've got so much pressure coming from the top.'

'You didn't tell me that,' Angie said, shooting him a curious look. 'What're they after?'

'They want it all sorted as quick as possible,' he shrugged, leaning back in his chair. 'It'll be affecting their figures, won't it?'

'You'd think they'd want the job that's actually the best, not just the one that makes them look the best.'

He shrugged, apparently unphased by it. 'They do. But these are people who haven't been on the frontline in years, Angie; their priorities are different to ours.'

'So,' I said lightly, as Angie sat there, looking conflicted. (Roughly ninety percent of Angie's family have been in the Police; it's just in her nature to defend every part of it.) 'Do you have any idea where Knight is now?'

'No,' he said heavily, with a grim look at me. 'We don't. Every obvious lead we had has been exhausted, and it's hard going to find new ones. She's got no family. No friends. Anything we find out just seems to lead to a dead end.'

We both eyeballed him for a few seconds, taking that in.

From what he was saying, Knight and Lyme had just disappeared into thin air.

And I'm sure that was all part of Knight's plan. I'm sure she *wanted* people to think she could just vanish, like any witch worth her salt could.

But Knight wasn't a witch. And witches weren't real. So they had to be *somewhere,* and there had to some*thing* that led to that somewhere; it was just a case of getting that *one* piece of information that would help to work it out.

I leaned back in my chair, taking a gulp of sherry as I played her interview through my head again. Johnny had said that Pace didn't want to talk to anyone about what Knight had done to him. But what if it was the *thought* of talking about it that was getting to him? Or what if he didn't want to talk to other cops about something he thought made him look weak?

I guess what I'm getting at is, no-one knew how he'd react if a couple of civvies popped up, unannounced, and started asking about what'd happened in that interview room.

And as far as I could see, there was only one way to find out how that'd go down.

TWO

Working for the Police does happen to have its perks.

Don't get me wrong, the pay could be better. And I'd never say no to the discounts and bonuses that people working in the private sector tend to get. And if our bosses could start paying for everyone's drinks at the Christmas party on their company credit card, that would be *amazing*.

But we do have other perks.

Like, for example, the opportunity to *accidentally* stumble into the wrong system and *accidentally* search for someone until you *accidentally* find out where they live.

And it was as a result of one such opportunity that me, Angie and Squidge found ourselves outside of Pace's house after work the next day.

'This is wrong,' Angie said stonily, staring at Pace's house with her hands in her coat pockets as I unloaded Squidge from the boot of my car. 'So wrong. You're not even supposed to use the systems for things like this, Tidge, it's *literally* the first thing they tell you when you start working for the Police. You do realise,' she added over her shoulder, almost conversationally, 'that you could get sacked for this?'

'I'm not going to get sacked,' I told her, panting slightly from the effort of holding tight onto Squidge's collar with one hand, keeping him in the boot as I unwrapped his lead from around the headrest with the other hand. 'How could they possibly prove that it wasn't an accident?'

'Besides,' she continued determinedly, as if I hadn't said anything. 'Pace is on the *sick*. Do you really think he'll want to talk to two complete strangers about what happened to put him in that position?'

'I'm counting on it,' I told her frankly, as I finally unravelled the lead and locked the clasp onto Squidge's collar, letting him bound joyfully out of the boot. 'How do we know he's not itching to talk to somebody about what he happened, but he can't, for fear of being judged?'

She turned and shot me a sardonic look, but I barely noticed; I was too busy staring at Pace's house in mild astonishment.

I hadn't really looked at it when we'd pulled up, and I'd been too busy sorting Squidge out to take a good gander once I'd got out of the car. But now that I *could* actually look at it.... well, how the hell he could afford a place like that on a copper's wage was beyond me, let's just put it that way.

It was huge, easily the size of three average-sized houses crammed together. It was made of light, sandstone bricks with windows that were easily as tall as a person, and it had a perfectly manicured front lawn that easily set it back from the street by a good couple of hundred metres. It was surrounded by a tall wall with black iron wrought gates that opened onto a beige, gravel driveway that had pine trees stationed along it at perfect intervals, almost like a woody guard of honour.

I reached through one of the gates and cranked open the lever on the other side, pushing the gate far enough inwards that we could scurry through the small gap and onto the drive. We crunched up to the house in complete silence, too busy gawking at the landscaped front garden and the patches of flowers dotted around on it to bother saying anything to each other.

The plan was simple.

We were two lasses who were going door-to-door, looking for their uncle who'd left work early on Friday and hadn't been seen since. And if anyone asked why we thought he'd be in Habely, of all places, we'd –

Well.

We'd either blag it or change the subject.

I hadn't quite decided yet.

We reached the front door and banged against it with the giant, lion-shaped doorknocker, and waited for a minute or so with baited breath.

To be honest, the place was so grand that I was half-expecting the Queen to open the door. She did not do that.

Instead, the door was wrenched open by an irritated-looking man who was even taller than Hadaway, with thinning black hair, large eyebrows that were dangerously close to forming a partnership, and a thick, bushy black beard.

'What?'

I have to say, not someone who gave the impression of being particularly ill or delicate.

'Hello,' I said brightly, refusing to be daunted by the annoyed vibe he was giving out. '*So* sorry to disturb you, we're just –'

'You're just trespassing, is what you're doing,' he bit off, in that broad Yorkshire accent of his, and then he jabbed one finger over our shoulders. 'Did it not occur to you that those gates might be there for a reason?'

'Well –'

'Or is that it did occur to you, but you just didn't give a shit?' He drew himself up to his full height, looking even more angry than he had done a second earlier. 'Let me tell you, I don't like people just coming onto my land all willy-nilly, and I like being disturbed by people I don't know even less. Now, if –'

'We're *so* sorry,' Angie told him hastily, taking half a step forwards. 'We've obviously made a mistake. It's just – we're not from the area, and we were trying to help our aunty. No-one's seen our uncle in days, and we said we'd go around and ask if anyone's seen him, or even just seen something that'd help us find him. But we'll leave you to it, we really shouldn't have bothered you.'

She turned to go and I reluctantly followed suit, feeling a mixture of disappointment and frustration explode in my stomach.

I didn't *want* to leave; I wanted to find out what the hell Knight had done to him and Lyme, and if he wasn't going to tell me about it, then I wanted him to tell me how else I'd be able to find out.

So you can imagine how relieved I was when, just before I followed Angie off his giant doorstep, I heard him make a reluctant noise behind me.

'Alright,' he said grudgingly. Clearly, this was a man who had the same inability to take off his cop hat that Hadaway, Johnny and half of Angie's family have. 'Hang on a minute. Let's see what we can do. What's your uncle called?'

'Keith,' I told him, trying to keep the excitement out of my voice and off my face as I turned to look at him again. 'We're looking for Keith Lyme.'

Five minutes and a considerable amount of bullshit later, we were sat on one of the giant, overstuffed loveseats dotted around Pace's living room.

It was huge, stretching from the front of the house all the way to the back garden, with hardwood floors, huge windows that weren't far off going all the way from floor to ceiling, and dark blue walls offset with bright white skirting boards and windowsills. It had a small bar area opposite to the fireplace, well-stocked with plenty of whiskeys and rums, and a grand piano in the corner on the other side of the room, and the whole effect made me feel like I'd wandered straight into *Pride & Prejudice.*

'So,' Pace boomed, striding over to the bar as Squidge made it his top priority to explore every inch of the room, nose glued firmly to the floor. 'Remind me what your names are?'

'I'm Kia Lyme-Pine,' I said brightly, and out of the corner of my eye, I saw Angie turn to look at me in disbelief. 'And this is my cousin, Lemon-Anne Lyme.'

He eyeballed us uncertainly as he sloshed some whiskey into a glass. 'You're cousins, are you?'

Mmm.

Yeah.

I could see why he was having difficulties; me and Angie hardly have anything that could pass for a family resemblance, even if you suspend belief and squint really hard.

I'm five foot nine and slightly on the gangly side, with a heavy side fringe and curly black hair that reaches down to just above my elbows. I have light blue eyes that have just a dash of green in them (they *do*), a ski-slope nose and a chin that definitely errs more towards pointed than round. Angie, on the other hand, is five foot five and has undeniably green eyes and light brown, shoulder-length hair with a full fringe; her nose is the daintiest thing I've ever seen on another human's face despite being perfectly in proportion, and her eyelashes go on for miles (the lucky duck).

'The Lyme genes aren't very strong,' I explained hastily. 'We all look much more like the other side of our families.'

He grunted, fastening the lid back onto the bottle and walking back over to us, whiskey glass in hand. (I couldn't help but notice that we hadn't been offered a drink.) 'Right. Come on, then, tell me about your uncle.'

I exchanged a quick, apprehensive look with Angie.

I wasn't completely certain that telling him about Lyme going missing had been the right thing to do. For one thing, it wasn't public knowledge; the local papers hadn't so much as mentioned it, let alone written an actual article about what'd happened, and if it wasn't for Johnny, we'd have had no idea that Lyme had disappeared. And for another, what if telling him about it triggered some massive breakdown that we'd be totally useless at handling? After all, whatever Knight had done to him, the guy was too shaken and upset to face going back to work; how did we know how he was going to react to talking about what'd gone on? (I had a feeling that Angie would say these were things I should've thought about before we ever went to see him. And this why Angie has no idea, to this day, that those thoughts ever went through my head.)

'Well,' I told him hesitantly, turning back to face him. 'Like we said, we don't know where he is. He left work on Friday and no-one's seen or heard from him since. It's not like him at all, we're all really worried.' I blinked at him innocently, hoping that I was pulling the role of Anxious Niece off convincingly enough. 'I don't suppose you've seen anything that could help us?'

'I don't, I'm afraid,' he said, sitting down on the loveseat opposite ours with a heavy sigh. 'I haven't seen him since Friday myself. I work with him, y'see,' he added, as I frantically tried to make myself look the suitable amount of surprised and confused. 'We're in CID together.'

'Right,' Angie said slowly, frowning slightly. 'Well, that could be helpful. D'you know if anything happened that upset him? Anything that'd make him walk out and disappear?'

He was silent for a few seconds, staring down into his glass with a look on his face that I couldn't read, and we both watched him nervously, holding our breath and wondering if he'd worked out that we weren't Lyme's nieces at all, but just two nosey lasses who wanted to know what was going on.

'We did an interview together,' he said in the end, his voice thicker than it had been a couple of seconds earlier, and I felt the knot in my tummy unravel itself. 'That's the only thing I can think of. I didn't get chance to speak to him about it, I didn't see him after we finished, but I – it definitely got to me. It was the worst one I've ever done.'

'What happened?' I burst out eagerly before I could stop myself, feeling myself shoot forwards slightly. 'I mean,' I added humbly, slowly sinking back again as he stared at me, looking surprised, and I remembered that I was supposed to be mourning the disappearance of my beloved uncle. 'I'm so sorry, that must've been awful. Would you mind telling us about it, so we can work out if that's been the trigger for all this?'

He looked at me for a couple of seconds more, and I stared back at him, hoping that I hadn't just given the game away.

Now, I don't know if it said something about how good a Detective he was or if he *did* want to talk about it, but instead of demanding to know why I was so excited or trying to catch us out, he just cleared his throat and took a swig of whiskey before saying brusquely,

'There's been a few murders around here lately. Has anyone told you that? Well,' he added, when we realised that he was actually waiting for us to give him an answer and quickly shook our heads. 'There has. Bloody odd ones, as well. There's a lady going around, this Elodia Knight, and the word is that she's a witch.'

'But,' Angie said on cue, frowning at him slightly, 'she can't be. Witches aren't real.'

'That's what I said,' he told her, nodding. 'Right the way through, from us finding out that she was the one we were looking for. But late on Friday, we managed to find her and haul her in, and it was down to me and your uncle to interview her.' He broke off and stared at his whiskey for a few seconds, and then – just as I was about to nudge him along – he threw his head back and downed the glass in one go, making me wince slightly. 'I wish we'd never bloody done it. It was wrong from the start,' he explained, pushing himself up and striding back behind the bar. 'She didn't even let us get through the introductions before she was telling us that she wouldn't answer our questions, and she...' He stopped, staring down at his feet. 'I don't know how she did it, but she got into my head. She knew – she knew things that she shouldn't have known, things that I've never told anyone. And the last thing I remember, she was in m– well, in my soul. I could feel her in there and it was... horrible. Just awful. It was the worst thing I've ever felt, and I can't remember anything that happened after that.' He looked back up at us and shook his head, with his eyes surprisingly wet. 'The next thing I knew, I was back here in a right state. And there's no way... I can't go back to work after that. Not for a while, at least. I just can't face it.'

And without any warning – save for a weird noise that I can only describe as being somewhere between a gasp and a gulp – he reeled back until he was resting against the wall behind him, with his hands over his face as he let out these huge, raw, properly heartbroken sobs.

Full disclosure: I am not good with people crying.

Don't get me wrong, it's not as if I don't *try*. I give them a hug and pat them on the back and say soothing things like 'there, there' and 'it's not that bad' and 'I've got wine in the fridge, do you want to get hammered?' But the whole time, I'm just squirming uncomfortably and waiting for the whole thing to be over so that I can go and get that wine out of the fridge.

And while Angie's usually much better at it than I am, it turns out that ability doesn't quite stretch to huge men who we've only just met and who could probably pass for an upright gorilla on a dark night.

Instead of going over to comfort him or saying anything that might cheer him up, we just sat there, alternating between glancing at Pace to see if he was finished and shooting uncomfortable looks at each other.

I'd never seen someone have a meltdown before.

I didn't know how long you had to wait to interrupt them without it being impolite.

Squidge, on the other hand, had no such concerns.

During one of my uneasy looks at Angie, my eyes landed over her shoulder instead of on her face, and I clocked Squidge fervently sniffing a corner of the fireplace.

Half a second later – well before I had any time to react – he pulled back, repositioned himself so that he was lined up with it, and cocked his leg against the marble.

Shit.

'Ang– Lemon,' I burst out in a horrified, strangled voice before I could stop myself, wrenching my eyes off Squidge for long enough to give her a panicked look. 'Why don't you take Mr –' Ah, bollocks. He hadn't bothered to officially tell us his name '– Person to compose himself? Maybe get a nice cup of tea, yeah?'

She stared at me for a few seconds, looking mildly confused and just as irked. It wasn't until I'd nodded towards Squidge's puddle as subtly as I could for about the fifth time that she finally realised I was trying to tell her something and turned to see what was going on.

And the second her eyes landed on the puddle, her whole body tensed up.

'Ahh,' she said stiffly, still staring at the fireplace. (Squidge, by this point, was nowhere near it. He'd wandered over to the window on the other side of the room and put his front paws on the low windowsill, panting happily as he stared out at the garden) 'Mmm. Yes. Let's, erm... let's go and see if we can find the kitchen.'

A minute or so later, the two of them were disappearing through the giant oak doors between the bar and the piano, Angie half-guiding and half-leading Pace by his elbow. I waited for the doors to close behind them before launching myself off the loveseat, grabbing a clump of the black serviettes sitting on top of the bar and legging it over to the fireplace. I dropped down in front of it, paper towels at the ready, and Squidge immediately came trotting over to me, excited to see what my new game was.

'For God's sake, Squidge,' I told him, as he snuffled my ear, tail wagging furiously behind him. 'You're not young enough or old enough to get away with this. Why didn't you ask to go outside?'

He didn't answer me.

He just rested his chin on my shoulder, giving off a definite vibe of self-satisfaction as he watched me mop up his latest work.

The good news is that there wasn't much on the fireplace that the piss could do any damage to. Pace was clearly either a minimalist or so skint from paying that beast of a mortgage that he couldn't afford to decorate; instead of having ornaments or anything that he would've had to pay for dotted around, he only had four framed photographs lined up along the slab of marble jutting out in front of the fireplace, each one the exact same distance apart from the others.

The photo nearest us, to the left of all the others, looked like it was the one that was most special to him; it was in the fanciest of all the frames, and while the other three pictures had a slight film of dust over them, this one was wiped completely clean. It was in black and white and showed Pace – considerably younger, judging by the thickness of his hair and the size of the gap between his eyebrows – with a blonde lass in her mid-late teens who had a classic emo haircut and overly-thick eyeliner. They were stood in front of a wall of trees, each with an arm around the other and both wearing the same serious, miserable expressions that Victorians liked to use before they were told it was acceptable to smile on camera.

'Ti– *Kia.*'

I jumped so high that I could swear I actually left the ground and swung around to face towards the doors. Angie and Pace were stood in front of them, Pace looking red-eyed (but thankfully not crying anymore) as he clutched his cup of tea, and Angie shooting me a look that anyone would take for a smile if you didn't know her well enough to see it for the furious gurn that it really was. Clearly, I was supposed to have finished cleaning and been sat back on the loveseat by now.

'What're you *doing*?'

'Oh, hi,' I said brightly, grabbing the fancy frame off the fireplace as I scrambled to my feet and turned to face them, holding the clump of wet tissues behind my back so that Pace wouldn't see them. 'I was just looking at these photos. They're lovely.' I held out the frame towards them, as if they were stood close enough to see exactly which one it was. 'This one's my favourite.'

He nodded slowly as he padded across the room until he was close enough to take it off me. 'It's my favourite, too. That's the last photo I have of my niece, Kathie; she was just seventeen there.'

He stared down at the photo for a few seconds, looking so sad that I literally bit my tongue to stop myself from asking what'd happened to dear ol' Kathie.

Clearly, whatever it was, it wasn't good.

Instead, I grabbed Squidge by the collar and dragged him over to the loveseat that Angie had sat back down on, keeping tight hold of him to make sure he didn't run off and piss on anything else.

'So,' I said carefully, dropping down next to Angie. 'When you say that you felt this Knight lass in your soul, what exactly does that *mean?* Like... how certain are you that it wasn't just indigestion?'

His head snapped up from the photo frame, and I couldn't help but notice that he looked considerably more irritated than he had not even a second earlier. 'It was not indigestion.'

'I'm sure it wasn't,' I told him reassuringly, like I'd never suggested it. 'But I don't understand how someone can get into your *soul.*'

'I don't understand it either,' he snapped angrily, his hand tightening on the frame until his knuckles went white. 'But I'm telling you, it happened. I felt it, clear as day; it made me feel the worst I ever have, and it damn well hurt. It was a... it *burnt* me. There's nothing else it could've been.'

It genuinely sounded like it *had* been indigestion to me, but I had an inkling that pointing that out would not have worked in my favour.

I heard Angie *just* start to say something, but before she could get past what was more of a squeak than a word, he was pulling himself up to his full height again and saying brusquely,

'Now, listen. I've told you everything I can remember about the last time I saw your uncle, and I can't help you any more than that. It's past time that you left. Go and find someone who can tell you more than I can.'

I was still frustrated when we got back to the flat half an hour later.

And it hardly looked like that was going to change any time soon; if anything, it was building by the minute, so much that I could barely sit still.

Clearly, I'd managed to offend Pace by suggesting that he'd had a bit of heartburn instead of having his soul invaded, but to be honest, I was more bothered about the fact that he'd chucked us out before we could find out anything else from him.

Especially given that I still had the same number of questions that I'd had before we went to his house; if anything, I was even more confused about what she'd done to them.

Why was he so convinced that it was Knight who'd given him that burning feeling?

And why couldn't he remember what'd gone on in that interview room? Was it just shock? Because I have to be honest, it seemed really odd to me that he could remember everything up to her taunting him but nothing between that and getting home, save for this feeling of her apparently being inside him. So... what? Had she managed to sneak some really precisely-timed drugs into Custody and pour it into his tea without him knowing about it? Or had she just brought back so many bad memories that he wanted to block out, and he'd ended up shoving that part of the interview out of his head as well?

And I still didn't have any idea about what'd happened to Lyme. There was no doubt in my mind that he definitely was with Knight, but where they were was a mystery by itself, let alone *why*. Why did she want him? And why just take one of the Bobbies that she'd hypnotised, or whatever it was? If you're going to all of that effort, why not take both of them?

I didn't get it.

In fact, I didn't get it so much that it made my head hurt.

And the most frustrating part was, I'd ran out of ways to get answers to any of that.

Well, no.

That's not quite true.

I did have one option... but I was hardly a massive fan of it.

Because basically, if I wanted to find out anything more about this case – which I did – then I hardly had any choice but to try and get on Hadaway's good side.

THREE

I'll be the first one to admit that I'm hardly the most patient of people.

Once I get a bee in my bonnet about something, I find it incredibly hard to have to wait for an answer or a delivery or for something to happen. It's always been the same way; Christmas Eve was almost physically painful for Little Armitage.

Hence the fact that, at nine o'clock that night, my car was taking up one of the spaces in East District Headquarters' back car park and I was determinedly walking up the stairs to the CID office, carrying a Bag for Life full to the brim with boxes and loose cans of Brewdog (which, by the way, had cost me a small fortune). I was being followed by a highly amused Angie, who could insist that she was only there to quickly see Johnny all she wanted to; I didn't buy for a second that she wasn't just as interested in what was going on as I was.

I was hoping that landing a shit-ton of beer on Hadaway's desk would do a good enough job of distracting him and/or making him think that I wasn't so bad after all, and then I could quickly hit him with my questions about whether they were any closer to finding Lyme or if they knew what trick Knight had pulled in her interview. Maybe I could even maybe get a good look at the notes and pictures that CID always had pinned to their whiteboards and noticeboards. (I wasn't massively hopeful that it'd work. But Angie was still determined that I shouldn't ask Johnny any more about it, so what's a girl to do?)

It took me less than half a second after stepping into the room to realise that that wasn't going to happen.

For one thing, Hadaway wasn't even at his desk; in fact, almost no-one was at their desks.

While the small room next to the CID office is usually the Major Incident Room, this time the roles had clearly been switched around, and the number of Bobbies that you usually find in the CID office had at least doubled, if not more. Despite what time it was, there were cops buzzing all over the place, some in jeans and T-shirts while others were wearing suits and ties; some of them were stood in small clusters, looking very serious as they talked in low voices, while other people were stood in front of the boards, looking at the notes and the pictures and the maps that had lines and arrows scribbled onto them. There were a few people taking phone calls or tapping away at their computers with frowns on their faces, and just as many cops were poring over statements or inspecting what was in the evidence bags stacked up on the windowsill in the far right corner of the room.

'Johnny,' I called as we made our way over to his desk, where he was leaning over another map with both hands on the desktop. 'What's going on?'

He glanced up at us for the briefest of seconds as we reached him, looking grim and exhausted. 'They've found another body.'

'What d'you mean, another body?' Angie demanded sharply, as I felt my stomach shift down by a good couple of inches. 'Another one in Habely Woods?'

'Yeah,' he told us in a low voice, after throwing the briefest of wary looks towards Hadaway, who was talking to another DC next to a whiteboard at the front of the room with a grim look on his face. 'Response did a patrol up there this morning and found another lad in the same place as the last three, with the exact same marks on him. She's fucking done it again, and we're no closer to getting hold of her than we were when the first body was found.'

I stared at him, my heart suddenly thudding in my ears. 'Haven't you got any leads?'

'No,' he said heavily, turning back to his map. 'Door-to-door isn't turning anything up, there's nothing on CCTV, and the appeals aren't getting people to come forward like we hoped they would. The only witnesses we have to any of this are Pettyfer and Eric, and neither of them want to talk.'

I swapped a quick, furtive look with Angie. We'd agreed on the way home that we wouldn't breathe a word about our visit to Pace to anyone; neither one of us could see it going down particularly well, even with Johnny, who's as laid back as a person can get.

'Has anyone tried talking to Pettyfer again?' Angie asked, frowning at him as I whirled around and squinted at the whiteboards, trying to make out what the different coloured scribbles were supposed to say. 'He must be the one who can shed the most light on it, right?'

'Josh and Liz pulled him out of his cell this afternoon, but they couldn't get him to do anything; I think he got himself too worked up, from what they said. They were at it for a good half hour before they called it a day.'

I scanned the whiteboards for a couple of seconds longer, trying so hard to read what was on there that it took me a couple of seconds to realise that Hadaway had clocked me; he was staring at me with his arms crossed tight across his chest, looking stony-faced, disbelieving and irritating all at the same time, and I got a vibe that I didn't have much time before he came over to pick up where we'd left off the night before.

I glanced over my shoulder at Johnny, barely even registering the thought in my head. 'Where is Pettyfer?'

'He's still in the cell downstairs,' he said absent-mindedly, glancing up from the map and tapping something into his computer, eyes fixed on the screen. 'We've arranged to keep him here for a bit longer, save us traipsing over to Watson House every time we need to talk to him.'

I turned back towards Hadaway just in time to see him excuse himself from the other Detective and start making his way over to Johnny's desk, sadly not looking any more pleased to see us.

Mmm.

Normally we had about a week, maybe a little bit more, between arguments.

As interesting as the case was, it wasn't worth dealing with two arguments in as many days.

'Listen,' I said quickly, whirling around on the spot and plonking the bag down next to Johnny's desk. 'Give that to Hadaway, will you? In fact, help yourself to a couple as well. Dish them out, if you like.' Hey. The plan was clearly a dud, and there was no point in giving a full supermarket shelf of beers to the man if it wasn't going to make a blind bit of difference to what he told me. 'We'll get out of your hair.'

I grabbed Angie by the wrist and dragged her through the office before she and Johnny even had time to say bye to each other, walking as quickly as I could and bursting out into the corridor without looking back to see if Hadaway was pissed off enough to follow us.

It was only when the door closed behind us that that hint of a thought at the back of my mind exploded into a full-grown idea.

And in that second, any intention I'd had of going back to the flat completely evaporated.

I wasn't ready to go home anymore.

No, I wanted to talk to Pettyfer.

Now, I don't know if you've ever tried to wheedle your way into the cell of a suspected murderer before, but let me tell you – it's not easy.

I mean, we could hardly go bouling into Custody and tell them that we were Bobbies. For one thing I'd worked at East District Headquarters for five years, and I hadn't changed much in the three years since I'd left to join the Typing Pool; a bit of weight loss and a couple of grey hairs was as far as it went, and neither of those things made me unrecognisable. For another, if we got lucky and the person manning the Custody Desk hadn't worked at East District when I did, we'd still have to give our names in; the second they looked us up on the internal system, they'd see exactly what jobs we did. (I didn't think that telling them that we were Johnny and Hadaway or whoever would quite wash.) And for a third thing, most people don't have an Angie trying to talk them out of it.

I didn't bother to clue her in on my plan before taking off from the CID office, and because I had a few inches and the element of surprise on her, I managed to put some pretty good distance between us. In fact, if it hadn't been for the Custody door refusing to accept my ID badge and let me into the airlock, she might not have even got to me in before I went inside.

As it happened, I was still stood at the end of the District Admin corridor on the ground floor, getting more and more frustrated as I tried to scan my card for a second time, when she caught up with me, charging down the corridor and grabbing my arm so hard that it felt like it was stuck in a vice.

I winced, looking down at my arm and then up at her face. '*Ow.* Jesus, Angie, that hurts!'

'What d'you think you're going to do?' she asked tightly, like I hadn't even said anything. 'Just go in there and ask to speak to the most high-profile person they've got?'

'Well –'

'Tidge,' she said seriously, staring at me with a look on her face that was somewhat dark and somewhat anxious. 'Why're you doing this? Why can't you just read the case in the paper like everyone else? I mean, surely it'd be a hell of a lot easier to *not* piss Hadaway off, and *not* get fired for using systems you shouldn't be and breaking into Custody?'

I looked at her for a couple of seconds, feeling some of the frustration and desperation to get answers melt away just a smidge.

I knew she had a point.

I wasn't a cop or a journalist.

I didn't know any of the victims.

I didn't know Knight or Pettyfer.

I had literally no reason or right to be sticking my nose in, but at the same time, I couldn't help myself. When was the last time something this interesting happened in Habely? Not even that, but when was the last time that something this interesting happened *anywhere* in Cattringham County?

And was it my fault that the papers were doing a shit job at reporting it? I knew what Knight was doing; what I wanted to know now was *why* she was doing it, and how the hell she was doing things that didn't make sense and convinced some people (Pettyfer) that she was an actual witch?

Bottom line, cards on the table, I couldn't help myself.

I wanted answers to the whole thing, and I was too impatient and intrigued to wait for the papers to print them.

Which you'd think that Angie would know. We'd known each other for ten years; it wasn't as if she hadn't seen exactly how nosey I've always been in that time.

I was just trying to decide whether I should try and explain all of that or if I should point out that I wasn't planning on *breaking into* Custody – and even if I was, it wasn't exactly possible to do that – when I heard the squeak of trolley wheels coming from the main hallway, which ran from the staircase at one end of the building right the way to the staircase at the other and connected to the District Admin corridor by a kind of T-junction. I whipped my head around to look past Angie just in time to see one of the caretakers round the corner, pushing a cart loaded with mops, toilet rolls and whatever else as he trundled towards Custody.

It took me a couple of seconds to realise that he wasn't one of the orderlies who'd worked there when I had.

And I think the rest of me realised what that meant before my brain caught on, because before I knew what I was doing, I was stepping forwards, one hand stretched out ready to shake his and a bright smile on my face.

'Hi,' I heard myself say cheerfully, as he eyed me uncertainly. 'I think you're expecting me. North District sent me across to help you out?'

The uncertain look changed into a frown as he chomped on his chewing gum, something he was apparently incapable of doing without opening his mouth as wide as it'd go with every bite. 'You're Dave?'

I blinked at him a couple of times, feeling my smile becoming decidedly more fixed.

What?

Dave?

Not that it wasn't a good thing that someone from North District *had* been sent across to help out, but if I'd given myself any time at all to think about it, I probably wouldn't have expected to play a Dave.

'That's me,' I told him slightly less cheerfully, feeling my smile waver and hitching it back into place. 'I know it's a bit of a strange name, but I've got used to it. Not like my brother; he's called Sue and he *really* struggles with it.'

I heard Angie let out a choking noise behind me as the guy stared at me, looking almost suspicious as he scratched his enormous double-chin, making it sway slightly.

He was enormous, 'round about five foot eleven tall and almost as wide, with arms a mile thick and legs like tree trunks. His hair was shaved to within an inch of its life, there was a small gold hanging from his right ear, and he had a couple of tattoos; one was a large D tattooed on the side of his neck in a nice calligraphic style, and the other was a letter on each finger of his left hand, spelling out the name Dean.

After a couple more seconds, he obviously decided he didn't need any explanation other than that. (Mind you, naming your son Sue and your daughter Dave is probably quite tame compared with some of the names you get lately.) Instead of asking any more questions, he trundled his trolley closer to the door into Custody, pulling his ID badge from a lanyard clipped onto his belt and making a noise at me that I can only describe as a phlegmy grunt.

'We've got a spare pair of overalls in our cupboard in here,' he told me, brushing his badge against the scanner so that the light turned green and the door clicked open. 'Go and get them on, and I'll meet you at the booking counter.'

Fifteen minutes later, I'd left Angie outside of Custody and was scurrying out of the cleaner cupboard, having managed to wedge myself in there with just enough room to get changed.

And honestly, those overalls were quite possibly the vilest things I've ever worn.

I can only assume that they were made for some kind of human beachball; the arms and legs were far too tight and stopped several inches short of where they were supposed to reach, while the torso area took 'baggy' to a whole new level. They were the same delightful colour as wet cement, and they were covered in stains from top to bottom, some clearly from food and others that'll always be a mystery. Not only that, but they had stiff patches in certain areas that I was trying hard not to focus on, partially because I knew that I'd leap to the worst possible conclusion, and partially because I was worried that it wouldn't be the *wrong* conclusion.

Custody's never as full as the rest of the building is, but by the time I stumbled back out of the cupboard, it was properly deserted; I couldn't see any Bobbies anywhere in the corridor or around the Custody Desk, and even Dean had done a decent impression of Houdini.

Not, mind you, that I was complaining. I'd have had a job to get past the Custody Sergeant without being interrogated, even in my overalls; anything that made the whole thing easier was peachy as far as I was concerned.

I shoved my hair down the back of my overalls and ducked my head down to stop the CCTV cameras from filming my face, and then I hurried down to where Dean had parked his trolley opposite the Custody Desk, grabbing a mop off it as I bustled towards the one locked cell, which – I was hoping – had to be Pettyfer's current home.

I shot one last, quick look around the corridor, trying to see if anyone was coming, and when I didn't hear anything except the kettle boiling in the office behind the Desk, I fiddled with the lock on the door and let myself in, holding my breath.

Me and Angie have always clashed on the interior decorating front. She likes to glue herself to *Home Makeover*-esque shows for full weekends at a time, and is genuinely never happier than when she's reshuffling her bedroom; I think the whole scene is a complete nightmare, and if you've found a wallpaper that works or you've managed to organise your ornaments in a way that looks good, you should never change it, ever.

Whoever had designed that room clearly had even less patience for it than I did.

It was literally a box room, small and perfectly square with a grey-green metal floor and walls more blank and empty than my mind whenever I have more than the ideal number of sherries. It had a chrome, seat-less toilet and a matching sink on the left hand wall, opposite a high mattress covered in a thick, blue vinyl that looked like it'd never been introduced to the concept of comfort.

And sitting on that mattress, looking just as depressed as the designer of the room obviously wanted him to be, was Pettyfer.

I remembered the papers saying that he was twenty-seven, purely because it'd seemed bizarre to me to think that someone only a year older than me and Angie could get caught up in something like what Knight was doing; but to look at him, you'd find it hard to believe that he was pushing twelve. He was reedy in every sense of the word, skinny and pale-skinned with greasy, light brown hair that flopped down over his forehead, a chin that looked like it'd barely developed, and an Adam's Apple that was giving its all to escaping from his throat.

'Top o' the morning t'you,' I beamed, shoving the door closed behind me. And then I kicked myself in a mixture of surprise and irritation. Why was I Irish? Why was I using any accent at all, when I'm so shit at them that it's a wonder I can pull off the accent I actually *have?* 'Do you mind if I mop in here?'

He blinked at me, barely even reacting to my horrendous accent. 'Who're you?'

'I'm Dave,' I told him brightly, scanning the room for the camera and spotting it in the corner of the room, up above the toilet. 'Cleaner Dave. It's a strange name for a girl, t'be sure,' I added cheerfully, strolling over to the toilet and shoving the mop against the wall behind it, working my way up towards the camera. 'But me parents didn't realise I was a lass until they gave me my first bath when I was two years old, and they says 'Glory be! It be a girl!' That's how they talked, you see,' I added after a slight pause, realising that I may have overshot Irish and landed more in the vicinity of Nursie from *Blackadder*. 'They thought they were pirates.'

I reached the camera and slammed the mop down on top of it, pushing down as hard as I could until I forced it downwards so that it was filming the toilet bowl instead of me and Pettyfer. The last thing I wanted was for anyone in the Custody Office to see me in there and come charging in to pounce on me; if nothing else, some of those people are heavy enough to do me some serious damage, and while I have every intention of coming back to haunt people once I die, spending all eternity in those horrific overalls was not something I wanted to do.

'So,' I said firmly once I was satisfied with how low the camera was, throwing the mop to one side and turning to face him. 'Word has it that you're in here because of this Elodia Knight business.'

He stared at me for a few seconds, apparently too perplexed to hear what I'd said. 'You don't mop walls.'

'It's a new technique,' I told him impatiently, wafting his words away with one hand. 'They taught us it at Cleaning School. What happened with you and this Knight lass?'

He slumped back against the wall behind him, arms crossed and a sulky impression on his face. 'Why would I tell you? So you can tell me I'm crazy like everyone else has?'

I tilted my head to the side, raising an eyebrow at him. '*Are* you crazy?'

'No.'

'Then what's it matter if anyone says you are? Look,' I added, crossing the room and perching on the edge of his mattress as he eyeballed me, looking like he didn't know whether he should be suspicious or not. 'What harm's it going to do to tell me what happened? Worst case scenario, you're right, and I'm just another person who calls you a loon. Best case scenario, I might be able to help you.'

The look on his face shifted more towards definitely suspicious. 'How?'

'Maybe I can look into things for you,' I told him, shrugging. 'Maybe I'm not as bound by processes and whatever as the cops are. The thing is, you're not going to find out if you don't talk to me, are you?'

I was talking shit.

Obviously I was talking shit. I barely even knew what I was saying; I was just coming out with anything that might get him to tell me exactly how he'd met Knight and been roped into the whole thing, and how she'd got him to agree to dump the bodies.

I mean, could I help him?

No.

But could I look into things that the Police couldn't?

Also no.

But the important thing was that *he did not know that*. And when it came down to it, he must've actually believed – or at the very least, *wanted* to – that this cleaner who murdered the Irish accent and didn't know that you don't mop walls could help with the investigation. Because after several long, silent seconds, he shot me a tearful look and said shakily,

'I can't remember much of it.'

Well, that made breaking into Custody worth it. 'Right.'

'I just remember...' he broke off, staring at the wall opposite us, and when he started talking again, his voice was even more wobbly. 'It felt like she was inside of me. Not inside of my head, it wasn't like that, it was... it was more like she was in my *soul*. That's the only way I can describe it. I felt like I was burning all the time, like every bit of my insides were on fire, and all I knew was that she was there, she had something to do with it. She knew things that I've never – I've never told *anyone*, and she kept talking to me about them, kept making me... she kept making me remember. And I didn't want to remember those things. I never have.'

He swallowed hard and ducked his head down so I couldn't see his face as I sat there, staring at him in shock as something icy-cold washed over me.

He felt like she'd been in his soul.

One person saying that, you can write it off as them being overly-dramatic and never having experienced heartburn. But *two* people? Two people who might never have met who were talking about the same person, and describing what she'd done in the exact same way?

No.

You couldn't brush that away.

There was something to it.

'She kept me in this room,' he carried on before I could think of anything to say, so quietly that he was all but whispering. 'And she'd come in every morning and read this – this *stuff* to me.'

'*Read*?' I repeated sharply, frowning at him. Funny, but I'd never really thought about psychopathic lunatics enjoying a good book. 'What was she reading?'

'I don't know,' he told me helplessly, glancing up at me as he shook his head. 'It never made any sense to me. It wasn't English, though, I can tell you that. I don't know what it was.'

He slumped back against the wall behind us, staring into space and looking completely miserable, and I eyeballed him thoughtfully, chewing on my lip and wondering if he was going to have a reaction similar to Pace's when I asked my next question.

One crying person was hard enough.

I wasn't sure I could handle two in one day.

'What makes you so certain that she was in your soul? It's just,' I explained, when he blinked at me in surprise, 'it's not something you hear about, is it? You hear plenty about people getting into other people's heads, but no-one ever goes around saying that someone was in their *soul*. How d'you know?'

He thought about that for a couple of seconds with a slight frown on his face. And then, just when I thought he might actually shine a light on the whole thing, he shrugged and shook his head wearily. 'I couldn't tell you. You just *know*. It's not a feeling you can forget.' He looked at me, the expression on his face definitely more thoughtful than disappointed. 'You think I'm insane.'

'No,' I told him, giving my head a little shake and surprising myself as I realised that I was actually telling the truth, and not just trying to keep him talking. 'I don't. I just don't get it. I mean... how much do you remember of the time you were with Knight for? D'you remember killing those lads?'

'No,' he said bluntly, 'but I don't remember taking the bodies away either, and we both know I did that.'

Mmm.

Couldn't exactly deny that one.

'Y'know,' I said, suddenly realising that I hadn't used my Irish accent for a while and quickly hitching it back on. Shit. Maybe he hadn't noticed. 'There's been another body found this morning.'

'What?'

'Aye. So either she's dumping the bodies herself now, or she's found someone to do what you used to.'

Lyme, I suddenly thought. What if she was making Lyme do it now? Was that why she'd taken him?

'Can you remember anything,' I asked quickly, taking the uneasiness that'd come with those thoughts and shoving it away somewhere deep in my belly, 'that she said or did that'd explain why she needs someone to take the bodies away? I mean, why can't she just do it herself?'

'Probably because of her followers.'

I blinked at him a few times.

Did he just say followers? Or was I having a stroke?

'What?'

'Yeah, she has followers,' he told me, as conversationally as if we were talking about whichever TV shows we'd been watching lately. 'Couldn't tell you what they look like, I never saw them. But I know they were there whenever we – whenever it happened. We were never alone up there.'

'How d'you know that if you never saw them?'

'Well, I *must* have seen them,' he explained patiently, suddenly the calmest I'd seen him. 'It's obviously one of those things that I don't remember, that's all. But I remember them chanting. Something I'd never heard before, something... eggo dabbo teeny Mam may I, or maybe may I esta dee mature. I don't know. I can't remember exactly. I just know it was something like that.'

'Right,' I said slowly, nibbling on my thumbnail as I thought about that. I wasn't exactly sure what I was supposed to make of it, to be honest. 'And this book that she used to read from. I know you said you don't remember it, but... are you sure about that? You don't know what it was called or anything?'

He made a little noise that was somewhere between a snort and a laugh. 'Now you're asking.'

He leant his head back against the wall and closed his eyes, frowning from the effort of thinking so hard. And while he was doing that, I just sat there and stared at him, feeling a swirl of panicky impatience mix with the curiosity raging through me. The fact that she had followers *(plural)* had blown me away, but it wasn't as if I could start going around Habely, knocking on every door I came to in the hope that someone would answer holding a spellbook and a black cat and wearing a 'I Heart Knight' T-shirt. If he could give me something that I could actually follow up on, that'd be brilliant.

And if he could do it before the Custody officers realised that they were watching a toilet bowl and came bursting in to find out what was going on, that'd be even better.

I was just contemplating reaching out and giving him a little shake when he lifted his head back up off the wall, shooting me a happily surprised look that – if I'm being completely honest – didn't really sit too well with what we were talking about.

'I do remember,' he told me lightly, sounding like he was almost dazed. 'I can't remember what was in it, but I can tell you what it looked like. It was grey or white – some pale colour, anyway – and it was bloody beast of a thing with a right long title. *Learning the Gainful Skill of Witchcraft and Mastering Your Abilities.* That's what it was called.'

FOUR

Mmm.

Yeah.

Call me a cynic, but having a book like that hardly smacked of being a witch to me.

I mean, don't get me wrong. I grew up on *Sabrina the Teenage Witch* and *Harry Potter*; I knew that fictional wizards and witches liked to have spellbooks, and it'd only make sense that Knight – yet another pretend witch – would want something along the same lines.

But I don't know.

If Pettyfer was right and that *was* the title of the book she used, then it sounded a lot less like a spellbook and a lot more like an instruction manual to me.

I have to be honest, the more I found out about Knight, the more questions I had.

Things like why Pettyfer and Pace were both so adamant that she'd wormed her way into their souls. What'd even put that idea in their heads? And how did they know that she wasn't still there? Was it an assumption they made when the burning stopped, or did she only have a hold over people in a two-mile radius?

And why she hadn't been bothered about Pettyfer seeing the book she was using when she was supposed to be this all-powerful witch already? Did she think that whatever she'd done to him would leave him so out of it that he wouldn't notice, or that – if he did – he wouldn't remember anyway? Or had she been she planning to do away with him as well, ideally before he had chance to mention it to anyone?

And who were these *followers* that he'd mentioned? Had they been following her right from the start, since the first lad was killed? Or did it go back further than that? Or not that far? Either way, who were these people who happily supported someone who spent her time either thinking about killing young lads, actually killing young lads, or hiding away after having been out killing young lads?

And right there, right at the base of it all, was the question that I *really* wanted the answer to: what the hell was she *doing?* And *why?*

I hadn't had chance to ask Pettyfer any of those questions.

For one thing, I didn't think that he was emotionally or mentally strong enough to deal with a complete barrage of questions from me.

And for another, I'd just been about to try asking anyway when there'd been footsteps outside of his cell door, and I'd took that as my cue to scarper once the corridor running between the cells was quiet again.

So, no.

Despite Angie insisting on it from us leaving East District right the way through to us calling it a night, I couldn't put the whole thing out of my mind.

I still had questions, and by the time we turned in for the night, I'd convinced myself that the only other thing that might help me get some answers was going up to Habely Woods.

I mean, I wasn't expecting to get much from it. For one thing, I didn't know where the bodies had actually been found; I just had a really vague idea from what'd been said in the papers. And for another, even if I did manage to find the place, what exactly was going to be there to help me get to the bottom of it? A gnarled old man who knew everything and talked in riddles, because according to the films, that's what wise men do? A carving in a nearby tree saying 'Knight woz here'?

Yeah.

I didn't think so.

But somehow I couldn't shake the nagging feeling that I should go up there anyway.

Hence the fact that, at half past eleven that night, I was standing by the front door of our flat, doing my best to keep Squidge quiet and trying to clip his lead onto his collar, two things that were harder than they sound, given that he likes to bounce and wriggle all over the place when he's excited.

I felt a little explosion of frustration and dragged him a couple of steps away from the doorframe, trying to stop his tail from frantically beating against it, but before I could remind him that this was a *secret* midnight walk – for the sole reason that, even though I knew it wasn't the best idea I'd ever had, I didn't want to get talked out of it – Angie's bedroom door opened on the other side of the living room and she stuck her head out, blinking and squinting against the light.

'What're you doing?'

'Nothing!' I told her brightly, beaming at her as Squidge whirled around and padded back to the door, jamming his nose against it as he let out a loud whine. 'I think Squidge needs another wee, so I'm just going to pop him out in the back garden again.'

She shot me a suspicious look as she took a couple of steps into the living room. 'And you had to get dressed to do that?'

'Yes.'

'You had to take off the pyjamas you were wearing when you last put him out for a wee, and instead get fully dressed – including your coat – just to do exactly the same thing?'

I eyeballed her warily, wondering if there was any smidge of a chance that she was going to buy this. 'Yes.'

'You can't actually expect me to believe that,' she said impatiently, coming dangerously close to glaring at me as she took a few more steps forward. 'Seriously, where are you *going?*'

We stared at each other for a few seconds, and I wondered if there was any way out of this that meant I didn't have to tell her that I was going up to Habely Woods.

I knew she'd try to stop me from going, and I knew that the most sensible thing to do would be to let her. But what was the point? All it'd lead to was me tossing and turning all night, not sleeping, wondering what Knight's game was and why she'd picked Habely – of all places – to play it in.

And I knew that going up to Habely Woods in the hopes of finding an answer or two was a long-shot. I knew that I'd come home just as clueless and even more frustrated than ever, but given that the obvious routes of trying Pace and Pettyfer hadn't gone the way I'd hoped, I didn't see what harm it'd do to try something slightly more out-there.

'Fine,' I told her reluctantly in the end. Because what choice did I have, really? The only thing she was going to believe was the actual truth. 'I'm taking him up to Habely Woods.'

She looked at me for a couple of seconds longer before letting her head fall back with a frustrated groan. 'Jesus, *Tidge*. What happened to staying out of this whole Knight thing?'

'I never agreed to that,' I pointed out defensively, over Squidge's second, longer loud whine. 'And if people would just give me answers, Angie, I wouldn't have to do it. But,' I continued hurriedly as she opened her mouth, no doubt to tell me that I didn't actually *have* to do anything, 'Pace and Pettyfer weren't much help, you won't let me talk to Johnny, and Hadaway'll have my head if I try to ask him anything else. So what d'you expect me to do?'

'Follow it in the papers like everyone else is.'

'No,' I said stubbornly, shaking my head. 'It's too interesting. I just want to know why she's *doing* it, that's all. I don't know why that's such a problem for everyone.'

She brought her head back up and frowned thoughtfully at me, with her eyes narrowed slightly. 'And you think going up to Habely Woods will help you find that out?'

'No,' I admitted frankly, 'but I think it's worth a shot.'

'And it can't wait until morning?'

'Well, it wouldn't make sense to. I won't be able to sleep, and Squidge isn't going to shut up until I take him somewhere now.'

He emphasised my point by choosing that second to let out a third whine, this one even longer and louder than the other two, going on for – well, probably not far off a minute.

'This is a bad idea,' Angie told me bluntly, looking decidedly unimpressed. 'And I want you to remember that I *told* you that it's a bad idea.' She paused slightly, looking more stern and serious than I could ever remember seeing her. And then she let out a heavy, reluctant sigh and gave her head a grim shake, almost like she was letting herself down. 'Give me five minutes. I'm coming with you.'

Habely Woods start about a quarter of the way up Habely Moor, right on the other side of the village to our flat, but the place is so small that it only takes around twenty minutes to walk between the two places.

We took the usual route, following the wooded path that runs along the side of Angie's old school and cutting through the cornfield behind the school field until we crossed one of the main roads into Habely and reached the muddy, gravel track that wound its way up to the Woods.

It's so gorgeous during the day that it's way up on the list of my favourite places, but at night?

I won't lie, I couldn't wait to get out of the place.

'So,' Angie said lightly, as we followed the track through the Woods, heading for the place where we thought the bodies had been found, pointing the lights from the torch apps on our phones into the pitch-blackness in front of us. 'What exactly is the plan here, Tidge? What are we looking for?'

'I don't know,' I told her, shaking my head slightly. 'I don't even know if there'll be anything there, I just wanted to take a look. I just don't *get* it,' I added exasperatedly, after a few seconds. 'None of it makes any *sense*. Pace and Pettyfer *both* said that they felt her in their soul, and I can understand getting something in your head –'

'I've noticed that, actually.'

'– because everyone does that, that's *normal*. But when does anyone ever say that they can feel something in their sodding *soul*? What does that even *mean?*'

'You can't feel something in your soul,' she said flatly, as I gave Squidge a hard yank away from the rabbit hole he was investigating. 'It's like saying that you feel something in a sock that's been lying on your bedroom floor for two weeks; it's not possible.' She shot me a sideways look. 'Do you believe them?'

'No, of course not. I don't even know how you'd *know* if you feel something in your soul. But you have to admit, it can't just be a coincidence that the only two people to say that have come out with it in relation to Knight.'

'I don't believe this,' she said, stopping dead in her tracks, and when I turned to shine my torch light on her, she was staring at me incredulously. 'You *do* believe them.'

'I do not *believe* them.'

'Yes, you do! You do!' She bit her lip as she shook her head in mock-disappointment. 'Shame on you, Armitage Black. *Shame.*'

'I do not believe them,' I repeated, laughing. 'I just think it's too weird to let slide. There has to be something she did to them to make them think that that's what happened. I mean, when was the last time that you had a feeling that you weren't too sure about and thought 'well, shit, guess someone's in my soul'?'

'All the time,' she said dryly, without missing a beat. 'My soul is constantly getting invaded.'

I laughed again as I turned away from her and started walking, following Squidge's lead and the sound of his happy snuffling and panting not too far ahead. It wasn't until I'd taken a fair few steps that I realised that Angie wasn't following me. Instead – when I turned around to see what she was doing – she was stood frozen to the spot, her head turned to the left as she stared up at the trees a couple of metres up the slope next to the track.

'What's wrong?'

'There are lights,' she murmured, so quietly that I had to strain to hear her.

'What?'

'Lights,' she said again, in a voice that was minutely louder, and then she pointed towards whatever it was that had her so mesmerised. 'There are lights up there.'

I scurried back to where she was standing, pulling Squidge with me and trying to move as silently as possible as my heart started thumping in my chest and ears. I followed her finger the second I reached her, and sure enough, she wasn't wrong; six dots of glowing, flickering light were making their way along the bit of the path that jutted out from the rest of the hill, moving in the same direction that me and Squidge had been walking in.

We watched them for a few seconds, both of us completely silent as what I can only describe as an excited dread started fizzing in my tummy.

Habely Woods aren't as popular at night as they are during the day; as far as I know, only teenagers who're looking to getting pissed and start fires, get drunk and have sex, or get hammered and do both go up there after a certain time. But even still, I felt like we would've heard if those drunk and horny arsonists had seen a bunch of random lights silently and somewhat eerily making their way through the trees.

And maybe they had seen them and told people, and word just hadn't reached us yet. But if not...

Well, how realistic was it that these lights would turn up in the same place that Knight was killing people when it was the middle of the night and while the bitch was still at large?

Just like Pace and Pettyfer being so convinced that she'd got into their souls, how much of that could be a coincidence?

Yeah.

None of it.

As far as I'm concerned, it wouldn't have made sense *not* to follow them.

What I hadn't realised is exactly how steep that slope was.

Not only that, but the thing was a bloody minefield.

It must've took us a good five minutes to scramble up the hill, not because it was that high, but because it was made of soft, wet mud that kept making us slide a good way down whenever we'd managed to pull ourselves more than a couple of feet up. And when we weren't slipping all over the place, the stupid thing was going on the offensive.

I'd impaled my hand on a bunch of thorns lying across the ground.

Angie had face-planted a rock when both feet shot out from underneath her.

I'd banged my head against a tree, purely because I'd been so busy looking for more thorns that I hadn't thought to check where I was going.

Angie had slid straight into a tangle of bushes and came dangerously close to having a meltdown when she struggled to get herself out of it.

All in all, not the most fun journey I've ever had.

By the time we finally dragged – literally dragged – ourselves onto the track that we'd seen the lights moving along, Squidge was standing there with his tail slowly wagging and his head tilted to one side like he was trying to work out what'd took us so long, and the lights were much further down the path; in fact, if I hadn't glanced to my right in time, I probably would've missed the last one rounding the corner a few metres ahead of us.

I stayed on my hands and knees for a couple of seconds, staring after them as I tried to catch my breath, and for one tiny second, I seriously considered just leaving them to it and collapsing face-down on the gravel.

But no.

We couldn't do that.

If nothing else, Johnny had said that they didn't have any leads; what if this was the one chance we were going to get to actually help with that?

I hauled myself to my feet and took off running after them, hoping that I wasn't wheezing and panting as much as I thought I was, and after a couple of seconds, I heard Angie let out a particularly enthusiastic choice of words before she came pelting after me.

I rounded the corner at top speed and hit a wall of disappointment, stopping dead so abruptly that Angie couldn't stop in time and slammed into me with enough force to send me stumbling forwards

But to be honest, I barely noticed.

I was too preoccupied by the fact that we were too late; the lights had completely disappeared, and all we could see was the pitch blackness stretching out ahead of us.

Shit.

'Where'd they go?'

'I don't know,' I said, fishing my phone out of my coat pocket and turning the torch back on.

I scurried to the edge of the path and glanced down at the trees and bushes, trying to see any sign of the flickering lights. And when that didn't turn anything up, I whirled around on the spot and glanced at the trees further up the side of the hill, wondering if they'd gone up to a path that was higher again.

It was completely possible that they had, but hell if I could see them; all my torch was showing me was trees and darkness.

I turned back to Angie, who was staring at me with a baffled frown on her face. 'They can't have just *disappeared.*'

I shrugged, trying not to seem as disappointed as I felt. 'Apparently, they have.'

She pulled her own phone out of the pocket and lit her own torch, shaking her head slightly, and I knew what she was thinking.

We hadn't been far enough behind those lights that they'd had time to vanish completely. There should've been some sign of them *somewhere,* even if it was just a slight glow from around another corner or in all the trees.

So what were they?

Usain Bolt?

'We should probably go back,' Angie said reluctantly, after a few seconds of staring into the darkness like we expected something to happen. 'At least we've got something to give Johnny and Hadaway, anyway.'

I looked at her incredulously. 'And what exactly have we got to tell them? That we saw some lights moving through the Woods, but we don't know what they were or where they went, and actually they could be nothing to do with Knight at all? Aye, I'm sure they'll be really grateful for those little nuggets, Angie.'

'Well, what else can we do?' she asked defensively, flinging her arms up in the air in exasperation. 'Follow them if you want, Tidge, but we don't know that they've stuck to the path, we don't know if they've heard us and are just waiting to pounce on us, and we don't know – you said it yourself, we *don't know* if they're anything to do with Knight! We've got something that *might* help CID, and if that's the best we can do, then what's the point in staying up here?'

'We haven't been to where the bodies were found yet.'

'And I'm not comfortable trying to find the place knowing that we're not the only ones up here.'

We eyeballed each other for a couple of seconds, Angie looking just as frustrated as I felt, and I realised that I didn't have much of a choice but to back down. I can't tell you how much I wanted to find those lights and see what they were up to, but if they weren't going to make a difference – and they obviously weren't, or they would've shown up by now – then I didn't know how I could do that. And if I'm being completely honest, those lights had put the heebie-jeebies into me; based on nothing but how unexpected and out of the ordinary they'd been, I had a bad feeling about them, and a small part of me was saying that trying to track them down probably wasn't the smartest of ideas.

'Fine,' I muttered in the end, not even trying to stop myself from sounding disappointed and frustrated. 'We'll go back. Just give me a second to sort my shoe out.'

I started to crouch down to tighten my left trainer, which had become uncomfortably loose while we'd been dragging ourselves up the hill. But before I could get as far as bending my knees, the light from my torch landed on the muddy grit next to me, and I completely froze, staring at the ground with my face tingling.

Footprints.

Of course there were footprints.

We'd *literally* just seen people walking around up there. Why hadn't it occurred to me to look for their footprints?

They ran along the track in a single line, coming from behind where we were stood and disappearing into the darkness in front of us, and while the footprints on the left were always perfect and identical, the footprints to the right were slightly scuffed, like whoever'd left them wasn't picking that foot up properly. Without saying a word to Angie or without even really knowing what I was doing, I slowly started to follow them, eyes and torchlight glommed on the prints. I heard Angie let out an exasperated sigh and start to crunch after me, but by that point, I was already a way ahead of her down the path and rounding another corner, heart thumping hard in my chest – but instead of going all the way around the bend, like the track did, the footprints led straight to the grassy edge of the moor and disappeared, so that it looked like they'd dropped down into the trees below us.

I frowned slightly and nibbled on my bottom lip as I followed the footprints over to the verge, wondering why I was bothering to look when I already knew that I wasn't going to see anything; I'd looked over enough verges and rounded enough corners to know that those lights did not want to be seen.

Or at least, they hadn't.

This time, apparently, they'd had a change of heart.

They were right at the bottom of the slope, with the people holding them still in that single line as they slowly wound their way through the trees and followed the lower track into a fairly small clearing, where even more flickering, glowing flame torches were being held in two large circles, one inside the other.

I was close enough to them now that I could make so much of them out in the light bouncing off the torches, and I felt a squirm of icy unease as I realised that they were all wearing identical, dark red cloaks that went all the way down to the floor and didn't look too dissimilar to what old-timey Monks liked to wear, with their huge hoods more than covering their heads.

What *was* this?

Meeting in the Woods in the middle of the night was weird enough, but why did they have to use the same slow pace, wear the same outdated outfit and carry flame torches?

Was this something to do with Knight?

Or did Habely have an underground cult who didn't believe in electricity?

I was leaning towards hoping it was the first one. One bizarre thing happening in Habely was enough to blow my mind; two at the same time might fry it altogether.

'*Jesus*, Tidge,' Angie breathed as she joined me at the top of the hill, moving so quietly that I jumped in surprise. 'What the *fuck* is going on?'

I shook my head, still mesmerised by what was happening in the clearing. 'I have no idea.'

From the number of flame torches we could see, there must have been at least sixty people down there, maybe more. But none of them seemed to be *doing* anything; apart from the flickering of the flame torches and the six cloak-covered figures we'd followed moving around to join the outer-circle, the clearing was completely still and silent, with everyone facing into the centre of the circles.

I tore my eyes away for long enough to throw half a glance in Angie's direction. 'We need to get a closer look.'

'We do not,' she hissed shortly, flinging a sharp look at me. 'Do they look like people who'd appreciate being interrupted, Tidge? Do you think they want people knowing they're here?'

'Well, we won't *let* them know we're here,' I whispered back, already taking a couple of slow, tentative steps onto the crest of the slope. 'I'm not saying we go bouling in there and ask to play with them, Angie, I'm just saying we get a bit closer.'

She lurched forward, grabbing tight hold of my arm with her free hand. 'For God's sake, Tidge, *no.* We can't –'

'*This* is what we give to Johnny and Hadaway,' I told her sharply, keeping my voice as quiet as I could and shooting her a hard look. 'This has got to mean something, Angie, and if we can tip them off about it, then it might just give them a lead, don't you think? Turn your torch off,' I added quietly, when she did nothing but stare at me for a couple of seconds. 'We don't want them to realise someone's here.'

I turned my own torch off and pocketed my phone as I started to move down the hill again, but before I could take more than two or three careful steps, she whispered stubbornly,

'Why don't we just *call* Johnny and Hadaway? Let them know what's going on?'

'And say what, exactly? 'Yeah, hi, there are a bunch of people wearing cloaks having a meeting in Habely Woods, and we don't know what they're doing or if they're anything to do with Knight at all, but we wanted to let you know about it before we could give you any details whatsoever'.' I shot her a sardonic look. 'Let's just take a second to imagine how well that'll go down with someone who already doesn't like me.'

She stared at me, looking livid. 'Whatever they're up to has to be linked to Knight. It *has* to be. Going down there is fucking suicide.'

'But it's alright for the Police to go in?'

'They're *trained* to deal with shit like this!' she whisper-yelled at me, and even though she was starting to irk me, I couldn't help but admire the control she had over keeping her voice so low. 'They have tactics! They know what they're doing! We have *nothing*, Tidge! We'd be like lambs to the slaughter if we go in there!'

I opened my mouth to tell her – again – that I wasn't planning on going *into* the clearing, and that she could sod off home if she was so dead-set against it, but before I could get any words out, a rumble suddenly came from the clearing.

It was an odd one, slow and droning, and it wouldn't have been loud enough for us to hear it if the rest of the Woods weren't so silent.

It took me longer than I'd like to admit to realise that it wasn't a rumble at all, but the Cloaks starting to chant.

They were chanting in complete unison, all of them using the same inflictions and the same monotonous tone, and I felt the hairs on the back of my neck stand up.

This was beyond creepy.

It was beyond weird.

It made a good 90% of me want to call the whole thing off and sprint home, but that last 10% was too stubborn, and I couldn't help myself.

Angie could say what she wanted to, and she could argue with me as much as she liked.

She could even actually go home if she wanted to, I didn't care.

But there was no way that she was going to stop me from finding out exactly what was going on in that clearing.

FIVE

While most of Habely Woods is made up of sycamores, ash trees and birches, the Cloaks had managed to find themselves a clearing surrounded by different, slightly bigger trees. The ashes had been swapped for a few horse-chestnut trees that were weighed down with conkers liable to give you a mild concussion if they dropped on your head; the sycamores had been ditched for a couple of oak trees that erred most definitely on the huge side; and instead of birches...

Well.

No.

The birches were still there.

Turns out birches are stubborn little bastards.

Basically, what I'm saying is that the Cloaks had found the one clearing in Habely Woods where it would be relatively easy for any passers-by to spy on them.

Before Angie had chance to stop me, I wrenched my arm away from me and took off, all but throwing myself over the side of the hill and scrambling (see: tumbling, with very few, fleeting moments where I was in anything remotely resembling control of the situation) through the soggy mud, sticks, leaves and occasional stones until I landed in something of a heap the bottom of the slope, feeling (surprisingly) out of breath and (less surprisingly) bruised in every part of me that didn't seem like it was on fire, with a very excited Squidge prancing around me, having realised that I'd dropped his lead and chased me down the hill to find out exactly what game we were playing.

I sat up within a couple of seconds of hitting the ground, grabbing Squidge's collar to keep him under some control and staring towards the clearing with my heart pounding in my ears, trying to keep the panting as quiet as possible.

There was no way that the Cloaks hadn't heard me.

Even with all of that wonderfully monotonous chanting going on, *someone* standing at the back of the circles must've heard the commotion of a random woman bouncing down the hill... and if they hadn't, they can't have missed the noises of a desperately happy Black Labrador pounding after her.

But apparently, the whole thing had gone right over their heads.

And if it hadn't, then no shits were given.

I must've sat there for a good five seconds, my eyes glued to the opening to the clearing and my heart pounding – while Squidge alternated between licking my face and whacking me in the head with his tail, as Angie furiously hissed my name from somewhere up the slope that was suddenly somewhere to my left – before I realised that, actually, no-one was coming to see what was going on.

From this, I can only assume that either I bounce very quietly, or chanting is life.

I shoved myself up to my feet as silently as I could, grabbing tight hold of Squidge's collar at the same time, and shot a glance up the slope just in time to see a dark, blurry outline of Angie making her way down towards us.

Slowly.

Very slowly.

Far too slowly for me to hang around to find out if she was coming down to take Squidge off me so that I could go and take a closer look from somewhere discreet, or if she was going to try and convince me to go home.

'Alright,' I breathed to Squidge, shortening his extendable lead until it was right at the knuckle and locking it into place, tightening my grip on the handle as we started walking towards the clearing, as quickly and quietly as you can with a thirty kilo Black Lab who's desperate to charge off and play with the people in strange clothing. 'Just be quiet, Squidge.

Be *quiet*, and if we're lucky, we won't find ourselves in a situation where we're likely to get dead.'

Whether I was holding him so tight that he didn't have a choice but to do what he was told or whether his doggy mind could somehow comprehend the danger of the situation, I'm not sure. Either way, the closer we got to that clearing, the quieter he got; he stopped straining against his collar and panting like a freight train, and instead, he glommed onto me, sticking so close that my left leg kept bumping into his shoulder, nervously licking his lips every couple of seconds and tucking his tail tight between his legs.

We snuck into the cover of the nearest horse-chestnut tree, crouching right down to duck beneath the lowest branches and doing our best to ignore the fact that they were draped in silvery cobwebs as we all but crawled to the other side of the tree, right to the very edge, until we had the best possible view of the Cloaks.

They were still chanting in that eerily monotonous tone of voice, and still fixated on something in the dead centre of their circle. I dropped my shoulders lower, letting my chest drop into the wet mud and straining my eyes as hard as I could to look through their legs, trying to work out what it was that they were all so mesmerised by.

It took me a few seconds to realise that they were staring at a tree stump.

Now, admittedly, it was an impressively large tree stump.

But if it walks like a duck, and it talks like a duck, then there's no getting away from the fact that it was a fucking *tree stump*.

And honestly, I had no idea what they were expecting it to do.

'*Armitage.*'

I jumped about a foot in the air, narrowly avoiding whacking my head against the branches and silently thanking every higher being that there was for the fact that I'd somehow managed to avoid literally shitting myself.

I whipped my head 'round so fast that I could swear I heard my neck crick, and found myself staring at Angie. She was crouching at the other side of the tree, looking more nervous than I'd ever seen her with her eyes wider than I'd known they could get, keeping herself steady with one hand as she held the other one out towards me.

'Let me take Squidge,' she whispered, so quietly that I had to strain to hear her. 'I don't think he likes it, let me take him back out of the clearing and we'll wait for you there, I promise.'

In all honesty, I can't say I wasn't a little relieved. Squidge was flat on his stomach next to me, panting fast through his nose as his whole body trembled.

Squidge never shakes. Not unless it's thundering, and even then, he'll calm down if someone's touching him. He's just not the kind of dog who scares easily, and I felt just as guilty about him being scared as I did baffled by the Cloaks.

I held his lead out towards her and her hand fastened around the handle – and at that exact second, the worst silence I've ever heard fell across the clearing.

All at once, every bit of chanting stopped.

It just stopped, without any no preamble to it.

It wasn't like most people stop, where one or maybe two people are half a second behind everyone else. No, this was practised down to a T; every last one of the Cloaks fell silent in the same heartbeat, leaving behind a heavy stillness filled with anticipation, and suddenly I couldn't feel anything but dread.

My head turned almost by itself to see what was going on, and for reasons that I can't explain, I felt like one half of me knew what I was going to see before the other half of me did.

The Cloaks were still in their circle, still facing into the middle of the clearing.

But they weren't just staring at a tree stump anymore.

No, no.

This time they were staring at Elodia Knight.

Given the weirdness of the situation, you'd think that I wouldn't be *too* surprised by the fact that she'd actually turned up.

You'd think wrong.

I froze.

For a few seconds, I couldn't move.

I couldn't think.

I'm not even 100% certain that I was breathing.

And in fairness, I'd challenge anyone not to do the same, because take out the fact that you're staring straight at the most dangerous person your town – in fact, your whole county – has seen in God knows how long, and you're still left with the rather large question of how the *hell* she got there.

Let's take a look at the facts, shall we?

Knight had not been in that clearing when I'd been peering through the Cloaks' legs.

Granted, I hadn't had the best of vantage points, but I'd been able to see the stump well enough that there was no way I'd have missed anyone standing anywhere near it. And if she'd been standing on top of it the whole time...

No.

No way would I have missed her.

But even putting that aside, there was the slight issue of clothing choice. Whilst all the Cloaks were dressed in dark red, Knight's robe was pure white, with a thin piece of gold rope tied around her waist. She stood out like a sore thumb – unquestionably by design – so much so that even if I *hadn't* been able to see the tree stump, it would have been far too easy to spot her.

But I hadn't. Because *she hadn't been there.*

So how the hell did she do it? How had she just appeared out of thin air?

The easy answer would be that she'd been standing with the Cloaks the whole time, and that she'd managed to pull off the slickest of costume changes from red robes to white ones before she jumped onto that tree stump. Considering the Cloaks were obviously there because they were stupid enough to believe she was an actual, real-life witch, I couldn't see her having any issues in getting away with that plan.

But... I don't know.

Knight might've been a delusional psychopath, but there was no getting away from the fact that she was clever with it. She wanted people to believe it was real; she wanted them to believe that she was a witch, that she was something to be scared of and amazed by all at the same time, and she'd have had something crafty up her sleeve to make them think that. Something as simple as a costume change didn't sit right with me.

I just couldn't for the life of me think what else she could've done.

'My children,' she said silkily, shooting a serene smile around the clearing as she spread her arms out wide. 'Thank you for joining me here tonight. You have been so loyal, and I could not have got this far without your belief, your support... and your conviction. It has been difficult and trying, but our journey is nearly at an end. In just a few days, everything we've been working towards will be in our grasp, and those who try to stop us will find themselves faced with a force they cannot begin to imagine!'

As if on cue, the Cloaks thrust their flame torches up into the air triumphantly at exactly the same time, all of them letting out something that I can only assume was meant to be a cheer, but actually sounded more like the noise that a cow makes while it's giving birth.

'Tidge,' Angie breathed, so close behind me that her breath brushed across my ear. 'We have to leave.'

'We have gathered our four advocates,' Knight continued calmly, still smiling that horribly peaceful smile as the Cloaks settled back down into creepy silences. 'And our fifth is readying himself for the procedure. By week-end' – the word was drawn out more than I'd ever heard before – 'under the light of the next full moon, we will achieve our aim.'

'Seriously, Tidge,' Angie murmured urgently, grabbing hold of my coat sleeve. 'We can't stay here. We need to go, *now*.'

'I know,' I whispered back, keeping my eyes glued on Knight and the Cloaks.

And it's true. I did know.

I knew exactly how risky it was to stay there, and I knew that the best thing we could do was to scatter before they ever realised we were there – but I was so morbidly fascinated by what was going on that knowing those things didn't do anything to make me move.

'You have served me well, my children,' Knight was saying smoothly, over the sound of the Cloaks' second attempt at cheering, 'and it will not be forgotten.'

'For *fuck's sake,* Tidge, do you have any idea how dangerous this is?'

'I will make sure you're rewarded more than you ever dreamed of.'

'We can't let them catch us here, we need to go and we need to go *now*.'

I started to turn my head towards her, ready to tell her to take Squidge back towards the hill outside the clearing and I'd be with them just as soon as I could tear myself away.

Except that before I could move too much, Knight froze on the tree stump. Her smile slowly faded from her face until she looked eerily blank, and before I even fully process that something was happening, she stiffly jerked her head to her left.

And stared right at our tree.

Fuck.

'You're right,' I whispered quickly to Angie, scooting back a couple of inches even as a tiny, defiant voice in the back of my head told me that it was just coincidence Knight was looking in our direction, and she had no way of knowing that we were there. 'We need to go now.'

'My children,' Knight said coolly, as we started to scramble for the other side of the tree. 'It would seem that we're not as alone as we thought.'

Angie and Squidge scurried out from under the tree, heading back to the path that we'd come from, and I started to scamper after them as quietly as I could – but before I could take more than a couple of steps, the branches of the tree started moving.

Which, I will give you, doesn't sound like anything worth mentioning. It was mid-September in North-East England; of *course* the branches were bloody moving. But here's the thing – the branches weren't moving in the wind. They were creaking and groaning as they moved *up*, as if someone with an insane amount of strength was lifting them by a few inches.

And as it happened, a few inches was all it took for me to be completely visible to everyone in that clearing.

I heard the Cloaks shuffling 'round to face me, and I felt my blood run cold as I realised that every single person there was staring at me.

And for the second time in a few seconds, I froze.

How I thought that'd help, I couldn't tell you. Was I going to blend in with the tree behind me? Make them forget that they'd ever seen me? I don't think so. I was wearing a red trench coat, for God's sake. And as far as I could remember, at no time had I been bitten by a radioactive chameleon and developed superpowers that let me camouflage myself whenever I wanted to.

I saw Angie spin around on the spot a couple of feet ahead of me, halfway between the tree and the slope that I'd all but fallen down, and even from that distance, I could see her eyes somehow get even wider than they already had been. She did a funny little jerk forwards, one foot awkwardly swinging out and stomping the ground in front of her, but before she could do anything more than that one step, I quickly shook my head at her.

Unlike me, Angie wasn't wearing a bright red coat.

Angie was wearing a navy blue quilted Barbour that seemed to make her invisible to people who like to use flame torches as their only source of light. It didn't seem to make sense to let them know that she was there if they hadn't already seen her.

I whipped around and shot a bright smile at the Cloaks and Knight, who had her left arm stretched out towards my tree, raised up a few inches with her palm pointing up towards the sky.

'*So* sorry,' I said chirpily, taking a few steps towards them until I wasn't covered by the tree anymore. 'I was looking for the meeting of the Midnight Tree Huggers, is this not them?'

'No,' Knight said drily after a little pause, lowering her arm back down to her side, and I heard the horse chestnut tree groan again as its branches obviously settled back into place. What the *fuck*? 'You missed them. They meet on Monday nights.'

'Ah,' I smiled pleasantly, sliding one foot back by a couple of inches as subtly as I could. 'That *is* disappointing. Well, I'll just get out of your hair and let you crack on, then. Again, really sorry to have interrupted you. You all have a nice night, and enjoy your...' I stared at them all for a couple of seconds, trying and failing to think of a word that summed up wearing robes, holding flame torches and planning a murder. 'Stuff.'

I whirled around on the spot, ready to hurry out of the clearing and hoping against hope that by some fluke, I'd caught Knight on a night when she was happy to essentially let me off with a warning. But before I could get very far, I heard her call lightly,

'I do hope you don't think you're getting away with that bullshit, Armitage.'

I stopped dead in my tracks as a huge, heavy dollop of dread clunked into my stomach, and then I slowly turned around to face her. 'I'm sorry?'

'Oh, come, now,' she said, fixing me with that same serene smile that she'd given the Cloaks a few minutes earlier. 'We're both too smart for you to try that one. I know who you are, Armitage. I know exactly why you're here. And I have to say, I don't appreciate being spied on.'

'I don't appreciate you being a complete lunatic and turning Habely into the murder capital of the North East,' I shot back, before I could stop myself. 'But hey. C'est la vie.'

'One day quite soon,' she told me, with an edge to her voice that I could tell she was trying to hide, 'you and everyone else like you will see that what we're doing here is for the greater good. When we've achieved our goal –'

'But surely,' I interrupted mock-thoughtfully, tilting my head to one side, 'you can achieve whatever you're trying to do without all of this? I mean, I would've thought one of the perks of being a witch is that you can use your magic to do what you want when you want without any trouble at all. And you *are* a full-blown witch, right?'

Any pretence of calmness or pleasantness slid right off her face. Instead, she shot me a furious look, and for a second – one bizarre, disgusting second – I could see all the bones in her face sticking out, exactly like they had done in her Police interview.

Believe me, as disconcerting as it'd been on a screen, it was a lot worse in the flesh.

'Children,' she announced coldly, still glaring at me as her bones settled back down into their usual positions. 'I'm sure you've realised by now that Miss Black is here to stop us from achieving our purpose. We cannot allow this to happen. Bring her to me. *Now.*'

I heard the Cloaks start moving towards me, but before I saw a single one of them take even one step – in fact, probably before any of them had *chance* to take a step – I felt myself jerk into action, spinning around on the spot as quickly as I could and screaming for Angie and Squidge to go.

And then I ran.

Oh, I ran.

I don't think I've ever ran so fast in my life; my legs were moving so quickly that they didn't feel fully attached to me, and even though I could hear my feet pounding away, I genuinely couldn't feel them hitting the ground.

Instead of running straight up to where Angie and Squidge had been, I veered off to my right, somehow managing to realise that while the Cloaks obviously now knew that I wasn't by myself, they had no idea where Angie and Squidge were. And there was absolutely no way in hell I was going to lead the gits to them.

I dove into the trees at the edge of the clearing and shoved my way through the branches that were grabbing at me, stumbling over the occasional tree root and running blindly in the pitch black, far too aware of the fact that however many people were pounding after me, and just as conscious of how loudly I was breathing.

It was one of those weird things where it felt like I was running for ages, hooking a sharp turn to the side every so often to try and lose the Cloaks that were chasing after me – but really, it must've only been about five minutes before I put enough space between me and them that it'd be safe to stop for a few seconds.

I threw myself into a clump of birches growing close together, right on the edge of a big patch of felled trees, and put one hand against the trunk of the tree to my right, straining my eyes in the direction I'd come from as I doubled over and tried to (quietly) get as much air as I could past the hard, burning lump that'd made itself at home in the dead-centre of my throat.

For a few seconds, I didn't dare move. Somehow, the fact that I couldn't see any Cloaks moving through the trees around me didn't do a lot to calm me down. It was almost like I thought I hadn't lost them at all and they'd followed me all the way to where I was hiding, but instead of immediately pouncing on me and dragging me back to Knight, they were just waiting for me to let my guard down.

But no.

Apparently not.

Once I was confident that they definitely weren't just lurking in the darkness, I straightened up and leant against the trees behind me, closing my eyes and trying to stop myself from panicking as I took in the whole situation.

I had absolutely no idea where I was. I didn't know how to get back to where I'd left Angie and Squidge, and even if I could find my way there, it wasn't like they'd have hung around; they would've took off the second they heard me scream at them. Besides, going back meant trying to find my way through a forest full of psychopath-sympathisers who wanted nothing more than to take me back to their precious Knight, something that – funnily enough – did not appeal to me.

But staying where I was didn't seem like the best idea, either.

Not when there was nothing to say that they wouldn't eventually find me.

I craned my neck over my shoulder, peering at the felled area through a gap in my clump of trees. From what I could see, it sloped down towards the edge of the moor, opening up over some town lights, which I was really hoping belonged to Habely. I turned a tiny bit to my right, squinting as I tried to see whether there was any kind of path I could take down to the village and get the hell out of there, but before I could work it out – and just as I decided, sod it, I'd just have to go for it and see what happened – I heard a twig snapping a few feet away from me.

My breath caught in my throat, even as I tried to tell myself that there was every chance it was just a badger or a fox or something.

Snap.

And then again, a little bit closer this time.

Snap.

The thing is, whatever was walking over the twigs was moving too slowly for it to be a fox or a badger.

Snap.

I could try and kid myself all I wanted to, but it was too deliberate to be any kind of animal.

Snap.

I felt my heartbeat pick up as I forced myself to turn away from the clearing and instead look straight ahead, in the direction that the snapping was coming from.

And the second I did, I saw a Cloak making their way through a row of trees two rows away where I hiding.

I didn't move.

I barely even breathed.

I just stood there with my back pressed tight to the trees behind me and a panicked dread rising up inside me, feeling my heart thumping hard against my chest as I watched the Cloak slowly walk between the trees, turning their head from side to side as they passed each one.

Any second now, they were going to come a bit closer and spot my clump of trees. And while where I was stood did give me more cover than any of the single trees nearby would have, it didn't do a lot to disguise the colour of my coat.

It was simple: if they found that clump of trees, they found me.

So I had two options.

I could stay where I was and take the chance that they'd get distracted before they realised the clump of trees was there, and scarper as soon as I could.

Or I could make a run for it over the felled area, and just hope that not only could I outrun the Cloak, but also that there *was* some path or another down to wherever the clearing looked out over.

I hadn't quite decided which way I was going to play it before I heard a man's hoarse voice say abruptly,

'Any sign?'

My heart sank down to somewhere to the vicinity of my ankles.

Shit.

Shit.

There were two of them.

One, I could try and deal with, but two?

I was shagged.

'Nothing,' the first Cloak grunted, also undeniably in a bloke's voice, turning to face the second, taller guy, who was talking towards him from the left-hand side of my clump of trees. 'It's like she's disappeared.'

'Don't be an idiot, Burrows,' the second Cloak snapped impatiently, resting one hand above his head on one of the trees between him and my clump. 'She can't have; she doesn't have the same abilities as our Mistress. No, we'll find her. We've got the whole forest covered, and she can't keep going forever.'

'Then you tell me where she is. I've been up to the pond, she's not there. I saw Henley and Cowell on my way here; they've been along the higher track, and there's no sign of her. You've been down here. Have you seen her?'

'No.'

'No. So where the fuck is she?'

Not standing in this clump of trees, I can promise you that. No, no. You don't need to look. Just trust me.

'She must be in another part of the woods,' the second Cloak said curtly, after a tense pause. 'We can't have been chasing her like we thought; the dark must've confused us. Let's head back up to the grounds,' he added decisively, lifting his hand off the tree trunk and straightening up. 'Someone will have found her and took her back, I'm sure. And if they haven't, we need to decide our next plan of action. We are not letting our Mistress down.'

He moved past my clump of trees, walking in the same direction he'd come from and leaving Burrows to follow, and I felt a tiny pinprick of relief break through all of the panic pounding through me. But he hadn't got very far before I saw something change in the way Burrows was standing.

I don't think he moved, as such; he just seemed to straighten up a bit more and get slightly stiffer for good measure.

'Wait,' he called out, and at the same time, I realised exactly what was happening.

He'd been looking straight at the other Cloak while they'd been talking.

The other Cloak had been standing right in front of my clump of trees.

The Cloak had moved, and Burrows' gaze hadn't.

Which meant that he was looking straight at me.

'Wait,' he called again sharply, launching himself towards my clump of trees. 'Get back here, now. *I found her.*'

Before the other guy could come back, Burrows moved forwards, striding towards where I was stood, and I didn't bother to hang about.

I whipped around and shot through the gap in the trees, sprinting out into the felled area and slipping over the loose twigs and branches under my feet as I ran towards the edge of the moor. But the two of them were right on me, and although I could hear them stumbling over the fallen trees as well, there was absolutely no question that they were moving faster than I was.

I felt one of their hands brush against my back, trying to grab the belt around my coat, and without thinking about it, I ducked down without breaking stride and grabbed hold of the first stick, and then I whirled around and slammed it into the side of his head. He let out a loud grunt of pain and went down, falling onto the twigs with a heavy thud, and then there was a yelp and a smack of bone on bone as the other Cloak fell on top of him. I tried to jump out of the way and take off running again, but before I could go anywhere, one of them whipped out an arm, grabbing me by my ankle and giving it a good yank, pulling me off my feet and making me land hard on my left arm.

I heard myself yelp as the pain exploded in my shoulder, and when I twisted around, I saw that it was the second Cloak – the one whose nose was so big that it stuck out from under his hood, and who was either very fat or very muscled, judging by the way his cloak was stretching over his shoulders – who had my ankle in a vice-like grip, shoving Burrows off him and leaving him to writhe around on the ground.

I kicked out at him wildly as he started pulling me in, trying to grab onto anything that'd stop me sliding towards them. *'Get the fuck off me!'*

'I don't think so,' he hissed viciously, giving my ankle another hard yank so that I flew another couple of inches closer. 'My Mistress is going to be very happy with me for this one. You have no idea how she'll repay me...'

And I didn't think twice.

In fact, I don't even think I thought once.

I twisted further onto my back and brought my free leg up to my chest, and just as he let go of my ankle to grab hold of my legs instead, I kicked out towards him as hard as I could. My foot slammed full-force into his nose, and I didn't just hear it break; I actually *felt* the bones shatter under my shoe.

He let go of me with a horrible howl of pain, both hands flying towards his crushed nose, and the second he did, I was up, scrabbling to my feet and hurtling towards the edge of the moor, taking off before I was even fully upright.

At the exact same second I took off, I saw two more Cloaks step out from the trees on the other side of the felled area and start coming towards me, picking up speed with every step. Whether they'd heard me yell and come to see what was going on, or whether they'd stumbled across us on their way back to the clearing, I didn't know and I didn't care; all that mattered was getting the hell away from the lot of them.

'Henley!' Burrows bellowed from behind me, and when I threw a frantic look over my shoulder, I saw him clambering to his feet, completely ignoring the Cloak splayed out on the floor in front of him. 'It's her, she's the one we need! Get hold of her!'

I threw myself forward, forcing myself to go even faster and desperately trying to stop slipping and stumbling on the bits of felled trees as I heard Henley and the Cloak with him – who I was guessing must be Cowell – start gaining on me.

I chanced another peek, this time over my right shoulder, and saw that the two of them had spread out slightly; one of them was coming up straight behind me, while the other was running along the treeline to my right, obviously hoping to grab me if I suddenly changed course and tried to get away through the trees. I could hear Burrows chasing after me too, his feet pounding the ground somewhere further back and to the left of me, so that the only option I had was to keep charging straight ahead, towards the boulders that were coming into view, overhanging the edge of the moor.

I was going fast, but they were doing a bloody good job of keeping up with me; every now and again, I'd feel someone's fingertips brush against the back of my coat, trying to grab hold of my belt or my collar, and it'd make me shit myself enough that I'd sprint even faster. I didn't dare look behind me again, partly in case it slowed me down and partly because I didn't want to know if even more Cloaks had joined in. I reached the boulders and scrambled up onto the biggest one as quickly as I could, shuffling as close to the far edge as I could and frantically trying to spot any kind of path that I could use to get out of there.

It wasn't until that point that I realised we weren't facing Habely; instead, we were looking out over Crambledon, the village a few miles up the road from Habely that just so happened to be where my parents were currently living.

Of course, my parents had gone on a three-month tour of America six weeks earlier, which meant that – if I'd been stupid enough to have *any* inclination to get them involved in the whole situation – they weren't going to be much help to me. But if I could get myself down off Habely Moor, if I could force myself to run for another mile or so and get myself to the local pub – which, if I was lucky, would be having one of those stoppy-backs it was so famous for – I'd be able to use their phone to get hold of...

Well.

Hadaway.

In the middle of everything, Hadaway was the only person I could think of who needed to know what was going on.

And as much as I wasn't looking forward to telling him about what'd happened, it turned out to be a moot point anyway. No matter how hard I looked – with and without using my torch app – I couldn't see any paths leading down from the boulders, not even any questionable ones.

So, basically, my options were to jump into the heather eight feet or so below the boulders and hope that I didn't find myself with broken bones or dead, or to force my way back through the Cloaks and hope for exactly the same.

I wasn't sure which one was more unlikely.

I whirled around to face the Cloaks to see what the chances were of getting past them, and felt my heart hit my boots as I realised that it was never going to happen. Three of the Cloaks were stood at the base of my boulder, clearly ready to catch me if I ran, while the fourth was heaving himself up onto the rock I was stood on.

Without even thinking about it, I strode fast across the rock and slammed my foot as hard as I could into his chin, so hard that the thud vibrated though my foot, and the Cloak immediately fell down onto the twigs below with a howl of pain. He'd barely hit the ground before the Cloak stood to the left of the others put his hands onto the boulder, ready to pull himself up onto the smooth rock, but before he could even start to climb up, I stomped hard on his fingers and pushed down with everything I had, making him let out a horrible kind of strangled scream.

'I'm not messing around,' I told them harshly, stepping harder onto the guy's fingers as I raised the stick I was still holding up to my shoulder. 'The next one of you to who tries to come up here is going to lose your face.'

'Just try it,' the Cloak in the middle sneered, sounding so full of cold that I could only assume that it was his nose that I'd put my foot through. 'The second you move, we'll have you. Our Mistress would like to meet with you, Armitage, and we are not prepared to let her down.'

Mmm.

Let's recap, shall we?

I was outnumbered four-to-one.

They had each other there as back-up, whereas I only had a stick, which – as solid and capable of rearranging faces as it was – was only going to get me so far.

And they were driven by some deluded but genuine belief that the woman they were bending over backwards to help was a full-blown witch instead of a bona fide psychopath.

I didn't particularly fancy the odds.

'Your boss mentioned a procedure back there,' I said, keeping my voice light and casual as I dug my foot further into the Cloak's fingers, stopping him from tugging them out from under me. 'What's that about?'

'That,' Bust-Nose Cloak said in a low voice, 'is none of your concern.'

'I'm going to disagree with you,' I told him kindly, somehow forcing myself to smile at him. 'I live in Habely. You lot are obviously wanting to kill me. I think both of those things give me the right to know if Knight's been performing illegal dental operations up here, or if 'procedure' is just a polite way of saying 'human sacrifice'.'

None of them said anything.

They just stood there, watching me in what would've been total silence, if it weren't for the grunts of pain coming from the Cloak whose hand I was squashing.

'Why does she even need to make a human sacrifice?' I pressed on after a couple of seconds, ignoring the vibes of imminent murder that they were putting out. 'I mean, she's a witch, right? So surely she can do what she wants without having to murder anybody?'

'The procedure is imperative for our Mistress's success,' the Cloak to the right of Bust-Nose

Cloak told me, taking half a step closer to my boulder. 'It won't be possible for her to reach

her goals without it.'

I tilted my head to one side, blinking at him. 'But you're telling me she's a *witch*. You're

telling me she's got all these magical powers and shit. So... what is it, exactly, that a witch

can't do without killing people?'

They all went silent again. Grunts and oh-so-manly squeals aside.

For a few seconds, we all just stood there and stared at each other. Whether I'd given

them food for thought, I had no idea; through all the running and fighting, their hoods had

stayed firmly in place, so I couldn't see enough of their faces to tell if anyone was having a

lightbulb moment. And while they were too busy being quiet to kill me, I thought it'd be best

to keep shtum myself, just in case any of them realised what a good point I'd made and

insisted that I be let go freely, i.e. without dying.

But before any of that could happen, there was suddenly an explosion of shouting coming

from the direction of the trees that I'd ran through. And just as we all jerked our heads

around to see what was happening, someone came bursting out of the trees and started

charging towards us, without even seeming to hesitate to check where we all were.

Bust-Nose Cloak and the Cloak who'd explained about the 'procedure' whirled around on

their heels and took off without a second thought, running towards the trees at the top of the

felled area, opposite the boulders and away from the person heading towards us, but the third

Cloak – the one who I'd booted in the chin – obviously had other ideas. He threw himself

forwards and hoisted himself up onto my boulder, clearly with every intention of dragging

me off it and back to Knight, and purely on reflex, I launched myself backwards.

And the next thing I knew, there was a whole lot of nothing underneath me.

For what seemed like a few bizarre moments but was probably only half a second – if that – I seemed to just hang in mid-air, staring at the Cloaks and getting a vibe that they were just as surprised as I was.

And then I was flying through the air, tilting just far enough back that I could see the star-dotted sky above the boulders and falling for what felt like at least a good hour or so.

In reality, it can't have been more than a second or two before I slammed down on my left side in the heather, hard enough that the force of it knocked all of the breath out of me and the sound of the thud made me feel sick.

I have no idea how long I laid there for, vaguely aware of more shouting coming from the boulders above me and feeling myself curl into a ball, clenching my hands into fists in front of my face and trying to remember how to breathe as I waited for the pain to hit me.

And all at once, it did.

It wasn't the nice, considerate type of pain that comes on gradually, so that you can get used to each level of it before you move onto the next one. No, this was a tidal wave of pure agony crashing over me.

Every single part of my body hurt, even – I swear to God – my eyelids and my fucking *ears*; some places were throbbing, some places were aching, and then there were some other places that had decided to do both.

I squeezed my eyes tight shut against it all, clenching my teeth together even as I heard myself letting out little squeaks as every bit of pain hit me again and again, completely unable to think about anything other than how much it all hurt – Christ, it hurt – and the fact that I needed to breathe, that I'd be alright if I could *just fucking breathe.*

At some point, a realisation that I still needed to get out of there broke through the fog. I didn't know where the Cloaks were. I didn't know who the hell had came running out of the trees, or – for that matter – what they were doing up there. I'd seen enough of them to know they weren't wearing a robe, but that didn't mean shit; what were the chances that they weren't another murderer wandering around in the woods, picking out their next victim? (High, actually. Once again – this is Habely.) And I could hear someone slowly crunching through the heather towards me.

'Armitage.'

I felt panic start to mingle with all of the pain coursing through me, desperately trying to make myself *do* something, but there was no way it was going to happen.

I hurt too much to move.

And I hurt too much to say anything.

'*Armitage.*'

All I could do was lay there, listening to whoever it was getting closer, and wondering if my parents realised that I was serious when I said I wanted my funeral to be fancy-dress.

I heard the heather crunching as whoever it was made their way to my side, and just as they put their fingers on my neck, clearly feeling for a pulse, I finally forced myself – with a ridiculous amount of effort – to open my eyes.

And immediately kicked myself for doing it.

Hadaway was crouching next to me with his fingers on my neck, looking more concerned than I'd ever seen him and just the tiniest bit paler than usual. Which was weird, considering the fact that his current life situation would drastically improve if I wasn't around to keep sticking my nose into the whole Knight case.

'Jesus Christ, Armitage,' he said, sounding out-and-out relieved as his face softened a smidge. 'I thought you'd got yourself –' He cut himself off and took his hand off me, blowing a heavy breath out through his nose as he ran one hand across the lower half of his face, still looking more concerned than I'd have ever expected. 'Jesus. How bad are you hurt?'

I did try to tell him.

I tried to say that everywhere hurt, that even my internal organs were hurting or throbbing, and that I was fairly convinced that I was never going to be out of this pain and this was me for the rest of my life. (Without even a hint of being dramatic, either.)

But it turns out that, actually, it's pretty hard to speak when you're hurting that much. Because when I opened my mouth to say all of that to him, the only thing that came out was a very eloquent kind of,

'Guhhhh.'

And then my eyes rolled into the back of my head.

And everything went black.

SIX.

I woke up feeling a lot more comfortable than I had been when I'd passed out.

Instead of having rough heather stick into me, prickling and itching every last bit of me, I was sinking into something warm and squishy, feeling deliciously snuggly and warm instead of cold and mildly damp. And the more I drifted to, the more I realised that there was something just as warm and comfortable draped over me as well, to the point where I felt like I was wrapped up in a giant burrito made purely of marshmallows.

But as nice as waking up on a bed of mallows is – and I can't stress this enough, it really is lovely – it didn't stop me from noticing, as I became more and more awake, that every inch of my body was quietly throbbing.

It was getting worse by the second, until it was definitely much more of a horrible dull pain than anything else; my back was as heavy and stiff as a concrete slab, and everywhere else felt like it had a severe tooth abscess and bad period cramps all at the same time. It was my left shoulder that hurt the worst; it was pulsing almost as much as my back was, and aching so much that I gritted my teeth against the pain before I even opened my eyes, breathing hard and fast through my nose.

And somehow, through all that, it filtered through to my brain that there was some kind of warm, not unpleasant pressure on my chest. Once I noticed that, I realised that there a slight breeze on my chin as well, one that alternated with something cool, moist and somehow solid but squishy at the same time pressing against me.

And when I cracked open one eye to see what was going on, Squidge was standing next to me, his chin resting on my chest as he stared at me with excited, expectant eyes and panting gently as he patiently waited to find out what game I was playing and how, exactly, he could join in.

I was laid on the settee in the flat, with a fluffy blanket stuffed underneath me and two more thrown over the top of me, and – I didn't know what made me happier, Squidge or this – a wine glass full to the brim with sherry on the coffee table in front of me.

'Hello, you,' I murmured, shooting him my best attempt at a smile as I lifted one hand up (with what I can only describe as a gargantuan effort) and ran it over his head.

He didn't say anything back.

He's a man of very few words, is Squidge.

I started to half-push, half-wriggle myself into a sitting position – grimacing in pain all the while – and he jumped up, panting excitedly with his mouth stretched into a huge doggy smile and his tail going like the clappers, clearly convinced that I was getting up from my nap to finally play with him.

I didn't bother explaining to him that he was wrong. As soon as I'd struggled far enough up to be officially classed as among the sitting, I nudged him out of the way and launched myself forward, clumsily grabbing hold of the wine glass and gulping down as much sherry as I could.

'Tidge,' I heard Angie say seriously, just as I came up for air. And when I dragged my head around to my right, she was stood halfway between the settee and the opening to the kitchen, looking more anxiously concerned than I'd ever seen her. It took me another second to realise that Johnny and Hadaway were stood not too far behind her, their faces far more grim than I really had the energy to bother with. 'How're you feeling?'

I managed to flash her a bright smile. Or at least, I tried to; I have a feeling that it came out more as something between a wince and a grimace. 'Dandy.'

Normally, she would've rolled her eyes at that, and/or flicked a dry little comment back at me. She didn't do that this time. Instead, she took a few steps forward and perched on the coffee table, looking so serious and so worried that it made me a little uncomfortable.

'No, come on, Tidge,' she said, as I took another huge swig of sherry. 'Be honest with us. If you need to go to hospital, you need to tell –'

'I don't need to go to hospital,' I blurted out, so quickly that she almost got showered in sherry. Nope. No hospitals. Not for me, thank you. 'Look at me, I'm fine, why would I need to go to hospital?'

There was a pause while she eyeballed me, looking less than convinced that I was, in fact, fine, and I frantically tried to think of an escape route in case the three of them tried to ambush me and take me to hospital by force.

Given how I could feel myself getting stiffer by the second, I didn't think that just running away would be as easy as it sounded.

'There's bloody good reason to take you to hospital,' Hadaway said, sounding almost impatient as he strode over to join us and fixed me with a slight frown. 'D'you remember what happened?'

I blinked up at him a couple of times, wondering what the hell he was talking about.

And then suddenly, in one big rush, it all came back to me.

Seeing Knight in that clearing.

Getting chased across Habely Moor by the Cloaks.

Clambering up onto the boulder so that they couldn't get me.

And accidentally throwing myself off said boulder when they tried to grab me anyway.

Mmm.

Yeah.

That explained why I hurt so much.

'I'm fine,' I repeated, sitting back against the settee and pulling my knees up to my chest. And then quickly putting my feet back on the floor when I realised that moving more than I had to was definitely not the best idea. 'I'll have a hot bath and I'll be back to normal, I don't need to go to hospital.' I blinked down at my wine glass, which had somehow emptied itself without any of us noticing. 'I wouldn't say no to more sherry, though.'

I saw Hadaway and Angie exchange glances, Hadaway looking out-and-out exasperated while Angie's face was somewhere between reassured and mildly annoyed.

'You're telling me,' Hadaway said, in the very brusque voice that he usually saves just for me, 'you don't think she needs to go to hospital.'

'At what point did I say that?' she demanded hotly, as Johnny brought the bottle of sherry over and topped me up, filling my glass nearly all the way to the top. Johnny Wallace, patron saint of the sherry lovers. 'At what point did I say *anything* other than she clearly *does* need to go to hospital? I'm with you, Ade, but what would've been the point in taking her when we didn't know what exact part of her needed checking out? And what's the point in her taking her in awake when she won't tell them that anything's wrong with her?'

I glanced up at St Johnny in surprise, but instead of shedding any light on why Angie and Hadaway were suddenly arguing – something I hadn't seen before – he just shook his head, with a look on his face that can only be described as exasperatedly grim.

'She just fell eight fucking feet,' Hadaway bit off, looking more irritated than exasperated as he crossed his arms across his chest. 'All of her needs checking out.'

'How would it have looked?' she asked testily, as her face started to fill with a dark red flush, the way it always does when she's pissed off. 'Come on, you're a copper. Tell me. How would it have looked if three people, none of who are paramedics, pitch up with an unconscious lass and some cock-and-bull story about her falling off a moor, but – oh – we can't tell them what moor she fell off, what the hell she was doing up there in the middle of the night, or how she even fell off the fucking thing? Would people not have immediately thought that we had something to do with it?'

'Right,' Johnny interjected wearily, as Hadaway opened his mouth to bite back, looking even more irritated than just the sight of me usually makes him. 'Enough. You've been having this argument for long enough now, it's a safe bet you're not going to agree. It's three o'clock in the morning,' he added, raising his voice just the tiniest bit as Angie made a funny little noise in the back of her throat, looking for all the world like she wasn't quite ready to drop it. 'Let's just get some rest, and if you still aren't happy, we can talk about it then. On the proviso,' he added, turning to look at me, 'that you be honest with us about whether you need to go to hospital or not.'

I nodded enthusiastically, too busy enjoying the warmth of the sherry that I was inhaling to take the glass away from my mouth, and he turned back to Angie and Hadaway with a look on his face that made it blatantly obvious that the conversation was over.

'Right,' Angie announced briskly, clapping her hands together as she jumped up from the coffee table. 'Fine. I'll go and run you a hot bath, Tidge, see if it stops you stiffening up too much. What're you going to do?' she added, turning to Hadaway before I had time to point out that having a bath wasn't *quite* what I wanted to do at three o'clock in the morning. 'Are you going home, or do you want to stay here?'

'Aye, go on,' he said after a couple of seconds' pause, and when I managed to tear my face away from the sherry enough to glance up at him, he was frowning slightly at me, looking no less convinced that they shouldn't be whisking me off for a full MOT at the hospital. 'I'll have a couple of hours here before we crack on.'

I felt myself give an inward little grown as Angie scurried off to the bathroom and Johnny followed her to get some spare bedding out of the boiler cupboard, leaving me alone with Hadaway (something that – let's be honest – never seems to end well). He sat down on the settee next to me, looking just as concerned as he'd looked on the moor and grim even for Hadaway, which...

Well, it was a bit off-putting, to be honest.

I was used to him glaring at me and looking like I was pissing him off. Looking at me like he actually gave a shit was so unprecedented that I didn't know how I was supposed to act.

'Honestly,' I told him, shooting him the best smile I could manage. 'I'm fine. You can go home, Angie and Johnny are here if I need anything.'

'No,' he said wearily, letting himself by coaxed into scratching Squidge's ears almost like he hadn't noticed that it was happening. 'It makes more sense to stay here, I'll be heading up to the Moor first thing. And,' he added, shooting me a faint smile, 'I won't have to worry about you as much if I'm here.'

I blinked at him a couple of times, coming over all warm as I felt a funny kind of flutter somewhere low down in my tummy. I had no idea what I was meant to say. I didn't know what I was supposed to *do*.

Hadaway was worried about me.

Hadaway was smiling at me.

Hadaway was showing himself to be an actual human and not an angry robot whose entire purpose was to shag every woman in the Cattringham County area, something that genuinely made me wonder if the force of the fall had knocked me clean into a parallel universe where a Hadaway who was moderately nice actually existed.

And for reasons that I can only assume were down to pure shock, I suddenly felt an overwhelming urge to cuddle into him, bury my head in his neck and maybe try to get a peek at exactly what was going on under his polo shirt.

'Listen,' he continued, as I blinked in horrified confusion at the thoughts popping into my head. Since when did I care what Hadaway looked like without his top off? 'I'm going to need to know what happened between you and Knight.'

This time my blinking was directed at him. 'I thought Angie would've told you that.'

'Angie wasn't there for everything. She's told us what she can, but we need to know what happened to you.'

I tilted my head to one side as the thought finally occurred to me. 'What were you and Johnny doing up there tonight, anyway?'

'Stakeout,' he said, flashing me a wry grin. 'We drew the short straws. Go and get your bath,' he added, in a voice that can only be described as final. 'We'll talk about what happened in the morning.'

I didn't sleep well that night.

Part of it was due to the 'responsible adults' in the flat point-blank refusing to let me have any painkillers with my sherry. Neither would they let me have another glass of sherry after my bath, something that meant I had nothing to save me from the waves of pain that hit me once the sherry I *had* had had started wearing off. And believe me, those waves were *massive*.

Big, stonking tsunamis of pure agony.

It was fun.

Another part of it was because I couldn't stop bloody *thinking*.

Whatever procedure Knight was planning was going to happen that weekend. A quick look at my phone in the bath had told me that the next full moon was going to be on Friday, which – if my app could actually be trusted – meant that somebody else was going to die in three days.

And part of me knew that I should've been thrilled. Not, of course, because someone else was going to die, but because I'd actually got information that could help with the investigation.

I just didn't feel like I'd found out *enough*. I mean, we didn't know who was lined up to be Knight's next victim. We didn't know where Knight *or* this person was. We had no idea what this procedure was, or why Knight had them all believing that she needed to do it.

Basically, we knew how Knight was going to be spending her Friday night.

That was it.

I finally gave up on sleep around six o'clock and dragged myself out of bed, groggy as hell and so stiff that after thirty seconds of slowly inching towards my bedroom door, all I wanted to do was crawl back into bed and sleep until I was less rigid than a brick wall again. In fact, if it wasn't for the fact that anyone who's had a fall like I had is entitled to sherry for breakfast, there's a very good chance that I would've done exactly that.

Hadaway was already awake when I dragged myself into the kitchen. Not only that, but he'd made himself perfectly at home, drinking a black coffee and munching on toast as he flicked through a newspaper that I was fairly certain we hadn't had the day before.

I stopped in my tracks and blinked at him. 'Where'd you get that?'

'I walked your dog down to the high street. How're you feeling?'

'My dog is called –'

'I'm not saying your dog's name,' he said dryly, closing the paper. 'How're you feeling?'

'Shit,' I said lightly, eyeing up the alcohol cupboard and wondering whether he'd let me get away with a morning sherry. 'I didn't sleep at all and everywhere hurts.' I flicked my eyes from the cupboard to him and back again before a tiny but firm voice somewhere at the back of my head said, *Sod it.* 'I'm having a sherry,' I told him defiantly, taking one small step towards the cupboard.

He shot me a faintly amused look. 'Good to know.'

'After last night,' I carried on defensively, although God knows why I was being defensive when he wasn't doing anything to stop me, 'I deserve a sherry.'

'I never said you didn't.'

I looked at him suspiciously for a couple of seconds, waiting for the catch. And when it never came, I took another small step towards the cupboard, just to see exactly how serious he was about not stopping me. Meanwhile, he was still sat at the kitchen table, looking even more amused as he took a swig of his coffee.

'Sit down,' he said eventually, standing up from the table when I didn't move any more than that, still unconvinced that he wouldn't pounce on me as soon as I opened that cupboard. 'I'll get you your sherry. But not a word to Angie,' he added dryly, opening the cupboard door as I waddled over to the kitchen table and eased myself into a chair, too surprised to do anything other than what he told me to. 'She'll have my head for it.'

'Angie just doesn't appreciate sherry.'

He gave his head a single shake as he fished my sherry glass out of the cupboard and filled it to the brim. 'You're the only person I know under ninety who appreciates sherry.' He handed me the glass and watched me inhale it, leaning back against the counter and crossing his arms across his chest as his usual slight frown slipped back onto his face. 'I had an interesting phone call this morning.'

The fact that he thought anything before six o'clock was part of the morning was interesting enough to me, but somebody else being awake enough to phone him so early was fairly intriguing as well.

'Really?' I held my empty glass out for him to refill. 'Lucky you.'

He topped my glass up roughly halfway, and watched me seriously as I eyed it up disappointedly. If I'd known that was all I'd get for a second glass, I would've made the first one last longer.

'James Pettyfer's asked for another interview.'

I blinked at him in surprise.

Then I blinked at him a couple of times more.

And then again, just for good measure.

'What?'

I'd never heard of anyone asking for another interview before. Usually, the people are just taken down to the interview room, and all they do is sit there and take their solicitor's advice to go 'No reply', something that I can't help but feel doesn't warrant a hundred quid an hour. Even when people come in for voluntary interviews, they don't ask to come *back*; if the Bobbies need more information, then it's *them* who arrange a second one. It's never the people being quizzed.

'Apparently,' Hadaway continued, his voice becoming something between dry and irritated as he leaned forward to pick his mug up off the table, 'he won't talk to anyone but Cleaner Dave.'

My heart stopped in my chest. 'Oh.'

'Oh.'

I flashed him my brightest smile, like Cleaner Dave meant nothing at all to me. 'Well, it's nice that he's managed to make a friend in there.'

He fixed me with a hard stare for a couple of seconds, and I frantically tried to think of any excuses or cover stories that might remotely work.

But nope.

No way out of this one.

'When they brought Cleaner Dave in,' he carried on eventually, definitely sounding more irate than dry as he scratched the left side of his jaw with his right hand, 'Pettyfer wouldn't talk. He said that it was the wrong Cleaner Dave. The Cleaner Dave he wanted was some lass with curly black hair and an accent he couldn't place, who mopped the walls and had parents who thought they were pirates.' He raised an eyebrow at me, his jaw suddenly looking quite tense. 'Any idea who that could be?'

I gave him the most innocent look I could manage. 'I couldn't even guess.'

He threw back what was left of his coffee before glaring at me, with a vein in his neck doing a funny little twitch. 'Why the *fuck* have you been talking to Pettyfer?'

I blinked at him again, feeling my breath catch slightly in my throat as I wondered if he actually expected me to answer that, or if he just wanted me to know that he knew that I was Cleaner Dave.

There was a little pause while we stared at each other, Hadaway's jaw so clenched that I was a little worried his teeth were going to shatter, and I wondered how he'd react to me changing the subject slightly to ask for another sherry.

Most likely: *not well.*

'Right, look,' he bit off impatiently, when it became apparent that I wasn't going to answer him. As if I could say anything that wouldn't piss him off even more, anyway. 'Forget about why you did it. The fact is, we've got a problem now, because he won't talk to us without you there. So' – he shot me a grim look that made it obvious that he couldn't believe what he was about to do, blowing a short breath out through his nose – 'how d'you feel about a run over to East District?'

Two paracetamol, one tiny sherry and forty minutes later, me and Hadaway were sat in an interview room at East District, across the table from Pettyfer. He somehow looked even reedier than he had the day before, keeping his head ducked so that he didn't have to look at either of us and wringing his hands together as he rested them on top of the table.

'You told me you were a cleaner,' he muttered, once we'd all introduced ourselves and Hadaway had gone through his legal rights.

'I also mopped your walls and told you my parents thought they were pirates,' I pointed out lightly, barely managing to stop myself from rolling my eyes. 'Did you work out that I might not have been telling the truth?'

Hadaway glanced at me with a grim frown on his face, and I sent him an innocent, wide-eyed, *'What?'* kind of look in return.

But come on.

If the guy really didn't have the brains to work out I'd been spouting bullshit, then I think we'd worked out the mystery of how Knight had got to him.

'Alright,' Hadaway said heavily, turning back to Pettyfer after a slight pause. 'You've asked for this interview. What d'you want to tell us?'

'Since I spoke with Da– with you,' he said shakily, knotting his hands together so tightly that his knuckles turned white, 'I've been having a think. I've been trying to remember what happened while I was with her... with Knight. It's not been easy, but last night, I remembered something. I remembered what I saw.' He lifted his head up, looking Hadaway dead in the eyes, and suddenly he didn't sound so reedy. He didn't sound shaky or scared. If anything, he sounded almost confident. 'I didn't kill those lads.'

Hadaway leaned forwards slightly, resting one elbow on the table as he ran a hand over his stubble. 'Last time we interviewed you, you said you *did* kill them.'

'I know, but that's –'

'What's changed?'

'I've remembered,' Pettyfer said defiantly, fixing him with a look that could almost be classed as angry. 'I know what I saw. And I did *not* kill them. They killed themselves.'

We both stared at him in slight confusion.

Officially, I didn't know too much about how Knight's victims had been killed. I hadn't been to any crime scenes. I didn't have access to any photos of the bodies. I *definitely* (thank

God) hadn't been invited to any post-mortems. And obviously I hadn't been eye-witness to any of it. As far as Hadaway and Pettyfer knew, I only knew what'd been printed in the papers.

Unofficially, thanks to Johnny being less tight-lipped with us than Hadaway probably would've liked – because according to Johnny, 'if you didn't work for the Police, it'd be a different story. But you're both vetted to the right levels to know' – I knew exactly what injuries those lads had been found with.

The symbols that had been carved into them were pentacles, huge ones, etched across the whole of their chests, and each of the lads had had Latin phrases carved into their backs, right between their shoulder blades. Not only that, but they'd all had a strange mark just above their collarbones, and the Police were still trying to work out what had caused it.

Their throats had all been cut right down to the bone, something that Johnny had said knocked even some of the hardest Detectives sick. And these were the cops who'd been there since time and memoriam, the ones who you'd think would've seen everything.

And the significant injury to their arms that the papers had reported was actually a ceremonial dagger buried deep into their left forearm, the tip of the blade right down to their wrists and the handle resting against the crook of their elbow.

'Look, mate,' Hadaway said steadily in the end, a hint of something on his face that made it obvious that that was the last thing he'd expected Pettyfer to come out with. 'I saw the bodies. There's no way those injuries were self-inflicted, no-one could've done that to themselves.'

'No-one in their right minds could do that to themselves,' Pettyfer corrected him, and this time there was no 'almost' about it; he sounded more confident and self-assured than I would've thought him capable of. 'These lads were with Knight for a good few days before they died. Now, I only saw them in that clearing, so I don't know if she did to them the same as what she did to me or if they got something different, but' – one skinny finger jabbed the top of the table – 'she did something that made them kill themselves. She handed them those knives and they went to town on themselves.'

'So, hang on,' I said, frowning at him. 'They just started hacking away at themselves? She didn't tell them what to do or start them off?'

'No,' he said flatly, giving his head a slow shake. 'And that proves it, doesn't it? If she hadn't done something to them, how could they all have hurt themselves in the same way without being told what to do? How did they know?'

There was another short pause while we stared at him, and while I obviously can't speak for Hadaway, I for one was struggling to take it in.

Whatever the guy said, Knight wasn't a witch.

She wasn't.

But if he was right, and if his memory wasn't so distorted by whatever she'd done to him that he was remembering things that hadn't happened, then he had a point. How *had* the lads done exactly the same thing to themselves?

Given that she'd had the lads for however many days before they'd died, it wasn't outside the realm of possibility that she'd managed to brainwash them into doing it. But wasn't that a bit risky for someone who was trying to make it seem like she could cast spells over people? What would've happened if the brainwashing hadn't kicked in by the ceremony, and instead of killing themselves, the lads had just stood there, awkwardly staring at the Cloaks? How'd she made sure that that hadn't happened?

'Alright,' Hadaway said eventually, sounding half exasperated and half like he was just humouring the lad as he leaned back in his chair, arms crossed across his chest. Say they did do it to themselves. How'd they manage it?'

Pettyfer blinked at him, looking mildly surprised. 'What?'

'Well, none of these lads were gymnasts, James. None of them worked for sodding Cirque du Soleil. How did they managed to bend far enough over'- he leaned forward again, rifling through the papers in front of him until he whipped out a photograph of one of the bodies and slapped it down in front of Pettyfer – 'to carve a fucking Latin phrase the right way up in their own backs?'

'I told you,' Pettyfer said, looking at him like it should've been obvious. 'They just did it.'

'Come on, mate. People don't just carve things into their own skin because someone hands them a knife.'

'I don't think they were really people anymore by that point,' Pettyfer told him slowly, shooting him a thoughtful look. 'Whatever she'd done to them... it changed them. It was like they were in some sort of a trance, almost. There was no fight in them, no resistance. It was like they were already dead.'

Well.

That wasn't creepy at all.

'What about this procedure?' I asked before I could dwell on that too much, frowning slightly. 'I came across Knight and the Cloaks in Habely Woods last night, and they kept bringing it up. What is it?'

'It's not a procedure. I don't know why she calls it that. It's a ritual. The people who go to the ceremonies would be standing there, chanting, and she'd be chanting too, but she'd be getting the lad ready at the same time. She'd dust them with something and help them up onto that tree stump right in the centre, where everyone could see them. And then she'd give them the knife.' He glanced down at the photo on the table, swallowing hard. 'I don't know how she got them to cut their backs. It was like they were contorting; they'd bend in ways that you've never seen, and they didn't even blink at it. They didn't react to any of it. Even when they cut their own throats.'

He bowed his head as he bit his lip, and I felt a wave of nausea sweep through me as I pictured those lads hurting themselves.

Even still, I wasn't completely sure what to think; it was one of those things that managed to sound like total bullshit but be completely believable all at the same time.

Knight had already put two Police officers into a trance. She'd convinced two people that she'd been inside their souls. And if that wasn't weird enough, she'd somehow appeared out of thin air. So what was to say that Pettyfer wasn't just spouting any old rubbish to get himself out of a murder charge, and Knight *had* had a way of getting those lads to hurt themselves?

'Right,' Hadaway said heavily, after a silence so long that whoever transcribed the interview tape was going to think that something had gone wrong with the equipment. 'Look, we have reason to believe that someone else is going to be killed this weekend. Is there anything you can tell me that'll help us stop that from happening?'

Pettyfer looked at him for a couple of seconds, slightly moist around the eyes as he slowly shook his head. 'You can't,' he said flatly, and I felt my heart drop by a few inches. Not quite what I'd been hoping he'd say. 'If she's planning on killing someone else, she'll already have him. She'll have got a grip on him. And there's nothing you can do to stop her.'

Three hours later, I was back at the flat, perched on the edge of my bed and feeling both drained and dazed, wishing that the can of coke on my bedside table was something a bit stronger. (Hadaway had banned me from having any more sherry.)

Within ten minutes of Pettyfer telling us that, basically, we were screwed, Hadaway had wrapped up the interview, led Pettyfer back to his cell and bundled me into a different interview room, brusquely muttering something about having to take a statement off me.

And for the next two hours, we'd gone over everything that'd happened the night before.

All of it, every minute detail, from when I decided to take Squidge up to Habely Woods right the way through to waking up in the flat.

And just when I thought we'd done one bit of it to death – or that his hand must be hurting so much from all the writing that he'd want to take a break – he'd go over the whole thing all over again, just with very minor tweaks to the questions he was asking me.

Don't get me wrong, I got it. I got that they had to get every detail absolutely spot on, and that there was no room whatsoever for making mistakes. But by the time we finally left the interview room, I felt absolutely wiped, so knackered that I was barely even aware of where we were going.

Whether that was why the drive back to the flat was so quiet, or whether it was because Hadaway's head was whirling with everything Pettyfer had said just as much as mine was, I couldn't tell you.

I mean, I did *try*. Somewhere roughly halfway between Habely and East District, I'd managed to pull myself far enough out of the fog to take my forehead off the passenger-side window and turn to look at him.

'Listen, Hadaway... what Pettyfer said about Knight and this next bloke. You don't think it'll be *Eric*, do you?'

There'd been a heavy pause while he stared straight ahead, looking even more grim than I was used to, with his jaw suddenly looking considerably tense. And just when I'd thought he was going to completely ignore the question, he'd given his head one single shake and said darkly,

'I don't know. We've got people out looking for him, but no-one's seen or heard from him since he left the station. He could be anywhere.'

And that was it.

Neither of us spoke again until we got back to the flat, at which point Hadaway handed me a can of coke and some more paracetamol and firmly told me to go and get some kip, which you'd think – between the lack of sleep I'd had the night before and the completely exhausting interview – would be the easiest thing in the world.

You would be wrong.

Hence the fact that I was sat staring into space with my mouth hanging open, vaguely registering the sound of Hadaway making phone phone calls in the living room and absent-mindedly fondling Squidge's ears as he happily rested his chin on my lap, wondering – somewhere right at the very back of my mind – if I was drooling.

How the hell he expected me to sleep, I have no idea. My head was too full of everything that Pettyfer had told us and everything I'd had to remember from the night before, and no matter how many times I tried to switch off, I couldn't snap myself out of it. And at some point, it occurred to me that if I could get it all out of my head, I might be able to stop thinking about it for long enough to actually sleep.

The problem was that I didn't really have anyone to empty my head *to*.

Who could I talk to about it, really? Angie? She was at work, and even if she hadn't been, anything I tried to offload would lead to her telling me to stop obsessing about the case and keep my head down.

Or Hadaway? Let's face it, I wouldn't even get chance to open my mouth before he was giving me the exact same orders, probably in a much less polite and friendly way than Angie would.

There was Squidge, but I could barely keep his attention long enough to throw a ball for him; keeping him still for long enough to go through the ins and outs of the murders would be challenging to say the least.

Nope.

Clearly, I was going to have to come up with another way of getting it all out.

I thought about that for a couple of seconds, and before I'd even realised that the idea had occurred to me, I felt my head slowly turn itself to my left, towards the flowery, garish 'feature wall' that the sons of our landlady, Mrs Miller, had installed when they converted the Tudor-style house into two flats, a downstairs one for Mrs Miller and an upstairs one that me and Angie had ended up renting.

I'd always hated that wallpaper.

It was in our tenancy agreement that we couldn't redecorate, but in reality, how would anyone ever find out? Mrs Miller was hardly strict on flat inspections, and on the rare occasion that she *did* get lost and wander upstairs, how many times in the last eight months had she ever been in my bedroom?

Never.

Exactly.

So provided that I could find an equally terrible wallpaper to stick back up once we were done and dusted, what was the issue with me stripping that wall?

Before I had chance to change my mind, I shoved myself off the bed and stiffly dragged myself across the room, stuck my finger into the only loose bit I could find in the seam, and gave it a good hard yank.

And then another one.

And several more, tearing off strip after strip and getting really into it, barely even noticing how much I was pulling off or how long I'd been doing it for, or even whether –

'What the *fuck* are you doing?'

I jumped about a foot in the air and whirled around, my heart going like the clappers in my chest. Hadaway was standing in my doorway, one hand on the door handle and the other clutching a cup of black coffee as he stared at me in what can only be described as a furious disbelief.

'Oh, hi,' I beamed brightly, airily waving at the wall with one hand, like suddenly ripping all of your wallpaper off for no reason was the most normal thing to do. 'I was just thinking that it'd be good to have somewhere to write down what we know about the Knight case. Like those whiteboards you have at East District, except... well.' I shot a quick glance over my shoulder. 'A wall instead.'

This didn't seem to a reassure him. If anything, all it made him do was look at me in even more disbelief.

And a lot more anger.

'Why the fuck,' he demanded tightly, his voice surprisingly steady for someone who looked like they were about to have an aneurysm, 'do you want something to do that on?'

'Well, because –'

'You're not working the fucking case, Armitage. You don't need a goddamn wall or a whiteboard, you – for *Christ's sake,* you need to keep your fucking nose out of all this and leave it to us, alright?'

I stared at him indignantly for a couple of seconds, feeling mild irritation start prickling at my insides. 'No! Not sodding *alright*, Hadaway! If it wasn't for us going up there last night, would you know that Knight has a bunch of followers? Would you know about this *procedure* that she's convinced them all she needs? And how do you know, Hadaway, how d'you know that if it wasn't for me being Cleaner Dave, Pettyfer would've ever remembered all that stuff he told us today? So are you really going to stand there and tell me that I'm not fucking *helping*?'

'All you're doing is giving us more work,' he bit off furiously, as a muscle on his jaw did a couple of twitches in quick succession. 'I should be back at the office, not stuck here babysitting you –'

'*Babysitting?*'

'It's not a fucking *game*,' he snapped, slamming his mug down on my chest of drawers as he stormed towards me, looking very much like he wanted to give me a good shake. 'We don't know where the hell Knight is or what her next move is, we don't know why she's doing it, and you sat in that interview room and told me that she knows what you look like, what your name is and where you fucking live!'

'She doesn't know *where* –'

'How many people called Armitage d'you think live in Habely?'

'It doesn't *matter*,' I shot back angrily, feeling my hands clench into fists as he stopped right in front of me, crossing his arms tight across his chest so that his biceps bulged in a very distracting way. 'It's not common knowledge where we live, Hadaway! She'd have to ask one hell of a lot of people to find out my address, and I can't see Knight going door-to-door, can you?'

'Look –'

'Even if she did, she's not going to pitch up in the middle of the day,' I said shortly, pinching my thumb and forefinger together and jabbing them at him. 'When has she *ever* turned up *anywhere* except at night?'

'Right. So do I need to stay here again tonight?'

I felt my insides give a funny little lurch. 'That is absolutely not what I'm saying.'

He frowned at me for a few seconds, looking more concerned than anything else, and then he blew a grim sigh out through his nose as he took another step closer to me.

'Look,' he said gently, reaching out and tucking some of my hair back behind my ear, making a jolt of surprise shoot through my stomach. 'We just want to make sure you're safe.'

'I *am* safe,' I told him, in a voice that was meant to be bright and jaunty, but actually came out weirdly high-pitched. 'And I'm hardly going to be more safe than when I'm updating my wall, am I?'

He eyed up the wall behind me, still looking vaguely irritated but a lot more resigned than he had a few seconds earlier. 'Is there anything I can say that'll stop you from doing this?'

I glanced over my shoulder at the giant bald patch that I'd created. 'Well... I've already pulled the wallpaper off. It'll just be a waste of time if I don't write on it now.'

His mouth did the quickest, tiniest of twitches, almost like he'd come dangerously close to grinning but managed to catch himself just in time. And then the second was over, so fast that I wondered if I'd imagined it, and he was giving his head a weary shake instead.

'When Angie asks,' he told me dryly, turning away from me and picking his coffee back up on his way back to the door, 'I knew nothing about it.'

He'd barely left my room before I stared scribbling away, using a bingo marker that I'd found in my nightstand drawer and that actually wasn't a bad alternative to a whiteboard marker.

Everything that we knew about Knight was going on that wall.

We knew that she was trying to sell that she was a witch, and that this procedure – this ritual or whatever it was – did something to help these powers that the Cloaks were convinced that she had. We knew that there were at least two people who felt like she'd been inside their soul, and that she knew things about them that she had no way of knowing. We knew that she could put people into trances, and that she was the last person who Lyme was seen with, which – logically, especially given that his family had still heard absolutely zilch from him – could well mean that he was still with her, wherever she was.

But that was it.

That was all we knew.

And it didn't feel like enough.

Not even close, especially given that what we didn't know way outnumbered it.

We didn't know whether Knight was deranged enough to actually *believe* that she was a witch, instead of it just being one big act.

We didn't know why she wanted Pettyfer and Lyme. Unlike all of the victims, neither of them were eighteen – although we could probably let her off for thinking that Pettyfer was, given that he'd barely hit puberty – and their backgrounds didn't match those of the lads *or* each other's. So why was it important for her that these two people were so different from the victims? And for that matter, why was it so important for all of the lads she killed to be *so* similar? None of them looked alike, but they'd all been the same age, with decent part-time jobs and a good group of mates. Why had she wanted people who fit that profile, and *only* people who fit that profile?

It probably goes without saying that the biggest thing we didn't know was *why* she was doing it. For God's sake, what did she think was going to come of her murdering four lads and making however many gullible idiots believe that she was a witch? Power? Or a Court-ordered long stay in a mental hospital? What was she planning that meant she saw *any* of this working in her favour?

And then there was this book that Pettyfer had mentioned. This *Learning the Gainful Skill of Witchcraft and Mastering Your Abilities* book. Wherever she'd got it from, it wasn't

Amazon; I'd checked the night before, and it wasn't listed. So was it something that she'd made herself? Or was it written by a bespoke author who only shipped to people's houses or maybe to small, independent bookshops? And why did she *need* it? Even if witches *were* real, surely they'd just *be* witches and they wouldn't need some book to teach them how to do it? So why have it?

'*Oh my God.*'

For the second time that day, I jumped out of my skin, feeling a massive sense of deja vu as I whipped around to face my bedroom door. Except this time, I didn't find myself looking at a furious Hadaway; instead, it was Angie, staring at my wall with her mouth hanging open and her face a good few shades paler than it normally is.

'Hi,' I said quickly, pushing the lid back onto my bingo dabber and checking my watch. One o'clock. Far too early for her to have finished work for the day. 'What're you doing home?'

'I...' she gestured wordlessly at the wall, looking almost desperate. 'What... why have you...' And then she seemed to shake herself out of it, and all of the desperation was replaced with a horrified irritation. 'Armitage, what the *fuck* have you *done*?'

'Do you like it?' I asked happily, turning back to the wall and fondly running one hand over my scribbles. 'I call it Scribble Chic.'

'No, I do not *like* it!' she burst out angrily, her eyes popping slightly out of her head. 'Armitage, you can't just go around ripping wallpaper down, we're not allowed to redecorate! We'll be lucky if this doesn't cost us the sodding tenancy! What the hell were you *thinking*?'

'Well,' I said hesitantly, realising for the first time how weak an excuse it was going to sound. 'I was thinking Mrs Miller wouldn't find out.'

She gaped at me for a couple of seconds. 'What?'

'How often does she come up here, Angie?' I asked, trying to keep the defensive note out of my voice. 'She hasn't been up the whole time we've been in. What're the chances of her suddenly being able to get up the stairs again?'

'What if she gets a chairlift?'

'That would be unfortunate.'

She whirled around to look at Hadaway, who'd wandered over to stand behind her, holding a half-eaten cheese sandwich and looking mildly interested in all the goings-ons. 'Did you know about this?'

'No idea,' he said tonelessly, taking another bite of his sandwich. 'I'm as shocked as you are.'

I tilted my head to one side, frowning slightly at him. 'Where's my sandwich?'

'You were busy.'

'I'm never too busy for food.'

'*You*,' Angie bit off accusingly, narrowing her eyes at him, 'should've stopped her! Why the hell did you let her do this?'

'I didn't *let* her do anything,' he told her exasperatedly, as I felt myself bristle. Why did everyone suddenly think it was OK to act like I was a five-year-old who needed watching at all times? 'I thought she was asleep. I came in to make sure she was still breathing, and she'd already ripped it all off.'

'It doesn't *matter*,' I bit off hotly just as Angie opened her mouth to fire back, glaring at the pair of them and crossing my arms tight across my stomach. 'There's no point in arguing about it, or treating me like a bloody *toddler*. It's happened. The paper's already off. So don't you think we might as well *use* it, instead of letting it all be for nothing?'

They both stared at me, Angie looking like she hated it and wanted nothing more than to keep kicking off, and Hadaway with a vaguely longing look on his face that made me think that he wanted to find a way to attach me to the wall so that I had no choice but to stay out of the case until it was all over.

Or maybe wring my neck.

Either one.

'Fine,' Angie said reluctantly, obviously realising that yelling at me wouldn't make the paper stick itself back onto the wall and stomping towards me, shooting me a look that said she was far from happy about it. 'What else do you want putting on the stupid thing?'

By the time we finally called it a day, Hadaway had long disappeared back to East District, Squidge had eaten about six pieces of wallpaper, and me and Angie had filled the wall with considerably more scribble.

We'd added everything we knew about the Cloaks. How there were at least sixty of them, all of whom believed so blindly in Knight and whatever she was up to that they'd decided that murder was a perfectly acceptable hobby. How they must've had a way of communicating with her, because otherwise they wouldn't know when they were supposed to turn up in the clearing. (We assumed. It was hard to picture Knight wrapping up their little meetings by asking for Any Other Business and reading the next date out of her diary.) But we didn't know what that communication *was;* a massive group chat in WhatsApp hardly seemed very witchy, and I couldn't see Knight going door-to-door or making phone calls to everyone. And how exactly had she recruited the Cloaks in the first place? Did she just go up to them in the High Street, tell them they should come and watch her murder someone, and then be like 'Be there or be square'? How do you *possibly* pull together a group of people who're happy to be involved in ritualistic murder and not bat an eye at it?

And how had they all known where the clearing was? I'd been taking Squidge up to those Woods for months, and not once had I stumbled across it. And given that Knight wouldn't have wanted to get found before she was ready to – or rather, she wouldn't have wanted to get found before the latest lad was dead – then she would've made sure that her clearing was hard to find. So how did all the Cloaks make it there? Did she draw them a map? Or did they just wander around aimlessly until they found other people wearing robes and carrying flame torches?

And how had the whole thing *started?* How long did it go back? The first meeting can't have been when the first murder took place; for one thing, the Cloaks knew what they were doing far too well to have only been to the five gatherings, and for another, you can't get a bunch of random people together, murder someone in front of them, and then have those same people turn up for a second meeting when they know that exactly the same thing will happen. No, she must've been prepping them for months, at least, before the murders actually started. But how? And why? What purpose did the Cloaks actually serve, apart from to give her an ego-boost and possibly stop the guy escaping if he tried to make a break for it?

'I don't get it,' Angie burst out eventually, taking a step back and putting the lid back on the second bingo pen we'd found in my drawer. 'The more we find out, the more we don't know. Is this making anything clearer to you?'

I flicked my eyes over the scribbles, taking them all in again. 'No.'

There was something we weren't getting.

It was something really obvious, and it was there, staring us in the face.

We just couldn't see it.

And it was winding me up.

'Let's take a break,' she said wearily after a few seconds of silence, tugging my marker out of my hand. 'Let's just relax and put it out of our heads, and if you really want' – said with a stern look that made it clear I should not want – 'we'll have another look at it tomorrow night. Alright?'

No.

Not alright.

I didn't *want* to leave it; I wanted to know exactly what it was that we didn't know.

My eyes landed on the notes I'd made about Knight's book, and I frowned thoughtfully at it as I nibbled on my thumbpad.

Say it *was* written by a bespoke author who sold to independent bookshops.

Habely had an independent bookshop.

And given that Knight was operating in Habely and obviously knew the place, I didn't think it was that far outside the realm of possibility that she'd been there.

So what if Habely Bookshop was where she'd bought it from?

Would they be able to shed some more light on the whole thing? Maybe give us a nudge in the right direction to find out what her big plan was, or – better yet – give us her address?

Either way, whether they knew something or nothing... how much harm would it to do to go down and ask the questions?

SEVEN

Habely Bookshop is just off the High Street, about halfway down a busy little side-street. It's bigger than you'd expect a local, independent bookshop to be – easily twice the size of the Waterstones in Exleigh Town Centre – but it's painted a murky shade of green that somehow makes it blend in, to the point where you'd easily walk past it if you didn't know it was there, especially if you weren't actively looking for the word 'bookshop' spelt out in big, tarnished gold letters. It's mainly used by older people – probably because they're the only ones who don't have to re-mortgage their houses to shop there, and possibly because a good 75% can't hear the irritating bell that jingles for ten minutes every time someone opens the door – and on that particular night, it had a bland-looking lass in her late twenties or early thirties standing behind the till, staring at us in blatant shock.

To be fair to her, I'm pretty certain that no-one had ever stepped foot inside it dressed like we were.

Angie was wearing the knee-length black dress with a jagged hem and a bodice top that I'd bought for Halloween a couple of years earlier, with a witch's hat perched on her head and a broomstick in one hand. And I'd thrown on the purple, glittery, velvet dress that'd been the right size when I'd bought it at fifteen but was now almost indecently short, with a matching hat of my own and a glittery, star-topped wand that had loads of differently-coloured ribbons hanging down from it.

And as good as our outfits were, I have a feeling that it was for that reason – or maybe because we asked for books about witchcraft the second we reached the counter – that we were hastily directed to the office at the back of the shop, and *not* because 'Mr Daniels will be the best one to help you'.

Mr Daniels turned out to be a fifty-something-year-old man whose width more than made up for what he lacked in height. He had a weak jaw perched on top of a gently wobbling double-chin, an undeniably rat-like nose and the most desperate attempt at a comb-over I've ever seen, with glasses so thick that I couldn't help but think they must be painfully heavy on his face. He wore shabby clothing and dirty shoes, and when we walked into the office, he was methodically plastering giant red stickers onto the stacks of books surrounding him, looking like it was a job that didn't bore him into insanity, and he was so engrossed in it that it took him a good couple of minutes before he noticed us standing in the doorway.

It turns out all the throat-clearing and 'excuse me's' in the world can't distract from the excitement of putting price reduction stickers onto countless books.

'Hi!' I said cheerfully, when he finally jumped slightly and blinked rapidly at us, looking more than a little surprised and just as alarmed. '*So* sorry to interrupt, I can see how much fun you must be having. We're just looking for a book on learning witchcraft, and they said at the counter that that you're the best person to help us.'

'We understand if you don't have it,' Angie added earnestly, with a tiny hint of reluctance in her voice that I doubt anyone else would pick up on. (You have no idea how hard I'd had to work to persuade her to come with me.) 'The lady at the till did say that you don't stock books on things like witchcraft.'

He snorted as he heaved himself out of his chair and slowly shuffled towards yet another stack of books, this one on a table on the other side of the room. 'That girl doesn't know anything. If she listened, she could've told you that we have the books, but we took them off the shelves because they weren't selling. We keep them back here on the off-chance anyone asks for them.' He picked up a couple of books from the piles and turned to face us, holding one in each hand. 'We have '*Witchcraft for Dummies*' or '*The Ultimate Guide to Being a Witch*'. Are either of those what you're looking for?'

We stared at him.

I won't lie, I hadn't been expecting that.

Maybe I'd been naïve, or maybe the witchcraft business was bigger than I'd realised, but somehow it hadn't occurred to me that there'd be more than one instruction manual for witches. Who knew it was such a common topic to write about?

'Erm,' I said hesitantly, 'no, actually. It's a book that our friend recommended to us, apparently it's the best out there. '*Learning the Gainful Skill of Witchcraft and Mastering Your Abilities*'. Or something like that,' I added blithely, like I hadn't memorised the title as soon as Pettyfer had told me what it was.

For a couple of seconds, Daniels just stood there and stared at me with the tiniest of frowns on his face, and I couldn't help but notice that something about him changed while he was doing that.

Just the tiniest bit.

I couldn't put my finger on exactly what it was, but there was no denying that it was definitely there.

Something just to say *off*.

'I'm sorry,' he told us tiredly in the end, putting the books back down on the table behind him and rubbing one hand across his forehead. 'It's a very unusual book. We've only ever sold one copy of it, and that was a good while ago. I haven't had anyone ask for it since.'

I felt a little leap in my stomach as my heart launched into an excited dance in my chest, pounding so hard that it was almost hard to breathe, but before I could say anything, I heard Angie ask carefully,

'The person you sold it to... I don't suppose you can remember their name?'

Elodia Knight.

He was going to say Elodia Knight.

He'd say they sold it to Knight, we'd somehow use that to find a way to get to Knight and stop her before she managed to kill anyone else, and Hadaway would have no choice but to admit that my nosiness *was*, in fact, helping with the case.

'That's a very strange question.'

'It's a bespoke book,' Angie explained casually, with a delicate little shrug. 'If it was our friend who bought it from you, then we'll know it's definitely the right one.'

He squinted at her warily, looking like he wasn't sure whether he should believe her or not, and I held my breath while I waited for him to say Knight's name. 'It was a lady called Goldin, if memory serves. Probably about your age, actually,' he continued, as I felt my heart stop dead mid-dance and instantly plummet several inches lower, until it was bobbing about near my bellybutton. 'Will that have been your friend?'

'That's the one,' Angie smiled brightly, letting her face relax so convincingly that *I* nearly believed that she was friends with this Goldin lass. 'Fantastic. I don't suppose you have any copies left in stock?'

He looked at her for a second longer before turning on his heel and shuffling through the door behind him, presumably going to check the stocks in some dusty old storeroom, and I shot Angie a disappointed grimace as I sagged against the doorway to the office.

It would have been *so* easy if Knight had bought that book.

But no.

All we knew now was that there was someone else wandering around Habely and pretending to be a witch, because no-one had had the decency to tell her that the role of Local Psychotic Lunatic had already been filled.

So.

No further forward.

Goddamnit.

It was a good couple of minutes before Daniels came shuffling back out of the storeroom, coughing slightly on the dust and clutching a grey book, which had its title etched on it in pale silver lettering and a thickness that put *War & Peace* to shame.

And he was limping slightly.

Limping on his right leg, so much that he had to drag his foot slightly across the floor. And just like that, it all fell into place.

The scuffed footprints we'd seen in Habely Woods. The fact that we'd been sent straight to him as soon as we asked for books on witchcraft. The way that he'd changed when I'd told him what the book was called. The mud on his shoes.

Daniels was one of the Cloaks.

'Thanks,' I croaked, somehow mustering a smile as he handed me the book. 'We really appreciate it. You know, rumour has it that this is the same book that Elodia Knight uses. I'll be over the *moon* if we can reach her level. Have you been following the case?'

'I have,' Daniels said after a slight pause, just a touch too lightly and a smidge too nervously. 'It's certainly intriguing.'

'Mmm,' I murmured carefully, forcing myself to stay calm as I glanced down at the book, which was so heavy that my arms were already starting to ache from holding it. 'She's so talented. Although I have to admit, I do think it's a shame about the missing Policeman, don't you?'

'I do,' he agreed hurriedly, nodding frantically as his eyes widened slightly. 'It's very worrying. His family must be beside themselves.'

I heard Angie do a sharp intake of breath as I felt something explode inside of me so forcefully that it almost knocked me off-balance, in the same way a headrush does.

Fucking *yes*.

See, Lyme's disappearance wasn't public knowledge. Cattringham's finest were keeping the whole thing tight under wraps, so much so that the only people who knew an officer had gone missing were the people who actually worked for the Force.

But Daniels wasn't a Bobby. He wasn't Police Staff. And unless he was made of granite, he couldn't be related to Lyme; otherwise, surely, he would've shown a scrap of one emotion or another when I mentioned the disappearance.

So the only way he wouldn't be shocked was if he already knew about it.

And the only way he could know about it was if he was one of Knight's followers.

'It really is a shame,' I said again, and then I lifted my head and fixed him with a grim stare. 'Because you were *so* close.'

Before he could say or do anything else, I heaved the book as far back as I could over my right shoulder and launched it forward, putting everything I had behind it. The front of the book smacked hard into his left cheek, making a dull, heavy *thwack* that echoed around the room, and before Daniels could react, before he could make a sound, he was arching to his right, slamming very solidly onto the thinly carpeted floor.

Pretty sure it's safe to say he was out cold before he even knew what hit him.

In the five minutes or so it took him to pull 'round, me and Angie had locked the office door and – in the absence of rope, string or any other alternative – Sellotaped him to the desk chair he'd been sat on when we'd first walked into the office.

'This is *insane*,' Angie said breathlessly, not for the first time, taking a step back from the chair and dropping her roll of Sellotape as Daniels started to wake up. 'Tidge, this is – we should never have done this. Why can't we just get the Police to come and deal with him?'

'We don't need the Police yet,' I told her harshly, too busy glowering at Daniels to even glance at her, and just as his eyes fluttered open and he fixed me with a groggy glare, I straddled him on the chair, pressing the spine of the book hard against his throat. 'What the fuck do you know about Keith Lyme?'

He spat at me, nice and frothy. 'Fucking *bitch*.'

I shot him a humourless smile as I pushed the book further into his neck. 'Come on, Daniels, you can play nicer than that. You obviously know what's happened to him, and we're not going anywhere until you tell us what that is. So,' I added, swapping the smile for a look so hard that I can only assume I was channelling my inner-Hadaway, 'try again. What's Knight got planned for him?'

He chuckled in a way that you would never expect of a man who took such pleasure in putting stickers on books. 'And why should I tell you that?'

'If you don't, this book is going down your fucking throat.'

He sneered up at me, choking slightly but smug nonetheless. 'D'you really think someone like you could understand my Mistress's plans? You're weak, Black. You're too closed-minded to listen to us. And even if you *weren't*, why do you think you'd ever be worthy of knowing her plans?'

Before I realised what I was doing, I'd pulled one hand up and given him a swift backhander, hard enough that my hand smarted from the force of it.

'We're not fucking around,' I bit off furiously, pushing the book further into his throat as he blinked against the pain, gasping slightly. 'If you don't tell me what you know, make no mistake, I *will* strangle you with this fucker of a book.'

'Tidge –'

'We've got a Bobby missing,' I said steadily, as Daniels stubbornly stared up at me, slowly tuning a delightful shade of purple, 'four people dead, and someone else who's going to die on Friday. So if you don't tell us how we can stop your little Mistress right *fucking* now, we're going to tell the Police exactly how involved you are in these murders. How you know what's going on, but you won't tell anyone because you've somehow convinced yourself that fucking *murder* is alright. And believe you me, as harsh as any jury will judge Knight, as harsh as any sentence she'll get, yours will be worse, because you're actually *sane* and you *still* support this shit. So tell me, Daniels, do you really think your precious *Mistress* is worth it?'

He stared up at me with his eyes burning, swallowing hard against the book, and I couldn't tell if he was thinking about what I'd said or if he was trying to decide how he'd most like to kill me.

'I can't tell you anything,' he wheezed, craning his head slightly to his right as he tried to get away from the book. 'She'll know. She knows everything. I've seen what she does to people who've betrayed her, and I'm telling you, she'd kill me. Maybe you should go back up to our clearing,' he added croakily, as I forced the book as far as I could into his neck. 'I know you were there the other night. Maybe we left something behind.'

I fixed him with a harsh stare for a few seconds longer, watching his face turn even more purple, before reluctantly yanking the book away from him and hauling myself off the chair.

One of two things was going on here.

Either he wasn't close enough to Knight to know anything, and he was trying to save face by pretending that he was.

Or he *did* know something, and he was too scared of what might happen to him to tell us.

Whatever the case, it hardly got us any further forward.

And more importantly, either way, I was pissed off.

These murders were probably the worst that the whole of Cattringham County had ever seen. Not only that, but the lads were getting killed for no reason at all. And this guy was too busy worrying about his own skin or his own sense of importance to help them.

What a fucking *dick*.

'Fine,' I told him coldly, hugging the book tight to my chest as I took a few steps back until I reached Angie. 'Have it your way. I hope you get everything you deserve, I really do.'

I eyeballed him for a couple of seconds, seriously tempted to leave him taped to his chair until someone happened to come into his little office and find him like that. With a bit of luck, it'd be a while. A good couple of days, maybe. Three, if we were lucky.

But in the end, I couldn't do it. He didn't deserve to be left there, stuck to his chair until someone found him ad just let him *go*.

He deserved the proper punishment.

'OK,' I said calmly, turning to look at Angie. And after a couple of seconds of staring at Daniels, breathing heavily through her nose, she slowly turned to face me, too. 'Let's give Johnny a call.'

EIGHT.

A couple of hours later, I was curled up on the settee back at the flat, quietly making my way through Knight's favourite read – which, if anyone asked, the bookshop had given to me a goodwill gesture and I had *not* stolen – while Angie sat next to me, glowering at the TV as she flicked through the channels with one hand and almost absent-mindedly fondled Squidge's ears with the other.

From what I'd been able to hear of their phone call, although Johnny had agreed to go down to the bookshop, he hadn't been too overly-impressed by the fact that his girlfriend had been prancing around Habely, pretending to be a witch and Sellotaping people to chairs, all in the name of detective work that – technically speaking – she shouldn't be doing. And from the way she'd fell into an angry silence as soon as she got off the phone with him (one she refused to come out of except to explode with things like 'he's such a *twat*' and 'seriously, he's being a dick' and 'why is tea taking so long?'), I felt like it was safe to say that Angie wasn't too overly-impressed by Johnny not being overly-impressed.

So.

I thought it was best to keep out of the way.

I also thought that – given that I'd read the stupid thing cover to cover once already, and found not a single reference to anything that Knight might be doing – Pettyfer must've given us the wrong book title.

'Frustrated' doesn't even begin to cover it. I'd even gone as far double-checking and *triple*-checking the overall contents, the contents list for each individual chapter *and* the glossary before I'd started reading through it for the second time. And it was all just a complete waste of my life.

'I don't know what you expected,' Angie told me flatly when I said that to her, keeping her eyes steadfastly glued to the TV. 'Pettyfer had already told you that he didn't remember much, and for all she's a raving lunatic, you can't deny that Knight's clever. Maybe she put

the dustcover of one book onto a completely different one, so that Pettyfer *couldn't* tip

anyone off about what book she was using.'

'She wouldn't just let him go after everything he'd seen though, would she? So why

bother doing that if she was planning on killing him?'

'I don't know what you want me to say, Tidge,' she said tonelessly, turning the TV

volume up by a couple of notches. 'I'm not Knight. I don't know how she ticks.'

There was a slight pause while I stared at her, she carried on stubbornly staring at the TV,

and Squidge decided that this was the perfect the time to climb up onto the settee so that

Angie could get better access to his ears, wedging himself into the gap between us and

panting happily, completely oblivious to the tension in the room.

'Good chat,' I said sardonically in the end, feeling a few prickles of irritation. 'Well

done.' She shrugged nonchalantly, her eyes still glued on the telly, and that just made the

prickles explode into little fireballs of irritated exasperation, so much so that I suddenly heard

myself burst out with, 'You know what, Angie, I'm not *Johnny*. I'm not the one who had a

go at you. I've sat here all night and let you sulk to your heart's content, so can you pack in

taking the whole thing out on me when I haven't done anything wrong?'

Her head moved half a millimetre towards me. 'You haven't done anything wrong?'

'No!'

She looked at Squidge. 'She hasn't done anything wrong.'

I felt my teeth clench themselves tight together. '*I haven't.*'

'You made me go down there!' she yelled suddenly, jerking her head around to glower at

me furiously, flinging one arm up in the air in frustration. 'You made me Sellotape that

dickhead to a chair! It was all of *your* ideas –'

'My *ideas*,' I interrupted sharply, seeing her glare and raising her one angrily indignant stare. 'Yeah, Angie, I suggested going to the bookshop, and yeah, it was me who found the Sellotape, but for God's sake, I didn't *make* you do anything! You could've let me go down the bookshop by myself! You could've called Johnny when I was taping the guy to the chair! How the hell is this *my* fault? You're not even mad at me,' I added accusingly, as she stared at me with wide eyes and her mouth hanging slightly open, like she couldn't believe that I had the nerve to argue with her. 'You're mad at yourself for going along with it and you're mad at Johnny for being angry with you, and it's easier to put the blame at my door than it is your own.'

She pretended to think about that for a second. 'No, I'm definitely mad at you.'

'Then be mad at me all you want,' I bit off angrily, slamming the book shut. 'But the fact still stands that I did not *make* you do anything. You came with me tonight because you want to know what's going on just as much as I do, you just don't want to *admit* it. I'm going to bed,' I added harshly, as she opened her mouth to shoot back. 'I'll see you at work.'

I must've got about an hour's sleep that night.

I was so angry with Angie that there was no sleep in me for a good couple of hours. And just as I calmed down enough to actually drift off, the painkillers wore off and I was stuck in the awkward position of being too warm and comfortable to move, but having a back that was too stiff and sore for me to sleep.

But despite being angry and despite being in pain, I must've gone over eventually, because I remember abruptly waking up around three o'clock in the morning.

For a couple of seconds, I just laid there, frowning at my bedside clock and wondering why I suddenly felt so wide awake.

My back didn't feel brilliant, but it wasn't hurting enough to have woken me up; it was just pulsing slightly, like it had its own little heartbeat. I couldn't remember having a bad dream, and if some loud noise had woke me up, Squidge would've heard it too, but I couldn't hear him moving around; the whole flat was completely silent.

I pushed myself up in bed, wondering if I should see if Angie was awake too or if it was best to keep out of her way, before I decided that – sod it – let her be annoyed at me, and flicked on my beside lamp.

And found myself staring at Knight.

I felt a horrible jolt in my stomach and completely froze, staring at her in horrified shock as my heart started pounding so hard that I didn't think I'd be able to hear anything over the sound of it, and I was mildly worried it was going to do some damage to my ribs. She was standing at the foot of my bed, wearing a long black dress with wizard sleeves and giving me a smile that can only be described as creepily serene.

'Good morning, sleepyhead,' she said softly, putting both hands on the foot of my bed and leaning forwards. 'And how are we this morning?'

I knew exactly what I needed to do.

I knew I needed to launch myself out of that bed, rugby tackle her to the floor and sit on her while I called the Police to come and get her.

Or – alternatively, and just as appealing – I needed to throw myself out of bed, rugby tackle her to the floor, hit her over the head with the nearest blunt object a few dozen times and call the Police to tell them that there'd been a terrible accident and I had no idea how it had happened, but somehow Knight was dead in my flat.

But I couldn't move.

I couldn't take it in.

Knight was in my flat.

No, no. Knight was in my *bedroom.*

What the fuck was Knight doing in my bedroom?

'Oh, come now, Armitage,' she said silkily, blinking slowly and tilting her head to one side, still giving me that horrible smile. 'It's not like you to be shy. What's the matter? Cat got your tongue?'

'What the *fuck*,' I finally choked out, more breathlessly than I would've liked, 'are you doing here?'

Just as importantly, how did she know where we lived? And how did she get *in*?

There was no way she'd just *walked* in; Mrs Miller was so paranoid about being burgled that there were three deadlocks on the front door *and* back doors to the house, deadlocks that were dutifully locked every night. And while it was completely possible that she'd just broken a window to get in, she wouldn't have been able to do it without at least one of us hearing her – but if that's what'd happened and I *had* heard her, and that was what woke me up, why hadn't Squidge heard her? And how would she have got from the window to my bedroom in roughly a second?

It didn't make sense.

So how the hell had she managed it?

The smile got wider. 'I thought it was time that we had a little chat. You see, I'm getting really tired of you sticking your nose into my business. It's took a lot of time and hard work for me to have achieved what I have, and I'm not prepared to let some nosey little girl ruin this for me. So I'm telling you now.' She dropped the serene smile and the floaty voice, and instead gave me a look so cold it felt like the temperature in my room actually dropped by a few degrees. 'You take your nose out of my fucking business or I'll make it my personal mission to make sure that you don't have a nose to poke around. Do you understand me?'

'I thought your personal mission was to kill any innocent eighteen-year-old lad you don't like the look of.'

I have know idea where it came from.

I couldn't even tell you if I thought it before it popped out of my mouth; all I knew was that one second, I was sitting there and staring at her in total shock, and the next, I heard someone say this sarcastic little comment in a voice that sounded freakishly like mine.

In an instant, that cold look she was giving me disappeared, and the serene smile was back in place. 'Those men died for a reason, Armitage. We needed them to serve a higher purpose. I can understand how it looks from your point of view, but I promise you, the day will come where you understand all of this.'

'I do understand.'

'You do.' It wasn't quite a statement, but it wasn't quite a question, either. If anything, I'd say she sounded just the tiniest smidge uncertain.

'Mmm, I do. I understand that the reason these men died is because you're a fucking lunatic.'

She stared at me for a couple of seconds, her face totally unreadable, and I took the opportunity to weigh up my options.

I have to say, they were pretty limited.

If I wanted to get to my bedroom door and out into the living room – which I did, very much – I was going to have to bolt past her, and something told me that she wouldn't take too kindly to me doing a runner before she was done with me.

If I wanted to get out of there without going past her, the only option I had was to smash my window and hope for the best when I jumped. It's just that jumping really didn't appeal to me. For one thing, there was no way I could afford to replace that window, and Angie would be well pissed off with me if I chucked our deposit away. For another, hoping for the best is all good and well, but it doesn't stop you from breaking a bone or three when yo ˎ the ground. I'd already had one big fall and walked away without any major injury; somehow I didn't think I'd be lucky enough to have it happen twice in a row. And for a third thing, I couldn't see smashing a window being a quick job. The book on witchcraft was right next to my bed and heavy enough to cause some damage to a window, but it weighed so much that swinging it at the glass would take some effort, and then I'd have to take some time to clear all the shards remaining around the edge of the window frame before I finally got around to the jumping bit. All while she was, what? Standing there, watching me? No. I didn't think so.

And then there was Option Number Three: I could just smack the bitch.

It was only my second favourite of the three, but it definitely seemed like the most inevitable. If I tried to get out of the door, Knight would go for me and I'd have to smack her. If I tried to get out of the window, Knight would go for me and I'd have to smack her. So wouldn't it make sense to just cut out the middle man and skip to the part that – going off the hard glint in her eyes – we both knew was going to happen?

She made a funny little noise in the back of her throat, almost like a short chuckle, and the look on her face hardened as she widened her smile at me. 'Don't call me a lunatic, Armitage.'

I smiled back at her, tilting my head to one side. 'What should I call you? A psychopath? Delusional? Or just some evil little cow who thinks that going around killing people makes her a wi-'

Quick as a flash, her right arm shot out and smacked me hard across the face, so hard that it took me a second or two to catch my breath. She moved from the foot of the bed to the side of it, looking furious and holding one hand out, obviously ready to go for my throat, b before she could do or say anything, I went for her, launching myself out of bed and grab ιe arm that she was stretching towards me, forcing it away as I punched her once, twice to the face. They weren't brilliant punches, and my hand instantly had a sharp ache because of them, but they seemed to shock her enough for me to grab her by the hair at the back of her head and slam her head into the wall to my left as hard as I could, hard enough for there to be sickening crunch. She sagged slightly and I let go of her, letting her slide down to the floor as I threw myself towards my bedroom door, but when I was about halfway there, I felt her hand fasten around my ankle and give it a rough yank, and I hit the floor hard, whacking my right shoulder off one of my bedknobs at the same time, so that a sharp, solid pain shot through me. I flipped onto my back as I hit the ground and saw her scurrying towards me, so furious that her face at least two shades paler than it normally was, save for the big red patch where I'd punched her and the equally red, slightly bloody mark that the wall had left on her. And before I could do anything, she was on top of me, kneeling on my arms so that I was pinned to the floor, and one hand tight around my throat as she punched my left cheek once, then twice, then again, and again, and again, making a noise that was a cross between a grunt and a scream every time she made contact, and I couldn't do anything to stop her, because all of her weight was on my forearms, surprisingly heavy for someone so thin, and not only could I not pull them out from underneath her, I also couldn't tell which hurt more – the punches or her legs pushing down on my arms.

She tightened her grip on my neck slightly, clenching her teeth as she swung for me again, and I wriggled around desperately, tossing my head from side to side to avoid the next punch and rocking my body as fast as I could, bucking at the same time, trying anything I could to get her the fuck *off me,* because while her grip wasn't so tight that I couldn't breathe, I knew ːactly where she was heading with it, and believe you me, those punches did not feel good. ᴀanaged to buck so high that her left leg flew off my arm, and before she could land back ι on it, I whipped it up, smacking my hand palm-first into her face and working my fingers into her eyes as hard as I could, gritting my teeth against the solid bu..

of it. She screamed and shoved herself off me, scrambling to her feet and backing

the backs of her legs bumped into my bed, hands over her face, and I shoved myself

feet, breathing heavily through my nose. I could hear Squidge scratching at my door,

alternating between whining and growling, and as much as I wanted to be out there with him

and have the whole thing be over – as much as the whole left side of my face was aching and

throbbing like a bastard, as much as my right shoulder was killing me, as much as my arms

felt like they were going to drop off and frankly I wouldn't be *that* sorry if they did – instead

of bolting for the door, I took the couple of steps towards Knight, propped my foot up on the

side of the bed just next to her, grabbed her head with both hands and slammed it into my

knee. Hard. As hard as I could. I shoved her head back up and she pulled her hands away

from her face – whether in shock or whether to stop me, I'm not sure – but before she could

do anything more than that, I yanked her head back down onto my knee, even harder than the

last time, and even in that second, I felt some thick, warm liquid start soaking through my

pyjama trousers.

I shoved her away from me and she landed on her back on my bed, both hands clamped

over her mouth as she let out a low moan, and I quickly scrambled on top of her, shoving one

knee into her stomach as I wrapped one hand around her neck and used the other to grab hold

of both of her wrists, dragging her hands away from her mouth, which was pouring with so

much blood that she looked more like a vampire than a witch.

'You tell me what the fuck you're up to right now,' I hissed furiously, bringing my face

slightly closer to hers as she glowered up at me, definitely struggling, but too weakly for it

have any effect. '*Why* do these lads have to die, Knight? Why does being a witch have

anything to do with *murder*? And what's the fucking plan, hm? Kill a couple more lad

convince a couple more people you're a witch, and – what? Walk away scot-free beca arrest a witch? You've told all your precious followers that it's all going to be done with this weekend, so what happens after that? What do they think this is all building up to? *What the fuck are you playing at?*'

She spat at me, a mixture of frothy spit and gooey blood, and it splatted onto my right cheek, making me flinch slightly and blink in surprise. And the worst part was, I couldn't wipe it off; to do that, I'd have to let go of her in one way or another, and the second I did that, she'd get the upper hand again.

And I wasn't going to let that happen.

For a split-second, I froze, wondering what the hell my next move was going to be and hoping more than anything that her spit wasn't going to trickle down towards my mouth. And then that split-second was over and there was a little knock on my bedroom door, and Angie's sleepy voice was coming from the other side.

'Tidge?'

'Get in here!' I screamed frantically, craning my neck around until I could see the door, behind me and to my right. 'Angie, it's – she's in here, it's –'

The door burst open with so much force that it bounced a few inches back off the wall behind it, and Angie came charging in, Squidge sticking his head through the door behind her, ears back and head low to the ground as he nervously licked his lips.

Chicken.

For half a second, we all froze. Angie was darting her eyes between me and Knight, looking just as stunned and panicky as I'm sure I did, and me and Knight staring right back at , almost with an air of 'well? What are you going to do?'

nd in the next second, Angie was charging towards us again, almost like she'd never her face getting paler by the second and her arms outstretched like she wanted to help 't sure how, crying,

'*Oh my God!* How did she – what is she – what's going on? How did she – *how the –*'

'I don't know,' I told her breathlessly, panting slightly, but before I could say anything more than that, and just as Angie reached the bed, Knight wrenched both of her arms out of my grasp, so quickly that I didn't know what was happening until it was too late, and before I could take it in, she'd shoved me off her, flung herself up into a sitting position and whacked Angie across the face, so hard that I could see the redness forming on her face almost immediately.

Angie stumbled back a couple of steps, clearly slightly stunned by the force of it, and Knight threw herself off the bed, racing towards my bedroom window, clearly with one thing in mind.

'*Don't!*' I bellowed furiously, and the next thing I knew, I'd launched myself off the bed too, landing on top of her and sending us both to the floor with a thud solid enough to make my wardrobe vibrate. And then suddenly Angie was there too, throwing herself down across Knight's legs, but before she could get into a better position to hold her down, Knight had thrown her off and thrown another punch at me, using my duck as an opportunity to push me off her, too. She dove for the window again, but before she could get very far, Angie had her arms wrapped around her waist and was dragging her back, back towards my bedroom door, frantically bending from left to right to avoid the wild punches and slaps that Knight was blindly hurling towards her, clearly trying to twist around to face Angie so she'd have a better aim, but Angie was holding her so tightly that she didn't have enough room to do it.

And I didn't think twice.

I dove for the book on witchcraft, heaved it up over my shoulder and whirled around to face Angie and Knight, keeping my grip as tight as I could even though my hands were already starting to ache from the effort of it.

'Angie!' I yelled frantically, starting to move towards them, fast. 'Get out of the way!'

She turned her head slightly and I saw her eyes get even wider as she saw me coming towards them, but in the next second, she'd hit the deck and I was swinging that book as hard as I could in Knight's direction. It slammed into her head with a satisfying, dull, heavy thud and Knight half-stumbled, half-fell into my wardrobe doors. For one long second, it was like she was frozen; she stayed exactly where she'd landed, sprawled out against the wood with her arms splayed and her cheek pressed against the doors, her face turned towards the window that she'd been trying to get out of. And then, very slowly, she slid down the doors until she was laid in a heap in the front of the wardrobe, completely motionless.

Completely out cold.

For a couple of seconds, neither of us moved; we just froze where we were, panting heavily and staring at her wearily like we were expecting it all to be a trick, and she was going to spring back into action just as we let our guards down.

And when it became obvious that – thank God – she *wasn't* faking it, I glanced over at Angie just as she turned to look back at me.

'Fancy that,' I said lightly, shooting her the best smile I could manage. 'Turns out this book isn't completely useless after all.'

We stuck her in the wardrobe.

Well, what else were we supposed to do? Neither of us had ever had a murderous psychopath break into our house in the middle of the night; we didn't know what protocol dictated we do with her until the Police pitched up, especially since – bizarrely – Mrs Miller's sons hadn't thought to build a jail cell in when they were converting the house.

The wardrobe just seemed like the most natural place to put her.

Hence the fact that, half an hour later, all my clothes and shoes were piled on my bed and Knight had been shoved into the now-empty wardrobe – the doors of which had been tied together with at least five hair bobbles – and me and Angie were sat at the kitchen table, edgily waiting for Johnny and Cattringham County's favourite manwhore to turn up.

I would just like to say that it hadn't been my choice to call Hadaway. I was all for calling 999 and letting Response come and pick the bitch up, like anyone who didn't have a direct line to East District CID would. It was Angie who insisted – while handing me a ridiculous amount of ice-packs, when she must've known that what I really wanted was countless glasses of sherry – on calling him, because 'at the end of the day, Tidge, he's one of the main Bobbies working this case. And he's not going to have any number of calls coming in to him like Response will, is he? He might even get here quicker than they would'.

So.

No.

I wasn't happy.

And I was even less happy when – once he'd turned up at the house and pounded so hard on the door so hard that our *flat* door had shuddered – he followed Angie into our flat, looking even grimmer than he normally did and mildly irritated, but also disturbingly fit, in a dishevelled, 'I rolled out of bed and shoved on the first things I saw. I didn't have time to shave either, have you seen how sexy my stubble is?' kind of way.

I mean, credit to the man, he must've absolutely floored it to get there as quick as he had; Hadaway lived slap-bang in Exleigh Town Centre, about half an hour away from Habely, and yet he got to the flat barely fifteen minutes after we'd called him; he even managed to beat Johnny, who lived on the opposite side of Habely, which actually *is* fifteen minutes away (if you can avoid the drivers who think thirty miles an hour means fifteen miles an hour). But for Christ's sake, did he have to look *so good* that early in the morning, and when I couldn't have been less in the mood for it? And did he have to stop dead the second he got into the flat and stare at me in that mixture of anger, shock and concern?

'Jesus.'

I forced myself to smile at him, even though it made a sharp pain shoot through my left cheek. 'Nice to see you too, Hadaway.'

Well.

OK.

In fairness, I was a bit of a mess.

I knew I must've been a mess from the way that Angie had insisted – far more than she needed to – that I didn't look in the mirror. The thing is, the more times she told me not to, the more I wanted to, something that she really should've known me well enough to work out. So of *course* I'd waited roughly two seconds after she left the flat to let Hadaway in the front door before I dove into the bathroom to find out exactly what had happened to my face.

And by saying 'face', I'm being a bit *too* generous. What I was looking at probably sat better under the category of 'pulp'.

My left cheek was already a delightful shade of purple and easily twice the size of my right one, so swollen that my left eye was half-closed. The bruising was already spreading up to my eye and down towards my jaw, and when I tried to smile – just, you know, to see if I still could – the corner of my mouth gave a funny little twitch but otherwise stayed exactly the same, like the dentist had gone mad with the anaesthetic and given me enough to make a bear go numb.

Not only that, but I also had bruises in definite finger marks around my neck, I'd somehow managed to get a carpet burn along the right side of my face, my right shoulder was covered by a huge red patch that clearly wasn't going to be saying its goodbyes any time soon, and the whole inside of my forearms were just to say starting to darken into bruises, right from a couple of inches above my elbow right down to my wrist.

That's right, kids.

The phaaaaaaantom of the opera is heeeeeere. Bom-bom-bom-boooom.

'For fuck's sake,' Hadaway bit off, snapping me out of my thoughts about the state of my face and whether Phantom of the Opera masks only came in white, or if I could get a more colourful one to cover it all up. He came over and crouched in front of my chair, looking disconcertingly concerned again as he ran one thumb over my cheek, so lightly that I wasn't even certain he'd touched me. 'What the fuck did she do to you?'

I flashed him my shiny-new, mutated smile. 'You should see the state she's in.'

He blew a long, heavy breath out through his nose, giving me a look that was somehow grim and dry at the same time, before twisting around to face Angie, who was still hovering at the gap in the wall where our living room met the kitchen. 'Where is she?'

'In Tidge's wardrobe,' she told him anxiously, squeezing the fingers of one hand tight with the other. 'We didn't know what to do with her, and that was the only place where we could lock her in, so... that's where she is.'

Not being a Bobby, I can't say how often you get told that the perp is locked in a wardrobe, but Hadaway seemed to take it totally in stride. Without another word, he shoved himself up and strode out of the kitchen towards my bedroom, leaving me and Angie to hurry after him as we heard any number of Police cars pull up outside the house, sirens blaring. (Clearly, Hadaway had made a few calls on his way over.) In fact, the only time he seemed to bat an eyelid was when he walked into my room and saw exactly what we meant by 'Knight is locked in the wardrobe'.

'What?' I said defensively, when he stopped dead and turned slightly, shooting us an incredulous look. 'The doors don't lock, it was the only way we could make sure they stayed shut. And it's done the job, hasn't it?'

Hadaway shook his head wearily, like he couldn't believe what he had to put up with, but for once, he didn't actually say anything. He took a few steps towards the wardrobe, pulling his handcuffs out of his back pocket at the same time, and then he tugged the bobbles off the double doors and yanked them open.

And froze.

I got a funny, prickly feeling somewhere in the pit of my stomach.

What was he doing? Why wasn't he diving in there and slapping the cuffs on her? I mean, I knew my wardrobe wasn't in the best of shapes, but was he really going to put the biggest arrest of his career on hold just so he could spend a few seconds staring at the damage I'd done over the years?

And then, just as I opened my mouth to ask if he was still with us, just as Johnny burst into the flat with Response officers and the odd CID officer behind him, he finally turned to look at us, looking thunderous. 'What the fuck are you playing at?'

'We didn't have a choice, Ade,' Angie said uneasily, as the prickly feeling exploded out of the pit of my stomach and hit the back of my throat, burning everything it passed on the way and making all of my organs sink down until they reached somewhere in the region of my ankles. Something wasn't right. 'She just kept coming at us, and we had to do *something*. It was a choice of letting her go or letting her keep going at one of us while the other one called you lot. What would you have had us do?'

He stared at her in furious disbelief, like he hadn't expected her to actually have the gall to say that to him, and I felt my legs start to carry myself forward by themselves, which was interesting, because I didn't seem to *have* legs anymore. That pesky dentist must've been at them as well; I couldn't feel them at all.

I heard Hadaway snap at her as I reached his side, but I didn't take in exactly what he said. I was too busy peering around him to see inside the wardrobe.

My stomach gave a giant lurch, so that any internal organs still hovering around it were thrown all over the shop, making me feel sick and empty all at the same time.

I couldn't breathe.

I had to grab tight hold of the bottom my pyjama top to stop myself from physically rubbing my eyes in disbelief.

I couldn't breathe.

This couldn't be right. It didn't *sense*.

But there it was, right in front of me. Plain as day.

The wardrobe was completely empty.

And Knight was gone.

NINE

An hour later, me and Angie were still sat on the settee, both of us staring straight ahead of us, in far too much shock to barely even think, let alone talk. Let alone even look at each other. I have a feeling we were sat there with our jaws hanging wide open, as dignified as ever, and everyone who was there that night has just agreed that they'll never tell us about the drooling.

Most of the officers had drifted home or gone to other jobs after half an hour, when it became apparent that Knight definitely wasn't there, but a few Bobbies had stayed on, triple-checking every corner and examining every inch, nook and cranny of the flat for any ways that Knight might have got in and/or out of the flat.

I was vaguely aware of Johnny perched on the sofa arm next to Angie, his arm slung across the top of the settee as he murmured into her hair.

I can't remember where Squidge was.

He was probably helping them, mostly to be fussed over and partly because helping *them* didn't have a risk to it.

Someone wouldn't be getting their nightly cheese for the next week.

It didn't make sense.

How the hell could she be *gone?*

Let's look past the fact that she was out cold, because of course there'd *always* been the chance that she'd wake up before the Bobbies turned up. But we'd *locked her in.* We'd been *in the fucking flat.* How had she got out of the wardrobe? How'd she done it without us picking up on it, or without Squidge noticing? Yeah, the kitchen is snuggled between my bedroom and the landing outside the flat, so you can't see who's coming in and out of my room from there – but the place isn't *soundproofed.* Surely at least *one* of us would've heard *something?* And for that matter, how had she got back *out* of the flat without us noticing anything, either? It wasn't like she'd just waltzed out through the flat door with a 'bye, guys!' and a cheery wave; you *have* to walk past the kitchen to get to the door, and between the gap in the wall and the empty window frame over the kitchen counters, looking out into the living room, you can't miss anyone coming or going.

See, that's the bit that properly gave me chills.

Pretend to be a witch all you like, but the idea that she'd been able to sneak around the flat while both of us were home and awake and neither of us had heard her... that was out-and-out *creepy*.

I didn't snap out of it until I noticed Hadaway sitting on the coffee table in front of me.

I have no idea how long he'd been sitting there for, watching me with a grim look on his face as he ran one hand across his mouth, jaw and anywhere else with stubble, but by the time I realised he was there, it was only the five of us in the flat.

'Alright,' he said heavily, when he realised that I'd come to. 'Tell me what happened.'

I told him everything.

I took him through how I'd woke up to Knight standing over me, and how she'd threatened me to keep my nose out of what she was doing.

I told him about how the fight had started, how Angie had got involved, and how no-one could give Squidge any attention for the rest of the night because he'd turned total traitor on us.

And I explained about how Angie being there hadn't stopped her, how she'd clearly been trying to get out of my bedroom window, and we'd finally knocked her out and stashed her in the wardrobe.

And the whole time I was talking, not once did he tell me off.

Not even a hint of it. If anything, there was a tiny second after I told him about hitting Knight with the book where he almost looked like he wanted to laugh, and frankly, I'm not sure who was more surprised by this new Hadaway – me or him. (Let's face it, probably me.)

For a few seconds after I finished talking, he didn't say anything. He just kept running his hand across his stubbly area, staring at me with that look that somehow managed to be too serious and too grim even for the situation.

'How'd she know where you live?'

'I don't know,' I told him honestly, and a second later, I felt myself prickle. 'What do you think? That I *told* her where we live?'

'That's not what –'

'Even if I'd had the *chance* to tell her,' I continued hotly, vaguely aware of Angie stiffly turning her head to look at me, 'why the hell *would* I? She's an out-and-out psychopath, Hadaway, she's hardly someone I'd want –'

'Armitage,' he interrupted, in a voice that somehow managed to be grim and gentle at the same time. 'Look, I'm not having a go.' Oh. 'I'm fucking *worried*. If she knows where you live, either she's got eyes on you or she knows someone who knows you.'

I blinked at him a couple of times, feeling something that could well have been my heart fall into the bottom my stomach, landing with a solid *thunk*.

I hadn't spent a lot of time trying to work out how Knight knew where we lived; the fight and her disappearing act had put all of those questions out of my head. All I'd been able to think about was the fact that she'd managed to get in without any explanation, and the fact that she'd managed to get back out without any explanation.

But he was right.

If she wasn't having us watched, someone we knew must've been helping her out.

Except that...

Well, except –

'No-one would do that,' Angie told him faintly, looking a couple of shades paler than she normally does. 'This is our family and our friends you're talking about, Ade. They're people who give a shit about us, not people who want us dead.'

'Right,' he said in that same half-gentle, half-grim voice, turning his head slightly to look at her. 'But until we know who Knight's got on side, we can't rule anyone out. The chances are they don't have anything to do with it,' he added hastily, when Angie made a funny little squeak in the back of her throat. 'But we need to look at everyone who knows where you live, just to make sure.'

'If you ask me,' Johnny said carefully, 'it's more likely that you were followed home from the bookshop tonight.'

We all turned to look at him, and at the same time, I felt a little whoosh of confusion, mixed with a few prickles of irritation. The last time we'd seen Daniels, he'd been taped to a chair, waiting for Johnny himself to turn up. So what was he saying? That he hadn't gone to the bookshop after all? That by the time he got there, Daniels had been cut free and done a runner? *What?*

'Hang on a minute,' I said slowly, frowning slightly at him. 'We *called* you from the bookshop. Wasn't Daniels there when you turned up?'

'He was,' he nodded, as casually as if we were talking about what we were going to watch on TV. 'And now he's at East District Headquarters, waiting for his interview. But there's nothing to say that he was the only one of Knight's supporters there.'

Angie whipped her head around to face me, her eyes a good couple of inches wider than they normally are, and I knew her mind had flown to exactly the same place mine had.

What if the people behind the bookshop till *hadn't* sent us to see Daniels so quickly because they were freaked out by the two lasses dressed as witches? What if they were just as involved as he was, and they'd wanted to get us out of the way as soon as possible so that they could – I don't know, tip the other Cloaks off? Make a plan to follow us home? Work out how they were supposed to deal with people who were clearly poking around in whatever Knight was up to?

I mean, they were the only other people who'd been in the bookshop that night.

And we hadn't even given them a second look.

'All I'm saying is,' Johnny continued easily, shifting his weight slightly on the arm of the settee, 'Knight's actively recruiting these followers of hers, they're not just turning up out of nowhere. And if she's not knocking on people's doors to get them involved, who d'you think's doing the legwork for her?'

Angie turned back to face him. 'So... what? Daniels has pulled the others into whatever Knight's doing, and they're the ones who followed us home and told her where we live?'

'Well, we won't know for definite until we can look into it a bit more. But that's my theory, aye.'

I turned away slightly, trying for the life of me to remember what the two people behind the counter had looked like, and immediately wished that I'd kept my eyes on Johnny. Because, of course, Hadaway was still sitting on the coffee table, straight in front of me. But instead of looking at me with the half-grim, half-gentle expression that'd matched his voice to a tee, he'd turned his head to his left to frown at Johnny.

'What went on at the bookshop?'

'Nothing,' I blurted out quickly, at the exact same time that Johnny told him dryly,

'One of Knight's supporters managed to get himself Sellotaped to a chair.'

Hadaway turned to face me again, shooting me an incredulous look that bordered on angry, and I quickly shot him my nicest, most placid smile.

'It's not what it sounds like.'

'It sounds like you Sellotaped someone to a chair.'

Mmm. Not really any way out of that one. 'I mean... I didn't say it was *completely* not what it sounds like.'

'For Christ's sake, Armitage,' he bit off furiously, shooting up off the table as he fixed me with one hell of a glare. 'What the fuck's wrong with you?'

I felt my head jerk back slightly as I stared up at him, feeling a few prickles of indignant irritation. 'Excuse me?'

'How many fucking times do I have to tell you to keep out of this?' he bit off angrily, and this time, the muscle in his jaw wasn't just twitching; it was beating out a solid rhythm. 'What do I have to do get it through your head that you're not helping with the case? Jesus, all you're doing is obstructing the damn thing!'

'Obst–' I felt a dart of white-hot anger shoot through me, and for a couple of seconds, I couldn't talk. I could barely even breathe. God, he was a dick. He was *such* a fucking *dick*. '*Obstructing?* You think we're obstructing it?'

'What've you done to help?' he demanded harshly, opening his arms out at his side in some kind of half-shrug. 'All you've done is get yourself thrown off the moor –'

'I *did not* –'

'– and have the stupid bitch knock seven shades of shit out you! What the hell makes you think any of that is *helping*?'

'We got you a fucking *arrest*, Hadaway!' I yelled furiously, throwing myself off the settee so that we were stood almost chest to chest and jabbing one finger towards the flat door behind him, as if the bookshop was just on the other side of it. 'We handed you one of

Knight's followers on a silver platter! And you're really going to stand there and tell me that's not helping?'

'You fucking taped him to a goddamn chair!'

'*So what?*' I screamed, feeling my eyes pop wide open as my hands buried themselves in my hair and grabbed tight hold. God, I was angry. I was *so* angry. There was a definite tint of red to everything. 'Why does it *matter* how we kept him there? We got you a fucking *Cloak*, didn't we? You should be saying thank you, not going off on one!'

'What makes you think he's a Cloak?' he snapped furiously, the look on his face getting angrier by the second. 'C'mon, Armitage, you're so made up with your frigging *arrest*, where's your evidence?'

'He has a limp –'

'Right, well, there you go then. Guilty as fuck.'

'*He has a limp,*' I repeated doggedly from between gritted teeth, scowling at him, 'and he had mud on his shoes. He was *there,* Hadaway. I *told* you, the footprints we found in Habely Woods were scuffed up on the right-hand side, like someone was dragging their foot behind them. And he was limping *on his right leg!*'

He gave one grim shake of his head. 'It's not enough.'

'I know it's not enough,' I told him hotly, digging my nails into my palms. 'It could be a complete coincidence and I'm going after some poor, innocent bloke. Except that he knew about Lyme, didn't he?'

That one got him.

He seemed to pull back slightly, and suddenly he didn't look quite as angry anymore. Not that he looked as shocked as I probably would've expected, if I'd actually thought about he'd react; more than anything, he looked suspicious.

'What?'

'Yeah,' I snapped, feeling a good-sized dollop of smugness start to mingle with all of the anger bubbling away inside of me. 'I mentioned that Lyme had gone missing, and he wasn't surprised in the slightest. It wasn't news to him, Hadaway. And how could he have known about it if he wasn't involved with Knight?'

He ran one hand over his stubble, stony-faced. 'He couldn't.'

'Right,' I said shortly, feeling my lip curl. 'So tell me again that we're not helping.'

For a few seconds, we just stood there and stared at each other, standing close enough that I could feel the heat coming off him, with my heart pounding so hard that it was all I could hear and feeling some kind of fluttering going on in my tummy. Hadaway, meanwhile, looked like half of him was having an internal rant about what a pain in the arse I was, while the other half was running through a hundred and one things that he needed to do for the Knight case.

To be honest, I have no idea how long we were stood like that for. And actually, I don't know what would've happened if Angie hadn't snapped us out of it.

'You know,' she said lightly in the end, making us both jump slightly and turn to face her, 'if you want to have sex, we can easily get out of your way. Just say the word and the room's yours.'

We both jerked our heads around to stare at her what can really only be described as complete abstract horror.

Jesus.

It was hardly a secret that Angie was desperate for us to fall madly in love and start bopping like bunnies, but come *on*. There's desperate, and then there's filling everyone's heads with *very* unwanted images that just won't budge.

And alright, did I *want* to see Hadaway naked? Yeah, absolutely. Of course I did. But that wasn't an *attraction* thing; it was much more what I'd call a scientific kind of curiosity, just to see exactly what he had going on under there that made lasses go even more gaga for him *after* they'd done the no pants dance than they were before. (I did have some ideas. But it's always good to know for sure.)

Still, though.

I didn't want to be picturing that while I was stood right next to the man himself.

'Hilarious,' I told her in the end, my voice just a touch too strangled to come out as dry as I'd wanted it to.

She shot me an overly innocent smile, clasping her hands together as she stretched her arms out in front of her. 'I thought so.'

I rolled my eyes and turned back to Hadaway, ready to pick up where we'd left off and really tell him to piss off. He was already staring back at me, looking just as grim as he had before Angie's attempt at a joke, except that now he had a glint of something in his eye that I couldn't quite put my finger on.

But before I could bother to try and work out exactly what it was or why it made me feel so hot and prickly, all of the adrenaline from everything that'd happened with Knight and all of the anger from arguing with Hadaway just disappeared, literally like someone had flipped a switch inside me.

And instead, I just felt totally drained and absolutely knackered.

'Look, I've had enough,' I told him tiredly. 'You can get as mad as you like and shout all you want, but the fact is, we *did* help the other night and we *did* help tonight, and I don't know why you're trying to say that we didn't, other than being a knob is just a habit to you now –'

'I'm not being a f–'

'– but I'm not doing it. I've had the shittiest night, my arms are killing me, I look like Quasimodo's less attractive cousin, and all I want to do is get a pint of sherry and sit in the bath for as long as possible. So if anyone needs me' – I brushed past him and walked towards the kitchen, suddenly feeling my eyes prickling slightly in frustration – 'and I'd really recommend that you *don't*, that's where I'm going to be.'

Honestly, angry doesn't even begin to cover it.

I can't say I was raging, because it was that tired kind of angry, where chunter after rant after dramatic monologue were flying through my mind but my body was too exhausted to bother coming to the party. And while I was sat on the side of the bath – feet in the rising water and swigging sherry out of the bottle, like the classy bird I am – I even realised that I didn't know who I was more mad at: Hadaway, for acting like the dickhead that he'd dedicated his entire life to being, or Knight, for being *so fucking close* and then doing a bunk right when we were about to throw another, less literal book at her.

Or maybe at myself, for not being able to work out the hell she'd done it.

For God's sake, it wasn't like we'd knocked her out and then thought, 'well, that's that taken care of. No need to do anything more here, no no no'. Because of *course* we'd seen it coming that she'd try and wander off the second she woke up; it was so obvious that I'd bet good money that *Squidge* had probably seen it coming, and the poor lad will have just thought we were playing a game that, frankly, did not look like his idea of a good time.

And again, once we'd locked her in the wardrobe, we hadn't exactly gone *far*; we'd sat in the kitchen, barely talking and taking it in turns to check that the wardrobe doors were still locked shut, which – I'll just point out – they always were.

So... what?

Could the lass fricking *teleport?*

Were we looking at a bona fide alien abduction?

How in Christ had she *done* it?

I took another swig out of the sherry bottle, eyeing the bathroom window thoughtfully. Maybe I needed to get Angie to lock me in the wardrobe to see if I could get out, too. With hindsight, it wasn't *completely* outside the realms of possibility that just tying the doors with a bobble was too easy, and we should've propped stuff against the double doors that, if nothing else, would've made a bit of a bang when she pushed the doors open.

But to be fair to us, you don't think things through to the far end of a fart when you're freaked out, beaten up and panicking.

I took another swig of sherry and just to say started to lean forward, ready to turn the taps off and jump into the bubbles, when it finally occurred to me what I was looking at.

Our bathroom window.

Or, to be more specific, our bloody temperamental bathroom window, which dated back to at least the nineties and liked to open and close whenever it felt the need to, no matter which hole on the little metal bar you had it hooked onto. Our temperamental bathroom window that you could push open even if you'd locked it with a key.

Our temperamental bathroom window that was banging just the *tiniest* bit against its frame, like someone had pushed it as far closed as they could from the outside, so it was almost – but not quite – as locked as it had been before we'd gone to bed.

And before I'd leant more than a couple of millimetres forward, I completely froze in place, my free hand reaching out towards the taps and my eyes locked on the window.

Aha.

Witch, my fucking arse.

I dropped my sherry bottle down next to the bathtub and shoved myself up with my feet in the water, grabbing my phone off the side of the sink as I lurched over to the window, giving it a solid shove open with one hand. I fumbled with my phone to turn the torch application on, and then I leaned as far forward as I could, standing on my tiptoes and steadying myself on the windowsill with my spare hand as I shone the torch light straight down, towards the wooden beams built into the side of the house.

And almost immediately, I felt a huge explosion of excitement in my tummy, so huge and fizzy that a part of me was surprised that I didn't actually hear it happen.

Because there, hanging off the edge the beam closest to the window and only just visible if you were *really* trying to look for it, was a clump of mud.

Which, admittedly, hadn't necessarily been left there by Knight; given that I don't make a habit of hanging out of the window and examining the beams, it could've got there at literally any point. It could've been dropped by a bird and clung on for dear life or something, I don't know.

But my gut was telling me that that probably wasn't the case.

Especially when I wobbled slightly so that my torch light shone against the side of the house, so that I could see a streak of blood, an inch or two below the windowsill... almost like someone who'd got blood on their hands had tried to steady themselves against the wall while they were balancing – and how the hell they'd managed to do that is beyond me – on that muddied beam.

For a few seconds, I just stared there and stared at it, with my heart thumping hard in my ears as I tried to remember how to breathe.

Because *of course* this was how Knight had got in and out. It made absolute perfect sense, to the point where I couldn't believe I hadn't thought of it sooner. Did I like the fact that she knew that that window would let her into our flat? 100% not. Did I like the fact that she'd given away one of her little secrets, proven that she was much better at breaking and entering than she was at being a witch, and emptied my head of all the questions that would've kept me awake all night, sherry or no sherry? You betcha.

And maybe it was the excitement of working it all out, or maybe the man was just so at the front of my mind after being a dick earlier, I don't know. But the next thing I knew, I was unfreezing and shoving myself back away from the window, almost losing my footing in the bath as I whirled towards the bathroom door and heard myself yell (far too happily),

'*Hadaway!*'

Barely half an hour later, our ridiculously tiny bathroom was crawling with Forensics (by which I mean there were three of them in there), and me and Angie were stood in front of my Scribbley Wall with our bingo markers firmly in hand, while Johnny and an quietly grim Hadaway sat on my bed, watching us in what I can only describe as a resigned acceptance.

We knew that – contrary to what I'd told Hadaway that morning – Knight somehow knew *exactly* where we lived and had no issues with pitching up in the middle of the night, which could mean that she was still in the nearby area, if not in Habely itself; we knew that she'd managed to climb up the side of a Tudor-style house, apparently the only unnatural skill that she genuinely had; we knew that she could silently escape from bound wardrobe doors; and we knew that, as far as Habely Bookshop knew, Knight had never bought the book that Pettyfer had told us about. Admittedly, she could've bought it from somewhere else. And admittedly, given that Daniels was a raging Cloak, he could've lied to us. But since all we had to say that she had the book at all was Pettyfer's drugged-up memory, it was going on the wall.

The problem was that there was still a lot that we *didn't* know.

For example, we still had no clue where Lyme was or what Knight was doing with him. We didn't know exactly what Pettyfer and Pace meant when they said that she'd got inside their souls, and we still hadn't worked out how she'd made them feel like that or how she knew all of that information about them, stuff that they'd kept secrets for years. We didn't know how she'd got so many people to follow her like they'd follow a celebrity on Instagram; we didn't know what Knight was planning to do once she got this procedure thing over and done with; and we didn't know what the Cloaks had been chanting in the –

'Wait a minute,' I blurted out, feeling my marker skid across the wall as I whipped my head around to face Angie. 'You speak Latin.'

She shot me a dry look for a couple of seconds, clicking the lid back onto her own bingo marker. 'Yes. Regularly.'

'Well, definitely after a few glasses of prosecco.'

'I studied it at college,' she said, shooting me a wry grin that said she saw my bait and wasn't going to rise to it. 'I wouldn't say I *speak* it.'

'Hang on,' Hadaway said, eyeing her with something that bordered on caution. 'How good are you at reading it?'

'I don't know,' she told him nervously, with the air of someone who knows they're getting roped into something they'd rather stay out of. 'I haven't looked at it since I was eighteen, Ade, I'm hardly fluent.'

'But you'd know what you were looking at.'

'I might,' she said painedly, after a few seconds in which I *heard* several excuses fly through her head, 'be able to work it out.'

He ran one hand over his stubble, looking like he was torn between keeping us as far from the case as humanly possible or actually (whisper it) asking us for some help. But before he could decide which way he was going to jump, Johnny was telling us warily,

'We're having a bit of a nightmare getting hold of a Latin translator.'

'Johnny, I'm not -'

'If you could just take a look,' he interrupted coaxingly, pushing himself off the bed and coming over to put his hands on her shoulders. 'Just give us an idea of what it might say. It'd be a massive help, Angie.'

There was a long pause, in which Angie stared up at him, nervously nibbling on her thumbpad, and both of them stared right back at her, Johnny looking just as hopeful as Hadaway did wary. And while they were doing that, I kept my eyes glommed on her, holding my breath and desperately tried to send her a telepathic message to just *do* it.

If Angie said yes to translating the Latin, then we'd have an actual reason to hang around East District HQ and get the latest gen on what was happening. (You'd think that having the most wanted person in the North East break into your flat and try to kill you would give you in an in. Somehow I had the feeling that that wasn't going to be the case for as long as Hadaway was around.) Admittedly, it was an in with a time limit... but hey, maybe by the time they found a bona fide Latin translator, they'd be so used to us hanging around that they wouldn't notice if we just kept on doing it.

'Fine,' she agreed eventually, in the same way that someone would agree to go to the electric chair. 'I'll take a look. *But*,' she added warningly, before any of us could get too excited, 'you have to keep looking for an actual translator. I was never the best at Latin, Johnny, and I haven't looked at in years. I am *not* having this case get thrown out of Court because of my shitty Latin skills.'

I didn't dare look at Hadaway as Johnny promised her that wouldn't happen and dropped a kiss on her forehead. I didn't need to; I knew that he'd be looking as grim as anything about the fact that I'd been given the opportunity to shoehorn myself into the case, and I knew that I wouldn't be able to stop myself from flashing him a huge, happy grin the second our eyes met, something that would no doubt shove him into telling me that it was *Angie* who'd be giving them a hand, not me.

Please.

Like we didn't come as a package deal.

Instead, I turned back to the wall and flicked my eyes over all of the scribbles up there, nibbling on the cap of my bingo marker and frowning slightly.

Again, there was something we weren't getting.

Actually, there were several things that we weren't getting. But I had this niggling feeling that there was one big thing that was staring us in the face, something that would give us one hell of a break if we could just crack it... but we just weren't seeing it.

I snuck the tiniest of peeks at Hadaway over my shoulder. 'Has anyone spoke to Lyme's family in the last couple of days?'

'Andy Hopkins went to see them the other day,' he told me, sounding for all the world like I was the last person he wanted to be talking to about it. Which, in fairness, I probably was. 'There's no word from him, but they're getting some hope from the fact that we haven't found him yet.'

Found him as in found his body.

Right.

'What about Pace?' Angie asked curiously, while I had a second scan through the Scribbley Wall. 'Has anyone spoke to him yet?'

'Not yet.' Johnny shook his head as Hadaway shoved himself off the bed and came to stand behind me, getting a better look at all of our notes for himself. 'Skip's going to see him again later today. Him and Mr Evans think he should be well enough to talk to us by now.'

I turned on the spot to face Hadaway, only to stumble back a step when the heat rolling off him hit me full-whack in the face. Jesus, what was he? A human radiator? 'Which do you think is the best one to start with from the 'Things We Don't Know' list?'

'This one,' he deadpanned, and then he plucked the bingo marker out of my hand and leant past me, close enough to give me a good whiff of his aftershave, and wrote 'Why Armitage keeps involving herself in the case' on the wall, in handwriting that managed to be undeniably masculine even in bright purple ink.

'I don't,' I told him nicely, turning away from the wall to flash him my most patient smile. 'Knight involved me in the case when she broke into our flat and tried to kill me.'

'Victims don't tend to be involved in their cases, Armitage.'

'No, but they *are* kept updated on what's happening with it, don't they? So think of it as me saving you a job and getting my own updates.'

He shot me a look that bordered on warning, but instead of saying anything, he blew a grim sigh out through his nose and jabbed his finger against the note about Lyme. 'We start with Keith. We need to make sure he's safe, and unless Knight has stashed him somewhere out of the way, there the chances are, if we find him, we find her With a bit of luck, we can do it before tomorrow night.'

I felt my insides give a funny little spasm, almost like they'd been happily snoozing away only to be so deeply disturbed by their very unexpected, very loud alarm clock that they skipped being startled, skipped hitting the snooze button, and jumped straight to wondering where the hell this sudden, enthusiastic attack was coming from.

Shit.

Shit.

Whatever Knight was planning, it was happening tomorrow night.

Whoever they were going to kill, they were doing it *tomorrow.*

Somehow I hadn't connected those dots until Hadaway said it.

But it was true. We didn't even have two full days to find out who was going to get dead, find out where they were being kept, and them as far away from Knight and her followers as possible.

Fuck.

I gave Hadaway a thoughtful look as my organs settled back into their usual positions, confident that the attack was over but still on high alert. 'D'you know what'd be a good idea?'

'You staying out of this case.'

'Why don't I go and see Pace with Skip?'

He stared at me for a couple of seconds, looking like he couldn't believe I'd actually had the gall to ask that - but there was just the *tiniest* hint of amusement in there as well, for (I'm guessing) the exact same reason. 'Why the fuck would we let you do that?'

'I have some questions that I could do with asking him.'

He stared at me for a few seconds longer, and I knew the exact second he realised that I wasn't joking. The look on his face suddenly got one hell of a lot darker. 'No.'

'Pettyfer talked to me,' I pointed out stubbornly, crossing my arms and frowning up at him. 'Pettyfer would *only* talk to me. How d'you know Pace won't be the same?'

'Pettyfer wanted to talk to you because he thinks he can connect with you,' he said exasperatedly, and I felt my chin jerk back in irritated indignation. 'He thinks you're just as screwed up as he is, it's not a fucking compliment. Listen,' he added shortly, seeing me open my mouth to argue with him and cutting me off before I could get started. 'You've got two choices, alright? You can do what I'm telling you to and keep out of it, or I can arrest you and *make* you keep out of it.'

My insides gave another little lurch as I stared at him in shock, feeling my jaw drop open by a good couple of inches and my eyes pop wide open so that I probably looked like The

Mask when he sees Tina Carlyle at the Coco Bongo for the first time (minus, thankfully, the freakishly long tongue lolling out of my mouth).

Half of me thought he was bluffing.

The other half thought he sounded like he'd enjoy it too much to not follow through.

'You wouldn't.'

'I would.'

'For *what?*'

'Wasting police time. Obstruction.' He eyed me grimly. 'Anything that'll keep you out of the way until this is done with. Look,' he added in the same heavy tone, putting one hand on my shoulder and using the other to tuck some of my hair back behind my ear as I stared up at him, feeling my heart pounding in my chest and a wave of red-hot, rage-fuelled hate rising up in my throat until it was hard to breathe. Oh, you dickhead. You *dickhead,* Hadaway. 'If arresting you is the only way to keep you safe, that's what I'm going to do. At the end of the day, Knight came after you for a reason. D'you think she's just going to let it drop? Or d'you reckon she's going to keep coming after you until you're not a problem anymore?'

I blinked up at him thoughtfully, feeling my throat relax slightly. 'You think I've got her running scared.'

'I think you've done something to give her cause for concern.'

'So why don't we –'

'*No.*' His hands slid off my shoulders and suddenly any traces of concern were gone from his face, so that he was giving me a cold, hard frown instead. 'They're your choices, you stay out of it or we take you in. I'm not telling you again.'

Before I had chance to argue back, he was turning on his heel and marching towards the door, muttering something to Johnny about making himself a bed on the settee at the same time. And after giving Angie a quick kiss and giving me a big-brotherly kind of chuck under the chin, Johnny followed him out of the room, leaving us both standing in front of the Scribbley Wall in a silence so sharp it was like someone had been slapped.

After a couple of seconds, I glanced across at Angie, tucking my tongue into the corner of my mouth. 'Well.'

She turned towards at me, eyeballing me in a way that looked wary at first... until you noticed the same shock and anger that I was feeling bubbling underneath. 'Well.'

I felt a little eruption in my stomach, almost as if seeing those feelings on Angie's face gave me some justification for feeling them too.

How fucking *dare* he?

What if I hadn't been involved in the Knight case?

What if I hadn't worked with him? Or what if we weren't constantly thrown together because of our best friends?

What if I was some complete stranger who'd had their flat broken into by a random psychopath who'd then proceeded to kick seven shades of shit out of me?

He wouldn't have pitched up and made an already brutal night even worse. I knew he wouldn't.

So why the hell did he think it was OK to do that here?

'He's angry,' Angie told me, almost as if she'd read my mind. 'And he thinks you're getting yourself involved for the glory. Johnny told me,' she added almost apologetically, as I felt my whole body jerk in horrified surprise, so much so that I almost swallowed my tongue. 'He said Hadaway doesn't understand why you'd be so desperate to get involved if not for your fifteen minutes of fame as The Girl Who Caught Elodia Knight.'

I felt my throat filling up with rage again. 'I don't want *any* fucking glory!'

'I know,' she reassured me quickly, hurriedly coming over to me and giving me a quick, tight hug. 'I know, Tidge. He's obviously just never met someone who's this nosey just for the sake of it before.'

I could feel myself shaking slightly in anger.

In fact, for the first time ever, I was so angry that I couldn't talk.

The glory?

He thought I was so shallow and self-absorbed that I wanted the fucking *glory*?

I wanted to know how she was making herself look like a witch. I wanted to know why she was doing it. That it was *it*. I didn't want my face in the papers. I didn't want any awards. I didn't want anyone knowing that I'd been involved in the whole thing.

And if he genuinely didn't get that, then he could just *piss off*.

'So,' Angie said just a touch too lightly, turning back to the Scribbley Wall. 'What's our next move?'

'Habely Woods,' I ground out, turning around myself to glower at the Wall. 'We need to go back to the clearing and figure out what exactly was going on there. And the less Hadaway knows about what we're doing,' I added, dropping my voice slightly, so there was no chance of him hearing me, 'the better. There's no way in hell I'm giving that dickhead the pleasure of arresting me.'

When we finally called it a night at half past four in the morning (there's a contradiction for you), the plan was to grab a couple of hours' sleep and sneak out without a word, and just hope that Hadaway and Johnny - whenever they woke up, just assumed that we'd gone to work for the day.

The plan didn't work for two reasons.

One was that I was too fuming with Hadaway to get any sleep at all. Instead, I just laid on my bed, scowling at my ceiling and wondering how many javelins it'd take to make the man look like a human porcupine.

The other was that Angie had been really clever and set her alarm clock for the agreed time of six o'clock, which – of course – had woken Johnny up too. And in the brain-fog caused by her two-hour nap, she'd remembered what we were doing but forgotten that Hadaway and Johnny weren't supposed to *know* what we were doing.

So she told Johnny.

And Johnny told Hadaway.

And nothing, but nothing, we could do or say would stop the pair of them insisting on coming with us.

But hey, who was I to complain? In Hadaway's post-nap haze, he'd forgotten that he was supposed to be arresting me if I looked any further into the case, and hell as like was I going to remind him of that canny little threat.

Hence the fact that, at half past six that morning, the four of us and Squidge were back in the clearing that Knight and her followers had used on Tuesday night.

Within a few seconds of reaching the place, the blokes had switched straight into Police mode and snapped on a pair of plastic gloves each, carefully prodding through the ankle-length grass an inch at a time, looking for anything that the Cloaks had left behind that could count as evidence or – better yet – might have DNA on it. And while they were doing that, me and Angie had tied Squidge to a tree on the edge of the clearing and quickly plonked ourselves in the centre of the clearing, staring at the beast of a tree stump that Knight had appeared on top two nights earlier.

There *had* to be a way that she'd done it. However she'd managed to make it look as though she could just appear out of thin air, there *had* to be some explanation. And if there was an explanation, who was to say that there wasn't evidence of it?

I mean, Knight had left something behind at the flat without even realising it. Now, surely, when you're in a new place and trying making it look like you've appeared there out of thin air somewhat impulsively, you'd take extra care? You'd be *so careful*, because you wouldn't know what to expect in this new place and you'd need your little party-trick to be just as believable there as it was in the usual place you pulled it in... whereas in said usual place, you might get complacent, because you knew that place like the back of your hand, and you could always, *always* pre-empt anything that could happen there. And if you got complacent, then surely you'd get a little bit sloppy? Maybe more careless?

Or would it be the other way 'round? Would you always be careful pulling the same trick in the same place, because there was more of a chance of you getting caught there, and only make mistakes when doing it on the hoof?

My point is, either way, if she'd left evidence in one place, she could easily have left it somewhere else, too.

Not, admittedly, that there looked like there was any in the clearing.

Or at least, if there was, the tree stump wasn't giving it away. It just sat there, wide and short and silent, defending Knight just as much as any of her Cloaks would. In fact, if tree stumps could pull facial expressions, there was no doubt in my mind that we'd be getting the most fatal of death stares off the stupid thing.

'I'm stumped,' Angie said flatly after a few seconds of staring at it, and then we both laughed hysterically at the unintentional, brilliant pun before abruptly sobering up. 'No, but seriously. You said that she just appeared here, but… that doesn't make any sense. You can't *actually* pop in and out of thin air whenever you want to. So how'd she make it look like she did?'

'I don't know,' I admitted reluctantly, running one hand over my face as a wave of tiredness suddenly hit me. I needed a coffee. Or maybe a sherry. 'Let's recreate it,' I added decisively, shaking the weariness off me and beaming at her as I clapped my hands together. 'You can be me. Go and sit under that tree with Squidge.'

She stared at me, looking slightly bewildered. 'What?'

'We're going to recreate what happened on Tuesday night,' I explained brightly, still beaming at her as I limbered up, reaching for my ankle with one hand and bringing my other arm over the top of my head. 'I was under that tree, watching the Cloaks doing all their weird shit. So go and sit there with Squidge.'

She craned her neck around to stare at the tree for a few seconds, before turning back to me with a definite grimace on her face. 'That's a lot more cobwebs than I'm really comfortable with.'

'Angie, you'll be under there for five seconds. Do you think any of the spiders will even *notice* you in five seconds?'

'I'd rather not take the chance.'

'Squidge has already been under there for more than five seconds,' I pointed out, raising my eyebrows at her. 'And he hasn't been infested by spiders, has he?'

We both turned to stare at said doggy.

He was just sat there, staring back at us and panting happily with his giant pink tongue lolling out of his mouth, ears on high alert and his eyes shining excitedly. What a fun, strange game the humans were playing.

After a few seconds, she turned back to face me, grimace still firmly in place. 'Why can't *you* be you?'

'Because,' I told her patiently, pretending that I hadn't noticed Hadaway take a break from prodding around in the grass and stare at me, looking like it was taking a hell of a lot of effort to stop himself from laughing. 'I'm going to be the Cloaks.'

And then, before she could argue any more about how she didn't want to be go under the tree, I started cantering around the clearing in sidesteps, showing roughly where each the Cloaks had been stood.

I'll admit, part of me was hoping that being back there was going to give my memory a little nudge. I'd gone over what had happened that night *so many times* in my head – again and again and again, and then once more for good luck – and not once had I had any astounding revelations, or any sudden memories of something that I'd barely noticed on the night itself but would give us a hell of clue about what Knight was playing at.

So really, what harm was recreating it all going to do?

'Right,' I carried on breathlessly, as Angie rolled her eyes and stomped over to the tree, exciting Squidge no end. And while she was doing that, Hadaway and Johnny gave up on any pretence of searching for evidence and instead just stood there, watching us with their blue-gloved hands hanging loosely at their sides. 'So. I was under the tree. The Cloaks were in this big circle, two rings of them. And Knight was on that tree stump. But she wasn't even here at first, she just popped up there...' I stopped side-stepping just next to the tree that Angie was grumpily crouched under, chewing on my bottom lip as I stared at the stump. 'So clearly, something happened that I didn't see. But what *was* it?'

'I don't *know*,' Angie told me impatiently, using one hand to keep Squidge at bay as he pushed forward against her, desperately trying to inhale any scraps of earwax she might have. 'All I know is that the tree is *vile*. Look at it,' she added disgustedly, swiping at the silver strings over the branches with her spare hand. 'Have you *seen* how many cobwebs there are?'

And that's when it happened.

She hit the cobwebs, and the smallest of the lower tree branches moved slightly.

Not like when they're rustling in the wind.

No, no.

These gave just the tiniest rise and fall, like the tree was giving us the slightest of sullen shrugs. *What? Because Stumpy McStumperson over there wouldn't give her up, you just assumed that the rest of us would be the same?*

There was a little pause, in which we all froze on the spot and stared at the tree in complete silence. And then Angie raised her hand and swiped at the them again, grabbing at the silver string and giving it a good yank so that the branches rose by an extra quarter-of-an-inch more.

More silence. Even Squidge was completely still now, peering at the branches with his head tilted to one side and a curious look on his face.

'These aren't cobwebs.'

'No,' I agreed slowly, taking a few steps back from the tree and letting my eyes flick between the right and left of it. 'Doesn't look that way, does it? Hit them again for me.'

She pulled her arm back and used her open palm to hit a silver string wrapped around a couple of branches slightly higher up, and then she grabbed hold of the same string and gave it a good tug towards her.

On the slap, I saw the air to the right of the tree wriggle slightly, like a tight elastic band stretched between the trees had been twanged.

On the tug, I saw the tiniest branches of the tree rise up again, and this time the sun glinted off something in the air halfway between Angie's tree and the birch tree a metre or so to its right.

I heard someone – I think it might've been me – breathe, 'Oh my God,' and the next thing I knew, I was hurrying towards the gap between the trees. Even up close, it took me a couple of seconds to focus on it, it was so fine, but as soon as I saw it, I grabbed onto it with my forefinger and thumb and followed it, tracing it to the birch tree.

Oh my God.

Cable wires.

The tiniest, most delicate cable wires I'd ever seen, so thin that they were close to invisible and you'd think they'd snap if you pulled on them too hard, wrapped around the branches of the horse chestnut tree and the birch tree... and probably all the other trees in the clearing as well.

I whirled around to face Hadaway, so excited that I forgot I wasn't supposed to be talking to him. 'This must be how Knight made the branches up the other night! Little cable wires all over the place!'

He shifted his weight between his feet slightly, shooting me a doubtful frown as he crossed his arms over his chest. 'Knight wouldn't be strong enough to lift the branches of a tree by herself. She's skin and bone.'

I blinked at him, suddenly feeling all of the excitement evaporate.

I hated to admit it, but... good point well made, Mr Hadaway. But then –

'So why else would there be a load of cable wires all over the place?'

'I don't know,' he told me, shrugging. 'Some sort of conservation work, maybe.'

'They aren't doing any conservation work up here, mate.' Johnny comes from a long line of National Park Authority and National Trust workers. Actually, Angie had once told me that while his parents *were* proud of him for being a Bobby, they'd initially been a little disappointed that he hadn't followed in their footsteps. 'And these things aren't anything like what they use.'

'Look, I'm not ruling it out,' Hadaway said, clocking the little frown I was giving him. 'And I'm not saying we won't look into it. But I can't see anyone having the strength to move branches like that by themselves.'

'Angie did it.'

'They were only twigs really, Tidge,' Angie pointed out from under the tree. 'Do you really think I could make any of the big branches move.'

Erm, yes.

Angie might be slight, but she's got a freakish amount of strength when, say, she's tackling me in front of the fridge to make sure I don't get the last piece of chocolate.

For a few seconds, we all stood there in silence, looking at different parts of the clearing. (Apart from Squidge, who'd obviously got bored of this new game and gently laid down on the grass with a long, happy groan.)

Me, I was staring at the stump.

Knight *had* moved those branches by herself. I knew no-one was telling me that I'd been seeing things, but still, that was just a fact. She'd stood on that stump, raised her hand, and the branches of that tree had lifted high enough up that everyone could see me.

But Hadaway was right; Knight wasn't exactly The Beast.

So... how'd she done it?

'What about Pettyfer?' Angie asked thoughtfully, as I started marching towards the stump. 'Could he have helped her?'

'Pettyfer'll break in the next strong wind,' Hadaway told her dryly. 'I'd be surprised if them two could lift a piece of paper between them.'

As I got closer to the stump, I could see another tiny cable wire running out from the trees behind it and over my head, back towards the trees on the other side of the clearing, and I could feel this kind of determined excitement bubbling away inside me, building up to the point where I was pretty sure I was vibrating with it.

In fact, I was so excited about finding out exactly how Knight had pulled her little trick that instead of just stepping onto the stump like a normal person would, I decided to launch myself onto it from about a foot away,

And for half a second after I landed, everything was fine.

Well, it was a little bit weird. Everything seemed to slow down until it was frozen, even the leaves rustling in the occasional breeze. But it was still *fine*.

And then in the next half second, three things happened all at the same time.

One was that Squidge let out a deep bark, but because my head hadn't caught up with what was happening, I couldn't tell if it was meant to warn us about something, or if it was because he was bored and wanted to remind us he was there.

Another was that I heard an equally deep voice that I can only assume was Hadaway's shout something that I couldn't quite make out, sounding considerably more alarmed than Squidge did.

And the third was that the world was suddenly doing a funny jolt so that the trees in front of me were a hell of a lot higher than they had been a couple of seconds ago, and the ground wasn't under my feet anymore; instead, I was falling through the air, just dropping and dropping into darkness. Something hard conked me on the top of my head as I fell, and I must've titled slightly, because my right shoulder smacked into what felt like a sodding *wall* with enough force to send a sharp pain shoot down my arm, making it feel all tingly and weak – but before I could really even notice either of those things, my right leg was abruptly slamming down onto something *ridiculously* solid.

And it's funny, but at first I didn't even feel the pain.

I mean, I knew that there *was* pain, because my foot had just hit what could only be a tank so hard that my ankle had moved in with my knee, and suddenly I couldn't breathe, and I could barely see in front of me because of all the stars that had exploded in front of my eyes.

But I couldn't *feel* it.

What I could feel were my legs buckling underneath me so that I slowly keeled over onto the ground of wherever I was now. I could feel some slightly moist coolness on the left side of my face, and I could feel it seeping through my coat and my jeans. And then I could feel some warm, fairly large hands on me, gently turning me until I flopped over onto my back like a massively oversized ragdoll, only to find myself staring up – once again – at Hadaway, who was leaning over me with that new concerned look he seemed to have these days and saying something that I couldn't hear as he cupped one side of my face in one hand. I must've felt more than heard the ground thudding slightly as Angie and Johnny hurried over to wherever we were and dropped down next to me, Angie's face suddenly filling my vision next to Hadaway's, except that hers had a glint of amusement in it, which I remember feeling vaguely indignant at.

But the pain?

Nah.

Not until the sound suddenly came back on and my head finally caught up with what was going on.

That's when a nuclear bomb of hurt suddenly went off in my leg.

And funnily enough, that's when I started screaming.

I have no idea how long I kept screaming for.

It must've been a while, because Angie later told me that it was like watching the live version of the Screaming Sun from *Rick & Morty*, something that only made the bizarre, ridiculous image of me randomly bolting across the clearing, leaping through the air and disappearing into the tree stump even more hilarious. Judging by the looks that I saw Johnny and Hadaway exchange over my head – the ones that were warning each other not to cave and start laughing, like Angie had already done – that was the general consensus.

Honestly.

The sympathy.

The concern.

It was overwhelming.

'Jesus, Armitage,' Hadaway said in a voice that was slightly choked, clearly from the effort of trying to not to laugh. 'What the hell were you doing?'

No, no.

I'm fine.

Thank you for asking.

'Well, obviously I was trying to be Super fucking Mario, wasn't I?' I bit off loudly, moving seamlessly from the scream into the talking and glowering up at him, because really? Did they think I'd fucking *planned* that? 'What the hell do you *think* I was bloody doing?'

The three of them exchanges glances over my head that blatantly said the Super Mario thing wasn't too hard to believe, Angie still happily chortling away, but none of them were stupid enough to actually *say* that. Good for them. It didn't matter that my right arm had dissolved into jelly, that my ankle had merged with my knee to form a kneekle, or that I was hurting so much I was pretty sure I could actually *see* the pain. I still could've whacked them one. (Cheerfully.)

Instead, Hadaway pulled back slightly and put his hands sideways across his thighs, so his elbows were jutting out slightly as he knelt next to me. 'Where're you hurt?'

I stopped writhing around for a second and stared at him in disbelief. *Seriously?* 'God, I don't know, Hadaway. How about my fucking earlobe?'

He made a noise that sounded suspiciously like the start of a laugh, but credit to the man, he managed to cover it up with a cough quick-sharp. 'Armitage.'

'My leg,' I told him from between gritted teeth, as I started to rock from side to side slightly. It hurt too much to stay still. 'My right leg. I think my ankle's moved up to my knee.'

'Alright,' he said, starting to lean forward, one hand reaching towards my leg. 'Let me take a look –'

My jellified right arm suddenly flung up and pressed itself against his chest, trying to hold him back. '*No!*'

'Look, I need to make sure –'

'You're not touching it, Hadaway! It fucking knacks as it is, I'm not having you prodding at it and making it even worse!' And then, just as he opened his mouth to undoubtedly argue with me, I struggled up onto my elbows and looked around, squinting slightly. 'What the hell *happened?*'

I craned my head around to look behind me and felt myself blanch when I saw a big, vaguely oval-shaped piece of wood that looked *very* similar to the top of the tree stump lying a couple of feet away, bathed in a big pool of light.

Jesus.

Had I *fallen through* the tree stump?

I mean, yeah, I'd eaten a bit more cake in the last couple of weeks than I probably should've. But I was hardly heavy enough to make a *tree stump* collapse.

I hoped.

'We'll talk about that in a minute,' Hadaway told me impatiently, easing me back down so that I was flat on my back again. 'We need to take a look at your leg before we do anything else.'

'And how exactly *are* you going to look at my leg?' I asked just as impatiently, shooting him a half-curious, half-sarcastic look as I tilted my head to one side. 'What's the plan here, Dr Hadaway? Are you going to take my jeans off?'

His eyes locked on mine, and for a couple of seconds, his face was totally unreadable. Also in those couple of seconds, this bizarre little thought popped into my head, out of nowhere, saying *I wouldn't mind you taking off my jeans, actually.*

Which... well, obviously I didn't *want* Hadaway to take my jeans off.

Maybe it was that conk on my head.

Maybe it'd given me concussion.

In fact, it *must've* given me concussion, because before I could correct my poor, confused little head, it followed itself up with *Maybe I should take your jeans off, too. Fair's fair.* And that in turn was followed up by images of what Hadaway might look like without his jeans on, and then what he might look like without other pieces of clothing on too.

Not, you know, that they were exactly *bad* images.

Of course they weren't. Hadaway's a very good looking man.

They just weren't images that I wanted in my head.

And I *definitely* didn't want to find out if they were anything close to accurate.

No thank you.

'I think you want to take each other's jeans off,' Angie commented lightly, and when I whipped my head away from Hadaway to glare at her, she was very casually examining her fingernails. 'But what do I know? I'm just a casual bystander to all this sexual tension.'

Oh, for God's sake.

'I'll be fine,' I said waspishly, snapping myself back to sanity and wafting his hand away from me. 'I'll get an ice-pack on it and a glass of sherry when we get back to the flat.'

I clambered to my feet, wincing against the pain and desperately trying to keep the weight off my bad leg, mentally adding *See if the NHS do kneekle separation surgery* to that list. Hadaway stayed where he was, staring at my leg with a grim, unconvinced look on his face, and when I glanced down at myself, I couldn't exactly blame him; my right knee was easily three times bigger than my left one, and I had a feeling that it was only going to get bigger yet.

'Anyway,' I said brusquely, limping over to the piece of wood, keeping my right leg straight at all costs and feeling my breath catch every time I put weight on it. 'What *is* this?'

We were in a small, firmly square, muddy pit that smelt of damp earth and had metre-wide wooden beams running from the floor to the ceiling in each of the four corners, propping up the horizontal beams that surrounded the opening directly above me – and sat on top of those beams was the now-hollow tree stump, letting in enough light that we could see, but not so much light that it could be classed as anything but dingy. There were two more wooden beams on either side of a decrepit-looking ladder to my right, which started just below the horizontal beams and which I could only assume that the other three had used to come down into the pit, based purely on their lack of kneekles. At the base of one of the beams, there was a small bundle of dark clothing and a silver pulley with a wire looping around it and going back up through the stump, and straight ahead of me, on the other side of the pit, there was an equally square tunnel entrance with the remnants of old railway tracks running into it, disappearing into a wall of solid blackness.

'Seriously,' I said, turning back around to face the others. 'What the hell is it?'

'Well,' Johnny said carefully, pushing himself up off the ground and pointing towards the tunnel, 'that looks like it goes into the old mines. They might've come here for fresh air after being underground for however long.'

Angie blinked up at him, frowning slightly. 'Isn't this a bit of a random place to have a mineshaft?'

'Not that random, really. The Old Railway Line won't be too far from here. What do you think was one of the things they used that for?'

I tilted my head at him. 'I thought mineshafts go into the side of hills and whatever. I didn't think they were buried in a hole on moors.'

'Well, I don't think this would've been the official entrance, as it were,' he shrugged, shoving his hands in his pockets. 'Like I say, it might've been some sort of break area. I'm just guessing,' he added almost dryly, when we just looked at him. 'I obviously wasn't around when it was in use.'

'What I want to know about is this,' Hadaway grunted, coming to stand next to me and giving the wooden slab a light kick with the side of his foot. 'I can't see an operating mine planting a tree over one of its entrances.'

'No,' Johnny agreed slowly, frowning up at the hollow stump. 'And it will've been a hell of a job to hollow it out while it was still in the ground.'

Somehow I thought that hollowing out a tree would be a hell of a job wherever it was, but I had the feeling it'd be pointless to point that out. 'So... what are we saying? Knight chopped drown a tree, dug out the roots, carved out the centre and then re-planted it in a different part of the woods?'

Because Knight had to have known that the pit was there.

If nothing else, she'd probably fallen into it herself a couple of times.

But why?

What did she use it for?

Was this where naughty Cloaks went until they promised to behave? Was it where me and Angie would've ended up if we hadn't got away from them on Tuesday?

Or was it just her little hidey-hole?

'I think what's probably happened,' Hadaway said, after we'd all spent a few seconds silently staring at the stump or its lid, 'is that the tree's been uprooted when she's come across it. Must've just fell right into her hands.'

I had a sudden image of Knight standing, arms outstretched, at the foot of a large tree that promptly fell over and squashed her flat.

It made me feel all warm and fuzzy inside.

Angie scrunched her nose at him. 'Doesn't seem very witch-like.'

'No,' he agreed, glancing at her without really moving his head. 'And it's not something she could've done by herself, either.'

I glanced over at the pulley near the ladder. 'D'you want to know what I think?'

I felt Hadaway tense slightly next to me. 'No.'

'I think this is where Knight hangs out while she's waiting for the Cloaks to turn up. Look,' I added, more to Angie than anyone else, pointing at the pulley. 'That's got wires wrapped around it. So maybe she wears a little harness or something, attaches it to that wire coming down, and hoists herself up through the stump.'

'I dunno,' she said, shooting me a doubtful look. 'The Cloaks are obviously complete idiots, but wouldn't they notice her coming out of the ground?'

'Maybe she comes out of the ground really, really quick.'

'Wouldn't they notice her coming out of the ground really, really quick?'

I frowned back down at the pulley, chewing on my bottom lip.

Would they notice her coming out of the ground?

I mean, sure, there'd be no way to hide it in broad daylight. But what about in the middle of the night, when it was pitch black and the only thing to see by were flame torches?

Although even then, what about the Cloaks stood nearest to the stump? Surely there was no way that they'd miss her coming out of the ground, if there was nothing to block their view of the stump? For God's sake, the woman wore *white*. It wasn't as if she was camouflaged.

'I don't know,' I said slowly, glancing back up at Angie. 'But you know how meticulous she is; she'll have found a way to do it without them seeing where she comes from, so it looks like she's just appeared out of nowhere.' I whipped my head around to look at Hadaway, shooting him a bright smile. 'There you go. No magic at all. She just lurks down here until it's time to pop out.'

'No shit.'

Oh. 'Sorry if I've announced the obvious,' I told him sweetly. 'I must be a bit distracted by my new kneekle.'

His whole face did this funny little twitch, leaving his jaw tensed up considerably more tense than it had been a couple of seconds earlier, and I realised that I probably shouldn't have brought my leg into it when he had, to be fair, tried to insist on helping me with it. But props to him, he didn't point that out; instead, he turned to Johnny and said curtly,

'We're going to have to call this in. Scenes of Crime will have to come take a look, maybe get the dogs here too, and –'

'Hang on a minute,' I interrupted incredulously, leaning forward slightly to get a better look at his face. 'Can't we just do whatever needs doing? Since we're already down here?'

He swung around to face me again, suddenly looking furious, and I realised that saying 'we' probably hadn't been the best move.

Shit.

I really hoped he didn't remember to arrest me.

'No,' he bit off, as the muscle in his jaw gave a couple of funny twitches. 'We're going to head back to the office and get this looked at. You're going home to sort that leg out.'

'We don't know how safe it is down here, Armitage,' Johnny said calmly, with another little shrug. 'We don't know how stable it is. We're going to have to come up with a plan to get SOCO down there.'

'It can't be that unstable if Knight's using it every week.'

He gave his head one shake, with his mouth set in a grim line. 'We can't just take that as read, unfortunately.'

'Right then,' Hadaway announced firmly, as if everything had been decided. 'We'll get you two dropped off at the flat on the way to East District.' He shot me another one of those concerned looks. 'D'you think you're alright to walk?'

'I'm fine.' I was not fine. 'But actually, I was thinking I might as well give Squidge a walk while we're up at here. I mean, he's come all the way up here with us,' I added, when they all stared at me incredulously, 'and he's just been left there, tied to that tree, when he's obviously been expecting to go for a good run.' I glanced up at the stump, through which we could hear Squidge snoring in the clearing. 'He's so excited.'

'He's had a walk,' Hadaway pointed out impatiently, frowning at me. 'Walking up and back down is his walk. You need to rest that leg or you'll make it worse, and then how're you going to walk him?'

'No,' I said stubbornly, folding my arms and frowning back at him. 'If you'd let us walk up here from the flat, then fair enough. But no, you insisted on driving up and parking in that clearing you used for your stakeout, and now you're saying that he can only walk from that clearing to this one and back. That's ten minutes all in, if that. He needs more than that.'

'Both make very good points,' Angie told Johnny, in a light, thoughtful kind of voice. 'And yet both are so stupidly determined to disagree. Look,' she added, rolling her eyes when me and Hadaway both started to protest that. (Why would I agree with him when he was wrong?) 'Yes, Tidge needs to rest her leg. And yes, Squidge needs a walk that isn't ninety percent car ride. So why don't you leave Tidge up here with me, and I'll give Squidge a decent walk and call my Dad to pick us up when I'm done?'

It makes sense,' Johnny shrugged, after a couple of seconds of us all staring at her, Hadaway looking critical and me feeling little crackles of excitement starting in my tummy. I quite liked the idea of being in that mineshaft without Johnny and Hadaway there. 'It'd let us crack on, and I'm sure Armitage can make it to that clearing on her bad leg. It's only five minutes away.'

Hadaway raised one eyebrow, looking just a smidge frustrated. 'And you trust her not to come back down here, do you?'

'I trust her not to be that stupid, aye.'

'She's won't be coming back down,' Angie told them patiently, and I snuck a quick wink at her. Of course, giving that I've never really cracked the whole winking thing, it's possible that she just thought I'd got something in my eye. 'She's going to sit in that other clearing while I walk Squidge, and then she's going straight to get her leg checked out. I promise.'

Hadaway shifted his weight from foot to foot again, folding his arms across his chest so that I had to try very hard not to notice those lovely biceps of his. 'All due respect, Angie, I'm not bothered what you can promise us. I'm bothered what *she* can promise us.'

I shot him my sweetest smile, so sugary that he was danger of developing diabetes. 'I can promise that you're a dickhead.'

'Armitage.'

'Why is everyone suddenly so determined that I'm going to come back here?' I demanded, spreading my arms at them all in the most innocent way I could. 'I only asked if we could do anything to help SOCO, and you started talking Policey stuff at me. What makes you think I'd come back the second your backs are turned?'

The ironic thing is, I hadn't started thinking about going back the second their backs were turned.

Not until they all started acting like that'd been my plan all along.

I was a little disappointed it hadn't been, to be honest.

Surprisingly, my little objection seemed to do the trick. After what seemed to take an absolute *age* but was probably only a couple of minutes, with a lot of suspicious looks shot in my direction by good ol' Hadaway, it was finally decided.

Johnny and Hadaway were going back to the office.

Angie was in charge of me and Squidge.

And I was the innocent invalid who'd only do exactly what she was told.

Which was true. I *would* only do exactly what I was told.

But only after I'd had a better look at that mineshaft.

ELEVEN.

I'd like to think I was clever about it.

I mean, I clearly wasn't, because I knew right at the start that I wasn't going to have the time to be as clever about is as I would've liked.

But still.

I started by playing my role of Innocent Invalid very well.

I let them help me hop up the ladder, even though Hadaway insisted on staying one rung behind me with his arms on either side of me, ready to catch me if I fell. (I didn't fall. Not even close. I think I was so distracted by the heat rolling off him and how close he was to my bum that my brain was knocked out of Clumsy Mode for the first time ever.)

I hobbled out of the clearing with them, into the muddy clearing where Angie and Squidge had stumbled across Johnny and Hadaway two nights earlier.

I let them position me on a dry patch of grass at the edge, leaning against the biggest tree there with my bad leg stretched out across the mud in front of me.

I waved bravely as Hadaway and Johnny piled into Hadaway's Audi and headed out, reversing up to the point where the clearing met a dirt track and effortlessly spinning around to face forward at the last minute.

I waved just as bravely as Angie and Squidge left the clearing by a little uphill trail opposite the dirt track, Squidge stopping every few seconds to shoot anxious looks back at me, like he was wondering why I wasn't coming to play with them.

And then, after sitting there for a few seconds to make sure that I was definitely alone, holding my breath as I strained to hear any sounds of anyone coming back, I hauled myself to my feet, keeping my gammy leg stretched straight out as I used my good leg and the tree behind me to half-push, half-drag myself up into something mildly resembling an upright position.

I paused for a couple of seconds, holding onto the tree as I caught my breath from the effort of it all and winced against the pain in my kneekle, which didn't seem to be in any hurry to piss off. I glanced over my shoulder towards the track that Angie and Squidge had disappeared along, making sure that they were absolutely, definitely not making any surprise trips back.

And then, the second I realised it was safe, I was off, shoving myself off the tree with both hands and throwing myself towards the dirt track that we'd all just walked along, the one that led back towards Knight's clearing, hopping as fast as I could with my bad leg stretched out straight to my side.

Of course, I had to stop every few steps to catch my breath, because frankly hopping is too close to exercise for my liking, and anything resembling exercise should not be allowed before lunchtime. But it was fine. Every time I stopped, it gave me chance to glance over my shoulder, checking for any sign of the Audi coming back or of Angie bursting out of the muddy clearing and hurtling after me.

Nope.

Home free.

By the time I reached Knight's clearing, both of my legs were aching like hell and I'd resorted to flapping my arms madly through the air, which seemed to help me push myself even further forward on each hop. I was also pretty sure I had a six-pack developing, so maybe there was something to this hopping malarkey after all.

I hopped over to the stump and spent a good few seconds just standing next to it, twisting this way and that, trying to work out if it'd be better for my kneekle to go down facing outwards or inwards. It'd be easier to climb onto the ladder and keep my leg held out if I went down facing outwards, but there was also a very good chance of me falling off the ladder, either while I was mid-hop between rungs or if my heel slipped off one of them –

which wouldn't be too hard, given that each rung was only made up of a thin, narrow fence panel. It'd be easier to balance on them if I went down facing inwards, like you're supposed to go down a ladder, but I wasn't sure exactly how to get onto the top rung if I was climbing onto it backwards; I'd either have to put weight on my bad leg or bend it to get inside the stump, neither of which was massively appealing. I spent a few seconds hopping backwards and forwards next to the stump, trying to figure out the right angle, and then decided, sod it, I'd just put weight on my kneekle and have an extra glass of sherry for the pain when I got back to the flat.

I swung my bad leg over the side of the stump and slowly lowered it down towards to ladder, thinking that I could keep the weight off it for longer if I put that one down first, but the second it made contact with the top rung, there was a massive shout of,

'Tidge!'

I jumped in surprise, nearly losing my footing at the same time, and when I whipped my head towards the entrance of the clearing, where the shout had come from, I saw Angie and Squidge running towards me, Squidge out in front and looking deliriously happy, and Angie flat-out sprinting with a furious look on her face.

Shit.

'Oh, hi!' I called back cheerily, waving at them. 'This *is* where we said we'd meet back up, isn't it?'

She reached the stump and grabbed hold of my arms, scowling at me with her face the dull shade of red it always goes when she's angry. 'What the *fuck* do you think you're doing?'

I felt my heart drop by a couple of inches.

Unlike me and Hadaway, who're self-confessed potty-mouths and fully embrace our hypothetical ability to make a sailor blush, Angie's much more restrained on the swearing. If she starts dropping F-bombs, it means she's either talking about her younger brother, or she's seeing nothing but red.

'I just –'

'You are *unbelievable*,' she snapped, in exactly the same tone that she always talks to Calvin in. 'Un-*fucking*-believable, Armitage. You made all that fuss about how *dare* we think that you'd come back as soon as we weren't looking, and then what do you go and do?'

I squinted up at her, tilting my head to one side. 'I think we have very different memories of that conversation.'

'Did you or did you not say –'

'I didn't, actually,' I interrupted smugly, hauling my bad leg back out of the stump so that we were back on level ground. Looking up at Angie was just too *weird*. 'I only asked why everyone thought I was going to go back down there. At no point did I say I wouldn't.'

She stared at me, her eyes flicking backwards and forwards by millimetres as she obviously replayed the conversation in her head, and her eyes became slightly heavy-lidded when she realised I was right. 'You are *such* a dick.'

'You're one to talk. What happened to walking Squidge?'

'Squidge had a guilty conscience about leaving you behind,' she told me, letting go of my arms and folding her own. 'He didn't want to walk without you, and when I let him off the lead he bolted straight back to where we left you.' She gave me a tight smile. 'I thought there was only one place you'd be when I saw you weren't there.'

'Well, come *on*, Angie,' I burst out, dropping all pretences and coming dangerously close to stamping my foot. (I might have actually done it, if I had a left leg that was in any way useful.) 'Are you not at all curious about what this is all about? About what Knight's keeping down there, or she gets up to in it?'

Her eyes flicked from me to the stump and back again in roughly half a second. 'No.'

'Alright then.' Let's try a different tack. 'D'you – be honest, d'you really think that if we're good little girls and do as we're told and ask nicely, Johnny and Hadaway are really going to tell us *anything* about what's going on?'

She gave me a look that probably wasn't as convincing as she wanted it to be. 'Do we *need* to know anything about what's going on?'

'I don't know,' I told her mock-thoughtfully, crossing my arms and giving a little shrug. 'Does the Government *need* to keep putting up the retirement age? Do Boohoo and ASOS ads *need* to keep popping up on my Facebook feed? Does my sister *need* to lecture me about calories every time I eat something that isn't a salad in front of her? No, but they do it anyway. Listen,' I added after a few seconds of staring at each other, letting my forearms flick up towards the sky. 'I don't care anymore. I'm going down there whether you're coming or not.'

I hopped about pathetically next to the stump for a couple more seconds, trying to get my positioning right, before I realised that there was, in fact, no way in hell I was going to be able to manoeuvre this with only one operational leg.

I glanced back at Angie, shooting her what I was hoping would be a very sweet, innocent look. 'If you could just give me a hand getting down the ladder, though...'

'*Fine*,' she snapped, rolling her eyes as she stomped the couple of steps closer to the stump. And then she did a tiny little shake of her head. And then another one. And then she rolled her eyes again. And then, finally, she looked me dead in the eyes, looking like she was just as annoyed with herself as she was with me. 'But I'm probably going to be able to help you down better if I'm already *in* the pit.'

I have to be honest, I really didn't get why that pit appealed to Knight so much.

Maybe it was because I'd never been anywhere near a mine before that morning, so all my ideas were based on Disney, and there was not one single diamond nor a singing dwarf in sight. Or maybe it was because Knight always seemed to be so *meticulous* in what she did and how she did it, and this just seemed to be lacking that psychopathic, delusional charm that she pulled off so well.

Don't get me wrong, I got that no-one wants to dig out a giant hole in the ground, and it was clearly the perfect place to leave her stump.

But it stank. And it was dark. It was dark at seven o'clock in the morning, so God knows what it was like in the middle of the night. Knight had bigger balls than I did if she could lurk down there when it was pitch-black above ground, never mind below it.

For all her murderous tendencies, for all she'd put up one hell of a fight earlier that morning, for some reason – probably because of how delicate she looked – Knight struck me as that girl everyone went to in primary school, the one who'd squeal when she saw a worm and was horrified at the mention of a fart. I just couldn't see that little girl growing up to enjoying wallowing in mud, unless maybe it was in a spa bath.

For a few seconds, we just stood there, taking it all in through the gloominess.

'Well,' Angie said in the end, in a voice that was light and dry at the same time. 'This is even nicer than I first thought.'

'Very cosy,' I agreed, eyeballing the entrance to the mine tunnel warily. Something about it gave me the heebie-jeebies. 'I love what she's done with the place.'

She started slowly wandering around the pit with the air of someone mooching around a museum, and I watched her for a couple of seconds, wondering if she was going to tell me that there was clearly nothing there and we should just head back to the flat. And then, when it became obvious that she wasn't going to do that, I glanced down at the bundle of clothing to my left.

'It seems like a weird place to keep a change of clothes.'

'This is Knight,' she pointed out, barely glancing over her shoulder at me as she drifted over towards the tracks. 'If it wasn't weird, she wouldn't do it.'

True story.

I bent over and grabbed hold of the bundle, whipping it up off the floor for a better look. Except that, as it turned out, it wasn't technically a bundle at all; it was one long, *just* to say see-through sheet of black material that'd been neatly folded over and over onto itself, which unravelled itself as soon as I picked it up. It wasn't a dress or a robe or anything like that; it was more like a big cape, with a loosely shaped hood on the front of it, two long pieces that could pass for sleeves, and a thin, solid belt running horizontally through the middle of the fabric, with a silver clip on one end and a substantially larger, equally silver hoop on the other.

No harness with it.

But to be fair, there was nothing to say that she wouldn't take the harness home with her.

'Think about it, though, Tidge,' Angie said conversationally after a few seconds, as I eyeballed the piece of cloth. Why would Knight leave this here and not the harness? 'You said she was wearing a white robe the other night. She wouldn't walk around the Woods in a white robe, is she? Any of one of her Cloaks could decide to follow her if they saw her wandering about, and besides, it'd get all muddy. Of course she'd have a change of clothes here.'

'Right,' I nodded thoughtfully, glancing up from the black sheet to look at her and deciding not to point out that her logic seemed to be lacking. Why would Knight bring a change of clothing with her so she could sneak in and out of the clearing – and then leave it *in* the clearing? 'Except that it's not a change of clothing.'

She stopped dead on the other side of the mine pit, looking mildly surprised. 'Oh. Then what is it?'

'I don't know,' I told her, shrugging. 'It's just one long thing. It's like some kind of cape that she keeps down here, or something.'

'Why?'

I stared at her. 'D'you really expect me to know the answer to that?'

We looked at each for a couple of seconds, probably feeling just as confused as the other. And then, when that didn't turn up any groundbreaking ideas, I turned back to the weird sheet I was holding, thinking as hard as I could.

The hood was facing the wrong way. And the belt didn't seem to have much of a purpose. But Knight clearly had this here for a reason, so –

An idea suddenly popped into my head, and my eyes darted from the sheet to the silver pulley. And then they flicked up along the wire above it, the one that ran all the way down from the top of the stump and looped around the pulley before shooting back up again.

Nah.

No way.

Surely that was far too simple?

'Knight wears a white robe,' I said slowly, turning back to Angie. 'But none of the Cloaks seem to realise that she comes out of the ground. It's the middle of the night,' I added even more slowly, because it was obvious from the way she was looking at me that she needed me to spell it out for her. 'It's pitch black. Knight's wearing a white robe, and yet no-one notices her coming out of the tree stump that they're all staring at.'

Her eyes flicked from me to the cape and back again. 'You think she covers herself up in that before she goes up there?'

'I can't see what else it's for.'

'But... she wouldn't. There's no way she'd do something that straightforward.'

I tilted my head at her. 'But why not? If it works, why not use it?' I slipped the cape on, shoving my arms through the loose arm holes and fastening the belt before throwing the backwards hood over my face. 'What d'you think? Would this stand out if it's pitch black and the Cloaks only have flame torches to see by?'

There was silence, and I could just tell that she was chewing on her bottom lip. 'Well... they'd be a lot less likely to see you than they would if you popped up in a bright white robe.'

'*Exactly*,' I beamed, yanking the hood back off my face as I felt a little eruption of excitement in my stomach. By jove, Jeeves, you've hit it! 'This is it, Angie. *This* is how she does it. She puts this on,' I explained patiently, when she stared at me, looking unconvinced. 'Clips it together with this nice little belt.' I demonstrated as I was talking her through it. 'And then she clips herself to the pulley and takes herself up. All she needs to do is unclip herself when she gets to the top and let the cape go off wherever the pulley takes it. They're all holding those stupid flame torches, there's a bit of a distance between them and the stump, it's the middle of the night – how well are they going to see what's happening up there, really?'

'I don't know, Tidge,' she said uncertainly, frowning slightly. 'How does she unclip herself from the wire without them seeing it? How does she unclip the *cape* without them seeing?'

'Maybe she's slight of hand. Or well-practiced. Or both. Or maybe,' I added, raising my eyebrows at her as the thought occurred to me, 'part of it is that they see what they want to see. I mean, they all believe she's a witch. Maybe they see her be a witch because they *want* to see her do it.'

She grimaced at me. 'It just seems too *easy*.'

Hollowing out a tree stump and planting it over a mine shaft didn't seem particularly easy to me, but hey-ho. Different standards and all that. 'I know.'

'I don't trust it.'

'Not everything has to be complicated, Angie,' I pointed out, shrugging. 'Sometimes the easy way is the only way. Everything points to it,' I added, when she still looked unconvinced. 'The pit, the cape, the pulley. All we're missing is whatever it is she uses to clip herself onto it.'

'And how she manages to make the trees move.'

I stared at her, feeling myself falter.

Shit.

In all the excitement of getting my kneekle and working out how Knight made it look like she appeared out of thin air, I'd forgotten how we'd ended up in the pit in the first place.

'It must have something to do with the cable wires,' Angie continued matter-of-factly, and I glanced back down at the pulley, wondering when I'd become someone who forgot what they were curious about. 'But I can't put it together. No matter how much she pulls herself up that wire, she can't be strong enough to make trees move by herself. And there's nothing down here that'd let her do it, so... how?'

I felt my eyes widen as an idea leapt into my head.

I didn't know how plausible it was... but at the same time, it would make a lot of sense.

'What if she's working with someone?'

'What?'

'What if she's not in it by herself?' I said, whipping my head around to look at her. 'What if she's got a couple of people helping her, who stay down here or somewhere in the background while she's talking to the Cloaks and pull the wires however she needs them pulling?'

I didn't know how they'd do it without being seen.

I didn't even know if they *could* do it.

You'd have to be pretty strong to move tree branches, right?

So... what? Had she recruited a couple of caber-tossers to help her?

'I guess it's possible,' Angie said slowly. 'Not my favourite idea, but it's more likely than her doing it all by herself.'

'Hadaway said himself that she couldn't have moved that tree trunk by herself,' I reminded her, feeling something I couldn't quite put my finger on start to bubble up inside me. 'And if he's right, and we're right... she's had help all the way along.'

We stared at each other for a few seconds, taking it in, and I felt that bubble inside me pop in a fizzy explosion of excitement and shock.

It hadn't even *occurred* to me that Knight might be getting help.

But of course she was. Logically, she *had* to have someone helping her.

She must've had help in recruiting the Cloaks. There were too many of them for Knight to have talked them all 'round by herself, and it clearly wasn't a word of mouth thing; the way Daniels had acted in the bookshop alone told us that.

And like Hadaway had said, she must've had help getting that tree stump hollowed out and burying it over the mine; there was no way that one average human could do that by themselves. Besides, it'd take *ages* to get those wires arranged right, to make sure they were laid right and strong enough to pull whichever tree needed pulling. And Angie wasn't wrong, either; no how many times Knight hauled herself up and down those wires, she wasn't strong enough to lift those branches without showing *some* sign of exertion. Which, in fairness, she *hadn't* showed on Tuesday night. She hadn't even been *holding* anything, from what I can see. She'd just lifted her arm, palm up, and the trees had followed suit. So that must've been a signal to whoever it was that was helping her, wherever they were hiding.

Even kidnapping the lads. Johnny had told us, right after the second lad had been found, that the toxicology reports from the post-mortem showed that *some* kind of drug had been found in both of the bodies. I hadn't really been clear at the time if he meant that the lads had taken something on their night out or if Knight had given them it, but if she *had* drugged them and they collapsed, how would a skinny little thing like her carry the dead weight of a six-foot-something unconscious bloke to wherever she needed to go, especially without anyone seeing them? And if she hadn't, how'd she got them to go with her? Pretended that she wanted a quick shag back at her place? But the CCTV from the clubs showed the guys leaving *alone*. So had she approached them on the street? Was it *normal* to get offered a one-night stand on the street? (I'd never had even a hint of a one-night stand. I'd have to ask Hadaway.) Or did Knight and her buddies just lurk until they saw a guy who fit the bill by himself, and then pounce and drag him away? And even after she'd took the lads, how would she have stopped them from knocking her out and doing a runner in the days before she killed them?

Jesus.

I couldn't believe it hadn't occurred to me sooner.

'Let's go down that tunnel,' I said impulsively to Angie, jerking my head towards the mine entrance. Suddenly it didn't give me the heebie-jeebies anymore. 'Let's see where it leads, or if there's anything in there that might help.'

She glanced at the tunnel and then back at me, frowning slightly. 'I don't think so.'

'What if there are things in there that tell us who's helping her?' I asked, feeling even more excitement at the idea of it. 'Or what if it leads us to them? To their house, or their... camping ground, or whatever.'

'Tidge, you do understand that mines go *underground*?'

'There could be more holes like this. Surely this isn't the only place they could come for fresh air?'

Maybe it was, actually.

I had no idea how big Habely Mine was.

I hadn't even known there *was* a Habely Mine until half an hour or so ago.

'What about Squidge? Are you just going to leave him up there for however long?'

'Squidge is fine,' I told her impatiently, because once again, I could hear Squidge snoring by the tree we'd tied him to. 'And I can't see anybody swinging by and stealing him, no-one's *here*. Look, Angie, what's the worst that could happen?'

'The tunnel could collapse.'

'We either find nothing in there, in which case we go home and tell no-one. Or we find *something* that tells us who's involved and we take it straight to East District. I mean, if we find them, we could find her, right?'

That'd show Hadaway and his little 'you're not helping' spiel.

Ha.

She shook her head, looking a mixture of grim and unconvinced. But before she could say anything, I felt a small snap in my tummy, and suddenly I'd had enough.

I'd had enough of being told I was wrong, or that I should leave the whole thing alone. Knight had come after me. She'd threatened to kill me. Not Angie. Not anyone else. *Me.* And if people thought that didn't give me the right to find out what the hell that bitch was up to and how she was doing it, they could piss off.

I saw Angie open her mouth, no doubt to tell that it was time to go home – but I wasn't giving her the chance. Instead, I dropped the cape to the ground and whirled around to my right, keeping my kneekle leg straight and wincing every time I had to put weight on it as I marched towards the tunnel, determined to see what was down there. I heard her say my name as I reached the tunnel entrance , but I completely ignored her, fishing my phone out of my back jeans pocket and turning my torch app on as I threw myself into the darkness.

It was that horrible kind of darkness that just swallows everything up, so the light didn't go as far as I'd thought it would. Still, though, I could see far enough to know if someone was coming at me, or if I was about to stumble over a dead body.

For a few long seconds, there was nothing behind me but silence, and I suddenly got a horrible feeling that she was actually going to let me explore the tunnel by myself. (Turns out I did still have some heebie-jeebies about it. And also, this was a terrible time for *The Descent* to pop into my head.) But then, just as the path as I was following started to slope downhill, I heard her let out a groan back in the pit. And then I heard her footsteps behind me, hurrying to catch up with me as she told me to wait, and I felt a smug little smile spread itself over my face.

She could pretend that she was too sensible to be interested in this case all she wanted. We both knew it wasn't remotely true.

I have no idea how long we were walking for.

I don't think it was *that* long, maybe ten or fifteen minutes. But when you're in a pitch black tunnel that's full of unexpectedly heavy air and reeks of dust and damp mud, with a phone that won't keep the screen and the torch app on at the same time, it's surprising how quick you lose track of time. Or maybe constantly waiting for Cloak-wearing psychopaths to jump out of you just makes it seem like you're walking for a lot longer than you actually are. (In fairness, I wasn't really expecting Knight or any of the Cloaks to be hanging out in that tunnel. But you never know, do you? Maybe hanging out in underground tunnels is the number one hobby for psychopaths.)

But however long it took us, we did eventually reach another break-out area.

It was connected to the mine by a walkway to our left that curved up a gentle slope, and it was a lot lighter and smaller than the one we'd just left. Not only that, it was much emptier as well; the four beams were there, built into the four corners and propping up the muddy roof above us, and there was another decrepit wooden ladder – this one much more like a steep staircase than the ladder in the first pit – leading up to the woods through a an opening that was so overgrown, chunks of long grass were dangling around the entrance to the pit.

'I prefer this pit,' Angie said with satisfaction, when we'd took a couple of seconds to glance around the place. 'Knight should've picked this one, it's much nicer.'

I mentally compared the two pits side-by-side.

With the way the light was trickling down from the entrance, brightening up the place and making the dust floating around almost look sparkly, it definitely reminded me of somewhere you'd see fairies prancing about on a kids' TV show.

The pit we'd just come from though, with its moisture and its gloominess (which was probably much darker in my head) and its delightful smell *absolutely* screamed WITCH in comparison.

'Mmm,' I told her, scrunching my mouth to one side. 'I'm not sure this one has the vibe that Knight's going for.'

I wandered over to the ladder and put my hands on either side of it, when Angie took a couple of surprisingly quick steps towards me and put one hand on my arm.

'Wait a minute, Tidge,' she said, frowning slightly. 'I know we said we'd see where the mine led to, but... are you sure this is a good idea?'

My eyes darted to the opening and then back down to her. 'I can't see Knight or any of the Cloaks being up there. It's broad daylight.'

'We don't know what's up there,' she reminded me, raising her eyebrows. 'We could be popping up into a Cloak compound, for all we know. I'm just worried about your leg,' she added, when I blinked at her a couple of times. A *Cloak compound?* 'We should be getting home and resting it, really, all this dragging it about isn't going to be doing it any good. And can you really see Knight having something else set up in the woods? Can you really see her pulling the same trick twice?'

I blinked at her some more.

I won't lie, my leg *did* hurt. And the thought of going home and lying on the settee, getting waited on hand and foot with all the sherry I wanted was really tempting.

But so was finding out where that ladder led to.

Because what if Knight *did* have something else set up there?

How was I supposed to rub Hadaway's face in the fact that we *were* helping in the case if I didn't find out?

'I'll just take a peek,' I told her, taking another couple of steps up the ladder. 'One tiny little peek. And then we'll go home, and you can play Nurse to your heart's content. OK?'

Hmm.

That sounded a little bit wrong, actually.

But never mind. She knew what I meant.

I scurried up the next few steps as fast as you *can* scurry when you're dragging one leg behind you and using your arms to help yourself hop from step to step, and as soon as I was close enough to do it, I poked my head out through the opening.

You know.

Slowly.

Just in case.

But instead of coming up to a load of Cloaks waiting to pounce on me, I found myself staring at... trees.

Lots and lots of trees.

Of course I did.

Whoever came up with the name of Habely Woods was clearly a creative genius.

I'd popped up in a much smaller clearing that was massively overgrown, so much so that when I climbed up to the top of the ladder, the grass easily reached my knees.

I slowly shuffled around on the ladder until I'd done a 180, keeping my eyes peeled for any sign of Cloaks or delusional murderesses. But no. There was nothing. Clearly, it was far too early for the psychos to be out and about.

The trees at the south of the clearing were a lot more sparse than the ones I'd been facing when I'd popped up, only about three or four rows thick, and behind them, I could see the felled area that I'd ended up in on Tuesday night.

I had a second glance around the survey, feeling more disappointed than I'd expected to be. I mean, obviously I'd known that the tunnel wasn't really going to lead us to Knight or any of her Cloaks. *Obviously.* It just would've been nice if it had told us *something* about what they were up to, or how exactly Knight was making that pulley system work for her, *or* – better yet – who the hell was helping her.

'Well?' Angie demanded expectantly, peering up at me from the foot of the ladder. 'What's up there?'

'Grass. And a lot of trees. I can't see anything to Knight and the Cloaks use this place, Angie. It doesn't look like anyone's been here in years.'

The *tiniest* flicker of disappointment shot across her face in less than a second, but before I could anything more than blink at her, wondering if it'd really been there, she was holding a hand up to help me back down the ladder. 'C'mon. Let's go back to the flat and get you good and drunk.'

I grinned. 'My kind of Thursday.'

I pushed myself to my feet, wincing slightly against the pain in my kneekle as I started to turn around so I could hop down the ladder in reverse, hands on the rung in front of me and arse sticking in the air like the bow of the sinking Titanic. (Who says I'm not dignity personified?)

It's just that, before I could turn more than half an inch, I heard a sharp crack come from the dense trees behind me.

A crack that sounded very much like a twig getting snapped.

I could feel my heart picking up speed as I whipped around to stare into the trees, so quickly that I didn't have chance to balance properly so the weight was kept off my kneekle, which suddenly felt like someone had shoved a red-hot poker into it.

But that barely even registered.

I was too busy staring at the Cloak lurking around the trees in the second row.

He was huge, almost as tall as Hadaway and easily twice as wide. His hood was pulled up over his head so that all I could see was the point of his nose and his jaw, and even that was a challenge, given how much shadow he was standing in.

But what I *could* see, much more than I wanted to, was his right hand.

Or rather, I could see what he was holding in his right hand. The thing that was glinting slightly in the very little sunlight that was managing to fight its way through the trees.

The thing that looked very much like a gun.

I froze.

I just froze, staring at him with my heart thumping in my ears, beating so hard against my chest that it was painful. And from what I could tell, he seemed to freeze too; for a few seconds, he just stared back at me, almost like he was trying to work out if I'd seen him or not.

It wasn't until I heard Angie hissing my name in the pit that I remembered I could move. Only it seemed to take me *ages* to turn my head to look at her; it kind of felt like I was trying to force my head through a boulder of treacle.

She was still stood at the foot of the ladder with her arm outstretched, but now she looked a little bit urgent. Clearly, I wasn't subtle about the fact that something was going on. 'What're you doing?'

I let my head drift back towards the Cloak. 'Erm...'

Shit.

Shit.

What did we do?

Where did we g*o*?

More importantly, *how* did we go?

I mean, it wasn't like I could *crawl* to safety; he'd have shot me five times before I was even on my knees.

No, no. There was a very unfair disadvantage here, and it wasn't in my favour.

He had a gun.

I had a kneekle.

I wasn't a big fan of those odds.

'Tidge! *What's going on?*'

I felt a horrible, cold jolt as the Cloak took one slow, silent step towards me.

I didn't know what to do.

I didn't know what my options were.

Crawling made me too easy a target. Running was going to be a challenge. *Walking* out of there was clearly not doable, because there was no he'd just *let* me do it. And hopping...

Well, hopping didn't seem quite *right*, given the situation. Besides, it wasn't going to give me any better chances if I had to stop to catch my breath every few skips.

And anyway, where would I hop *to*? This clearing was much more enclosed than the other one; it didn't have any handy gaps in the trees to let people in and out. I could probably get myself to the felled area, but then where was I going to go? Over those boulders again?

No thank you.

Once was more than enough fun.

'Right,' Angie said firmly, when it'd been a few seconds and I hadn't answered her. 'Sod it. I'm coming up there.'

'*No!*' I burst out frantically, and then I kicked myself.

I didn't really have any doubt that the Cloak had been lurking there the whole time we'd been in that clearing, and I was fairly sure that he'd have known Angie was in the pit. He must've been in the clearing on Tuesday, so he'd know that I had a friend. And no matter how long he'd been in those trees for, he would've heard us talking to each other. But still, if there was *any* tiny chance at all that he hadn't put two and two together, that he'd forgotten that there were two of us there on Tuesday night and he thought I was just chatting away to myself as part of some mental break... I didn't want to be the one who put him right.

The last thing I wanted was to be the reason Angie came up that ladder and got hurt. (Actually, the last thing I wanted was to get shot. But Angie not getting hurt was a close second.)

I also didn't want to be the reason why the Cloak went *down* the ladder and hurt her.

So I did the only thing I could do.

'No,' I repeated, more calmly this time, eyeballing the Cloak warily as I took the tiniest of side-steps onto the grass next to the ladder. 'No, Angie, you stay down there. And just... give me a couple of minutes.'

I held the Cloak's gaze for another second more, bracing myself on my good leg. And then, before I could think too much about it, I whirled around and took off, running as fast as I could, wincing and – as much as I hate to admit it – letting out a little whimper every time I had to put weight on my kneekle. I heard Angie shout me from the pit and I heard the Cloak take off after me, his feet pounding across the grass, and I desperately tried to pick up speed, but it was hard to do that when I was down to one good leg; it wasn't so much a *run* as a high-speed hobble.

I reached the thin clump of trees at the bottom of the clearing and threw myself into them, but before I could make it past the second row of trees, something fastened like a vice around my upper arm and suddenly I was getting yanked backwards, so hard that I was nearly pulled off my feet.

And the next thing I knew, I was getting turned out around to face the way I'd just come, and something hard, round and cold was pressing against my left temple.

And I couldn't breathe.

'Oh, my Mistress is going to be *very* happy with me,' the Cloak breathed, as I stood there, frozen on the spot, staring at him with wide eyes and my mind blank with shock. 'She's a bit sick of you, y'see. Said she doesn't care what we do, as long as we make sure you're out of the way.' He gave me a sick smile as he pressed the gun harder against my head. 'I'm going to have a good time taking you out of the way.'

I wasn't particularly fussed on finding out how much he'd enjoy it.

Which is probably why, before it'd even occurred to me to do it, one hand came up to give the gun a harsh shove away from my temple, while my other hand was curling into a fist and slamming hard itself into his stomach.

He doubled over with a choked kind of grunt and doubled over, clearly winded, and I caught a glimpse of Angie stood frozen at the top of the ladder, staring at us in shock. I yelled at her to get back down into the pit, but before I could see if she did or not, I whirled around and took off again, sprinting into the felled area.

And this time, the kneekle wasn't a problem.

I had so much adrenaline pumping through me that I couldn't even feel it. All I could think about was getting away from that Cloak.

Get across the felled area.

Get back to Knight's clearing.

Get Angie and Squidge, and hightail it to the nearest Police Station.

That sounded like a plan.

Some of the smaller branches slipped and rolled under my feet as I ran over them, slowing me down when I slid and stumbled every few steps, but even still, I must've been a good metre or two into the felled area before there was a sudden, huge boom behind me, cracking through the air, and I immediately hit the ground, knocking the breath out of myself as I landed on the logs underneath me.

I twisted around to stare over my shoulder, back towards the trees I'd ran through. The Cloak was stood right in front of them, the hand holding the gun outstretched towards me.

Fuck.

He readjusted his aim, and I forced myself to move, scrambling to feet as quick as I could and veering off to my right, towards the boulders I'd flown off two nights before, thinking that a zigzag approach might just save me from getting shot. A second later, there was another huge crack behind me, and then I heard him making his way across the logs and branches. I heard Angie shout my name, and when I turned around – more on instinct than anything else – I saw her racing out of the trees, slipping and sliding just as much as I was as she headed right for the Cloak.

My mistake was stopping.

It can only have been for a second or two while I opened my mouth to scream at her to go back, but that was obviously all the time the Cloak needed, because before I could shout anything to Angie, he slammed into me, as solid as a brick wall, knocking me to the ground and coming down with me so that I was squashed underneath him. Pain shot through the entirety of my back, my bad shoulder and my kneekle, but before I could let myself feel it too much or push the Cloak off me, he was sitting up, straddling me on his knees and leaning over me as he pressed the gun to my head against my forehead.

'It was a nice try,' he told me smugly, wheezing slightly from his stint at running. 'But you're an idiot if you thought this would end any differently.'

I struggled against him, bucking and kicking to try and get out from underneath him, but it was pointless.

He was too heavy.

There was no way I was going to be able to get him off me.

He gave me that sick smile again as he gripped the gun with both hands, pushing the gun hard into my forehead, but before he could pull the trigger, there was a dull thud from my left – and suddenly he'd disappeared.

It was so unexpected and so abrupt that it took me a second or two of lying there, blinking in surprise, before I realised that a pale, furious-looking Angie had materialised next to me, the leg that she'd used to boot him in the head just coming back down to the ground.

She leapt over me and pounced onto the Cloak, who was sprawled out next to me with his head pointing straight at the trees to my right. I saw her dive for the gun, which he was still clutching in his hand, but the Cloak was just stunned, not knocked out; the second Angie's hand fastened around the gun, he jerked into action, pulling the gun out of her grip and weakly waving his arm around so that she had to weave about to try and get hold of it again.

I laid there for a couple of seconds, feeling slightly dazed and watching them struggle for the pistol, before I gingerly pushed myself to my feet, fully intending to whip the gun away from both of them – but I didn't even get close before the Cloak had a burst of energy and gave Angie swift smack to the jaw, so hard that there was a crack loud enough to knock me sick.

I threw myself on top of him as Angie reeled backwards, both hands clamped to one side of her face, and before he had time to realise that we'd effectively swapped places, I had one hand wrapped around his thick neck, squeezing as hard as I could while my other hand reached for the gun.

I don't know if everything that'd been going on was catching up with me or if it was seeing him hit Angie so hard that I was expecting to turn around to see half of her jaw hanging off her face, but I was filled with this white-hot kind of *rage*. I'd never felt anything like it, before or since, even in all the arguments I'd had with Hadaway – but whatever the reason it was there, it wasn't a bad thing. It made my hand fasten around his neck like a vice, so that no matter how much he tried to buck me off, no matter how much he swung at me with his free hand, making me duck and weave like a pro, I stayed very firmly in place. Our other hands were wrestling for the gun, my hand catching hold of his wrist every now and again before he wrenched his arm out of my grasp, but before I could get a firm hold on it, Angie's foot appeared from somewhere to my left, smashing into the Cloak's forearm and forcing it down to the ground. She pressed down hard, making him scream out with the pain, and then she leant down to pluck the gun from his hand in very much the same way she pulled dandelions out of our garden.

'*Right*,' she bit off breathlessly, aiming the gun at the Cloak as I let go of his wrist and yanked his hood off his head, exposing a head full of curly, bright ginger hair. 'You *fucking dickhead*. You're going to tell us what the hell you think you're playing at and you're going to tell us right *fucking* now, unless you want this piece of shit emptied into that insane little head of yours.'

I felt myself slowly turn to stare at her, wondering where the hell *this* Angie had been all this time, and then I quickly yanked my head back down to the Cloak before she decided to threaten to kill me as well.

He was only a young lad, at that special age in his twenties where men revert to looking like they're twelve, with a bright orange moustache, a crooked nose and pig-like, panicky dark eyes that darted from Angie to me and back again as his face slowly turned the colour of red wine.

'Let go of him a bit, Tidge,' Angie added to me casually, after a few seconds had passed and all the Cloak had done nothing but making choked gasping noises as us. 'I think you're holding him too tight for him to say anything.'

'You know, I disagree with her,' I told him conversationally, slacking my grip on his throat slightly as my free hand settled into that ridiculous nest on his head, gripping tight in case I needed to yank a good clump of hair out. 'I don't give a shit why you were shooting at us, really. What I want to know is, where the hell is Keith Lyme?'

Because who was to say he didn't know?

He knew Knight was after us.

He knew who we were.

He knew those things for a reason, and that reason could only be

> A.   Knight was a big fan of sharing and she'd shown all of the Cloaks photos of us, or
>
> B.   He was in Knight's inner-circle and had been picked to act as hitman.

Either way, you had to think that if he knew about us, he'd know about Lyme.

'I don't know what you're talking about,' he told me wheezily, making a feeble attempt to wriggle his arm out from under Angie's foot. 'I've never heard of Keith Lyme.'

I yanked on those stupid curls, so hard that his whole head jerked to his right. 'Maybe you should have a *really* good think about that.'

He paused for a few seconds, obviously taking in the situation.

It was two on one.

I was prepared to pull every strand of hair out of his head, and could easily shift one of my legs to do some serious damage to his favourite place.

Angie was pointing a gun in his face.

He didn't exactly have the advantage.

'I don't know,' he croaked helplessly in the end, as the most pathetic look spread itself across his face. Being a Cloak is all fun and games until you're at risk of having your meat and veg shoved back inside your body. 'I'm not close to the Mistress, I don't know where she's keeping him. I just know that Mr Lyme is now where Mr Pettyfer used to be.'

'What d'you mean?' Angie demanded harshly, sounding slightly confused. 'Is he helping her now? Did Lyme dump that last body?'

'Mr Lyme has a coveted role,' he told us loftily, sounding like he was reading from a script. 'He helps our Mistress by taking care of the Selected Ones to ensure that they give us their essence. And once he has done this, he and the Mistress will complete the Procedure together.'

More staring at him.

More confusion.

And honestly, where had that come from? Was he quoting a recruitment flier at us? Did the Cloaks have *recruitment fliers?*

'Nothing you just said makes sense,' I said, almost conversationally. 'What the hell is their *essence?* What do they have to do to complete this stupid Procedure?'

'And,' Angie added, as the Cloak blanched at me calling the Procedure stupid, 'what happens to Lyme *after* the Procedure?'

He stared at her. 'Oh. Well... I dunno. She hasn't told us that. I guess we'll have to... put him somewhere.'

Put him somewhere?

That was the big plan?

They were going to *put him somewhere?*

That didn't seem witchy at all.

At least, it didn't until a couple of seconds later, when something clunked into place in my brain, just as Angie asked in confusion,

'Why would you need to put him somewhere?'

'He doesn't mean put Lyme somewhere,' I told her, feeling panic rising up inside me as I twisted to look up at her. 'He means what's *left of* him. Whatever they think they don't need for this pathetic Procedure they're all so obsessed with.'

She stared at me, a couple of shades paler than she normally is. 'What, you mean – you think they're going to... they haven't cut anyone up before, Tidge! Why would they do it to Lyme?'

Oh God. Oh God, that was exactly the question I was trying not to ask myself.

I mean, the only reason I could think of was so that Knight could eat some part of him, most likely – I was guessing, purely because there was a lot more symbolism around eating one bit of the body than most other parts – his heart.

But was she really going to try *cannibalism* as part of this whole thing?

Jesus.

Just when I thought she couldn't get any more insane.

'It's her big finale,' I reminded Angie. 'She's going to want to do something big so that it's not just the same thing again, something that will make the Cloaks believe that she's really got witch powers. And she'd have to do something different, wouldn't she? Otherwise they'd start questioning why she got powers this time when the other rituals haven't made a blind bit of difference.'

We stared at each other, and I could tell that she suddenly felt just as daunted as I did.

Whatever Knight's exact plan was, we only had until the next night to find Lyme, get him away from her, and make sure that she didn't spontaneously find someone else to kill in his place... which was a tall order, given that there were absolutely zero clues about where she was keeping him.

And for the first time, I felt like there was a very good chance that we weren't going to manage it.

In hindsight, we probably should've had a plan about what we'd do if we bumped into a Cloak or Knight.

We hadn't bothered to do that.

We'd just gone bouling in all willy-nilly, and I'll be honest, dragging a Cloak about with you when you haven't got a solid, well thought-out Psychopath Contingency Plan makes everything one hell of a lot harder.

And obviously there was no way we could let him *go*. For one thing, Johnny and Hadaway were going to enjoy a nice chat with him, and I was quite looking forward to handing the Cloak over as proof of how we weren't helping the case at all. For another, if we let him go, he was only going to go running back to Knight to tell her what had happened, and I didn't fancy my chances in another fight with her now I had my kneekle. And for a

third... well, I really wanted to shave all those stupid curls off his head.

But Christ, I had *definitely* underestimated how much trickier everything was when we

were keeping him with us, with his hands tied together behind his back with the belt from my

red coat.

Getting back into the tunnel was fine, thanks to the genius who'd decided to install stairs

instead of a ladder – but climbing up the rungs in the pit that Knight used was a bloody ball-

ache. Because neither of us were happy about untying the Cloak's hands to let him climb up

through the stump himself, we had to essentially drag him up the ladder. Angie went first,

one hand pulling herself up on the rungs while the other reached down behind her to hold

onto the Cloak's hood, and I followed behind, my feet a couple of steps below the Cloak's

and one of my hands pressed against his back to help Angie keep him upright.

And then, once we'd heaved the Cloak out through the stump and untied the deliriously

happy Squidge from his tree in the clearing, we realised that we hadn't actually realised what

we were going to *do* with the git. (The Cloak. Although Squidge does thoroughly enjoy

being a git, he was actually being quite a good boy at that point.)

We could take him back to the flat and get Cattringham County's finest to come and pick

him up... but the thought of having a Cloak where we lived made both of our skins crawl, no

matter how much I wanted to get rid of that bright orange hair. As well as which, knowing

our luck, Hadaway would be one of the Bobbies who pitched up to arrest him, and I was

getting really tired of being shouted at all the time.

We could call Angie's Dad and ask him to take all four of us down to East District

Headquarters, but neither of us wanted to run the risk of getting Angie's family involved and

having Knight target them as well. Besides, that was only going to raise all sorts of questions

that we didn't want asking, especially given that – as a retired copper – her Dad would only give us the same spiel about keeping out of it that Hadaway loved so much. (That was probably more my gripe than Angie's.) And unlike with my parents, who're always so vaguely distracted, there was no way we could've convinced Graham that the Cloak was our new friend who liked fashion choices that were outrageous enough to distract from the crime against humanity that was his hair.

So. That left us with the option to drag him through Habely High Street and drop him off at the satellite Police Station, which had about two coppers and three PCSOs on duty at any given time, and was only open for six hours a day.

It wasn't the best choice, given that we didn't know what time the Police Station opened and there was nothing to say that the two cells in its tiny Custody area wouldn't already be full.

But it didn't seem like we had any other options, really.

And on the plus side, there was no CID at the station, so my chances of getting told off were slim to none.

We made our way over to the muddy clearing that Johnny and Hadaway had left us in an hour or so earlier, thinking that the dirt track leading out of there would fit all three of us abreast better than the paths that we took through the Woods. And I'll be honest, by the time we reached the trees surrounding the entrance, I was already flagging; all I wanted to do was get back to the flat, grab a vat of sherry and sit in a steaming hot bath until that bottle was good and empty.

When we took a couple of steps into the clearing, I felt even worse.

Hadaway's black Audi A6 was sitting there, parked right in front of the dirt track.

Even worse, the man himself was climbing out of the driver's seat, his left leg still in the footwell.

We all froze on the spot, staring at each other in a horrified sort of shock. I'm not really sure was more stunned – Hadaway, at seeing us there with a Cloak; us, at the fact that he was there at all; or the Cloak, who'd just found out how his precious Mistress made it look like she appeared out of thin air, and it wasn't because she was a bona fide witch.

And then suddenly we finished playing that game, and Hadaway was slamming his car door shut and striding towards us, looking beyond furious, with that muscle in his jaw doing a dance that looked very much like the cha-cha.

'What the fuck,' he bit off tightly as he reached us, 'are you playing at?'

I swapped a nervous look with Angie, even though – frankly – we had nothing to be nervous *about*. We'd given him his second Cloak. Not only that, we'd given him his second Cloak in *twenty-four hours*. He should've been thanking us on bended knee, at the very least.

But still.

There was something about that clipped, slightly too controlled voice that was worse than him just coming out and bollocking me.

'I –'

'You told us you were going back to the flat,' he continued, and it was like he was so angry that he couldn't get out more than a few words at a time. 'That was the fucking deal. What the hell are you still doing up here?'

'Hadaway, we –'

'And what the fuck were you doing?' he added, turning to Angie, looking just as furious with her as he was with me. 'You were supposed to make sure she went back. What's she still doing up here?'

'I tried!' she said defensively, her face matching her voice to perfection. 'I took Squidge for a walk but he wouldn't settle without her, and when we came back, she was already in the other clearing, climbing into the tree stump!'

'So you just let her carry on, did you?'

She didn't seem to know what to say to that. She just stared at him for a few seconds, opening and closing her mouth but not making any noise, and when it became obvious that she wasn't going to get any further than that, I offered feebly,

'We have a Cloak.'

He looked at me, and I felt my stomach drop by a good couple of inches. I'd seen Hadaway angry before, but this was something else. This was livid at the bare minimum. His face was almost blank with anger; his jaw was so tense that a part of me wondered if he'd be able to prise it open again; his face was *just* to say paler than normal; there was a vein standing out on the side of his neck; and his eyes were much, much colder and harder than I'd ever seen him.

Without saying a single word, he tugged his rigid handcuffs off his belt and yanked the Cloak around to face the trees behind us. He pulled my coat belt off the guy's wrists and thrust it at me, not giving me another glance, before he clapped the handcuffs on in its place and swung the Cloak around to face the car.

'He's got a gun,' Angie told him quickly, as if she'd only just remembered, carefully covering her hand with her coat sleeve and pulling the pistol out of her coat pocket. 'He, erm, he shot it at Tidge. I don't know how much he can tell you about Knight, but I bet you'll be able to get him on this, if nothing else.'

He grunted, giving her a curt nod. 'I'll get you an evidence bag.'

We stood there and watched as he marched the Cloak over to his car, opened one of the back passenger doors and helped the bloke get into it before straightening up and looking back at us, his face still angrily blank.

'C'mere.'

I glanced at Angie, and I could tell that she was thinking the exact same thing that I was; we did *not* want to be the ones who lit Hadaway's fuse while he was this het up. Hence the fact that, without a second thought or saying anything to him, we obediently trotted over to his car, Squidge glommed to my side like even *he* understood that we all had to be on our best behaviour.

Hadaway held out an evidence bag to Angie as we reached him, and once she'd dropped the gun into an evidence bag, he silently opened the back passenger door for her – but just as I was about to follow her in, he gave the door a hard shove shut and leaned in slightly, his hand resting against the part where the top of the door met the car roof.

'I warned you, Armitage,' he said in that horribly clipped tone, but this time his voice was slightly lower, 'that I'd arrest you if you didn't keep out of it.'

Shit.

He *had* remembered.

'But then we found another Cloak for you,' I pointed out brightly, flashing him my widest smile. 'That cancels out the need to arrest me, right?'

He eyeballed me, looking far less than impressed, and out of pure nervousness – and also in a mad attempt to distract him from locking me up – I suddenly found myself telling everything that'd happened after we'd gone into the mine.

I told him about the robe we'd found, and how Knight must wear it when she was coming out of the stump to meet the Cloaks.

I told him about the other clearing, and how it didn't look like anyone had been there in a long time, but it'd be a handy way for Knight to get in and out of the pit under the stump without anyone seeing her.

I told him how the Cloak had found us and about the fight we'd had, and I told him what the Cloak had said about what would happen to Lyme.

And by the time I stopped talking, he didn't look quite as angry anymore.

Don't get me wrong, he still looked pissed off, like he could quite happily throw me off the moor and be done with the whole thing. But he clearly wasn't seeing red anymore.

In fact, he almost looked like he was – whisper it – *listening* to me.

'Right,' he said when I was finished, in a surprisingly matter-of-fact voice. 'Well, we already worked out that she's working with someone.' Oh. 'What I'm worried about is how she knew where you live, or how this prick knew where you'd be this morning. Think about it,' he added, when I blinked at him. 'The chances are, you could've come here any morning this week and not had to deal with any of these idiots. But the one time you're up here, one of Knight's people is lurking about. Does that seem like a coincidence to you?'

I felt something cold drop into my stomach as I remembered what he'd said way back in the early hours of that morning, about how *'if she knows where you live, she's got eyes on you'*. And I hadn't even *thought* about what the chances were of a Cloak turning up on the same day we'd decided, on a whim, to go back to the clearing.

Admittedly, the guy could've been prowling around up there the day before as well, and he just got lucky (or not, as the case may be) on his second try.

But no. I had a horrible feeling that Hadaway was right, and it wasn't a coincidence at all.

I tilted my head at him, trying to be optimistic. 'Are we sure she's definitely watching us? I mean, maybe we're just easily findable. *You* knew where we were.'

'I knew where you were because I went back to your flat and you weren't there,' he told me, almost dryly. 'I don't reckon this git will've done the same thing.'

Ah.

No. Probably not.

'Look,' he said grimly, folding his arms across his chest so that I had to work very hard to keep my eyes off his biceps. 'If you keep going like this, you'll get yourself killed.'

'I won't,' said the girl who no longer had a separate knee and ankle, who'd fallen several feet off the moor and whose face sadly still resembled a pack of mince.

'You will, Armitage. It's what Knight wants, and you just keep on handing her opportunities.'

'*I do n–*'

'I'm not taking the risk anymore,' he interrupted flatly, as I stared at him in complete outrage. 'I'm sick of watching you get hurt. I'm putting you under House Arrest.'

TWELVE.

House Arrest?

There was one day left to find out where Knight was hiding and make sure she didn't kill anyone else, and he was putting me under *House Arrest?*

Honestly, I was fuming.

Half an hour later, we were back in the flat. Angie and Squidge were happily sprawled out on the settee, Angie taking up two seats as she laid on her back, with her head resting on the arm, and giving Squidge an ear massage as they watched *Friends.* Josh Grey and Graham Mackle – two of the three lads in East District that I'd never quite warmed to, and who Hadaway had asked to cover the first stint of babysitting us – were making themselves at home in our kitchen, talking about the latest footy scores and which of the lasses at East District they'd be up for shagging. And I was stood in front of the flat door, glowering at it with my arms tightly crossed, even though Hadaway had disappeared through it a good ten minutes earlier.

I didn't w*ant* to be under sodding House Arrest.

I wanted to be outside, doing whatever the hell I needed to do to work out who Knight was working with.

Because it wasn't like it was going to be *easy.* If we'd had any way at all of just waltzing up to Knight and *asking* her what sadistic bastard had helped her set all of this up, that'd be just dandy, but here's the thing – that was never going to happen. Even if we knew where Knight was, it would never happen, because she'd have made sure we were good and dead before we'd got as far as opening our mouths.

Christ's *sake*.

I threw an irritated towards the entrance of the kitchen.

If Hadaway had asked anyone – literally, *anyone* – else to babysit us, it wouldn't be a problem. I'd got on brilliant with everyone when I worked at East District, save for these two and Hadaway; anyone else would've let me go on my merry way with a cheery wink and a promise that they'd cover for me with Hadaway. (Probably. I mean, for all he was a knobhead, he was really well thought of. And he *was,* in fairness, trying to stop a serial killer from getting to me. So maybe they would've had torn loyalties.)

But there was no chance with Josh and Mack around.

Oh, no.

Josh wasn't the worst person in the world, but he was a bit stand-offish and far too much of a stickler for the rules. And I was too angry to think up any loopholes that'd convince him that House Arrest didn't *really* mean we couldn't leave the flat. (He was also watching me like a hawk, so I wasn't going to be able to sneak out of the door, either.)

But Mack? I couldn't *stand* Mack. He was about an inch taller than me and squat, with salt-and-pepper hair and a horrible habit of all but hero-worshipping one Aidan Hadaway. If he saw me doing something Hadaway didn't want me doing, or if he caught wind that I'd even *tried* to do something Hadaway wouldn't want me, he'd be straight on the bat phone to the man himself.

And I'd had enough Hadaway for one day, thank you very much.

'Come on, Tidge,' Angie said placidly, looking up from the TV long enough to notice I was still standing there. 'He's not coming back anytime soon, not if he's interviewing that Cloak. Why don't you just come and chill out?'

'No.'

'Squidge wants you to.'

'No.'

'We have chocolate.'

'No.'

'I can get you some sherry.'

'No.'

There was a long silence behind me, and when I eventually glanced over my shoulder to make sure she'd given up, she was staring at me, looking absolutely flabbergasted.

'What d'you mean, *no?* Since when do *you* say *no* to *sherry?*'

'I don't want sherry,' I told her impatiently, finally turning away from the door. 'I want Hadaway to stop being a *dick* and let us out of the sodding flat.'

She rolled her eyes. 'He's not *being* a dick. He's trying to *protect* you. You said yourself that he told you he doesn't want you getting hurt anymore.'

'He *did not* say that he doesn't want me getting hurt anymore,' I countered immediately, suddenly feeling particularly stubborn. 'He said he's sick of watching me get hurt. They're two very different things.'

'They're not,' she told me pointedly, raising her eyebrows as she hit the pause button on the remote, 'and I think it's sweet. He's trying to protect you. Because he *li–*'

'If you say he likes me one more time, I'm going to rip that sodding tongue out of your mouth and feed it to Squidge.'

She blinked at me a couple of times, and I played back what I'd said, wondering if I'd reacted a tad violently.

But hey.

You have someone go on and on about how much you and another person like each other, when in actuality, you're very unlikely to ever be on even friendly terms.

It is *exhausting.*

'Fine,' she shrugged after a couple of seconds, turning back to the TV and hitting play. 'Suit yourself. But you're the only one who doesn't realise he's doing this for your own good.'

I scowled at her for a couple of seconds, but she was too distracted by Rachel's rapping to notice.

So instead, I watched Squidge as he slid off the settee and started sniffing around the coffee table for treats that he might've dropped, accidentally nudging my laptop further onto the bottom shelf as he tried to get his nose into the little gap between the –

I felt a little jolt as I realised what I'd just seen, surprised that it hadn't occurred to me before now.

My *laptop*.

Jesus.

I couldn't believe I hadn't thought of it sooner.

Hadaway might've banned us from going outside for however long – probably until the case had gone to Court and Knight was in jail – but there were no rules against using a laptop while you're under House Arrest, right?

I hadn't read the papers since Monday. What if there was something in there that I'd missed? What if there was a quote in one of the articles about Knight that'd unintentionally give us an idea about who was helping her?

I plonked myself down next to Angie with the sigh of someone who's reluctantly accepted that they have to be stuck in the same place for the rest of their lives, and then slowly pulled the laptop off the coffee table, trying to pretend that I was morose about House Arrest and not excited about the possibility that I'd found another way to look into Knight.

Not that I really needed to bother with the act.

There are very few things that Angie notices when *Friends* is on.

'You're still logged into Facebook,' I told her, when the laptop booted up on the screen that Angie had last had open.

'Oh, you can log me out. My laptop is ready for collection from the repairs shop, so I won't need to borrow yours anymore.'

I glanced down at the laptop screen, feeling a little stab of disappointment. I couldn't be arsed to get Facebook for myself, but it'd been a little fun to snoop on everyone that Angie had gone to school and college with. They all had very boring lives that they thought were very interesting.

'You've got a Friend Request from Kathie Goldin.'

She hit the pause button and turned to look at me, frowning slightly. 'Who?'

'Kathie Goldin,' I repeated helpfully, waving the laptop at her. How was *I* supposed to know who Kathie Goldin was? I'd only gone to our college for five minutes before I dropped out to get an apprenticeship, and there definitely hadn't been any anyone with that name in the one class I'd had with Angie.

She pushed herself up on the settee, leaning over my shoulder as I opened Kathie's profile to see a picture of a vaguely familiar-looking blonde girl. 'Oh, *that* Kathie. Yeah, I remember her. She was in my Latin class.'

I took a closer look the selfie that Kathie had used as her profile picture. She was definitely around our age – a year older, tops – and she leaning too close to the camera for anyone to see what was behind her. She was almost painfully skinny, with light blonde hair that stopped just above her elbows, heavy eyeliner, and killer cheekbones that – I'll be honest – made me a little bit jealous. I frowned slightly, wondering where the hell I'd seen her before. It *definitely* wasn't college; it felt more recent than that. I strained my brain, trying to think of anyone I'd ever come across who was called Kathie Goldin – or Kathie *or* Goldin, for that matter – but instead, all of these random phrases starting drifting through my head.

'My niece, Cathy. She was only seventeen there.'

'It was a lady called Goldin, if memory serves. Probably about your age, actually.'

'Yeah, I remember her. She was in my Latin class.'

And suddenly I couldn't breathe.

Oh my God.

I couldn't move. I couldn't speak. I couldn't do anything but sit there and stare at that photo, feeling myself break out in tingles of shock as my heart started thumping against my chest.

Oh my God.

'Tidge?'

I made a weird choking noise, wildly jabbing my finger at the screen.

'What?' She peered closer the screen for a second before shooting me a massively concerned. 'What is it?'

'That...' I'd gone from choking to rasping. 'It's *her*.'

Her eyes darted from me to the screen and back again, clearly not following. 'Yes, that's Kathie. Are you OK? Are you having a stroke?'

'I'm fine,' I told her impatiently, as my ability to talk came rushing back. '*That's* not Kathie Goldin. I mean, it is, but – Angie, can you not see this? It's *Knight!*'

Her face snapped in complete shock. I think her eyes might have even bugged out a little bit. *'What?'*

'Look at that photo! It's *her!* And think about it,' I added, springing to my feet and dumping the laptop on the settee, because suddenly I was too excited to stay still. 'The Cloaks speak Latin; she was in your Latin class. The bookshop told us that Knight never picked up the book Pettyfer said she used; a lass called Goldin did. And we've seen a photo of that lass *much* more recently than college. *It all fucking fits.'*

She stared at me for a few seconds, looking totally thunderstruck. I didn't blame her; I felt the same way myself. Who the hell would've thought that Knight was using a sodding *alias?*

She slowly turned her head to stare at the photo again, her mouth hanging open slightly. And suddenly she threw her head back against the settee, both hands shoved into her hair as she stared at me with wild eyes.

'Oh my God, Tidge. Oh my God. *Fucking hell.'*

I didn't even have to ask her. I knew she wasn't only talking about finding out who Knight really was.

Because that didn't *just* give us the link between her and that book on witchcraft. And it didn't *just* explain how all the Cloaks knew Latin, or why they'd been using it while they were in the clearing.

No.

Oh no.

It also told us that Pace was a hell of a lot more involved that he was pretending to be.

In our defence, we did *try* to tell Mack and Josh.

It's just that, every time we said that we needed to tell them something about the Knight case, they shut us down, telling us that we needed to do what Hadaway had told us to and stay out of it. Even when we tried to ignore them and keep going, actually *telling* them what we'd found out, they just talked over us, raising their voices just enough that there was no way they could've possibly heard what we were saying.

And we did *try* to tell Hadaway and Johnny, but neither of them answered their phones. Johnny did text Angie at some point to say they were really busy and he'd call when he could, but to be honest, I wouldn't have been surprised if they were ignoring our calls for the same reason that Mack and Josh hadn't let us speak.

So. What choice did we have but to sneak out?

In fairness, it wasn't like we went charging out of the flat on a whim. After Josh and Mack had shut us down, we barricaded ourselves and Squidge in my room and spent *hours* whispering about what we were going to do.

We needed *something* that would give us both a plausible reason to leave the flat – ideally at the same time, so that it wasn't completely obvious that we were sneaking out – and wouldn't make them feel the need to come with us. Stocking up on pads and tampons wouldn't do the trick; any man who has a wife or girlfriend or who's accidentally found themselves in the Feminine Hygiene aisle would know in an instant that it's not exactly a two-person job. There was no way they'd let us walk Squidge, given that he'd supposedly had a walk that morning – or if they did, they'd insist on coming with us. And similarly, we couldn't pretend that one of us had a family emergency and the other one needed to come along for moral support, because they'd insist on driving us to make sure we got there OK. (Angie did suggest trying to silently roll out of the car halfway there, but I quickly shot that one down. I get nervous trying to get off *cable cars*, for God's sake; did she really see me throwing myself from a moving vehicle?) And then what we would do when we pitched up at my parents' empty house and saw it was in complete darkness, or at Angie's family's house to find them alive, well, and completely confused about which one of them was supposed to be dead?

It was around six o'clock before we thought of something that they couldn't catch us out on.

And the best part was, it was so *easy*.

So bloody *simple*.

Honestly, it was a little embarrassing that it'd taken us so long to think of it.

'So,' I announced, striding out of my room and into the kitchen, with Angie right behind me. 'Not that we haven't *loved* having you here, but you two can go home now, if you like. We're having tea with Mrs Miller tonight.'

They lifted their heads up from the sandwiches they were eating (I couldn't help but notice that they hadn't offered to make us one, even though they were in *our* sodding kitchen) and looked at us. Unconvinced doesn't begin to cover it.

'No,' Josh said after a little pause, swallowing his bite of sandwich down with a swig of water. 'You're not.'

'We are, actually,' Angie told him brightly. 'We have tea with her every Thursday. We have done since we moved in.'

'Well, you're not going today,' he said bluntly, taking another bite. 'You're under House Arrest, not House Arrest Except for Tea Parties. You'll have to cancel it.'

'It's too late to cancel it,' Angie retorted indignantly, and I flicked my eyes towards her, wondering if she'd forgotten that we weren't *actually* going for tea with Mrs Miller. 'She'll have cooked. How would you feel, Josh, if your Mam had worked and slaved all day on some lovely, delicious, gourmet meal that she was really looking forward to serving up, and then the people that she'd been cooking for cancelled on her at the last minute? How d'you think your *Mam* would feel?'

'Ade said you're not to leave the flat,' Mack told us, in that broad Yorkshire accent of his. 'Therefore, you're not leaving the bloody flat. End of.'

'Hadaway won't give a shit if we leave the flat as long as we don't leave the house,' I said impatiently, rolling my eyes. 'That's why he said *House* Arrest, isn't it? Besides,' I added, before any of them could point out that that's not really what House Arrest means, 'what do you's think is going to happen? That we'll stage the Great Escape with our eighty-two year old landlady?'

There was silence while we all eyeballed each other for a few seconds. Josh and Mack didn't look any more convinced that we were telling the truth, and I was holding my breath, wondering exactly how this was going to go.

In my head, when we'd told them that they didn't need to hang about anymore, they were a lot happier to go along with it than they'd turned out to be in real life. There hadn't been any questions or any suspicion or anything like that; we'd basically said 'leave' and they'd basically said 'OK', and frankly, I found it really rude that they weren't sticking to the script that I'd written in my head.

But what if we couldn't blag it out? What if they refused to let us leave, refused to listen to us again, and we still couldn't get hold of Hadaway or Johnny?

What'd happen to Lyme?

'Call Hadaway,' Angie told them dispassionately, shrugging. 'Call Johnny. Or better yet, come with us and see for yourselves, because at least then you can explain to Mrs Miller personally why you're taking away the one thing that she looks forward to the most in life.'

Her pretend weekly dinner with us.

Her annual visit from her grandkids who lived in Cornwall.

Either/or, really.

'Fine,' Josh said firmly, pushing himself back from the table and standing up. 'Good idea. We'll come with you.'

I threw a wide-eyed, WTF-esque look at Angie, who suddenly seemed to falter.

Oh, yeah. Fantastic.

She'd got all carried away with her indignation, and what now? How were we supposed to get away from them?

I think it was at that moment that I decided Angie wouldn't have a speaking role in any of our future plans.

'Great,' I beamed, turning back to Josh and Mack and hoping that neither of them would notice me sweeping my car keys off the kitchen counter to my left. 'Let's... go and do that.'

We filed out of the door and traipsed down the stairs in complete silence, to the point where a small part of me wondered if they could all hear my heart beating against my chest.

You'd think that, after having faced off with the Cloaks and Knight herself, getting caught out in a lie wouldn't bother me. And in a way, you'd be right, because it wasn't the getting found out that bothered me; it was what happened *after* we got found out. What was the next level up from House Arrest? Actual arrest? Getting Hadaway to come out and light that fuse that he'd probably been holding onto since that morning? Banishment?

I was excited to find out.

And I *really* hoped Angie was kicking herself.

We reached the bottom of the stairs and I banged on Mrs Miller's door, hoping against hope that she'd be out at her weekly Bingo night and we could turn around to Josh and Mack and be all, 'Oh, silly us! We don't have tea with her on Thursdays, that's what we do on *Wednesdays!*' And then we could all laugh and go back to the flat, and me and Angie could think of another way to get away from them.

Like drugging them, maybe.

But no.

Barely a couple of seconds after I'd knocked, the flat door swung open and Mrs Miller stood there, beaming at us.

Mrs Miller is an absolute sweetheart. She's a small, slightly plump old lady with curly white hair who likes to rock out 80s' style glasses and always seems to be wearing an apron. (In fact, I wouldn't be surprised if she had a special one to put over her nightie.)

There was the tiniest of beats before she opened her mouth where I just stared at her helplessly, wondering if I had any chance whatsoever of telepathically telling her what was going on, but before I had chance to try it, she was declaring cheerfully,

'Oh, hello, dear! What perfect timing, I've just finished cooking the mince and dumplings.' Everything is *the* with Mrs Miller. *The* mince and dumplings. *The* Tesco. *The* Ant and Dec. 'Are you coming in?' And then she peered around the doorway to where Angie, Josh and Mack were standing in a single file to my right. 'Oh dear. Will your friends be joining us? I don't think I've made enough for everyone.'

'No, no,' I assured her hastily, feeling a giant wave of relief wash over me. Jesus. Was she always this happy to feed us, or *was* she telepathic? Or did she have our flat bugged, in which case she would've heard some *very* questionable singing on mine and Angie's monthly Drunk Karaoke Nights? 'Josh and Mack aren't staying, they're on their way out. Aren't you?'

They exchanged glances, and I felt a pang of irritation as I realised that they *still* weren't sure if they should believe us or not.

Don't get me wrong, I got that they had their orders, and I got that they knew those orders were for a reason. But let's be honest, it wasn't as if Hadaway could *do* anything if they bailed; he was their colleague, not their boss. They were doing him a *favour*. And really, what the hell did we think we were going to get up to? Did Mrs Miller *look* like someone who'd go off chasing serial killers?

'Right,' Mack said uncertainly, after a few awkward seconds of them two looking each other, having a conversation with their faces, and us three standing there, watching them expectantly. 'We'll get gone, then. If you need us for anything, we'll be in the car outside.'

I scrunched my face up at Angie as we followed Mrs Miller into her flat, feeling a drop of frustrated disappointment.

Damn it.

Sneaking out wasn't going to be as easy as I'd hoped if they were sitting right outside the house.

'Well, then,' Mrs Miller said happily, closing the door behind us and bustling towards her kitchen so that we had no choice but to follow her. 'Take a seat, girls, I'll bring it over to you. I've got plenty of sherry in, and I'm well stocked with gin if either of you want that. But first' – she put down the spoon that she'd been stirring the mince with and turned to face us, crossing her arms across her (ample) chest and looking surprisingly stern for someone so adorable – 'why don't you tell me what you've got yourselves caught up in?'

As it turned out, Mrs Miller had quite the knack for spotting a copper a mile off, even when they were off-duty. ('It's something in the way they carry themselves, dear. I thought about taking it on the Britain's Got Talent, but Ethel said that's not the talent they're looking for, you know.') And it wasn't even just the Bobbies themselves; no, Mrs Miller could pick an unmarked Police car out of a line-up of plain white Ford Focuses, 'and that one's been sat outside all day'.

Half an hour later, we'd told her everything, from me reading the paper on Monday morning right through to how we'd found out that Pace was helping Knight.

And credit to her, she never blinked. She just sat across the table from us, nodding slowly every now and again and letting us talk, and when we finished, she just said simply,

'Well, then. You can't stay here, can you?'

Her plan had been even simpler than we'd thought ours was.

She'd take a bowl of mince and dumplings out to each of them while we were 'eating', and while she was there – carefully stood at an angle that would keep their eyes off the house – she'd conveniently get carried away talking to them, telling them all about her family and what the Holly and Phil had talked about on their show that morning, and anything else that came to mind. Meanwhile, we'd be standing behind the gate that split our shared garden off the street, waiting for Mrs Miller to start telling them all about the dealings her son Andrew had had with the Police as a teenager, which was our cue to sneak out of the gate and leg it down the street.

I have to admit, a tiny part of me thought it was never going to work.

I couldn't have been more wrong.

I don't know whether they were so distracted by the mince and dumplings ('I put red wine in the sauce, love, that's what makes it so rich') or by what the Holly and Phil had been talking about on their show that morning, but either way, we made it all the way to Pace's house without seeing another Bobby or Police car.

It took us a good hour to walk there, maybe a little bit longer.

And we were both feeling half-frozen, it being a hell of a lot colder than it had been that morning and neither of us having thought to grab a coat before we left the house.

But it didn't *matter*.

We were *there*.

We eased open the iron gates scrambled over the iron gates and snuck up the gravel driveway, frantically – and quietly – trying to decide which of the plans we'd come up with on the way over was our best option.

All I wanted was to find out was whether Lyme was there or not. (And get him out of there. If he was.) I mean, he *had* to be there. It wouldn't make sense for him *not* to be there.

For one thing, Pace's house was unnecessarily big for just one person, and I was still curious about how he could afford it on his wage. But what if it wasn't *just* his house? What if it was Knight HQ, and whatever happened between meetings happened there? (Gads.

Were they one of those cults or whatever that had sex parties? Were we about to walk in on some sweaty, Cloaky *orgy?* I'd lose my mince and dumplings.)

For another, I couldn't see Pace helping Knight with only some parts of what she was doing; it struck me as a very 'if you're in, you're in, and if you're out, you're dead' kind of deal. No, he was involved in all of it. He had been right from the very start, that was how they'd set up that interview; that was how Knight knew so much about him and Lyme, and I'd bet anything he'd done something to the tape to make sure it stopped when she told it to. And they'd need *somewhere* to keep the victims before they got killed; why not in a house so huge that they couldn't be heard by any visitors outside of Knight's circle, no matter where they were and no matter where the visitors were?

And for a third, wasn't it a little bit like hiding Lyme in plain site? As far as I was aware, nobody but us knew that Pace and Knight were related; why would anyone even *think* that he was involved? Why would they consider that his house might be getting used as some kind of base? And let's not forget that, as far as they were concerned, Pace was traumatised by whatever Knight had done to him; they were hardly going to start poking around his house on the odd occasion that they visited him, were they?

Which brings me to the other thing. The thing that I didn't want to say to Angie in case it made her balk and demand that we get back-up. (Not exactly a daft thing to do, but any back-up that arrived was only going to pull us away before we could explain why we were there.) What if Pace *wasn't* there by himself, save for Knight's victims? What if the psychopathic cow was staying there with him? It was exactly the same as with Lyme and the lads they'd killed; nobody would know, because nobody had reason to suspect it.

'Shit.'

I jumped slightly as Angie grabbed tight hold of my arm, making me break out of my cloud of thoughts as she stopped dead on the spot.

'What?'

'Someone's here.'

What?

I whipped my head around to look in the direction she was staring in. We were close enough to the house by now to see the brick carport at the left-hand side of the house, and sure enough, one of the nondescript white cars that CID always use was sitting under it, next to the red sportscar that had been parked there on Tuesday afternoon.

Shit.

'What do we do?' Angie hissed, as we stared at the white car in horror. Somehow we hadn't been expecting this. 'Do we go ahead with the plan, or do we wait until they leave?'

The plan had been to resurrect Kia Lyme-Pine and Lemon-Anne, who would've been passing their good friend Pace's house when they realised that they needed the toilet, and they were *sure* that he wouldn't mind them coming in for five minutes. (Hey. It might've been a shit plan, but it was the best one plan we had.) But there was no way we could do that now. Whoever was in that car was bound to be from East District, and there weren't many people who worked there who didn't know me from my District Admin days. Angie had a better chance of getting away with it than I did, because she didn't know as many people there as I did – but even then, they'd started to recognise her more since she started seeing Johnny.

I glanced at my watch, wondering if we *could* wait it out, but it was already five to eight; if Josh and Mack hadn't realised we'd gone yet, it was only a matter of time before they worked it out and got search parties looking for us. And what if one of those parties happened to look for us at Pace's house, because they knew we'd been there before, and found us hiding in the bushes before we had chance to get into the house?

No.

I wasn't taking the risk.

'New plan,' I whispered back to Angie, setting off again. 'We're not going to the front door. Let's have a look 'round the back and see if we can get in that way.'

I heard her chunter something under her breath about me and my stupid ideas, but she still crunched across the gravel behind me.

We ducked into the carport and skirted around the side of the house, coming out into a garden that was at least three times the size of the front lawn. Even in the darkness, I could tell that it was big enough to build another huge house on, and you'd still have room to spare. There was a gentle slope leading down to a patio area towards the back of the garden, a pond that bordered on being a lake in the bottom right-hand corner, and there trees dotted all over the place, some of them good, sturdy, green trees and others covered in pink blossom.

Genuinely, I think Buckingham Palace would be underwhelming after visiting that place.

Why didn't Knight just do her meetings *here?* Why go to Habely Woods when this place *dwarfed* that clearing? She still could've dumped the bodies up there if she'd wanted to, and this way all the Cloaks could have a nice swim after their murder sesh.

I forced myself to stop drooling over the garden and looked up at the house instead (which, I have to be honest, did nothing to stop the drool). There were no doors out the back (weirdly), but there were plenty of windows, and every single light in every single room was blazing so that the place was lit up like a Christmas tree – except for one room upstairs, maybe three windows in from the other end of the house to where we were stood.

I glanced over my shoulder at Angie, who was staring out at the garden, slack-jawed. 'Any reason you'd have all the lights turned on except one?'

She wrenched herself away from the grounds and looked at the windows, scanning all of the downstairs ones first before flicking her eyes at the top ones. 'Maybe some of the lights have popped.'

Tch. No. 'Pretend that this is the house of a creepy psycho killer, and not a middle-class couple who like to use all the electricity they can because there just aren't *enough things* for them to spend their money on.'

She shot me a sardonic look before scrunching her mouth to one side. 'I dunno, Tidge. If that is the room that Lyme is in – and let me remind you, that is a *big if* – why would she want to draw attention to that room? Why wouldn't she stick him in one of the rooms that has all the lights on, so no-one suspects anything?'

I glanced around the garden a couple of times, wondering if Angie could see a house that I was too blind to spot. Whose attention was going to be drawn to that room? Even if they had any neighbours out the back, who had the *eyesight* to see *three miles* away, just to be all, 'Oooh, Frank, I think there's something going on at the Pace house. One room is a lot darker than all the others, maybe we should call the Police to look into it'?

Jesus.

You could tell Angie had grown up with a mother who was paranoid that they were their neighbours' only source of entertainment.

'Well,' I told her quietly, flashing her a bright smile. 'There's only one way to find out, isn't there?'

I scurried across to the tree that was planted outside of the dim window, ducking underneath any normal-sized windows and leaping past the floor-to-ceiling ones, Angie close behind me. I glanced up at the window as we reached the trunk, and felt a little explosion of excitement in my stomach.

Yes!

I could *just* to say see it over the slab of pale, perfectly square stone that acted as the windowsill, but there was no doubt about it; that window was open.

Only a tiny bit, from what I could see.

But that was fine.

That was all we needed.

'OK,' I whispered to Angie, beaming at her and patting the tree trunk. 'Up you go.'

She stared at her, her mouth hanging open slightly and her right eyebrow a tiny bit higher than it normally is. 'Excuse me?'

'Well, we have to get in there somehow,' I pointed out, blinking at her. 'And this tree's the only way up.'

'I am *not* climbing that tree. I'm not doing it, Tidge. You *know* I'm scared of heights.'

I only just managed to stop myself from rolling my eyes.

Angie's fear of heights is strangely temperamental. I've seen pictures of her having a whale of a time on the Stratosphere in Vegas, and looking out of the plane window during take-off is her favourite part of the flight. But ask her to climb up ten flights of steps to go on a particularly epic-looking waterslide or drive across a high bridge, and she'll all but have a panic attack.

'This isn't very high,' I told her, as kindly as I could. 'And I'm right behind you if you fa– if you need me. Look,' I added, moving to stand next to her and putting one arm around her shoulders, pointing with the other one. 'All you need to do is shimmy up the tree until you get to that nice thick branch.' It was basically another tree in itself, jutting out a couple of metres above us and stretching out to the very window we wanted to climb through. 'And then you just need to pop the window further open, and voila! You're in the room. You're done.'

I was hoping it was going to be that easy. To be honest, apart from short, skinny ones with really easy footholds, I'd spent a lot less time climbing trees than I'd always wanted to. Unlike Angie, I didn't have an older brother who'd shown me how to do it, or a younger brother who I could only get away from if I hot-footed it up the nearest tree; instead, I grew up with Coveney, who'd dedicated the first twelve years of my life to her pretence that that I was just another household item that our parents had bought.

'I don't know,' Angie grimaced, wriggling away from me so that her back was to the ground-floor window next to us. 'We don't even know if Lyme's *there*, do we? Can we not just try calling Hadaway and Johnny again, see if they can look into instead?' She looked at me expectantly, and then – when I didn't answer her – she frowned slightly, peering at me. 'Tidge?'

I couldn't speak.

I was completely frozen to the spot, staring at the window behind her in horror.

Because when she'd moved away from me and planted herself right in front of the stupid thing, so that I'd had no choice but to see what was behind it.

I was vaguely aware of Angie turning – like she was in slow-motion – to see what I was staring at. And then I heard her let out a sharp little squeak of shock as she saw what was on the other side of the window.

Namely, Johnny and Hadaway.

Both stood right in front of the window, each of them holding a mug and looking beyond thunderstruck as they stared out at us.

Shit.

Fucking *shit.*

It hadn't even *occurred* to me when we saw that unmarked car that *they* might be the ones using it. I mean, Johnny had said that *Carl Morskip* was going to see Pace that night, not them. So what they hell were they *doing?*

For a few long, silent seconds, we all just stood there and stared at each other in shock and – I'm sure I wasn't the only one feeling it – horror. In the end, it was Hadaway who snapped me out of it; he turned to Johnny and said something that we couldn't hear, his face going from shocked to thunderous as he put his mug down on the windowsill, and he turned around and strode away from the window, heading for the door of whichever room they were in.

'Haway, let's go,' I told Angie quickly, taking the couple of steps over to the tree and grabbing hold of it, bracing one foot against its trunk. 'I want to see what's in that room before I get arrested.'

I scrambled up the tree surprisingly quickly for someone who'd never quite cracked climbing the rope at school, grabbing onto any knobs or branches that I could and scrabbling to keep the bottom of my feet pressed firmly against the trunk of the tree. I could hear Angie right behind me, breathing slightly heavier than normal – whether it was from nerves or from climbing, I wasn't sure – and the second I reached that thick limb that led to the dark window, I threw myself onto it, straddling it with both legs and half-bouncing, half-shuffling my way along it.

Not the most dignified, I will give you.

But hey. If it works, it works.

I kept going until I reached the part of the branch where it fans out into different, smaller branches and gets a bit weaker, and then, trying not to think about what I was supposed to do, I pulled myself up so that I was balancing on the branch, with the toes of one foot touching the heel of the other. I threw myself forwards as hard as I could, squeezing my eyes tight shut and hoping for the best even as I braced for impact with the ground.

Except that that never came.

No, no.

Long-jumper Armitage Black over here, I cleared the rest of that branch and the gap underneath it like an absolute boss and landed on that ridiculously huge, inset windowsill with no problem at all.

Guaranteed I would never be able to do that again in my life.

But still.

The window was so huge that the lintel was a good couple of inches above my head, and there was a little bit of space between where I'd landed and the window itself, and for a second, I just stood there, feeling completely elated that I hadn't crashed and burnt and made it very easy for Hadaway to arrest me. I spun around to look at Angie, half-expecting to see her crouching by the tree trunk and holding up a scorecard – but before I could really see anything, a vaguely Angie-shaped blur slammed into me, hitting me so hard that I stumbled backwards into the bricks that were jutting out from the windowframe and very nearly lost my footing.

All I can say is, it was a good thing that these people liked to have actual paving slabs as their windowsills. I would not have been held responsible for my actions if I'd been made to have another fall that week.

'*Jesus,* Angie,' I hissed, shoving her off me (but keeping tight hold of her so that I didn't actually push her off the windowsill). 'Did you not *look* before you jumped?'

She stared at me indignantly as she took a shaky step back from me. 'No. I didn't. I was too busy trying to pretend that I'm not *scared of sodding heights.*'

Mmm. Of course she was. 'You did very well.'

'I know,' she told me snootily, smoothing her top down and coming dangerously close to sticking her nose in the air. 'My jump was well better than your jump.'

I couldn't quite stop myself from scoffing. 'It was not.'

'Yeah, it was. Of course it was. I was all sleek and direct, and you were flayed out like a flying squirrel.'

I shot her a tight smile that nearly reached my ears. 'At least I didn't nearly kill us both when I landed.'

Ha.

Couldn't argue with that.

I bent down and hooked both hands under the bottom of the window, giving it a hard shove upwards until the gap was wide enough for us both to slide through.

I'd only just followed Angie into the room when there was a huge bang on the other side of the room, and suddenly a furious-looking Hadaway was striding towards us, with that muscle already tapping out a steady beat on his jaw.

'What the *fuck*,' he demanded tightly, grabbing me at the top of my arms with a surprisingly tight grip, 'do you think you're doing?'

'Ade,' Angie told him quickly, as I blinked up at him. He'd appeared and crossed the room so fast that even though I'd been expecting him to pitch up, my brain seemed to be having a hard time in keeping up. Instead, all it could focus on was how nice its aftershave was. 'You have to listen to us –'

'I have to do fuck all,' he bit off, glaring at her as my brain finally clicked into gear. 'How many *fucking* times do I have to tell you two to stay out of this sodding case?'

'I know, and after this, I promise we will, but –'

'I don't give a shit what you promise,' he told her, staring at her incredulously, and she blinked at him a couple of times. Obviously, Angie had seen Hadaway furious several times before, but that was directed at me; she'd never been on the receiving end of it before. 'You promised me she wouldn't go into that mine pit this morning. What happened there?'

'When I told you,' Hadaway bit off, giving me a look so furious that it not only came dangerously close to melting my face off, but also convinced me that going in for a grope of his biceps wouldn't be the best course of action, 'to keep *the fuck* out of it, Armitage, what the hell did you think I meant?'

'Hadaway,' I said impatiently, knocking his hands off my arms and catching a grope of his biceps at the same time. (Accidentally. Of course.) 'You really need to listen.'

He looked at me, and I could see some – just a tiny bit – of the anger seep out of him. I don't know if it was the fact that I hadn't immediately started arguing with him or the fact that or if he'd liked the little squeeze of his biceps, but suddenly he looked like he was actually...

Well.

Going to listen to us.

I swapped apprehensive looks with Angie before locking my eyes onto Hadaway's. 'Look. You're not going to like this at all, but there's no way it can't be true. Pace is in on it.'

He stared at me, frowning slightly. But not like he was annoyed. More confused. 'What're you talking about?'

'Knight isn't using her real name,' I explained, as gently as I could. I mean, this was someone Hadaway had seen day in, day out for the last four years. (Well. Four days in and four days out, but that doesn't really flow the same.) This was someone that he'd gone *drinking* with. It was someone he got on with really well. He was hardly going to enjoy hearing about Pace's extracurricular activities. 'Her real name is Kathie Goldin. She's Pace's niece, there's a photo of her on his fireplace and everything.'

The frown deepened, and his eyes flicked across my face a couple of times, like he was looking for some sign of a joke. 'You're talking bollocks.'

'I'm not. I'm really not. It was Kathie Goldin who bought the book Pettyfer mentioned from Habely Bookshop. She sent Angie a friend request this afternoon, and it was that girl on Pace's fireplace, just a few years older. He's involved, Hadaway. She's his *niece*. He *knows*. This whole thing has been a complete act.'

We stared at each other, and I could tell that Hadaway was thinking back through everything that'd happened since Knight had first popped up, working out if Pace had done anything that tied in with what I was telling him. It took me a couple of seconds to realise that I hadn't knocked his hands completely off me; they'd kind of floated down to my waist. And in the meantime, my hands were still resting on his biceps.

Shit.

Angie was going to have a *field day* with this once Knight was out of the way.

'We tried to tell you when we first worked it out,' I added, hastily taking a step back from him so that we weren't touching anymore, 'but we couldn't get hold of you or Johnny. And we tried telling Josh and Mack, but they just kept talking over us and telling us to shut up. We didn't know what else to do except to come here and see what was going on.'

Well, wasn't that the wrong thing to say?

The second I reminded him that we were, in fact, at Pace's house, his eyes snapped back onto mine and his eyebrows came down as his mouth settled into a grim line.

'Right. Nice one. Go home.'

I stared at him in shock. That was *it?* Nice one, go home? No 'why don't you stick around, watch us beat the shit out of Pace'? No 'good work, we'll let you use Knight as a punching bag once she's safely locked away'?

What the *hell?*

But before I could tell them that we *weren't* going home, that we were going to stay here and see Pace caught in the headlights – ta very much – a funny little noise came from the far side of the room.

A noise a bit like a wheeze.

We all glanced at each other, Angie looking weary, Hadaway looking suspicious, and me feeling somewhere in between.

The room wasn't full, but it wasn't empty, either. There was a big, old-fashioned wardrobe to our left, exactly halfway between the door and the window; a matching writing desk snuggle away in the corner to mine and Angie's left; and on the other side of the room, not quite pushed up against the wall, was a double bed, hiding whatever was wheezing out of our sight.

None of us moved at first. I have no idea why, since we'd all clearly heard the same noise; but if they felt the same way I did, somehow it just didn't feel like it was *possible* to move, almost like I was rooted to the floor.

Until there was a second wheeze.

Hadaway whipped around and strode over across the room, leaving Angie and me to scurry after him, but before we even halfway across the room, he froze at the end of the bed, staring at something between it and the wall with a totally stunned look on his face.

And I just *knew*.

I hurried around him, stopping on his side nearest the wall, and felt my knees turn to jelly as I took it in.

He was bollock-naked, covered in scratches and bruises and tied to a fixing on the wall with the same type of cable wire that was draped over the trees in the clearing. He looked like he was close to unconsciousness, his head lolling against the wall as he leant against it, but I'd take that over dead any day.

But even with all that – even with the swelling to his face and how clammy and pallid he was – there was no mistaking who it was.

Keith Lyme.

Alive and barely kicking.

THIRTEEN.

None of us moved.

We all just stood there and stared at him in complete shock. Obviously I can't talk for Angie and Hadaway, but suddenly I was finding it hard to breathe.

I couldn't take it in. For all we'd gone over there to find out if Lyme was there, for all I'd spent a good chunk of the night thinking about how he *had* to be there, it turns out that there's a very big difference between having an outrageous theory and having it proved right.

To be fair, Lyme seemed completely oblivious to the fact that three people were ogling him like he was a particularly interesting Lion in the zoo.

He was slumped on the floor, the upper half of his back against the wall, and he was staring into the space in front of him with his mouth hanging half-open and a small trickle of drool slowly making its way down his chin; from the dried, white-ish marks around his mouth, it wasn't the first bit of spit to make that journey. He was shackled to the wall by a thick, rusty chain that was clamped around his right hand, and his legs were stretched out on the wooden floor in front of him, splayed wide open.

Yep.

There were no secrets between me and Lyme anymore.

I glanced at Hadaway, who was frowning slightly as he stared at Lyme, but before I could ask him what we did next, he was on the move, walking over to Lyme and crouching down in front of him, totally unphased by the display between his legs. (I've noticed that men have very different attitudes towards nudity than women do. Ours are normal. Theirs are just weird.)

'Now, mate,' he said in a voice that was half-gentle and half-grim, watching at him with concern written all over his face. 'Can you hear me?'

No response.

Literally, nothing. Not even a flicker of acknowledgement that someone was there, let alone that he recognised him.

And honestly, I didn't like it.

I mean, I don't think any of us *liked* it. But I could feel this intense dread pooling in my tummy, and the longer Lyme stayed there, all floppy and non-responsive, the more dread there was.

And I didn't really get why it was *dread*. Concern? Sure. Anger? Definitely. But we'd *found* him. We were going to get him out, and the lads were going to arrest Pace. There wasn't really anything to *dread* about the whole situation.

I glanced at Angie and Hadaway, trying to see if either of them felt the same way I did. Angie looked nervous, her eyes constantly flicking from Hadaway to Lyme and back again. Hadaway still had that concerned look on his face as he ran one hand over the stubble on the lower half of his face.

Neither of them seemed to be full of dread.

After a few more seconds, Hadaway stood back up and walked over to us, his face turning more grim than concerned.

'Right,' he said, sounding very much like he hated what he was about to ask us. 'D'you think you could manage to get him out of here?'

'Absolutely,' I told him quickly, even though Lyme looked like he weighed twice as much as me and Angie combined, and the heaviest thing I'd lifted recently was two bottles of sherry off the shelf at the same time. But hey. If we helped because he asked us to, his argument about us *not* helping was out of the window. 'No bother at all.'

I saw Angie shoot me a sidelong glance, no doubt thinking the same about the heavy-lifting as I was, but credit to the lass, she didn't actually say anything.

'Right,' Hadaway said again, throwing a quick look at Lyme over his shoulder, his hands on his hips. 'Good. I'll have to get downstairs and take Eric in.'

I felt a sudden pang of apprehension at the reality of it.

Hadaway was a good fifteen years younger than Pace and in much better condition, but Pace was going to have those extra two inches and blind panic on his side. There was no way that he'd go with them nice and quietly; no, the second he realised Hadaway was about to arrest him, he'd freak out like no-one's business. He'd try to run. He'd probably try to hit them. And let's be honest, there was no end to the possibilities of what else he might do.

Which – to be fair – Hadaway and Johnny were probably used to. I bet most people turn unpredictable when they're getting arrested, unless it's one of their main hobbies.

But still. I can't see arresting a six-foot-five bloke built like a brick house being something that happens every day.

'Just one quick question,' Angie said lightly, just as Hadaway took a step towards the bedroom door. 'How are we supposed to get him away from the wall?'

'What?'

'He's shackled to the wall, Ade. How the hell are we supposed to get him out of here without any way to unlock that handcuff?'

He looked at her blankly for a couple of seconds, as if what she'd said wasn't quite going in, and then he spun around on the spot and strode back to Lyme, and as soon as he reached him, he crouched down again, pulling Lyme's arm towards him to examine the cuff around his wrist.

'Fucking ridiculous.'

'What?' I asked eagerly, scurrying forwards to peer over his shoulder. 'What's ridiculous?'

'You'd think someone as organised as Knight would have a better way of locking her handcuffs,' he said dryly, shooting me a sardonic look over his shoulder as he held Lyme's arm up so I could see it.

It was a proper old-school handcuff, the kind that was you'd expect to see in dungeons or on the Rack or something; it had two rectangular pieces jutting off the part clamped around his wrist, and a metal hoop attached to one had been slid into a straight line cut into the other. But that was where Knight had given up on the whole historical vibe.

Well.

Unless they'd used modern handcuffs to keep people tied to the Rack, that is. Because instead of a padlock or whatever was usually used to clamp handcuffs like that together, a pair of Police-issued handcuffs had been fed through the metal hoop and fastened on the tightest setting, holding the shackle shut and dangling loosely from Lyme's wrist.

'Well,' I said, feeling slightly discomfited. How had I missed that? 'Maybe the Blacksmith was too busy to come out and weld it shut.'

He stared at me, looking like he had no idea what to make of that, and then he grunted and shook his head slightly as he turned back to Lyme, fishing his handcuff keys out of his jeans pocket and jamming them into the lock of the pair around the shackle. There was a sharp click, and the handcuff slackened off enough for Hadaway to pull it out of the shackle.

For a couple of seconds, nothing changed.

Hadaway shifted back slightly, reaching out to help Lyme get to his feet, but before he could even make contact, Lyme slowly turned his head towards him, with his head still lolling towards his chest and an eerily blank look on his face.

'My Mistress,' he croaked, a lot more articulately than I would've thought, but in a monotonous voice that was completely devoid of any feeling or tone, 'will not be pleased about this. My Mistress will not like it at all.'

My stomach shot down to somewhere around my ankle and a block of ice immediately took its place, but before any of us could move, Lyme suddenly lunged forward, surprisingly fast for someone who didn't look like they'd moved for a good while.

He barrelled into Hadaway and the two of them keeled backwards towards me; the back of Hadaway's head banged into my kneekle, and an explosion of pain shot through me, making so many spots of light burst in front of my eyes that I couldn't see; all I could do there was stand there, doubled over and trying to breathe and listening to the chaos that'd broke out. There was grunting, angry voices and dull thuds coming from the men on the floor, and I heard Angie make a sound that was somewhere between a gasp and a choking noise, and the next thing I knew, she was hurrying forwards, shouting things at them that I couldn't completely make out over the pain and the noises coming from the lads.

By the time the popping lights in front of my eyes finally pissed off, Lyme was straddling Hadaway's chest, with his leg pressing down on Hadaway's right arm and one hand tight around his throat while the other hand slammed into Hadaway's face again and again and again, always somewhere towards his right eye, which – from what I could see – was already starting to swell and turn a darker shade of red than the colour slowly filling the rest of Hadaway's face. Hadaway was fighting like mad, alternating between swinging for Lyme with his one free hand and trying to yank Lyme's hand off his throat, bracing his legs on the floor and obviously making one hell of an effort to haul himself out from under Lyme, and making the occasional choking noise that made little jolts of panic go right through me. Meanwhile, Angie was having a go at Lyme, frantically kicking and shoving Lyme to try and get him off Hadaway, and when that didn't work and Lyme stayed firmly in place, she was leaning down and trying to pull his hand off Hadaway's throat, wincing and occasionally yelping whenever Lyme's hand caught her arm instead of Hadaway's head. There was a strong enough smell of blood to knock me sick, and I could see Hadaway looking more dazed and fighting just a smidge less with every punch.

I picked my good foot up and booted him as hard as I could in the face, twice; on the first one, there was a sickeningly gross crunch, and blood started pouring from both of his nostrils when I kicked him for the second time, but he just kept swinging away, pounding Hadaway's face into a pulp with that horribly blank expression still on his face.

Angie gave up on pulling Lyme's hand away from Hadaway's neck and moved behind him instead, hooking her arm under his (multiple) chins and desperately pulling him back as hard as she could, but no matter how far she got him to reel backwards, he wouldn't let go; he just pulled Hadaway with him, lifting Hadaway's head up by a couple of inches before Angie lost her grip on him and he slumped back down, letting Hadaway's head bang against the floor. Meanwhile, I was trying my best to ignore the choking, gurgling coming from Hadaway's throat and the awful shade of purple he was turning, and leaping over them so that I could help Angie pull Lyme backwards. He swung his hand back to hit Hadaway again, but before he could do that, I'd managed – somehow – to catch him by the wrist. I quickly twisted his arm the wrong way and forced it down to the ground, pulling him to the side and fighting with him all the way, keeping as tight hold as I could to stop him from wrenching it away from me and socking Hadaway again. Angie gave him a hard shove in the same direction I was pulling him in and he slumped over onto his side, pulling Hadaway with him by the throat, but the angle that we had him pinned at let Hadaway wrestle one leg out from underneath him, and suddenly there was a large, trainered foot slamming hard into Lyme's face. Lyme sagged slightly, blood pouring from his mouth, and without even hesitating, Hadaway booted him again, this time even harder. There was half a second where Lyme froze, looking completely dazed – and the next thing I knew, his eyes were rolling back into his head and he was going limp again, his hand finally slipping off Hadaway's throat.

Hadaway scrambled to his feet surprisingly quickly for someone who'd just had the shit beat out of them, heading over to us and making a wheezy noise that I think was supposed to mean 'get out of the way'. We both dove away from Lyme, and Hadaway was on him in an instant, hauling his arms behind his back and locking his handcuffs onto his wrists. He threw Lyme's arms down onto his back and took a step back, and for a few long seconds, we all just stood there, staring at the unconscious kidnapped man, Hadaway panting as he stood with his hands on his hips and his right eye getting more swollen by the second, and me and Angie breathing almost as heavily as we alternated between shooting wide-eyed looks at Hadaway, wide-eyed looks at Lyme, and – just to mix things up a bit – wide-eyed looks at each other, not really daring to move.

It seemed like absolutely ages before Hadaway finally looked up at us.

'Right,' he said grimly, still breathing more heavily than normal. 'We're going to need a new plan.'

I opened my mouth to tell him it was fine, that Lyme turning out to be a psychopathic zombie didn't mean that we couldn't still get him out of the house while Johnny and Hadaway arrested Pace, but I didn't quite manage to get the words out before there was a little noise from the doorway.

And when we all jerked our heads around to see what it was, we saw Pace and Johnny stood in the doorway, staring at us with identical expressions of shock on their faces.

It was weird, but everything seemed to slow down.

I was vaguely aware of Hadaway doing a funny little jerk to my right, and then he was moving forwards, stepping over Lyme and towards the door. I saw Johnny slowly turning to look at Pace, realisation dawning on his face, and I could see Pace's face draining of colour. But it all seemed to take forever to happen.

At least, it did for a while.

Roughly up to the point that Pace whipped around on his heel and bolted down the hall, and suddenly it all kicked into hyper-speed.

He took off faster than I would've thought he was capable of, and before he'd taken more than a couple of steps down the hallway, Johnny and Hadaway were on him; Hadaway was brushing past me and charging out of the door, apparently well recovered from being strangled and adjusting well to having a face three time its normal size, and Johnny followed right behind him, looking like he still hadn't fully absorbed what was going on.

We heard the front door open and slam shut before opening and slamming slam again, this time with a slightly longer gap between them, and then we were alone in the house.

Just the three of us.

Me, Angie, and one still very naked, still very unconscious Lyme.

FOURTEEN.

I didn't know what to do at first.

I didn't know what'd *happened.* It'd gone too quick and lasted too long all at the same time, and I couldn't take it in.

One look at Angie told me she was feeling just as dazed as I felt.

'Erm... Tidge.'

I couldn't stop replaying the sight of Lyme's fist slamming into Hadaway's face over and over again, and my brain felt like it was sagging under the weight of all the questions flying around in there.

How had it happened? How had Pace become someone who'd agree to help his niece commit the worst crimes that Cattringham County had seen in living memory? How'd he got to the point where he was happy to keep someone he worked with, someone he *knew,* chained and naked in his house until it was time for Lyme to die? What has to happen to you for all of that to be completely acceptable? Was he getting a big backhander out of it? Was he getting the *house?* Or was the sadistic streak that Knight liked to flaunt a family trait that they both shared?

'Tidge?'

More to the point, how had they got Lyme into such a state that he could attack people trying to help him without even seeming to know he was doing it? Did he attack *them* if they ever untied him? Or did they have him so well trained that he wouldn't dare lay a finger on them? But if he was as out of it as he looked, how did he *know* who was trying to help him and who wasn't?

'Oh, for God's sake, *Tidge!'*

I jumped so high that – frankly – I should've been given an Olympic medal, and did some rapid blinking as I turned to look at Angie, blinking rapidly. She'd moved to stand in front of me, looking like she's been a couple of seconds away from giving me a shake, with an expectant and impatient look on her face.

'*What?*'

'We have to get him out of here,' she told me, jerking her head towards Lyme. 'And we need to do it quick, in case Pace comes back or one of the other lunatics pitch up.'

'Oh. Right.'

We both stared thoughtfully at Lyme, wondering how we were going to do it. He still looked unconscious enough, but let's be honest, he'd hardly been the definition of alive before he started knocking seven bells out of Hadaway; I didn't know how confident we could be that he wouldn't try to do the same to us, even with his hands cuffed behind his back. (Those shoulders looked like they could pack quite the punch, if they wanted to. And headbutting... well, headbutting exists.) And then, of course, we had the rather large issue of him being naked.

As nice a man as Lyme was, I was in no rush to touch him while he was starkers.

'I can't believe,' Angie burst out, jerking her head around to look at me again and sounding as if she'd held it in for as long as she could, 'that Pace is *actually* involved in this whole thing. Can you?'

'I dunno,' I said, shaking my head. I couldn't take it in that any copper would want to be involved in anything like this – especially not when you had people like Hadaway walking around, who very rarely snapped out of cop mode – but now that we knew, it made so much sense that I couldn't believe it'd taken us so long to realise it. 'I mean, looking back, the guy's a pretty horrific actor. Right,' I added firmly, after a little pause where we both stared at each other. 'Let's shift him.'

Five minutes later, we'd managed to get Lyme to his feet and half-carry, half-drag him to the top of the stairs a couple of metres down the hall.

I was fairly certain that he'd started to come to, but luckily for us, he'd hadn't flipped back into attack mode; instead, he was just as limp as he had been before Hadaway had unlocked his shackles, his head flopping down against his shoulder. Even luckier, Angie had found a slightly damp blanket that we'd managed to wrap around his waist, so we could almost – *almost* – pretend that he was wearing clothes. (Somehow, manhandling a naked stranger did not make me feel like someone my parents would be proud of.)

The three of us teetered at the top of the stairs, two of us staring down the stairs in a fair bit of concern and the third one blissfully unaware of what was going on.

You'd think – or at least, I did – that in a house that size, they'd have staircases built to proportion, that three people going down it abreast wouldn't be a problem and Joan Collins wouldn't look out of place walking down it.

But no.

Or maybe the staircases *were* in proportion, but the builders hadn't expected someone of Lyme's proportion to use them.

Me and Angie looked at each other across Lyme's vast chest, and I immediately knew what she was thinking.

'I won't trip over if you let me go at the back.'

'Yes you will,' she returned immediately, almost before I'd finished talking. 'Of course you will, and then I'll be squashed under the pair of you. *I'm* going at the back. I *definitely* won't trip.'

I couldn't quite stop myself from laughing. '*You* won't fall down the stairs?'

'No!'

'You? The girl who used her parents' staircase as a slide more often than actual stairs when we were in college?'

'It is not my fault,' she said stiffly, instantly looking defensive, 'that my parents decided to redo their stairs in the slippiest surface known to man. They could've *warned* me that I shouldn't wear socks on it!'

'They probably thought they wouldn't need to after the first time you went flying down them. They probably didn't expect you to do it *another five times.*'

We stared at each other for a couple of seconds longer, Angie looking like she was putting some serious effort into looking annoyed instead of laughing, and then I glanced down the stairs again.

'There is one other option.'

'We're not pushing him down the stairs.'

Damnit.

'Have you got any better ideas?'

'A much better one. I go at the back.'

I tilted my head at her. 'And what happens if we get halfway down the stairs and he snaps back into attack-mode? What if he flings one of us off him and does to the other what he did to Hadaway?'

I'll be honest, this was something that had been hovering in the back of my head the whole time we'd been carting him off down the hall. Hadaway wouldn't have got Lyme off him if it was just the two of them, and he was a hell of a lot stronger than me and Angie; what would we do if Lyme suddenly went for one of us?

'He won't,' Angie said, chewing on her bottom lip slightly as she gazed thoughtfully at Lyme. 'He would've gone for us already if he was going to.'

'We don't know that, though,' I pointed out, raising one eyebrow at her. 'Whatever state she's got him in, how do we know that how he reacts in one situation is the same as how he'll react in any other situation? We do it quick,' I added, when she just looked at me, looking like she was *just* to say on the edge of being convinced. 'And it won't hurt him. He's floppy. He'll bounce. No-one ever needs to know.'

She stared at me for a smidge longer. Then she glanced at the staircase. Then she flicked her eyes back at me, looking slightly exasperated and slightly grim. 'Fine. But not a *word* of this, Tidge, I swear to God.'

We shuffled him forwards by a couple of steps, glancing around all the time for anyone walking in on us, and as soon as his feet were halfway over the top step, right when it was our last chance to back out and come up with a new plan... we let go.

(If I'm being honest, Angie actually let go first. But you didn't hear that from me.)

Of course – because this is *just the luck we have* – the second we let go of Lyme, the second he started to pitch forward, the front door opened and Hadaway and Johnny stomped into the lobby at the foot of the stairs.

We all froze in place, me and Angie staring at Lyme's fat wobbling as he bounced from step to step, and Hadaway and Johnny also staring at him, looking incredulous as they watched him heading towards them, his blanket getting left behind so that he was back to being full-frontal.

He bounced off the second last step with a bit more force and took off enough to clear the bottom step, landing on his side in front of Johnny and Hadaway before rolling back onto his back, legs spread so that there was no pretending we couldn't see his downstairs situation.

None of us moved.

We all just stood there and stared at Lyme in complete silence, until Johnny and Hadaway eventually turned their heads to stare up at us, with matching looks of incredulity on their faces.

'Oops,' I said, in a voice that was unconvincing even to me . 'He slipped. What *happened?*' I added before anything else could be said about that, bounding down the stairs towards them as I realised that someone was missing from our little reunion. 'Where's Pace?'

'For Christ's sake,' Hadaway bit off, as if I hadn't said anything, glaring at me as I reached the bottom of the stairs. 'I asked you to get him out of the house, not *push him down the fucking stairs.*'

My stomach gave a funny little lurch and my breath caught in my throat as I looked at him, and for a few seconds, I couldn't get any words out.

For the first time in my life, Hadaway's face was making me go weak at the knees, and not in the same way as all those lasses who would've quite happily dropped their knickers right there in the pub for him.

His right eye was swollen completely shut, and the whole area around it – from just above his eyebrow to about halfway down his cheek – was twice the size it normally was, covered in a horrible, dark purple bruise that seemed to getting blacker by the second. The bruising had spread to his left temple and looked like it was starting to creep down towards his jaw, and there was a steady trickle of blood coming down from his eyebrow; Lyme must've broken the skin through pure force alone, because he definitely hadn't been wearing any rings that could've done it. His knuckles were scarped from where he'd tried to defend himself and he had five dark lines going horizontally across his neck, clearly left by Lyme using his throat as a stress ball, but those bruises were lighter and more of a reddish-brown colour, absolutely nothing compared to that storm cloud taking over his face.

And yet, somehow, he still managed to be objectively good-looking.

Talk about winning the genetic lottery.

'Oh my God,' I croaked eventually, reaching out to touch the storm cloud as lightly as I could, just as Angie scurried down the stairs behind me. 'Jesus, Hadaway, look at the state of you! Are you alright?'

A stupid question, to be sure, but hey. I'm British. We like to ask people who are clearly *not* alright if they *are* alright, because otherwise we'd feel very impolite and useless.

'I'm fine,' he snapped impatiently, folding his arms tight across his chest as he jerked his chin towards the staircase. 'What the fuck was that?'

'You said we needed a new plan,' I reminded him defensively, dropping my hand from his face and sweeping it towards the staircase behind me. 'Voila. New plan. You're welcome. *Where's Pace?'*

'He got away,' Johnny told us heavily, crouching down to make sure Lyme was alright, even though I thought it was obvious that he was. He was making wheezy, grunting noises that told us he was still alive, and he had enough padding on him that he wouldn't have any broken bones. 'We were right on top of him until we got to a field at the top of the street, but we lost him in some trees. We'll have to get people looking for him as soon as.' He straightened up and stepped over Lyme before grabbing Angie by the shoulder and pulling her in for a tight hug. 'Are you alright?'

'I'm fine,' she told him slightly breathlessly, pulling back just enough to look up at him. 'What about you? Are *you* alright?'

He nodded grimly, obviously grasping straight away that she wasn't asking how he was physically. No matter how angry Hadaway wanted to look, no matter how much Johnny wanted to do the whole stiff upper lip thing, it was obvious that they were both a bit shaken.

And why shouldn't they be?

Hell, I didn't even like half of the people I worked with, and I'd still be a bit taken aback if any of them turned out to have a starring role in the biggest murder investigation that Cattringham County Police had ever seen.

'Right,' Johnny said wearily, letting out a heavy sigh as he and Angie broke apart. 'I'll going to call this in to East District, and then I'm going to take Keith down to the hospital, get him checked over. In the meantime' – I couldn't help but notice he was talking more to Angie than me and Hadaway – 'can you take Ade back to your flat and get his eye sorted out?'

'Of course we can,' Angie told him firmly, cutting off Hadaway as he tried to say that his eye was fine (spoiler alert: it was not fine). 'Don't worry about it, we'll get him sorted.'

'I don't need sorting,' Hadaway bit off hotly, glaring at the lot of us, and I felt a happy smile spread across my face. It was quite nice to see someone else getting told to do something they didn't want to for a change. 'I'm *fine*. Look, mate, I'm better off coming with you. If he kicks off in the car –'

'He's not going to kick off,' Johnny interrupted patiently, and I felt a little jolt of eeriness as I realised that they were having the same type of conversation that me and Angie usually did. 'I've got handcuffs and leg restraints in the car, we'll get those on him before I set off. You're going back with the lasses,' he added firmly, as Hadaway stared at him, looking like he was feeling just as incredulous as he was pissed off. 'You're no good to anyone until you get that eye sorted out.'

It turns out that Johnny has an unexpectedly good 'that's final' voice. If he'd told us all the plan in any other tone of voice, or if me or Angie had decided what we were going to do, Hadaway would've told us that we were wrong and done whatever he wanted to anyway. (Basically, he would've done exactly what he kept bollocking me for doing.)

But no.

Because he'd used *that* voice, Hadaway had given up on any arguments he might've had about it.

Hence the fact that, twenty minutes later, I was leading Hadaway into the flat while Angie paid the taxi that we'd took from Pace's house to ours.

He'd been silent for the entire time we were in the car, and it didn't look like that was going to change any time soon.

I have to be honest, I didn't like Hadaway being silent.

You'd think that I would, given that the alternative was having him snapping at me or yelling at me or generally being a knob, but somehow... no. Angry Hadaway, I could deal with; Silent Hadaway put me on edge and made it very hard to think of anything that I could say to him. It didn't exactly help that I could tell that he was pissed off, but didn't have any idea what about. Nine times out of ten, I know exactly what he's raging about, because nine times out of ten, I'm the one who's made him angry. This time, I didn't know if it was something I'd done; if he was annoyed because he'd had to stick with us instead of going with Johnny and Lyme; if it was because Pace had been involved the whole time without anyone catching on, and because he'd managed to escape before they could catch them; if it was all of the above; or if it was something else entirely. (OK. So maybe I had a *few* ideas what it was about.)

For several long, silent and oh-so-painful seconds, we both stood awkwardly just inside the door, Hadaway pulling off the brooding look really well while I fussed over Squidge and glanced all over the flat, wondering if I should tell him to go and sit down or if I should just let him work it out for himself. (Hadaway. Not Squidge. Although the latter wouldn't have been the worst idea either, in fairness.) I can't tell you how relieved I was when Angie came bustling into the room, saying busily,

'Right, Ade, go and sit yourself down. Tidge can keep you company while I get you some meat for your eye, and then we can all have a drink and chat about what happened tonight.' She threw us a look that was almost dry as she kicked her shoes off. 'I don't know about you two, but I am *well* ready for a drink after that shit-show.'

'Angie, just leave it,' Hadaway told her flatly, taking a couple of steps after her as she scurried into the kitchen without waiting for either of us to say anything. 'I don't need any meat, I'm alright.'

'You are *not* alright,' I blurted out, staring at him incredulously. 'You're *not*,' I insisted, when he turned and shot me a half-irritated, half-exasperated look. 'Have you seen the state of you?'

'It looks worse than it feels.'

'How can you say that if you haven't seen it?' I demanded impatiently, raising one eyebrow at him as I felt a little burst of irritation. What is it with men not being able to admit that they're ill or hurt (with the obvious exception of the dreaded Manflu)? 'You can't *possibly* know if it looks worse than it is if you don't know how bad it looks.' And then, before he could say anything, I grabbed hold of his wrist and tugged him over to the mirror next to the TV. 'Look at it,' I ordered him, forcing him to stand in front of it. 'Are you really telling us that doesn't hurt?'

His good eye slid towards me. 'Leave it. I'm fine.'

I shook my head at him in disbelief, crossing my arms at him and coming dangerously close to stamping my foot in frustration. Did he think I was blind? Did he think I hadn't *seen* the tiny wince he'd made when he saw the state of his face? Or did he think I was too deaf to pick up on the tiny halting note to his voice, the type that people only get when they're in a hell of a lot of pain?

Please.

I've had cramps.

I've had toothache.

Sometimes I've been lucky enough to have them both together.

So, yeah.

I think I can tell when someone's in pain.

'Jesus, Hadaway. We get it, you've got big balls. Can you just take a break from the whole macho thing and admit that having your face smashed in bloody *hurts?*'

He stared at me for a few seconds with a look on his face that I couldn't quite put my finger on, and I used the opportunity to try very hard not to think about his balls.

Fantastic.

Well done, Armitage.

Well done for putting really unwanted images in your own head.

'Armitage,' he said gently in the end, pulling my mind out of his pants as he tucked some of my hair back behind my ear. 'Don't worry about it. It's just a bruise and a bit of swelling, it'll go down. I'm alright. Listen,' he added, his hand still in my hair, making my scalp break out in a hundred hot tingles. 'You did a good job tonight. We owe you one.'

I blinked up at him a few times, feeling a little explosion of mixed surprise and excitement.

Was Hadaway admitting that me and Angie had helped with the case?

Was he actually *recognising* that we weren't just getting in the way?

Did this mean –

'That doesn't mean you can keep involving yourself in the case,' he added dryly, flashing me that attempt at a grin again. 'I still want you to keep out of it.'

Shit.

'Right,' Angie announced breathlessly before I could anything back to that, hurrying out of the kitchen and over to the mirror, a beer in one hand and a bunch of ham in the other. 'Sorry it took me so long, I couldn't find any meat. Here.' She held the ham out to Hadaway, looking at him expectantly. 'Put this on your face.'

We both stared at her for a few seconds, and I suddenly found myself fighting a massive urge to laugh.

I didn't know what was funnier; the fact that she was expecting him to put ham on his face, or the fact that she was so completely serious about it.

Hadaway let his hand drop out of my hair, looking totally incredulous. 'No.'

'You have to,' she told him, frowning slightly. 'You have to put meat on busted eyes, it's common knowledge.'

'*Steak*, Angie. You can't just use any meat.'

'Well, we don't have any steak. We have some mince in the freezer and we've got a pack of ham, so unless you want a block of frozen meat shoved against your face, it's this or nothing.'

'I'm alright with nothing,' he told her dryly, reaching out to take the beer off her, but instead of letting go when he put his hand on the bottle, she just stared at him, stony-faced. If anything, I'm pretty sure I saw her *tighten* her grip on the bottle.

They looked at each other for a few seconds, both looking equally outraged, and this time I couldn't quite stop myself from laughing.

I wasn't sure whose side I could see more. Angie's, because Hadaway clearly needed to do something about that face, and if this was his only option, then this was what he should do; or Hadaway's, because no-one wakes up expecting today to be the day that someone forces them to put ham on their face, and also, if you've spent the evening getting your face smashed in, then the least someone can do is hand you the beer that they're dangling in front of you.

'Angie,' I said, trying and failing to keep the laughter out of my voice, 'give the man his beer. You,' I added to Hadaway, 'put the ham on your face.'

'There's no point. It won't do anything.'

'How do you know?' I asked, tilting my head to one side. 'What evidence is there that it *absolutely* has to be steak, and nothing else will work?'

To be honest, I've never understood why people put steaks on busted eyes. I'm sure it must do something for it even be A Thing, but to me, it's always just seemed like a waste of perfectly good meat.

'Listen –'

'Humour us,' I told him firmly, grabbing the ham off Angie and holding it out to him. 'Just for ten minutes, sit on that settee and put the ham on your face. Worst case scenario, you're right and it does nothing, and you get to gloat about it all you want. Best case, it actually works and you can open your eye again. What've you got to lose?'

He stared at me for a few seconds, looking like he couldn't believe that he was actually being made to do this, and I smiled patiently back at him, wondering if he wanted that beer enough to put the ham on his face.

'You can have it,' I said lightly, when I saw his good eye flick to the bottle in Angie's hand and back to the ham in less than a second. 'When you have this ham on your face.'

He shot me an impatient look that bordered on being angry, but suddenly all the fight seemed to have gone out of him. Because instead of saying anything, he just grabbed the ham off me and strode over to the settee, pulling the beer away from Angie as he brushed past her. He threw himself down in the middle of the sofa, flung the ham over his bad eye and just sat there, glowering at us in a way that would've been a lot more effective if he didn't have ham on his face.

I'll be honest, the man looked ridiculous.

But somehow I had a feeling that laughing wouldn't have gone down too well.

'Right,' I said to Angie, and then I had to break off, pressing one hand tight over my mouth. It was no good. I couldn't keep the laughter out of my voice. I had giant bubble after giant bubble of laughter rising up in my throat, making my shoulders jerk from the force of it, because of all people who'd do something as daft as putting ham on their face, it had to be him. It had to be the always-serious, always-practical Aidan Hadaway.

'Are you alright, Tidge?' Angie asked, looking mildly amused as she raised one eyebrow at me. She glanced over her shoulder towards my bedroom and then looked back at me, and I couldn't help but notice that she managed to avoid looking at Hadaway as she did it, even though he was sat right in her line of sight. 'Do you want to have a chat in your room?'

'I do,' I choked out, nodding frantically and barely daring to look at Hadaway as I started to move past the settee. 'I really do.'

It may have been a lie.

I wasn't that bothered about chatting in my room. I mean, did I want to ask her if she really expected the ham to make a blind bit of difference to Hadaway's eye? Yeah. Did I want to go somewhere that I could have a good laugh at Hadaway's expense without pissing him off even more than we already had? Yes. *Yes.* There are no words to describe how much I needed to do that.

But they were just little bonuses to going into my room. Because what I really wanted to do was update the Scribbley Wall with everything that we'd found out that night.

We hadn't found out as much as I'd hoped we would when we'd snuck out of the house earlier on.

We knew that Lyme was in a much stronger trance than Pettyfer had been; unlike Lyme, Pettyfer hadn't attacked the cops who'd caught him dumping the body and he was perfectly capable of talking to people who weren't Knight or Pace.

Obviously we knew that Pace was heavily involved in the whole thing, and was probably Knight's second-in-command person, not just because of their being related, but also because

Pace could influence the case in ways that no-one else could. I mean, it wasn't even limited to the fact that he could throw the cops off her trail as much as necessary; it was other things, like telling people how she'd got into his soul, and tampering with the interview tape, and pretending to be hypnotised in that interview room. And come one, now we knew the truth, *of course* he was pretending. I'd even go as far to say that his little act was the reason why Lyme had been so affected by Knight, because he'd seen – or thought he had – what she'd done to Pace and *expected* her to do the same to him. (Well. It was one of the reasons, at least. There was no doubt in my mind that something else was at play as well; knowing Knight, she'd want something to fall back on if Pace's act didn't work as well as they wanted it to.)

We knew that Knight was starting to get cocky, because there was literally no other reason for her to send Angie that Facebook request. But... why? Regardless of how good she thought her disguise was, why did she want to be Facebook friends with Angie? (Obviously I mean that in the nicest way possible.) Did she want to see what Angie was up to? I'll be honest, she'd be disappointed; all Angie really used it for was share pictures uploaded by Dogs Trust and the RSPCA, usually posted while she was drinking wine and crying her eyes out over the sad stories. Or did she *want* us to recognise her? In which case... *why?* Did she even recognise us from college? Or was this just part of being a psychopath?

We also knew that, for someone so different and creative with her lunacy, she was surprisingly uninspired when it came to her aliases. The girl had literally just rearranged the letters of her name. Kathie Goldin. Elodia Knight. Seriously, where was the thinking outside the box? Where was the imagination? Why had she done that instead of coming up with something completely original, something that people could never tie to Kathie Goldin? Unless... I have to go back to this one, did she *want* to get caught? But then why use an alias or a disguise at all?

And if she really was so uncreative that she couldn't think of a name that had different letters to her own, who'd really thought up this whole Procedure thing? Knight? Or Pace? Either way, *why?* Why couldn't she just kill them like a normal murderer would, instead of being so *theatrical?* And regardless of whose idea the whole thing, why would the other one go along with it? What did either of them have to gain from murdering a bunch of innocent lads and making people think there was a witch on the loose? Power? Fame? Notoriety? But if that's what they wanted, why keep Knight's real identity and Pace's involvement secret? (Except for, you know. The obvious arrest, trial and jail sentence.)

I took a step back, pushing the lid back onto my bingo marker and frowning as I looked up at everything we'd scribbled on the wall. Angie was still working away in complete silence, and the inside of my head hurt from all of the thoughts and questions that were flying around inside it, so much that I had no idea we weren't alone in my room until a deep voice immediately behind me said,

'How'd you know where Keith was?'

I would say I jumped, but that'd be a bit of an understatement.

What I did do was a damned good impression of *Tom & Jerry* Tom every time he gets startled.

'*Jesus,* Hadaway,' I said weakly, holding one hand over my chest as I floated back down to the ground, hopefully becoming much more human than cartoon cat with the bizarre ability to run around on two legs. 'You scared the shit out of me. What the hell are you doing? And,' I added, narrowing my eyes at him, 'where is your ham?'

He shrugged, shoving his hands in his jeans pockets as he looked over all of our scribbles. 'I ate it. What?' he added impatiently, when I blinked at him. Somehow it hadn't occurred to me that people would eat meat that had been on someone's face. 'I haven't ate since breakfast, I'm bloody starving.'

'There's some bread in the cupboard,' Angie told him lightly, fastening the lid on her own bingo marker as she turned around to join the conversation. 'You should've made yourself a sandwich.'

'I did. I'll have to buy you some more cheese, I used up what was left.'

I blinked up at him, feeling mildly irritated. Whether it was because he'd surprised me so much or at finding out that our cheese was gone, I couldn't tell you. 'Where are our sandwiches?'

'You were busy.' Christ's sake. What is it with coppers and refusing to make people sandwiches? 'C'mon. How'd you know where he was?'

'It was a lucky guess, really,' I admitted, shrugging. 'It just seemed to make sense, given that Knight is Pace's niece, and he's rolling around in that giant house all by himself. He could've been somewhere else completely, we just lucked out.'

'Right,' he said slowly, still scanning the wall, his face becoming more and more grim. 'And why'd she send Angie a friend request?'

'She was in my Latin class at college,' Angie explained, popping her bingo marker into her back pocket. 'I have no idea how she's recognised me though, she can't have got too good a look at me when she was here this morning.' Jesus. Was it really only that morning that Knight had broke into the flat? 'But it explains how she's got all the Cloaks chanting in Latin, doesn't it?'

He didn't even respond to that.

He just kept looking up at the wall, his jaw slightly more set than it had been a few seconds earlier.

'Whatever their endgame is, everything they're doing now depends on people believing Knight,' I told him, swapping an apprehensive look with Angie. I'd kind of been hoping that we'd seen the back of Silent Hadaway. 'That's why Pace had to be the lead Officer in her interview. I'd bet *anything* that he got her alone before they went into the room and told her everything that she needed to know about Lyme, everything that'd push his buttons. The things that she said about Pace probably aren't even *true*, they just needed something to make Lyme believe she could really get inside their heads. And it's the same with the Cloaks; they're seeing her do these things that they know are impossible and they can't think of any explanation for it. So in their heads, witches *must* actually be really and she *must* actually be one of them.'

For a good minute, he didn't move. He didn't say anything. He just stood there, staring at the wall with his face turning more thunderous by the second. And while he was doing that, we watched him, swapping the occasional look that said we were both wondering if we should say something or if we should just leave him to it. But just as I opened my mouth to ask him if he was alright, he suddenly came back to life, turning to his right and slamming his fist so hard into the wall that the thud echoed around the room.

'*For fuck's sake*!' he roared furiously, throwing his other arm up at the wall as we both jumped, Angie letting out a startled little squeak. 'How the *fuck* did we miss that?'

'Whoa!' I burst out in alarm, feeling my eyes widen as I ducked in front of him, grabbing hold of the fist that he was about to slam into the wall again. 'Hadaway, stop it! *Everyone* missed this! Do you really think we would've worked it out if she hadn't set Angie that friend request?'

'Not everyone's in the fucking Police,' he bit off furiously, his face somehow livid and stony at the same time, with a glint in his eye that almost seemed to border on manic. 'We're meant to cover all bases, we never even *considered* the possibility that she was using a fucking alias!'

I blinked at him a couple of times, and even as I realised that it was completely the wrong thing to come out with, I heard myself say,

'Well... didn't you do background checks?'

'Of course we fucking did!' he bellowed, and this time he wrenched his arm away from me and punched the wall again, even harder this time. I couldn't help but feel sorry for whoever had been tasked with doing those checks. 'Have you got any idea how much effort they've put into this? They've given her a whole fucking backstory, a whole life, nothing we looked into led to any fucking Goldin!'

We both stared at him in alarm, wondering what we were supposed to say to that. We knew from Johnny exactly how hard Hadaway was working on this case; as hard as everyone else was working on it, it was Hadaway who'd been forced to go home after close to forty-eight hours in the office, Hadaway who'd come back as soon as he could, and Hadaway who'd already filled two pocket notebooks with everything they'd found out. I mean, we knew from the amount of time he'd spent at the flat that he was hardly getting any sleep; if he'd got any more than I had that week, I'd be amazed.

So was it really any surprise that he'd finally reached breaking point? No.

Was it something we knew how to handle? Also no.

I saw Angie take a step forward, nervously opening her mouth to say something, but before she could get any words out, Hadaway had turned and strode out of my room, his shoulders rigid and his back ramrod-straight. And when we scurried after him after a couple of seconds' hesitation - which was spent staring at each other with huge eyes, Angie clearly wondering how we calmed him down just as much as I was – we found him standing in the middle of the living room, scrawling in one of the notebooks we keep lying around with a hell of a scowl on his face, apparently oblivious to Squidge watching him curiously from the other side of the settee.

'Here,' he grunted when he was finished, clicking the ballpoint pen off and thrusting the book at Angie. 'That's the Latin she's got her followers saying. It won't be spelt right,' he added brusquely, grabbing his jacket off the back of the settee and shrugging it on. 'But see what you can do with it.' And then, as Angie ducked her head down to look at what he'd written and I stared at him in a way that I *knew* was more 'what the hell' than I meant it to be, he turned and headed for the door, tossing over his shoulder, 'I'm going outside.'

He wrenched the flat door open and disappeared through it, slamming the door behind him so hard that the whole room juddered. And we just stood there, staring after him in the heaviest silence that I've ever known.

I'd never seen anyone reach that pitch before.

Obviously I'd seen him pissed off and worked up plenty of times; to be honest, it felt like I was seeing it on an hourly basis that week. But that was always directed at *me*; this time he was clearly mad at himself, even though – earth to Hadaway – he was not the only person working on the case, and he was far from the only one who hadn't known that Knight wasn't who she said she was. And while I'd thought I'd seen him reach his peak a couple of times that week – especially when he caught us coming out of Knight's pit and breaking into Pace's house – there was absolutely no doubt now that I very much had not.

This was the top-level anger shit. This wall-punching, manic-eyed Hadaway was clearly him at the angriest and most frustrated that he could be.

Him being mad at me was a piece of cake. I could shout back at him or smile at him or push his buttons or do all of the above, and then we'd get calmed down and crack on until the next time he decided to bollock me.

Him being mad at himself and the situation in general was something new, and I couldn't really see any of my usual tactics being any good in this case.

We gave him five minutes before me and Squidge followed him outside. He was stood just outside the front door, resting his head against the brickwork with his eyes closed and a half-burnt cigarette in his hand.

'Oi,' I said, blinking at him in surprise. 'Since when do you smoke?'

He lifted his head off the wall and looked at me wearily. 'Since I was seventeen.'

'I've never seen you smoke.'

'I packed in a couple of years ago,' he told me, shooting me a grim smile that had absolutely no humour or happiness in it. 'It's only been this week I've felt like I needed it again.'

I eyeballed him, chewing on my bottom lip and gracefully overlooking the fact that he was laying this little habit at my door. Judging by the three cigarette stubs littered around his feet, this wasn't his first cigarette of the night – but I was happy to let that slide, given that he looked a lot calmer than he had in the flat. In fact, he somehow looked even fitter than he had in the flat; I don't know if it was the angle of the nearest streetlamp or the lighting of it, but it highlighted all the angles of his face, especially in the jaw area. That jaw of his looked even stronger and more chiselled than it normally did.

'Listen,' I said as gently as I could, trying to ignore the fluttering that was suddenly going on in my tummy. 'Are you alright?'

'I'm fine.'

'Right. It's just, you know, the whole punching-the-wall thing made us think that you might not be OK.' I adjusted Squidge's extendable lead so that he could explore the front garden as much as he wanted to as I kept watching Hadaway, waiting for him to say something. And when he did nothing but take another drag on his cigarette, I continued firmly, 'You can't shoulder this case by yourself, Hadaway. You are *not* solely responsible for it, and you can't expect to know *every* little thing. It's only because Knight got cocky that *we* found out who she really is.'

'We're the Police. We're paid to know shit like this.'

'Yeah, the Police. Not psychic. You're paid to find out as much as you can and look into things as much you can, and correct if I'm wrong, Hadaway, but that's exactly what you're doing. *Stop beating yourself up.*'

For a good while, he didn't say anything. He just stared broodily at the houses on the other side of the street, blowing cigarette smoke out through his nose. And while he was doing that, I watched him almost nervously, wondering if I should carry on giving him a pep talk or leave him to it.

Just as I decided to let him get the brooding out of his system and go back into the flat, he blew a grim sigh out through his nose and dropped his cigarette to the floor, grinding it out with his foot as he immediately lit up another one.

'It's a fucking mess,' he told me heavily, his voice muffled slightly from the cigarette hanging out of his mouth. 'It's the biggest case any of us have seen, and we're not getting anywhere with it. We've got you two hanging around, thinking that you're helping; we've got the pricks at the top wanting us to get it sorted yesterday, so they can tell the Press that Knight's been arrested; and everything we find out gives us another ten lines of enquiry. And Eric...' He shook his head grimly, clicking the lighter off and shoving it back into his pocket as he pulled on his new cigarette. 'I knew something wasn't right. But if people tell you someone's ill, you give them the benefit of the doubt.'

I chose to ignore what he'd said about me and Angie only *thinking* we were helping.

I also chose not to point out that he'd as good as admitted that we *had* helped that night barely even an hour ago.

There'd be better times to remind him of those things later on.

'Well,' I said, mainly because I wasn't sure what else I *could* say. 'Everyone knows that you're all working hard on it. And if those pricks want a quick result instead of a good one, that's on their conscience, isn't it?'

He frowned at me, looking almost like that hadn't really occurred to him. Which, in fairness, I could more than understand; I've been under pressure from bosses before, and all I could focus on at the time was the frustration of it. I couldn't remember ever thinking about how badly it reflected on them.

'But smoking isn't going to make a blind bit of difference to any of it,' I carried on loftily, holding my hand out towards him, palm up. 'So why don't you let me look after your cigarettes, and the next time you really, *really* need one and we can't distract you from it, I'll give them back?'

He grunted, shoving himself off the wall as he dropped his latest cigarette to the floor and ground it out. 'I always really need one.'

We turned to go back into the house, Hadaway's hand bizarrely warm against the small of my back, but before we could take more than a couple of steps, his work mobile rang, and he answered it with another grunt that I think was supposed to be his name.

I hovered awkwardly in the doorway, reeling Squidge's lead in and wondering if we should wait for Hadaway, or if we'd be better off going back into the flat so that he didn't think we were eavesdropping on him. He'd taken a few steps away from us and was stood with his back to the house, but it was obvious that this wasn't a phone call he was happy to get; his entire body had stiffened up, his shoulders just as rigid as they had been as he'd stormed out of my bedroom.

'What the fuck d'you mean, *you don't know where he is?*'

And suddenly I gave up any pretences that I wasn't interested in that phone call.

I wandered slowly over to him, carefully making enough noise that he didn't think I was trying to sneak up on him so I could listen in. (I did want to listen in. Just not sneakily.)

He noticed me when I was a couple of steps away, snapping around to face me with an angry, disbelieving look on his face. But instead of shooing me away like I'd thought he would, he didn't react, save for keeping his eyes glued on me as I sidled even closer to him.

'Right,' he bit off shortly, shoving his spare hand through his hair impatiently. 'Do we know where it happened? Is there any –'

He was quiet for a couple of seconds, his jaw getting more and more tense as he listened to whatever the person on the other end of the line was saying, until he eventually hissed furiously, '*Fuck.*' And then, after a few more seconds of listening, he added grimly, 'Yeah. No, I'll be there. Give me ten minutes.'

He angrily jabbed his thumb against the End Call button and jammed the phone back into his jeans pocket, running one hand over his jaw as he glowered down at the ground. I just stood there and watched him, feeling more and more dread swirling around in my stomach as I waited for him to tell me what'd happened.

It was bad, that much was obvious. Even if I hadn't heard that tiny snippet of conversation, I'd have been able to tell it was more bad news just from the way he was standing; everything about him seemed to scream that something shit had happened, to the point where I didn't want him to tell me just as much as I was itching to find out what it was.

'Right,' he said grimly in the end, lifting his head up to look at him, and I immediately felt the dread inside of me double up. 'How do we tell Angie it looks like Knight's got Johnny?'

FIFTEEN.

I wasn't expecting East District Headquarters to be as busy as it was.

I don't know why. I mean, the place had been packed through the day ever since Knight had started this psychopathic hobby of hers; it wasn't as if anyone would be like 'oh, what's that? A Bobby's been kidnapped? Never mind, it's clocking off time, I'll deal with it tomorrow'. And it wasn't as if it was *late*; by the time me, Angie and Hadaway got there – barely fifteen minutes after that phone call, thanks to Hadaway's lead foot – it was only nine o'clock, and I knew for a fact that that was downright early compared to the time some of the people working the case had been going home.

Hadaway had all but abandoned our car in the front visitor car park and the three of us had charged through East District Headquarters until we'd reached the CID office on the first floor, Hadaway striding ahead of me and Angie so fast that we struggled to keep up, and Angie silent and pale-faced as she hurried along next to me.

I couldn't take it in. I could hear the words and I knew what they meant, but I just couldn't wrap my head around the fact that Johnny had been kidnapped. How the hell had Johnny been kidnapped?

Well.

Actually, I *knew* how Johnny had been kidnapped.

While we'd been flying down to East District, Hadaway had told us that Johnny had dropped Lyme off at the hospital with a couple of Response officers and then gone to East District to fill them in on what had happened at Pace's house. Once he'd done that, he'd headed back up to the flat, but before he'd got halfway there, his car had been ran off the road. By the time a Response car passed by chance, the car was in the bushes at the side of the main road between East District and Habely, with its left-hand side caved in and its driver's door wide open, and save for some blood on the steering wheel and dashboard, Johnny was long gone.

But still.

People you know aren't meant to get abducted.

People you don't know who live on the complete other side of the country are the ones who get abducted. Not people who are *real*.

The three of us burst into the CID office to find it jam-packed with a lot of officers that I recognised and even more that I didn't. Some of them were in plain-clothes, some of them were wearing the high-vis vests that Response officers have, and all of them perched on anything mildly resembling a seat, facing the giant whiteboard and noticeboards that were full of information about Knight and what she was up to. There was a smattering of quiet gasps and mumbles from the ones close enough to the door to clock Hadaway's swollen face, but whether he heard them or not, I couldn't tell you; without acknowledging a single person, he turned to his left and strode over to speak to Dave Evans, his Detective Inspector, who was stood by the whiteboard with Derek Farley, the Detective Superintendent in charge of the Murder Investigation Team. And while he was doing that, I led Angie over to the back of the room, towards a blond Response officer who'd let out a particularly violent swearword at the sight of Hadaway's face; namely, Luke Hadaway.

I have to be honest, I have a bit of soft spot for Luke. He'd worked at East District since before I had, and from my very first day there, he was like the big brother I never had.

He's fifteen months younger than Hadaway and much less serious, and while there's a strong enough resemblance that you can tell they're brothers, Hadaway had definitely made the most of his first dibs at the genetic market. Which isn't to say that Luke isn't good-looking in his own right, because he very much is (and he has a track record not dissimilar to his brother's to vouch for it). While his nose and eyes are exactly the same shape as

Hadaway's, his eyes are brown to Hadaway's gray; his jaw is fairly strong, but nowhere near as chiseled as Hadaway's; he wears his hair shorter; his shoulders aren't as broad; and while there's no denying he keeps himself in good shape, he is lacking The Biceps.

And... I don't know. There's just something about Luke that stops me from ever seeing him as anything other than a brother, and something about Hadaway that makes me... very much not.

'Now then,' Luke said without preamble, as we reached the windowsill he was sat on. 'What've you done to his face?'

'Not my work,' I told him, feeling my mouth pull itself into something resembling a smile as I hoisted myself up to sit next to him. 'He tried to get Lyme out of Pace's house, and Lyme had a *Rambo* moment. Have they said anything about Johnny yet?'

'Not yet. I think they've been waiting until everyone's here, there's a few people they had to call in.' He shot an uncharacteristically serious look at Angie, who'd pulled herself up into the tiny gap next to me. 'How are you doing?'

'Mhmm,' she squeaked bravely, nodding shakily and staring straight ahead. 'I'm OK.'

'He'll be alright,' he told her reassuringly, as I gave her hand a tight squeeze. 'They've got everyone this side of Exleigh looking for him, we'll find him. And Johnny's a good lad, he knows how to handle himself in a tight spot.'

She gave another tiny nod, making that 'mhmm' sound again – the shaky one that sounded like she was dangerously close to bursting into tears – and keeping her eyes front and centre, almost like she didn't want anyone to see how close she was to crying.

Before either of us could say anything else to her, my eye was caught by a movement at the front of the room. I turned my head just in time to see Hadaway take a couple of steps away from Evans and Farley, who clearly had some strong control over the room; one clear of the throat from Farley and a look around the room from Evans was enough to make everyone shut up.

And just like that, we were off and running.

Hadaway went first, explaining how edgy Pace had seemed when him and Johnny visited him that evening, and how Pace had done a runner when we'd found Lyme in one of his guest rooms. He told them who Knight really was and about how me and Angie had found out that she was related to Pace, and he talked through the likelihood that Knight was hiding somewhere in Pace's house, given how they were working together and how unnecessarily huge Pace's place was – and if she wasn't actually staying with him, she couldn't have been far away; she'd pulled a plan together too quickly and carried it out too soon to be much outside of Habely.

And then Farley stepped up, grabbing a marker pen from a nearby desk and circling three areas on the map of East Cattringham County that was pinned with magnets to one side of the whiteboard. One of the circles was slap-bang between East District and Habely, near where Johnny's car had been found; another was around Pace's house and the back road that led out of Habely and towards Ambledon; and the third ring was drawn around the whole of Habely Woods.

'This is where we're looking,' he boomed in that thick Irish accent of his. 'Based on what we know about Knight, we can safely assume that she's most likely to be in one of these areas. I want good, thorough searches in each place; I want door-to-doors, I want the dogs out looking for them, I want no stone left unturned. Now, we can't assume that anywhere's too obvious for them to hide; don't think they won't be sitting it out in Eric's house just because we had folk there earlier. There's every chance they've gone somewhere in plain sight.'

'Hang on, sir,' a lass with white-blonde hair in the middle of the room piped up, holding her hand in the air. 'Why are we assuming that Knight's still in the area? How do we know she hasn't gone into Yorkshire or headed for Newcastle? Don't you think it'd make more sense to look there?'

'We'll get word out to the other Forces,' Hadaway told her, folding his arms across his chest. 'But I'm quietly confident she'll still be in the area. Everything she's done has been building up to what she's got planned for tomorrow night; she wouldn't clear off when she's this close to it. At the very least, she wouldn't want to lose face in front of these people who believe her.'

'Well,' the blonde-haired lass said, frowning slightly, 'in that case, how sure can we be that they haven't took him into the Woods to do this Procedure tonight? She *has* to know that we'll be on her like white on rice now she's kidnapped one of us. Don't you think that they'd just get it over and done with before we could get close to her?'

'She wouldn't do that,' I pointed out before I could stop myself, and there was a little wave of noise as sixty-odd heads whipped around to look at me. 'She's been telling the Cloaks that this Procedure has to take place at the end of the week, when it's the next full moon. She can't just bring it forward all of a sudden, it'd knock her credibility. She needs them to believe in what she's doing, and they might question it if there's a last-minute change of plan.'

'Right,' Hadaway said grimly, nodding at me and looking less annoyed with me for interrupting than I'd expected him to. 'She's banged on about tomorrow night and she's shot herself in the foot. She hasn't got any choice but to do it as planned.'

Fifteen minutes later, the briefing had been wrapped up, Evans and Farley had separated the officers into teams – one for each area circled on the map – and the officers were flooding out of the office, group by group.

Hadaway was in the team going to the posh end of Habely to check out Pace's house, the park that he called a garden and the area around it.

Luke was in the group searching the fields and farmland around where Johnny's car had been found.

Josh and Mack were in the search party heading for Habely Woods, who'd had it hammered into them that there were mine pits up there.

And me and Angie...

Well, we hadn't been picked for shit.

It was just like PE class all over again. Except this time I wasn't hiding in the toilets, wondering if there was any chance of climbing out through the tiny window without getting stuck and keeping my fingers tightly crossed that no-one found me before it was all over.

This time, I actually *wanted* to be on a team.

And let's be honest, after everything we'd done, me and Angie *deserved* to be on one of the teams.

I slid off the windowsill and stood there, rooted to the spot with this angry indignation as I looked around for someone to raise hell with about it, but Farley and Evans were long gone, Luke – the one person I might actually be able to talk into letting us tag along with his team – had disappeared, and I didn't have a clue where Hadaway had gone to.

At least, I didn't. Not until I got lucky and spotted a familiar-looking bicep heading for the door in the last crowd of Bobbies.

Without even thinking about what I was doing, I launched myself towards across the office, joining the back of the crowd and shoving my way through it until I managed to grab hold of Hadaway's arm, yanking him back towards me just as he was about to walk through the door.

'What about me and Angie?' I demanded hotly without any preamble whatsoever, glaring up at him as he moved me out of the way of everyone trying to leave the room. 'What exactly are we supposed to do? Sit here quietly like well-behaved little girls until you get back?'

A pained look passed over his face. 'I was hoping you might.'

I felt my left eyebrow shoot halfway up my forehead. 'We're coming with you.'

'No, you're fucking not.'

'Yes,' I snapped angrily, scowling at him, 'we fucking *are*. Jesus, Hadaway, we've had just as much to do with this case as anyone else has! Why *shouldn't* we come with you?'

'It's too fucking dangerous,' he bit off, nudging me back into the room as that muscle started jigging away on his jaw. 'We have no idea what we're going to find, and if shit hits the fan, I'm not having you two running around, thinking that you're helping.'

'We do f–'

'What happens,' he asked tightly, taking a step closer to me and lowering his voice so that Angie couldn't hear him, 'if we find Johnny and he's not doing as well as we want him to be? How d'you think Angie would react to that?'

I blinked at him a couple of times, feeling a little bit of the anger seep out of me, but not enough to stop me from absolutely *hating* him in that second. I hated him for shutting us out of the case again and I hated him for pretending that we *weren't* helping instead of hindering, but mostly I hated him for being so goddamn *right.*

Because he *was* right. For all she was being an absolute trooper and trying to hide it, Angie was in no state to see Johnny if they found him after Knight had done whatever she'd taken him to do.

'What do you think about her taking Johnny about an hour after she lost Lyme?' I asked abruptly, folding my arms and shooting him a dark look. 'Do you really think that's just a coincidence?'

He eyed me warily for a couple of seconds, almost looking like he was trying to work out whether I was genuinely asking, or if I was trying some out-there new tactic of worming my way into going with him.

'No. I think she likes the idea of having a cop caught up in it.' He jabbed a couple of fingers in Angie's direction, already turning to walk out of the door. 'Don't let her think about it too much. Get her to translate that Latin for us, whatever you can to keep her mind off what's happening.'

Because clearly I would never have thought to do that by myself. 'We didn't bring that notebook with us.'

'Pettyfer's statement is on my desk,' he told me, stopping sideways in the doorway and nodding towards a desk behind me and to my left, which was covered in photos and neatly stacked, criss-crossing piles of paper. Clearly, Pettyfer's wasn't the only statement there. 'You should be able to dig it out easy enough, they're in order.' He paused for a second more, giving me a reluctant look as he ran one hand over the stubble covering the lower half of his face. 'Just do me a favour and stay here, alright? I'll let you know what's happening as soon as I can.'

I gave him a curt nod, but I don't think he even saw it. He'd barely finished his sentence before he was striding out of the door and down the corridor, leaving me standing there, glaring after him and feeling so frustrated, so wound up that my back teeth were weirdly tingly and my skin felt like it was on fire.

But before I could dwell on it for too long, a loud, drawn-out squeak erupted behind me. And when I whipped around on the spot, jumping slightly with my eyes popping wide open, I saw Angie kind of slumping off the windowsill and onto the floor, landing straight on her knees and resting her forehead on the carpet in front of her, and just dissolving into these huge, hysterical, body-shaking sobs.

I didn't move at first. I just stood there, frozen to the spot and staring at her with wide eyes as I felt myself fill with that awkwardness that always comes over me when I'm around crying people.

If she hadn't let out a particularly loud sob that went on for a couple of seconds longer than sobs are supposed to, I have no idea how long I would've stayed there for. As it happened, I was so startled that I accidentally jerked into action, hurrying over to where she was crumpled on the floor and dropping down next to her.

'Angie, it's alright!' I told her anxiously, leaning over her to give her something mildly resembling a hug. And when that more like I was just lying on top of her instead of doing anything to comfort her, I pushed myself back up to sit cross-legged next to her, stroking her hair the way my Mam used to when I was little and I'd cut my knee open. 'Look, *everyone* is out there looking for him! It's going to be *fine,* they're hardly going to come without him, are they?'

I hoped they wouldn't, anyway.

She lifted her head up and wailed something that was far too high-pitched and hysterical for me to understand, and I blinked at her a few times, feeling my eyes wider and wider. What was I supposed to do with that?

'Let's do something,' I told her firmly, grabbing her by the shoulders and dragging her up into a sitting position. 'Let's get your mind off it and focus on something else until they come back, OK? Let's...' I glanced around the room, trying to spot anything non-murder-related that we could use. And when nothing turned up, my eyes landed on the tower of statements on Hadaway's desk. Sod it. 'Let's read some Latin!'

I mean, I don't think being forced to read Latin is much more fun than finding out your boyfriend's been kidnapped. But it was either do that or let her stay there and flood the CID office.

I hurried over to Hadaway's desk and shuffled through the statements covered in Hadaway's handwriting, desperately fighting the urge to settle in and read them all as I flicked past name after name – Bewick, Black, Holland, Jones, Kendall, Mason, Mason, Norton and Partridge, all several pages long – before I finally reached the ones that Pettyfer had given. There were about five of his; the top one, dated a few days after he was arrested, was at least fifteen pages long, while the one from the interview with Hadaway and Cleaner Dave was the shortest of the lot, with a lot more words that I didn't recognise in it than the others did. I pulled it out of the pile and scarpered back to where Angie was sitting, still propped up against the wall and still sobbing hysterically.

Shit.

This 'keep her mind off it' lark really wasn't as easy as Hadaway had made it sound.

I stared at her for a few seconds, gripping the statement so tight with both hands that I was scrunching the paper up, and chewing on my bottom lip as I tried to decide what my best course of action was.

There was literally no-one but us around. I had no medical training. My family was, save for one person, incredibly undramatic. And I'd never known anyone who'd had someone they loved get abducted. I had absolutely *zero* experience with hysterical people.

It really isn't any wonder that I only had one idea and no clue as to whether it'd work or not.

'Angie,' I said gently, crouching down in front of her. And when she pulled away from the wrist she'd been resting her forehead on and turned to look at me, her face all crumpled up and drenched with tears, I –

Look, in my defence, it isn't my proudest moment.

But yeah.

I slapped her.

I slapped her hard.

And without missing a beat, she turned around and slapped me ten times harder.

'What the *fuck*,' she spat furiously, jumping to her feet as I let out a strangled shriek and went sprawling to my left, feeling very much like the wind had been knocked out of me and seeing stars, 'was that for?'

'I just –'

'My boyfriend gets kidnapped and you fucking *slap* me?'

'You were hysterical!'

'Yes! Because *my boyfriend has been kidnapped!* It's one of those situations where you're *allowed* to be hysterical!'

I propped myself up on one elbow, gingerly prodding at the right side of my face, which had broken out in painfully hot tingles from my temple right down to my chin. 'Am I bleeding?'

'I don't give *a fucking shit.*'

I blinked at her a few times, suddenly feeling a little bit upset. She actually meant that, as well. She had that special note of anger in her voice that people save just for when they really, *really* mean what they're saying.

And I got it. I really did. Her boyfriend had been run off the road and kidnapped by a delusional idiot who thought that murder was a hobby; no-one in their right mind would stop worrying about that long enough to give a toss if their best friend was bleeding.

But still, it wasn't like I'd slapped her for the *sake* of it.

'I was trying to help.'

'Well, remind me never to ask for your help again.'

'You were hysterical,' I told her shortly, shoving myself to my feet as I felt the upset give way to prickles of anger. 'I didn't know what else to *do*. Hadaway told me to keep your mind off what's happening, and I couldn't –'

'Since when do you do what Hadaway tells you to do?'

'– I couldn't even get you to *look* at me, Angie! What else was I supposed to do?'

'Google it!'

We looked at each other for a good while, probably close to a minute, with both of us breathing heavily and Angie looking even more pissed off than I felt, an ugly red blotch growing on her right cheek.

'I was trying to *help*.'

'I tell you what, Tidge,' she said coldly, giving me the stoniest look as she held her hand out towards me. 'Give me the statement and leave me the fuck alone.'

I shoved the papers at her, giving her a hard look of my own before I turned and marched away from her, heading for the whiteboard without really paying attention to where I was going.

Jesus.

That was the last time I slapped someone going through a serious emotional turmoil.

I glowered at all of the notes and photos that CID had pinned to their boards, reading them mainly so that I'd have something to look at other than Angie, and at first, I was too angry to really take any of it in. But the less my cheek hurt, the less angry I was, and before I even realised it, I was genuinely reading everything that was stuck up there.

A lot of it was similar to what me and Angie had written on the Scribbley Wall, but - probably not surprisingly – they also knew things that me and Angie had no way of finding out.

They'd drawn up a list of all the backgrounds of the lads Knight had had killed, highlighting the very few similarities between them. They'd all come from decent, stable families and only had one sibling, always a sister, be it younger or older than them; they all played for some local sports team or another, but not one of them played for the same team as any of the others; none of them had ever had a girlfriend, at school or since; and none of them had ever met a girl called Elodia, Knight or anything similar.

They had toxicology reports for each of the lads, showing that they all had traces of cocaine, roofies and ketamine in their system, and I wondered if Lyme's toxicology report would show the same things; after all, a cocktail like that would definitely explain how Knight had such tight control over them.

They had photos of all the victims, photos of the evidence collected from where the bodies had been found and other places that they'd been investigating, DNA test results, and –

'This isn't Latin.'

I blinked a few times as I whirled around on the spot, ripping myself away from the notes so abruptly that I felt slightly disorientated. 'What?'

'This,' she said, wafting the statement at me. 'Whatever Ade's written down here, it's not Latin. It's not spelled right.'

I stared at her for a few seconds, waiting for her to listen to what she'd just said. And when it became apparent that that wasn't going to happen, I pointed out dryly,

'Yeah, well, I don't think Hadaway *studied* Latin, Angie. It's not exactly a common subject. What about if you sound it out?' I added brusquely, before she could slap me again. 'Does it sound like anything Latin then?'

She looked back at the page. 'I don't know. I'm sure he probably has written it down as it sounds, but... 'may I esta dee mature' doesn't mean anything to me. It doesn't make *sense.*'

None of what Knight was doing made sense, but I didn't want to point that while we were talking and not yelling.

'That was from the interview I was in,' I told her, sidling over to her so that I could see the statement too. 'That's exactly what he said.'

She shot me a sidelong glance. 'You actually heard him say it?'

'Aye. That was the day he wanted to talk to Cleaner Dave.'

She pointed to the words on the page. 'Say that, but faster.'

'Mayiestademature.'

'Right,' she said slowly, staring at me like I was a moron. 'Let's try it a tiny slower and a lot more Exleigh-ish.'

'May-ah estah neema tour.'

'May-ah estah neema tour? You mean...' she glanced down at the statement, and her face cleared in recognition. 'Mea est anima tua?'

'That's what I said.'

'I actually know this,' she told me almost excitedly, instead of pointing out that that was not, in fact, what I had said. 'Some lass in my Latin class wanted something out there and 'romantic' to say to her boyfriend, and this is the only thing our teacher gave her that she decided was good enough. It wasn't Knight,' she added hastily, just as I opened my mouth to ask that very question. 'It was some creepy, intense girl who was properly obsessed with whichever boyfriend she had at the time.'

'Fantastic story,' I said politely, even though I'd heard better stories from her nephew. 'What does it *mean?*'

'Well, this bit means "my soul is yours",' she said, following the statement with her finger. 'And this first bit –' she let out a sudden giggle as she read the words. 'Eggo dabbo teeny Mam may I?'

'That's what he said,' I told her, suddenly feeling surprisingly defensive on Hadaway's behalf. 'That's exactly what it sounded like.'

'If I'm right...' she broke off and stared at the paper for a couple of seconds, chewing on her bottom lip. 'If I'm right, and Knight's just ripped all of this from what that lass wanted to tell her boyfriend, then I think he means ego dabo te anima mea. It's "I give you my soul."'

I blinked at her a couple of times. 'I give you my soul, my soul is yours?'

'Yeah. I remember it because it was so bloody *weird.* Why couldn't she just tell him she loved him like a normal person?'

I took the statement off her and stared at the words, feeling a little weirded out myself. What was it with Knight and souls? Why did she want people to think she could get into their soul, or actually *give* her their soul? And why would the Cloaks *want* to give her their souls? (Just to be clear, I do know that you can't actually *give* someone your soul. I mean, it's not like there are any Food Banks just for souls being set up anywhere, or last I heard, soul transplant operations do not exist. But still.)

The Cloaks had told me on Tuesday night that the Procedure would help Knight get to where she wanted to be. Is that what they thought the whole thing was about? That the lads were giving their souls to her? But surely they must've noticed that how the lads "gave" their souls to her and how the Cloaks did it were two very different things? Unless... was there supposed to be some kind of a difference between the souls that were happily donated to her, and the ones that she decided to take?

I didn't get it.

I didn't get it in the slightest, and trying to work it out was giving me a headache.

'Let's take a break,' I said abruptly, hoping that Angie wasn't having similar thoughts and realising that Johnny's soul was next on the chopping block. 'How about some coffee?'

Hadaway's team got back to the office around two o'clock in the morning, half an hour after the other teams had come back. And as much as everyone looked frustrated and disappointed after having found zero signs of Johnny, Pace or Knight anywhere, Hadaway was by far the most grim-faced out of them, even more than Angie, who – instead of going down the grim route – had just got quieter and quieter and looked more and more upset as each of the teams turned up empty-handed.

We handed over Angie's translations of the chanting and stuck around for the debrief, which was just five minutes of Farley thanking everyone for what they'd done that night, arranging for some night-shift Response officers to stakeout the places where Knight was most likely to turn up, and sending everyone else home to get some kip so that they (we) were ready for whatever they (we) would have to do later that day.

By the time we got back to the flat, we were all completely exhausted. We'd been awake for close to twenty-four hours and it'd been a hellishly long day, one that was only made even more tiring by finding out that Pace had been in on it the whole time and knowing that Johnny was stuck somewhere with the psychopaths. I mean, I was absolutely bone-tired, to the point where I felt like I was wading through knee-high treacle every time I tried to take a step; people have climbed Everest easier than I got up those stairs.

'Right,' Angie said tiredly, the second the flat door closed behind us. 'I'm going to try and grab a couple of hours. If you hear anything about Johnny,' she added to Hadaway, 'you'll wake me up, won't you?'

'Course I will.'

'D'you want me to bunk down with you?' I asked her, taking a single step forward as she headed for her bedroom. 'Keep you some company?'

She shot me a grim smile as she reached her door. 'Thanks, Tidge, but I'll be fine. I just want to get my head down and pull myself together.'

We watched her disappeared into her room, and in the fraction of a second before the door closed behind her, I saw her face crumple. I felt a little pang of guilt at not barging in and making sure she was alright, but in all honesty, I'd been friends with Angie long enough to know that I was doing the right thing; forcing company on her when all she wanted was a bit of privacy would not end well for me.

I turned around to face Hadaway, who looked like he was trying hard not to fall asleep on the spot. Johnny was the man's best friend; I thought it was only fair that someone checked up on him as well. 'And how're you doing? Are you alright?'

He grunted.

Fantastic.

Like I was supposed to know what that meant.

I glanced over at Angie's bedroom door and took a step closer to him, lowering my voice so that she couldn't hear me. 'Do you think they'll turn up anywhere we're watching?'

'No,' he told me grimly, after shooting a furtive look of his own at Angie's door. 'If they were going to do that, they'd have done it before now. I think they've gone somewhere we don't know about.' Hmm. Didn't really give me the heart-warming feeling I'd been hoping for. 'Go to bed,' he added wearily, putting one hand at the small of my back and nudging me towards my bedroom. 'You'll need all the energy you can get for tomorrow.'

I obediently dragged myself over to my room, too tired even to point out that we were actually talking about today and not tomorrow, suddenly more desperate for my sleep than I could ever remember being.

It wasn't until I'd closed the door behind me that I realised the room was in no way how I'd left it.

I hadn't left all of my dresser drawers open, with all of the contents rumpled up and spilling over the top of them.

I hadn't left my wardrobe doors wide open, or dumped all of my clothes on the floor in front of it.

And beyond a shadow of a doubt, I had absolutely not left Elodia Knight sitting on my bed.

SIXTEEN.

I whirled around on the spot and grabbed tight hold of the door handle, fully intending to storm back out and get Hadaway to slap some cuffs on the bitch. But here's the thing – my door wouldn't open. And while mine does like to stick in its frame every now and again, our bedroom doors are not the locking type.

I yanked on it a couple more times, making the door rattle against its frame, but it wouldn't budge. If anything, it almost felt like the stupid thing was stuck in that treacle I'd just been trudging through.

'It's not going to open, Armitage,' Knight told me smugly from the bed. 'I've made sure of that.'

I turned around to face her, keeping my back pressed against the door and making a mental note to fire Squidge as Guard Dog the second I was out of that room. 'Let me out.'

'No.'

'I wasn't asking. *Let me out.*'

'No,' she said again, looking far too comfortable as she sat slap-bang in the centre of my bed, cross-legged. 'Not until we've had a little chat.'

I felt an eruption of red-hot anger in my stomach, fizzing up until it burned the back of my throat and making my hands shake slightly. 'OK. Fine. Let's chat. Where's Johnny?'

'He's fine,' she told me lazily, finally unfolding her legs and pushing herself up off the bed. 'He's safe. I'm much more interested in talking about what *you* have of *mine.*'

'I don't know what you're talking about,' I told her coldly, and then I turned back around and yanked on my door a few times, as hard as I could. But nope. It still wouldn't budge.

What the fuck was wrong with it? What'd she done to my door?

'Oh, don't play dumb, Armitage,' she laughed, and she could sound breezy all she wanted to; I didn't miss that freezing cold note underneath it. 'Just tell me where it is and I won't get mad.'

'I don't give a shit if you get mad,' I snapped frostily over my shoulder, digging what little nails I had into my palms in frustration. This was just fricking... this was *shit*. How long had Hadaway and the others spent looking for the stupid bitch that night? Four hours? Four and a half? And what, had she just been sitting on my bed *the entire time?* 'I don't have anything of yours. I don't *want* anything of yours, except maybe your head on a block. So get as angry as you like, it's not going to make a blind bit of difference.' I pounded a fist on the door, just once, as hard as I could. 'Hadaway!'

'That's a bit of a risky thing to say,' Knight commented lightly, and when I glanced back at her, she was stood next to my bed, examining her fingernails. 'After all, I didn't say I'd get mad with *you.*'

I turned around again, feeling my stomach drop to somewhere in the region of my ankles. 'I swear to God, if you fucking touch him −'

'Armitage,' Hadaway's grumpy, tired voice interrupted me from the other side of the door. 'What the hell are you doing?'

'I'm not *doing* anything,' I told him shortly, turning my head slightly but keeping my eyes glommed on Knight. 'I just wanted to let you know that I found out where Knight is.'

There were several seconds of stunned silence before he said incredulously,

'You're fucking kidding me.'

'Here's what we're going to do,' Knight said lightly, before I could tell Hadaway that I was not, in fact, having his life. 'You're going to stop talking to your boyfriend out there. You're going to give me *my goddamn wand back*. And then you're going to take that pretty little nose of yours and put it somewhere that is *not* my business.'

I blinked at her, too surprised by one particular part of that sentence to pay much attention to the rest of it. 'Your *wand?*'

The door jolted against my back, and then it jerked against me again, and then Hadaway's voice was coming from the other side again, considerably more urgently this time.

'Armitage. Let me in.'

'Yes,' Knight said crisply, taking a step forwards. 'My wand. I know you have it, and if you hand it over now, it won't go anything further than that.' She shot me a tight smile. 'I'd rather avoid any violence, between you and me. I need to save my energy for tonight.'

'I *can't* let you in,' I snapped at Hadaway, as the door pushed against me again. 'She's done something to the door, it won't open. Christ, d'you really think I'd stay in here with her by *choice?*' And then I turned back to Knight, glaring at her as I heard Hadaway hiss a particularly enthusiastic swear word in the living room. 'I don't have your fucking wand. I've never even *seen* the stupid thing. But you're such a powerful witch, Kathie, why don't you just go ahead and do whatever you need to do without it?'

I saw what little colour was in her face drain from it, and suddenly she was pulling back slightly, lifting her chin up as she gave me a stony look. Clearly, this was not a person who appreciated the use of But before either of us could say anything, there was a massive thud from behind me, and at the same time, the door jolted into me so hard that it sent me stumbling forward a couple of steps.

Straight into Knight's open palm.

Her hand smacked into my cheek so hard that I couldn't see anything but stars for a good couple of seconds. and the left side of my face skin immediately erupted into a thousand hot, sharp prickles, like tiny little knives were stabbing me all over it.

There was another loud bang and even more swearing from the other side of the door as my vision cleared, and as the shock of being slapped wore off, all of that anger came back, so strong that I could feel it everywhere, to the point where my knees were like hot jelly and my fingertips were itchy.

It was like the anger had a mind of its own, and what that mind wanted to do was punch the bitch.

Hard.

My fist slammed into the side of her face so hard that pain shot through my knuckles, but before she could react more than shrieking and covering her face, before I could register how much my hand was hurting, I grabbed her by the hair and slammed her forehead down onto the nearest wooden bedpost. I was just hauling her head back up to do it again when she punched me in the stomach, hard enough to make me loosen my grip on her with a little grunt, and in what seemed like less than a second, she'd ducked away from me and slugged me to the chin with a killer upper-cut. I felt a sharp pop in my neck as my head rocketed back, and just as there was a series of fast, heavy thuds on the door, she flung herself on me, getting her arm around my neck and forcing me down until I was bent over, and then she dragged me onto the bed, scrabbling onto my back and pushing my face into the duvet as she wrapped her hands around my neck.

'I *want*,' she hissed viciously in my ear, squeezing, 'my wand *back. Now.*'

I tried to tell her again that I didn't have it, but my face was squashed into the duvet so much that I couldn't breathe, let alone make any noise, and she had me at an angle where it was hard to fight back against her; I kept trying to push myself up, but for someone so slight, she was surprisingly heavy, and I couldn't lift myself up very far before she managed to force me back down again. I could hear Angie frantically gabbling away to Hadaway over the thuds against the door, and I planted my feet on the carpet as hard as I could, trying to pull myself out from underneath her, but I had as much luck with that as I did when I tried to lift myself up.

And by this point, the panic from not being able to breathe was really starting to set in.

I swung both of my hands backwards, desperately trying to make contact something, but the first few times all I hit was air. It must've been on the fourth or fifth try that I finally caught her, and it wasn't hard by any stretch, but it was enough to startle her enough that she lifted herself up slightly, just by a couple of inches but enough for me to haul myself out from under her, ripping her hands off my neck at the same time. I shoved myself to my feet and slugged her again before she had time to react, hitting her in her nose – which, I have to say, looked more bruised and swollen than it had done before our scuffle a couple of nights earlier – so that she reeled backwards, blinking frantically and sounding like she was trying to gulp down air as blood shot out from her nostrils. I shoved my way past her, taking in as much air as I could myself as I darted towards my bedside table, where that stupid witchcraft book was still sitting. Except that before I could get my hands on it, before I could even reach the table, she came charging at me, slamming into me from behind and shoving into me almost immediately, so that I was sandwiched between her and the wall hard enough to knock the wind out of me.

You really do take this breathing malarkey for granted until you can't do it.

I tried to shove her away from me, but because I couldn't get any air back in my lungs, I hardly had the strength to do it, and suddenly she had one hand clutching at the hair around my left temple and her right arm around my neck, and before I could do anything, she was dragging me a few steps backwards, back towards the wardrobe we'd locked her in the day before, except that instead of going that far, she stopped right in front of my bedroom window. She smashed my head into the window, and then she did again, and then once more for good luck, and on the third time I heard a tinkling kind of crack and something warm and sticky started trickling down the side of my face.

I could hear Angie calling my name from the other side of the door, but I was too busy dealing with Knight to bother answering; just as she went to smack my head into the window for a fourth time, I grabbed hold of the arm she had around my neck and pulled it away from me, and then I moved, ducking away from her and whirling to my left, twisting her arm with me as I almost doing a complete 180, until I was stood more or less directly behind her. Her forehead was on my windowsill and her left arm was twisted right around, her elbow pointing up at the ceiling as I forced her arm up her back and leaned on her as hard as I could, growling,

'Where *the fuck* is Johnny? What d'you want him for?'

She let out a laugh, but it didn't sound like she found anything funny; it was short and halting, like she was in too much pain to pretend she found the whole thing amusing for very long. 'Do you really think I'm going to tell you that?'

I glanced up by a few inches, still leaning on her with as much force as I had and trying to catch my breath as I thought about what my next move should be – and completely by chance, my gaze landed on the window pane that she'd whacked my head into, which was considerably more smashed than it had been a few hours ago.

And by smashed, I mean that there was a wide enough hole in it that I could feel quite a nice breeze coming in from outside.

That's the only thing I could think of that could've given me the idea.

'Tell me the fuck where he is,' I hissed in her ear, tightening my grip on her hair as much as I could so that it would hurt her as much as possible, and I could actually hear strand after strand snapping away from her scalp, 'or I swear to God, Knight, I will throw you through this fucking window.'

She wriggled frantically, tossing from side-to-side so hard that a cowboy tackling a bucking bronco would have nothing on me, but I held on as tight as I could, and just as the wail of sirens filled the air – I could only assume that Angie or Mrs Miller had called for them, since Hadaway was still giving his all to booting down the door – I slammed *her* head into the window, as hard as I could. I don't know if it was because the window was already more weakened than it was supposed to be or because of the force, but the whole pane – right from the top of the frame down to the windowsill – shattered like an egg on impact, making any number of shards rain down onto the shrubs and pavement at the front of the house and letting an even bigger breeze into my room. I reeled her head back, and before I really had time to notice how floppy she'd gone, I smashed it into the next pane along; this time, even more glass pieces fired out into the sky before twinkling down to the ground below my window. But before I could shove her head through the third and final pane, she suddenly came back to life, shoving me off her with a surprising amount of force and scrambling up onto my windowsill, grasping onto the panes in a way that made it perfectly clear that she had no concerns about cutting herself on the leftover shards.

And suddenly three things were happening all at once.

One was that I heard the door *finally* explode open, and suddenly – without any hesitation whatsoever – footsteps were charging up behind me.

Another was that I saw, almost in slow-motion, Knight crouching down enough to crawl through the pane to the left pane of my window and making like she was going to throw herself through it, perfectly happy with her chances of hitting the shrubs below.

And the third was that – before I had a chance to think about it, and definitely before I knew what I was doing – I'd launched myself after her with both of my arms stretched out in front of me, determined that she wasn't going to be getting away this time, and catching hold of one of her ankles at the very last second.

She swung downwards, halted in mid-air by my hand, and I felt my feet leave my bedroom floor.

And the next thing I knew, I was following her out of the window.

For what felt like half an hour but could really only have been a second or two, we were flying through the air, and at first, my grip on her ankle as tight as ever; but somewhere between my bedroom and the ground, and for no reason at all, her foot slipped from my grasp, and I had no idea where she'd gone.

Luckily for me, I didn't get much chance to worry about that before I tumbled even further forwards – *literally* going arse over tit – and my head collided with something incredibly solid and just as rough.

And suddenly everything went black.

Fucking *again.*

SEVENTEEN.

I woke up however long later, feeling just as disorientated as I do after a heavy sesh and wondering why there were so many people milling about around me.

I didn't know where I was.

I had no idea how long I'd been there for.

All I knew was that the right side of my forehead was stinging like mad and I was terrified to check my phone in case I'd sent any messages that I was going to regret.

It took me longer than it should've done to realise that I was laid out on the settee in our living room, and that I had something cold and wet pressing against the sore part of my head and something much warmer and cosier across my knees.

I put one hand up to the side of my head, trying to figure out what was going on with it, but instead of touching skin, my fingers hit something that felt a lot like thick cotton that was soaking wet and filled with something solid and lumpy. Which was interesting, because I didn't remember anything like that growing out of the side of my head.

'Morning, sleepyhead,' a voice to my right said croakily, and when I whipped my head around to see who was talking, I saw Angie sitting on the coffee table, giving me a sad little smile and leaning forward slightly as she pressed the cold, lumpy thing against me. 'How're you feeling?'

I blinked at her, feeling even more confused than I had been a couple of seconds earlier. Why was Angie sad? Why was she pressing something cold onto me? 'What's going on?'

She shot me a tiny frown, suddenly looking a lot more concerned than she did sad. 'What do you think's going on?'

We stared at each other for a few seconds, and when I didn't do anything other than look blank, she pulled her hand away from me and put the flannel full of ice-cubes she was holding down on the coffee table.

'What's the last thing you remember?'

'I don't know,' I told her honestly, propping myself up on one elbow as I racked my brains.

Well.

'Racking' might be a slight exaggeration. I'd barely put any effort into remembering what'd happened when it all came flooding back to me.

Johnny getting kidnapped.

The search parties coming back to East District without him.

Walking into my bedroom to find Knight making herself at home on my bed.

Fighting with the bitch and trying to stop her from climbing out of the window, only to have her make me overbalance and fall out after her.

Shit.

'Where is she?' I demanded hotly, scrambling to my feet and dislodging Squidge, who'd been sitting with his chin resting across my legs. 'Where's Knight?'

'Tidge –'

She cut herself off and shot me a resigned grimace instead of actually breaking the news, and I felt that red-hot anger bubble up inside of me again as I stared at her incredulously.

'You're having me on.'

'I'm not. She'd already cleared off by the time we got to you, we don't know where she is.'

'By the time you got to me?' I blurted out in frustration, feeling my eyes get considerably wider. 'How long did you bloody *leave* me there for?'

'Well, it's not like you were there *hours*,' she said indignantly. 'We came after you the second we saw you go through that window!'

To be honest, I'd already stopped listening; instead, I was spinning around on the spot to looking for Hadaway.

As it turned out, all the people I'd clocked when I woke up were Bobbies; some were in plainclothes and some were in high-vis vests, and all of them were crawling all over the flat, putting things that had nothing to do with Knight in evidence bags, poking around in cupboards and under chairs, and dusting any surface they could find for fingerprints, DNA or footprint marks.

But none of them were Hadaway.

It's never hard to spot him; for whatever reason, the man stands out in any room like he's got a sodding spotlight on him. And even if he didn't, nobody else in the flat had biceps like he does.

'Tidge,' Angie told me patiently, reaching up to put one hand on my back. 'You need to sit down.'

'No,' I told her shortly, even though I really wanted to. Every inch of me was pulsing with a dull ache, almost like toothache. Except that instead of being in my teeth, it was everywhere but; genuinely, I think the only place where I didn't hurt was my fingernails. 'Where's Hadaway?'

'He's in the bathroom, fixing that stupid window. He thinks that's how she got in again. Tidge, come on, sit *down*.'

I did not sit down.

I didn't *want* to sit down. What I wanted was to find out exactly how the hell Knight had got away again.

It didn't make *sense*. I *knew* that Angie and Hadaway would've come and got me the second they saw me fall, even before Angie had told me that that's what they'd done. And let's say they'd come over to the window to make sure neither of us were clinging to the outside windowsill, or maybe they'd just stood there in shock before reacting. That gives us, what? Four seconds? Five? Add that to the fact that it takes roughly a minute to get from my bedroom to the front door, and you're giving Knight next to no time to get herself out of there. And I'm not just talking out of our front garden or out of the street, but out of the actual *estate*; I had no doubt that, regardless of what kind of shape I'd been in when they'd found me, Hadaway would've tried to chase after her, even if he'd only gone to the corner of the road to see if there was any sign of her. So how'd she managed to get herself up off the ground and high-tail it out of there *seconds* after falling out of the window?

How had not she not been *hurt?* Did the woman fricking *bounce?*

Why hadn't *I* bounced?

Before Angie could tell me to sit down again or say anything else, I dove into the crowd of cops filling our flat and shoved my way through them, trying to stop myself from feeling irrationally annoyed with her and Hadaway.

I mean, I *knew* it wasn't their fault that Knight had got away again. I *knew* they'd have done everything they could, especially given that they were by alone with an unconscious lass with a head injury. And I really didn't blame them for it. I was just so frustrated and pissed off with the whole situation that I needed someone *real* to take it out on, and unfortunately for them, they were the easiest targets.

I fought my way through the Bobbies until I reached the bathroom door, and before I'd fully registered the whole scene in the room, my feet stopped dead right where the carpet met the tiles.

Hadaway was stood at the opposite end of the bathroom to the door, wedged into the tiny gap between the toilet and the bathtub with an open toolbox at his feet. He was working hard on screwing something into the window frame, and I don't know *exactly* what he was screwing in or where he was putting it, but it was making the muscles in his biceps and arms flex in a very lovely way.

It made me feel warm in places Hadaway wasn't supposed to make me feel warm.

It also made it considerably harder to breathe.

'You're awake,' Luke said lightly, giving me a little jolt of surprise and snapping me out of whatever daze I'd been in. I'd been so mesmerised by The Biceps that while I'd been vaguely aware of a human-shaped blur to the left, I hadn't realised that it was Luke. He'd taken his high-vis vest off and was perched on the side of our bath, his arms folded over his chest and his head craned around so that he could see Hadaway work on the window. (Or he had been. Obviously he was looking at me now.) 'How are you feeling?'

'I'm fine,' I told him, my voice coming out a bit shorter than I meant it to. Why did people keep asking me that? 'Bit sore, but that's about it, really.'

He nodded at me, obviously meaning to point something out. 'Your head's a mess.'

'My head's been a mess since yesterday morning,' I told him dryly before turning to Hadaway, who'd put his screwdriver down and turned around to face me, his own arms crossed and a slight frown on his face. 'Angie said Knight got away again.'

He grunted, beckoning me over to him with two fingers. 'Let me see your head.'

'I don't understand how she did it,' I said, as I obediently trotted over to him. 'She must've had *some* kind of injury after falling out of that window. I don't see how it didn't slow her down. Unless...' I blinked at him as the thought occurred to me. 'D'you think someone else was with her and got her out of there?'

He shook his head grimly, just the once, putting one hand on my chin and using the other to brush my hair back off my face. 'No. I didn't see anyone out there, and there weren't any cars around. However she got away, she did it by herself.' He gently turned my head to my left to get a better look at my forehead, frowning slightly as he lightly brushed his thumb over the stinging patch. 'How's it feel?'

'Sore,' I admitted, letting him tilt my head back by a smidge. 'And a bit like it's on fire, but I'll live.'

He grunted again, his face becoming even more grim. 'You took a hell of a whack to it.'

'Did I?'

'Aye. It took us a good while to stop the bleeding. We didn't know whether we should take you to hospital or not.'

The look on his face told me that it was Angie who'd put the kibosh on that little idea.

'I'm fine,' I told him hastily, taking a step backwards before he could decide to throw me in the car and drag me to the hospital after all. And then, just to change the subject as quickly as possible, I added casually, 'Where'd those tools come from?'

'He sent me to get them from his house,' Luke said lightly before Hadaway could answer me, shooting me a bland smile. 'I didn't mind. Now, he never would've asked me to do it if there were any major cases going on, but' – the grin got a touch more mischievous – 'luckily that's not the case here.'

I felt a grin spread itself across my face, but before I could say anything, Hadaway was looking at him like he wanted nothing more than to give him a swift smack across the head.

'I dunno what you're complaining about. It got you out of doing some work, didn't it?'

A loud laugh burst out of me before I could stop it, and I tried to cover it up with a cough as quickly as I could.

Not that I didn't appreciate what he was doing, but I could see both sides.

I mean, given everything that was going on, it did seem like a bit of an odd time to start doing DIY.

But if Hadaway was right and Knight had got in through that window again – and why wouldn't she have, if she'd already done it once and knew it worked? – then yeah, I wanted it sorting as soon as possible. I didn't *want* her coming and going through it as often as she liked, like we had some kind of cat-flap that was just for psychopaths. And really, why *shouldn't* he be fixing it now? It wasn't like there weren't twenty-odd officers in the other rooms, already doing the only things that any Bobbies *could* do at that point. (To be honest, I had no idea why they'd insisted on having so many people there at the same time.) If you asked me, Hadaway had already done his fair share of work around Knight breaking into our flat again – after all, he was the one who'd kicked my bedroom door in; he was the one who'd came charging after me with Angie; he must've been the one who carried me back into the flat; and more likely than not, he was the one who'd got all the other Bobbies there. If he wanted to chill out with a bit of DIY, why not?

'So,' I asked Hadaway, before either of them could say anything else to needle the other. 'What're our next steps?'

He let go of my chin and folded his arms across his chest as he took a step back, fixing me with a hard look, and I felt a sinking feeling in my stomach as I braced myself for the inevitable reminder that there was no 'us', 'we' or 'our' in this case.

Except that, this time, it never came.

Instead, he told me grimly,

'I think we need to get everyone working the case 'round here for a look at your Wall.'

I blinked at him a few times, my face suddenly tingling with surprise.

What was going on?

When I'd hit the side of the house, had I knocked myself into a parallel universe where Hadaway actually *wanted* us to help with the case?

Or was he ill? Or too exhausted to know what he was saying?

Don't get me wrong, I wasn't *complaining* that he was happy to have us help. I was just more taken aback than I could remember being.

About anything.

Ever.

Luke glanced from Hadaway to me and back again, looking more than a little bit interested. 'What wall is this?'

'They've been making notes about the case on Armitage's bedroom wall,' Hadaway explained, without taking his eyes off me. 'It could be worth a look before tomorrow night, they've got some decent stuff up there.'

Something warm and fuzzy spread through my stomach as I beamed at him, suddenly feeling ridiculously proud of me and Angie. (I decided that reminding him Knight's grand finale was actually that night and not the next would ruin the moment.) At least, I did until he added baldly,

'It's not going to do any harm at this stage, anyway.'

Mmm.

OK.

Not a parallel universe, then. Or an unexpectedly nice Hadaway.

Just a 'we'll take what we can get' mentality.

'Fine,' I said shortly, feeling my face drop the smile and settle into a slight frown. 'And then what?'

He shrugged. 'Then we do what we can to find her. See if we can stop her from going to the Woods, and if we can't, we'll meet her there.' He eyed me thoughtfully for a couple of seconds, scratching the right side of his jaw with his left hand. 'How d'you feel about talking everyone through your Wall?'

'Peachy,' I told him coolly, even though I've literally had nightmares about public speaking. 'Although I don't know how you'll fit everyone in there.'

'Don't worry about that,' he said affably, and I felt a jolt of surprise shoot through all the irritation at how blasé he was being. 'We'll work something out. Right, then,' he added with an air of finality, grabbing the screwdrivers he'd been using off the windowsill and chucking them into his toolbox. 'I'll go and make some calls.'

I took a couple of steps backwards and squeezed into the gap between the toilet and the sink to let him past. He'd barely reached the bathroom door before something from earlier that night or morning or whatever time of day it was classed as – something that I'd forgot about completely – popped into my head.

'Hang on a minute, Hadaway,' I blurted out, without thinking about it. 'I don't know if you's have already got something on this or not, but... Knight said she came here to get her wand back.'

He stopped dead and turned to look at me, frowning slightly. 'Her wand?'

'Yeah. I don't know what she's talking about,' I added, when he didn't say anything. 'I've never seen anything even resembling a wand. But for whatever reason, she's adamant that I've got it.'

We stared at each other for a few seconds, Hadaway still frowning slightly and me wondering if he believed me or if he thought I was talking shit due to my undiagnosed concussion.

I had no idea why Knight wanted a wand. I had no idea why Knight wanted people to think she *needed* a wand, when she was so determined to make them think she was this all-powerful being. Wouldn't it ruin the illusion slightly if she was stood there, waving around the sort of toy wand you get with *Harry Potter* dress-up sets? (Obviously, I had no idea what it looked like. I was just guessing that's what she'd use, based purely on the fact that she was a stark raving lunatic.)

Unless that was what the whole procedure was *about?* Making them think she could do all things witchy all by herself, without needing anything to help her?

I couldn't help but feel like it was a hell of a lot of effort to go to when she could just pitch up to one of the meetings and be all, 'oh, guess what, I had a really good sleep last night and now I don't need a wand anymore'.

It was Luke who eventually broke the silence between us. 'Have you lot got anything on that, mate?'

'No,' Hadaway said brusquely, running one hand over his stubble (which, I have to say, was looking rather good). 'No-one we've talked to has mentioned it.' He eyeballed me for a second longer, and there was something in his face that told me it made just as much sense to him as it did to me. But before I could say anything else, he was shooting me a brief nod and telling me, 'Make sure you mention it in your briefing.'

I felt a little jolt of alarm. A briefing?

He thought I was doing a *briefing?* What'd happened to just talking people through what we'd found out? I'd thought that meant reading out the notes that they could easily read for themselves, not doing a *briefing*.

The thing is, I didn't quite manage to say that to him. Before I even got chance to open my mouth, he was turning around again and striding out of the bathroom, already pulling his phone out of his pocket as he disappeared into the crowd of officers on the other side of the door.

An hour later, I was feeling decidedly fuzzy from a lack of sleep and stood in front of my Scribbley Wall, facing a room full of officers.

There were Response officers, some wearing their vests and some not; CID officers; officers from the MIT who somehow had the energy to put on a shirt and tie at five o'clock in the morning; even Farley and Evans were there, squeezing together and cramming into any bit of space they could find with everyone else. They were sat on the floor, perched on the windowsill of my now boarded-up window, standing three deep around the walls, and about fifteen of them had managed to pile onto my bed, three of them even delicately sitting on my headrest. And even then, there were at least ten of them crowding around the other side of my door, standing on the tiptoes to peer over the heads of everyone who was stopping them from getting into my room.

I glanced at Angie, who was stood next to me and looking just as daunted as I felt. There must've only been the same amount of them that there had been in the CID office, but somehow – either because of how much smaller my room was or because of how nervous I was – it seemed like there was a lot more, maybe even double.

I took a deep breath, remembering what Hadaway had told me when he'd realised how nervous I was about the number of people pitching up ('look, everyone here's on your side'), and launched into it without any real preamble, because the idea of starting by welcoming them to Armitage's Room seemed like it'd stop them from taking us as seriously as we needed them to.

We went through everything with them.

We started with how I'd typed up Knight's interview and saw her make all the bones in her face stick out, and we talked them through it all; going to see Pettyfer and Pace, interrupting Knight and the Cloaks a few nights earlier, Knight breaking into our flat, finding out that Pace was in on the whole thing... everything, *everything*, right up to how Knight thought that I had this wand of hers.

And the whole time we were talking, none of them moved a muscle. None of them laughed, or asked why these two random lasses had been pulling together so much information about what Knight was up to; they just sat there, their eyes glued on us and the Scribbley Wall as they took it all in. I even saw a few of them taking *notes.*

'This is really good work,' Farley boomed from the back of the crowd near the door once we'd wrapped up, and there was a slight rumble as fifty-odd heads swivelled to face him. 'Very impressive. You should be proud of yourselves. Having said that,' he added sternly, fixing us with a frown before I could feel too thrilled about that, 'I don't know why you've got yourselves involved in this case.'

I blinked at him, opening and closing my mouth a few times as I tried to think of something to say that sounded better than 'because it's too interesting a case not to' and hoping against hope that he wasn't going to follow Hadaway's lead now that we'd handed over everything we knew. But before I could get any words out, he was carrying on, sounding for all the world like he hadn't just pulled off a magnificently dramatic pause.

'But since you have, I want to know what your feeling is.'

I blinked at him a few more times. 'My feeling?'

My feeling was tired, more than anything. Tired with a side dish of confusion about exactly what he was asking me.

'Aye. Of everyone in this room,' he added, when I just looked at him blankly, 'you're the only one who's met her. You're the only one who's spoken to her. What d'you think?'

'I think she's a raging psychopath,' I told him baldly, and then – when he looked at me in a way that said he wanted me to do more than state the obvious – I added, 'I don't think she's as clever as she thinks she is. She's so convinced that she's pulling off the most amazing thing anyone's ever thought of and no-one can see through it, but she's getting so confident that she's making daft mistakes. Things like sending Angie that Friend Request; we might never have realised who she really is if she hadn't done that. And kidnapping Johnny was a stupid move, because now she's being watched by the Police even more than she was before. Let's face it, she could've kidnapped any random person and we wouldn't have found out about it for hours, maybe even a couple of days – but because she's gone after another cop, you lot have found out about it pretty much immediately and been straight on her. And then there's this wand that she was banging on about; if she so desperately needs it, you'd think she'd have kept an extra-close eye on it. But instead, she's lost it somewhere.'

'You think she's unravelling.'

'Not *unravelling* as such,' I said carefully, frowning slightly as I thought about it. 'I reckon she could still throw something at you that you don't expect if you put a foot wrong. But she thinks she's beyond getting caught, and it's making her sloppy. Which begs the question,' I added, shrugging, 'that if tonight goes how she wants it to, how long she can keep going for before she has a major slip-up.'

I heard Angie take a sharp inhale, and winced slightly, kicking myself.

Shit.

I probably could've phrased that a lot better than basically 'how long after she's killed Angie's boyfriend will she cock up'.

'Well, we won't be waiting around to find out,' Farley said firmly, and then there was a small, oddly loaded pause as he squinted at me thoughtfully. 'D'you think she's expecting you to turn up at this Procedure whatsit tonight?'

I looked at him in surprise. To be honest, I'd never thought about what she was expecting. I think on some level I'd already decided that me and Angie would be in that clearing ahead of this stupid Procedure – but I couldn't say it'd been a conscious thing, and I definitely didn't know how Knight was going to react.

But before I could say anything, there was a sudden movement to my left. And when I looked, Hadaway – who was stood with his arms crossed and his back against the wall, closest to the Scribbley Wall and in the one spot where there weren't three or four other people stood around him – had done a funny little jerk forwards before stiffly turning his head towards Farley.

'Hang on,' he said incredulously, staring at him in a way that you don't really see DCs staring at their Supers. 'You're not thinking of using them as *bait?*'

'Not bait, no,' Farley told him lightly, stroking his short, bushy grey beard. 'But this lass has got one of ours on her side. He'll have told her all about what tactics we use, and they'll be expecting us to go down the normal route. If we don't want to end up on the back foot, we'll need to do something unexpected. We'll be with them the whole time,' he added reassuringly, as Hadaway's face started changing from incredulous to pissed off, his jaw getting tenser by the second. 'And we'll do a recce, make sure we know what they're going into. They'll be safe.'

'I'm sorry,' Angie squeaked, staring at him with eyes as big as dinner plates. 'Just to be clear here... are you thinking of sending us in *first?*'

'I'm considering it.'

I felt a massive explosion of excitement in my stomach, so violently that I was amazed I didn't make like a baby Squidge and piss myself right there and then.

He wasn't telling us to stay out of the case.

He wanted us *on* the case.

He actually *wanted* us to help!

Ha.

Suck it, Hadaway.

'Knight's a fucking lunatic,' Hadaway said tightly, his shoulders becoming considerably more rigid. 'We don't know what the hell she's expecting. We send them in there first and there's no way we can't guarantee they'll be safe.'

'We won't let anything happen to them,' Farley told him confidently, nodding slightly. (At what, I don't know.) 'We'll make sure they've got protective gear on, and we pull them out at the first sign of danger. I don't like this anymore than you do, Ade,' he added, obviously clocking that Hadaway looked like he couldn't believe what he was hearing and couldn't be more furious about the fact. 'It's not a route I want to go down. But I think it'll give us the best shot we have.'

There was silence for a few seconds, some people looking at me and Angie and others watching Farley and Hadaway, and I held my breath, wondering if they were going to dangle the dream and then snatch it away.

But really, the decision had already been made. I mean, Farley was the one leading the investigation from the top; what he said went, and if we said that we should be there, then we were going to be there.

'Right,' Farley said in the end, as Hadaway turned back away from him, the muscle in his jaw working and a vein standing out on the side of his neck. But what could he do? He was a DC. Farley was his Super. DCs don't argue with their Super. (At least, the ones who know what's good for them don't.) 'Now, there are going to be some ground rules. First of all, I want you to do exactly what we tell you to do, no questions asked. If we tell you to get out of there, you get out of there, is that understood? Secondly,' he added when we both gave him a nod, mine a lot more enthusiastically than Angie's, 'I don't want you two going off on a tangent. If you get any ideas, I want you to tell me, I don't want you running off like you did yesterday, alright? And lastly, if either of you have second thoughts about all of this, you let me know. I'm not putting you in a situation you're not comfortable with.'

Interestingly, I couldn't remember him asking us if we were comfortable with doing it in the first place, but I had a feeling that pointing that out would not go in our favour. So instead, I just nodded like a Churchill dog, catching Angie doing the same out of the corner of my eye. And just like that, we were dismissed; Farley was working his way through the crowd until he was stood at the front of the room, a few steps in front of me and Angie, and barking out orders for different teams.

I didn't dare look at Hadaway. (Not that I'd need to; I could take an educated guess at how his face would look anyway.)

I didn't even dare look at Angie.

All I could do was stand there, staring at my feet and biting my lip as I listened to Farley talking, with so many bubbles of excitement fizzing around in my stomach and already feeling the adrenaline I was going to need for that night pumping through me.

EIGHTEEN.

Just under an hour later, me, Angie and Hadaway were the last ones left in the flat.

All the Response officers who were due to come on duty that morning had been sent off on various stakeouts or inquiries; the MIT officers had gone to their office, deciding that it wasn't worth going home before the day really started; and everyone else had been sent home by Evans and Farley, with strict orders to get some rest before we went to the clearing that night.

Which was all good and well, but I couldn't do it.

I couldn't sleep.

I *tried*, believe me. I spent a good couple of hours tossing and turning in my bed, listening to Hadaway gently snoring as he napped on our settee and pulling every trick I could think of to make myself drift off, but every shred of the exhaustion I'd been feeling not so long ago had completely exhausted.

And instead, I was jittery.

I was checking the clock on my phone every ten minutes, thinking that it must be time to head up to the Woods by now.

More than anything, I was sat cross-legged on my bed, listening to the rain pelting down outside and entertaining Squidge – who'd been locked in with me well before he could decide to wake Hadaway up in the drooliest way possible – by tugging on his ears as I read every scribble on that Wall, trying to pick out anything that we might've missed.

I read the whole thing over and over again, until I could have recited it with my eyes closed. We hadn't got the answers to everything we didn't know, but for the most part, it was just the little things, like why she'd needed Pettyfer and Lyme or how she'd recruited the Cloaks; at this point, the only things I couldn't even guess at were what the hell this wand business was about, and what she was planning to do after she'd got this stupid Procedure thing out of the way.

Time obviously cracked on and I could hear Angie and Hadaway moving around in the living room, but I couldn't tear myself away from the Scribbley Wall. And neither could Squidge, apparently; while normally he'd be pawing at my bedroom door, crying and panting until I let him out to play with his new friends, this time he just stayed lying on the bed next to me, resting his chin on my knee as he stared at the Wall himself.

More time went past and Angie brought me in some food, trying to get me to go into the living room 'just for a little bit, Tidge, come and chill out for a bit', but I was too busy reading my Wall for the fifteenth time to bother listening to her. And then she left and Hadaway came in to try his hand at it; not that I listened to him either, but I *was* vaguely aware of him telling me I needed to clear my head before we went up to the clearing, which didn't even make *sense*. I just wanted to be as prepared as I could be for facing Knight, and even though I knew it was a hell of a lot more likely to get physical than not, I couldn't help but feel like going to face her without memorising everything we'd found out would be like going to a sword fight with a stick.

One or the other of them popped back into my room here and there through the day, but how often they did it, I couldn't tell you.

I didn't move, not even to look at them.

I don't even know if I was blinking.

I just sat there, reading and re-reading and re-re-reading the notes until there was a sudden banging on the flat door, loud enough to jolt me out of my obsession with the Wall and making me jump hard enough to almost send poor Squidge sprawling off the bed.

I whipped my head around to my bedroom door just in time to see Hadaway walking back through it. I blinked a couple of times, partly to clear my head and partly in surprise; to be honest, I hadn't even noticed him come back in that time.

'What time is it?'

He froze in the doorway and turned back to face me, looking almost as surprised as I felt. 'Half eleven. Nearly time to go.'

Shit.

Half past eleven?

Wow. Time really flies when you're catatonic.

I threw myself off my bed and hurtled out of my room, suddenly raring to go and itching to know why anyone had come to our flat. I came dangerously close to slamming into Angie, but it didn't even slow me down; I was too focussed on racing over to our door and yanking it open.

Evans was stood on the tiny landing between the top of the stairs and our door, looking even more grim than he had done that morning. 'We're heading up,' he told me without preamble, and then he handed me an envelope with my name written on it in smooth, curly writing. 'This was taped to your door.'

'It was?'

My bedroom is at the front of the house, facing out over the street; catatonic or not, wouldn't I have heard someone come into the house? And why had it been stuck to the door, instead of being slid underneath it?

'I don't suppose you recognise the writing?'

'No,' I said, shaking my head as Hadaway to stand behind me, clamping one hand around the open door. 'I don't know anyone who writes like that.'

It was just a little envelope, a small version of the long and narrow type, and it felt like it was empty save for a clump of something solid in the bottom right corner. And without thinking about it, without waiting for either of them to say something, I ripped the envelope open and tipped whatever was inside out into my open palm.

A slip of paper big enough for one sentence fell out onto my palm, followed by five fingernails.

Five full fingernails, right from the tip all the way down to the roots.

They were bloody and scabbed-over, with little clumps of flesh clinging to the back of them.

And they were definitely the right size to have come from a full-grown man.

Every single inch of me suddenly felt hot and prickly, and my stomach started churning like a washing machine on speed as something boiling rose up into my throat, burning it all the way down. And even though I didn't need to, I couldn't help myself from reading that note, just in case there was any chance – even just a tiny one – that those nails hadn't come from Johnny.

'Something for your friend to remember him by.'

Oh God.

'Erm...' Even to me, my voice sounded a lot deeper and throatier than it normally does. 'Where's Angie?'

'She went to get a coat from her room,' Hadaway told me, in a voice that was half shocked and something that was either anger or horror. 'Jesus, is that –'

'Yep,' I managed to eek out, and then I thrust the fingernails and the note at him, so abruptly that it clearly caught him off-guard. 'Don't tell her.'

Before either of them could do or say anything else, I whipped around on my heel and bolted for the bathroom, one hand clamped over my mouth as the churning in my stomach rose higher and higher and that burning feeling in the back of my throat reached my tongue.

I'd barely got the toilet seat up before it all exploded out of me, a fairly impressive amount considering that I'd only eaten half a sandwich all day.

Wave after wave came out of me, and I have no idea how long I was crouched there for, clinging onto the bowl for dear life, before I heard someone moving to stand behind me, and suddenly my hair was being pulled back from around my face and off my neck.

I waited until I'd stopped vomming before I twisted my head around to see who it was, partly because nobody – but *nobody* – needs to see my vom face, and partly because if they were being nice enough to make sure I missed my hair, then I probably owed it to them to make sure I didn't throw up on their shoes.

Hadaway was standing right behind me, my hair in his hands and a massively concerned look on his face as he frowned down at me. 'You alright?'

'Peachy,' I muttered, wiping my mouth with the back of my hand and flushing the loo before (I hoped) he could see what was in the bowl. 'Where's Angie?'

'Still in her room. It must be a hard coat to find.'

I didn't miss the dry note in his voice. I was just too preoccupied with what was going on to really register it.

'Why would she do that to him?' I asked as I sat down on the floor, twisting around so that my back was against the toilet and looking from Hadaway to Evans – who was stood in the doorway, holding the envelope – and back again. 'Why's she sent me that?'

'I don't know,' Hadaway admitted grimly, crossing his arms across his chest as he sat down on the edge of the bath. 'We all know she enjoys this shit, but it could just be to let you know she's serious. Look,' he added, after a little pause in which he and Evans swapped looks that I couldn't quite read. 'Armitage, it's not too late to back out. If you don't –'

'I'm not backing out!' I told him, my voice coming out a bit sharper than I really meant it to. But really? We were *this* close, and he was still trying to keep us out of it? 'What, d'you think that we're going to sit around and wonder what the hell's going on all night? D'you want me to turn around to Farley and say ta very much, but we can't really be bothered? Fuck that, Hadaway!'

His face clouded over slightly, but before he could fire back at me, Evans was saying, almost lightly,

'What I want to know is how she managed it. She can only have left that there today,' he added, when we both looked at him, 'so she must've done it while you were all here. Unless you went out at any point?'

'No,' Hadaway told him, with a little shrug. 'The only thing I can think is she's done it while we've been asleep.'

'I never went to sleep,' I said quickly, glancing between them. 'I was awake the whole time, and I didn't hear anyone come in. I don't know how she's done it.'

Hadaway shot me a sharp look, his face half-appalled and half-concerned, and I just knew that he was going to say something about how I couldn't go up to face Knight on such a lack of sleep. Luckily for me, for the second time in a matter of seconds, he was interrupted before he could get the words out; this time it was by Angie, who popped up at Evans' left shoulder, wearing a grey, chequered trench coat.

'I'm ready!' she announced in a voice that would've been bright if it wasn't so nervous, shooting us all a wobbly smile. And then she obviously took in the scene in the bedroom, because the smile slipped off her face almost straightaway, leaving her looking considerably more apprehensive than she was obviously trying to. 'What's going on?'

'Nothing,' Evans told her smoothly, tucking the envelope inside his jacket so swiftly that I don't think she even noticed he was holding it. 'We were just getting making sure we had everything.' He shot me and Hadaway a stern look that made it obvious that that was the official party line, and then he turned to Angie, clapping both of his hands onto her upper arms with a smile that you'd only expect to get off your Dad. 'Right, then. Time to go.'

Twenty minutes later, Hadaway was pulling Evans' unmarked Police car into the clearing that he'd parked in a couple of days earlier, easing it into a gap between two riot vans parked at the side. The four of us tumbled out of the car as soon as he put the handbrake on, straight into the pelting rain and an atmosphere so charged that I could feel my adrenaline start pumping as soon as my feet hit the ground.

There were Police cars and officers everywhere, all of them grim-faced as they darted from one side of the clearing to the other to speak to someone, or talking into their radios and listening intently to what was crackling back through, or stood in their own teams, clearly getting something of a pre-briefing-briefing. All of the Response officers were in their high-vis stab vests, glowing in the headlights of cars still pulling as close to the clearing as they could get, while the District Support Unit lads were standing around in their plain black vests, some of them pulling riot helmets and shields out of their own van. And then you had CID, all of them sticking out like sore thumbs purely because they looked like they weren't wearing any vests at all, when in actuality, they all would've been wearing the same under-the-shirt type that Hadaway and Evans had strapped on before we'd left the flat.

There was a definite throb in the air, the type that tells you in an instant – even if you come into it completely cold – that something huge is brewing, and that every single person there is ready for it.

The four of us had barely reached the back of the car before Farley materialised in front of us, wearing a high-vis coat that reached down to just above his knees, with what was left of his hair flattened against is forehead by the rain.

'So,' he boomed, fixing me and Angie with a look that was kind of stern, kind of satisfied. 'How are we feeling?'

'Fine,' I told him, flashing him a quick smile and ignoring Angie's nervous little squeak. 'When do we get to go in?'

'Soon,' he said, giving me a grim smile of his own, and then he shifted his attention to Evans and Hadaway. 'I'm not doing a briefing as such; we've been doing it on a team-by-team basis as they get here, so we can get everyone in place as quickly as possible.' He pointed towards the clump of trees behind us, which ran all the way down to our right, right down to the bottom of the fields and out of sight. 'We've got people in there already, keeping an eye on things. There's already been a few of these idiot followers pitch up, but there's no sign of Knight or Pace; we think they're waiting until everyone's there before they show themselves.'

I heard Angie let out another nervous squeak as she rocked forward slightly on the spot. 'Is Johnny there?'

He looked at her, and even in the darkness, I could see his eyes get considerably more gentle. 'We haven't got eyes on him yet.'

'How sure are we that this is a good place to be?' I wanted to know, even though I'd have hardly been able to offer an alternative if any of them had asked. 'I mean, what if any of the Cloaks come through here on their way to Knight's clearing? Do we just grab them all, or –'

'We don't think they know this clearing's here,' Hadaway told me, surprisingly easily for someone who was stood so rigidly, with the vibe I imagine a Lion does when he's on the hunt. 'On all the stakeouts we've done, we haven't seen them come this way.'

'We've got people in position to come in from every direction,' Farley continued, as if we haven't said anything. 'They're already set up to come in from the North, East and South, and this lot' – he indicated behind him, towards the Response and DSU officers who were starting to file out of the clearing – 'are going to come in from the West. We'll have DSU going in first, then Response, then I want CID coming in to tie it all up. But first of all' – and this is where he turned back to me and Angie, a hard frown on his face – 'I want you two going in. I don't want you to do anything other than talk to her,' he added harshly, just as I felt my eyes light up. 'I don't want you to get involved in anything, just keep her distracted. She'll be expecting us lot to turn up, but if you can keep her focus on you for a couple of minutes, it might just give us the chance to catch them on the back foot. We'll have eyes on you at all times, and we'll get you out of there at the first sign of trouble.' He eyeballed us for a couple of long seconds, looking like he didn't know if this was the best thing to do or if he was looking the end of his career dead in the eye. 'D'you think you're up to it?'

I felt like we were polar opposites in that second. She was clearly trying to hide it, but waves of nerves were just rolling off Angie and crashing in every direction; and in the meantime, I was trying to pretend I wasn't as excited as I really was, just in case anyone thought I didn't realise how serious this was.

Because I *did* realise how serious it was.

And I *did* realise how dangerous it could get.

But rightly or wrongly, we'd worked just as hard on this case as anyone else, and the fact that it was *this* close to being over had got me all raring to go.

'Of course we are,' I said, before Angie could give into the nervousness or Hadaway could try to persuade him to send us home. 'When do we go in?'

'Five minutes,' he grunted, turning to his right, ready to head over to the next clump of CID officers. But before he took a single step, he paused, looking at Hadaway and Evans. 'Get them kitted up.'

Almost exactly five minutes later, we were suited and booted and standing with Hadaway about a quarter of the way down the field next to the clearing, just in front of the trees that we were going to go through to get to Knight and the Cloaks. We were wearing the same white stab vests that CID use under our coats (I can't tell you how relieved I was when he said we didn't have to go further than that; the idea of whipping my top off in front of him was somehow more daunting than going in to face Knight) and we both had the retractable nightsticks on us that everyone in the Force used, Angie's placed carefully into her pocket and mine tucked into the belt around my red, felt trench coat.

I'll be honest, I had no intention of using it; it was a bit too thin for me to feel like I could do much use with it, but at the same time, it contradicted itself by feeling solid enough that I didn't want to see what damage it could do.

It was a metal *stick*, at the end of the day.

That shit could be lethal.

'I don't like this,' Hadaway said grimly, running one hand over his stubble as we waited for Farley's signal. 'It doesn't feel right.'

'It'll be fine,' I told him cheerfully, flicking my eyes around where we stood to try and find something I'd be more comfortable using instead of the Metal Stick of Doom. 'It's nothing we haven't done before, Hadaway. And we're not dead yet, are we?'

He grunted, and it said something about how much he did that around me that I could translate this one as meaning he wasn't convinced. I bent down to pick up a fairly thick stick a couple of inches inside the treeline, one that looked solid enough to give a good whack but not so much that it'd cave someone's head in, and by the time I stood back up, there was a torch flashing at us from the clearing; once, then three times, then once again.

'Is that it?' Angie asked sharply, whipping her head around to stare at Hadaway. 'Is that the signal?'

He gave her one short, grim nod. 'That's the one.'

I felt a huge jolt of something shoot through my stomach, and I couldn't tell if it was excitement, nerves or a bit of both.

'Well, then,' I said to Angie, shooting her a big smile as the adrenaline kicked in, making my heart start thumping and my hands start trembling. 'We best get cracking.'

We both turned so that our backs were to the clearing, ready to walk into the trees, but before we could take a single step, one large, warm hand wrapped around my upper arm and gently pulled me back. And when I stumbled back and turned into the pull, I found myself standing considerably closer to Hadaway than I'd expected to be.

'Listen,' he told me urgently, nearly dislodging my cloche as he tucked some of my hair back behind my ear. 'You don't owe anyone anything. If you get down there and decide you don't like it, or if you feel like you can't go ahead with it, just get yourself out of there. Or call me, and I'll come and get you out.'

'Hadaway, I –'

'You're not letting anyone down if you back out,' he said, lowering his voice slightly and somehow sounding even more urgent as he tugged me another step closer to him, and suddenly his face was tense in a way that I'd never seen before. 'Don't put yourself in that situation if you're not sure you can hack it, alright?'

I stared up at him, frowning slightly as I wondered where *this* Hadaway – the one who seemed like he was trying to give us a way out because he was actually worried about us, instead of trying to keep us away from the one interesting thing that'd ever happened because we were annoying him – had come from.

He just stared back at me, still with that intense look on his face, and just one tiny second, I thought he might –

Well.

I don't really know what I thought.

And it doesn't matter anyway; the whole moment was over as quick as it'd started, and before I knew what I was doing, my hand was coming up to pat him nicely on the cheek.

'We'll be fine,' I promised him, trying my best to sound reassuring as I gently tugged his hand off my arm. 'We've done this before, remember? You don't need to worry about us, we can deal with her.' I pulled myself away from him and started walking to where Angie was hovering, suddenly feeling suddenly weirdly surreal as I swung my stick up to rest against my shoulder and nodded towards the trees. 'OK. Let's go.'

We picked our way through the trees in complete silence, stepping over roots and brushing past branches, both of us staring dead ahead as we walked in perfect step with each other.

It didn't feel real.

The whole week had been building up to this, but it didn't seem like it was really happening; if anything, I felt like I was going to wake up in my bed any second now. And for the first time, I *really* realised what we were going into here.

I'd been focussing just on dealing with Knight, but she had an army almost as big as ours; what happened if she set the Cloaks on us? I knew Farley had said that they'd get us out of there at the first sign of trouble, but what if something went wrong and they couldn't get to us in time?

More importantly, what happened if we couldn't get to Johnny in time? What if she did whatever she was going to do to him the second we pitched up, and there was nothing we could do to stop her?

And what'd Ginger Cloak said the other day? She was going to *eat* him?

Shit.

I didn't want to see that happen.

I definitely didn't want *Angie* to see that happen.

So, yeah. I had a definite sense of foreboding mixing with the anticipation, and both of them got heavier and heavier the closer we got to Knight's clearing.

We reached the other side of the trees, passing officer after officer from about the fifth trees back, and stopped at the edge of the trees, lurking just far enough back that we could see what was going on without the chance of being spotted ourselves.

There seemed to be twice as many Cloaks as there had been the other night, standing around the centre exactly like they had on Tuesday, and Knight was already standing on her stump, making some kind of speech and holding her arms slightly out to her sides, pumping them up into the air so that she looked like some kind of raver ballerina. She was wearing the white robes that she had been the first time we'd been in the clearing, so light compared to everyone else that it almost made her look like she was glowing from the light their flame torches were giving out.

And immediately to her right, staring out at the Cloaks in front of him (and by default, due to the angle we'd come at, me and Angie) with his hands in shackles and an eerily blank look on his face, was a topless Johnny.

'We have succeeded!' Knight was crying ecstatically as we reached the clearing, and I saw Angie do a funny little jerk forward as she clocked Johnny. 'We have faced opposition and we have faced suppression, but we have stayed together and overcome all of it! Tonight, everything that we have worked for becomes our new reality, and those who opposed us will soon see the error of their ways!' She paused, flattening one hand against her chest as she shot them all a beatific smile, and I felt my top lip pull back as I watched her. Somehow I'd forgotten about the bizarre way of talking that she liked to use when she was standing on that stump. 'It would be remiss of me not to thank you; after all, you've been so loyal to me. And I *will* reward you for what you've done. But now is not the time for that,' she added after a little pause, and I saw her slip something that glinted in the torchlight out of her sleeve. 'We're here for a purpose, after all.'

She took a step closer to Johnny and pressed the shiny thing against his neck, and from her new angle, I could see exactly what it was; it was a knife with a chunky handle made of glass and a blade that was four or five inches long. I heard Angie start breathing more heavily, and before I knew what I was doing, before I'd even registered that *this* was the time to go in, I'd grabbed hold of her elbow and took a step forward, pulling her with me.

The second we stepped out from the trees, Knight froze, tilting her head to one side like Squidge does whenever anyone mentions cheese – but instead of drooling, she looked like she was listening intently to something. And then, so slowly it was almost painful, she turned her head, twisting it around to her left until she was staring straight at me and Angie.

'Ah,' she said softly, as the smile on her face turned cold. 'Our visitors have arrived. Don't be shy, Armitage!' she called out, suddenly sounding a lot more invigorated as she beckoned to us. 'Please, come and join us up here!'

I threw a grim look at Angie, who stared back at me apprehensively.

Putting ourselves slap-bang in the middle of the Cloaks didn't seem like the most sensible thing, but what else could we do? We needed to get to her and Johnny anyway, and it wasn't as if we had any number of ways to do that.

I started walking forward, my legs suddenly feeling like they weren't attached to my body anymore and making me go slowly and heavily, and I could hear Angie following right behind me. The Cloaks parted row-by-row to let us through, and I could feel my heart thumping hard in my chest and my ears as that sense of foreboding grew even more, to the point where I could feel it in the back of my throat.

I glanced at Johnny as we reached the stump, and for just one second, I could've *sworn* that his eyes had flicked towards us. But when I looked closer, it was clearly just a trick of the light; he was staring straight ahead again, still with that horribly blank look on his face.

'Well, isn't this a pleasant surprise,' Knight beamed, more to the clearing at large than to me and Angie ourselves. 'I'm so glad you could join us, Armitage. Did you get the gift I sent you?'

Out of the corner of my eye, I saw Angie stiffly jerk her head around to stare at me. Before I could say anything or do something more than glower up at Knight, the psycho clocked it as well, clapping her hands together and letting out a soft gasp of delight.

'She hasn't told you,' she cooed to Angie, and then she leant over to Johnny, pulling his right hand up with the back facing us so that we could see his fingers. 'It was a joint effort.'

We both stared at his hand, Angie making a strange, strangled noise as I felt a lurch of horror mix with a fresh wave of queasiness in my stomach.

Instead of fingernails, he had raw, bloody patches that looked like they'd only recently started to scab over, and it wasn't until I actually saw them that I realised how much I'd been hoping that the nails she'd sent me were just very convincing props instead of really being Johnny's.

'I did,' I managed to get out icily, forcing myself to turn my head back towards at her. 'Yeah. Lovely of you to think of me when you had all this to look forward to.' I glanced around at all the Cloaks, folding my arms as nonchalantly as I could and letting my stick dangle from one hand. 'So, what's the plan here?'

'We achieve the ascension.'

The – *what?* The *ascension?*

'What the *fuck*,' Angie demanded harshly, slowly turning her head away from Johnny, 'is an *ascension?*'

'We have been working hard to make sure I achieve my full abilities,' Knight told her pleasantly, like a teacher explaining something really simple to her Primary School class. 'It's taken some sacrifices, but we've made them with love, and we have finally collected all of the souls I need. The ascension will let me harness all of the powers they have gifted me.'

'Right,' I nodded, like she wasn't as insane as a person can get. Those lads had been killed *lovingly?* Did she really believe that? 'And you can't do that without doing this Procedure?'

'That's correct.'

'Let me ask you something,' I said, as if the thought had only just occurred to me, shifting my weight from one foot to the other. 'You've done this kind of thing before, right? So what's different this time? Why will this one give you extra powers when all the other times didn't?'

A hard flicker passed across her face, and I could just tell that she knew I was trying to make the Cloaks see the flaw in her plan, rather than actually asking. 'There are more requirements this time.'

'Why?'

She stared at me for a few seconds, her eyes bugging out slightly, and I realised that of everything she'd been expecting that night, this wasn't one of them.

Not only that, but she had absolutely nothing to say back to it.

Clearly, no-one had ever asked her the question before, and she hadn't bothered thinking up an explanation for it in case someone *did*. And it wasn't as if she could turn around and say 'because it does', could she? Not without losing some major face in front of all the Cloaks.

'Well,' I said breezily in the end, smiling blandly as I waved one hand through the air, like I was brushing the question away. 'Whatever the reason, I'm sure that wand of yours will help you.'

Her eyes turned hard, glinting at me as she clenched her teeth hard, so hard that all of the bones in her face were suddenly sticking out so that she looked like a living skull. I heard Angie let out a startled gasp and for the second time in a few seconds, I nearly lost whatever I had inside me, but before either of us could react more than that, she was saying tightly,

'Children. We have two more sacrifices for tonight. Kindly get them for me.'

I felt a wave of panic crash over me as the Cloaks took a step forward in unison, and then another one, and I didn't know where to look – at the Cloaks to stop them from grabbing us, or at Knight to make sure she didn't stab either of us. I whirled around, grabbing the bottom my stick tight with both hands, ready to swing it, and I caught sight of Angie whipping her baton out of her pocket and shaking it out to its full length, but just as the Cloaks took a third step forwards, there was a sudden explosion of shouting from the trees around the clearing, and suddenly wave after wave of Bobbies were storming into the clearing.

DSU came in first, banging on their plastic shields with their batons, forcing the Cloaks further into the circle, and Response were right behind them, some holding just their batons and some grasping their handcuffs as well. The Cloaks moved closer together and pushed forwards, jolting me and Angie closer to the stump, and I caught glance of Knight, staring at the officers with a stunned look on her face, like she couldn't take in what was happening. And the next thing I knew... it was just chaos.

It was one of the Cloaks kicked it all off; they panicked and launched themselves forwards, trying to sprint out of the crowd before DSU could close ranks, and suddenly most of the others were following suit, trying to force their way past the shields, and I saw the ones who managed it swinging at Response, who were chasing after them without missing a beat. More Cloaks charged in every direction just as CID came bursting out of the trees, but before I could see who was doing what, a hand fastened around my upper arm, so tightly it was painful, and when I whipped around – with my stick held up, ready to conk whoever it was hard to the head – I saw Johnny standing there, his other hand wrapped around Angie's arm as he stared at us, looking nothing short of livid.

'What the fuck,' he demanded tightly, dragging us a couple of steps away as a Response officer hurtled past, chasing a Cloak who was putting up one hell of a fight. 'What the *fuck* are you two doing here?'

'Farley wanted us here,' Angie told him over the sound of all the yelling that was coming from every direction, reaching out to touch as his face. 'Johnny, are you alright?'

'I'm fine,' he snapped, and I blinked up at him in shock, wondering how the hell he *was* fine. How'd he manage to stop Knight from doing to him what she'd done to Lyme. 'But I want you two to get out of here, I don't give a shit what Farley said. He should never have involved you.'

I opened my mouth to remind him that Farley massively out-pipped him, but before I could get the words out, a Cloak charged out of nowhere, slamming into Johnny with enough force to knock him to the ground. He pulled us so far with him before letting go, so we both stumbled a few steps to our right, nearly hitting the ground ourselves, and by the time I'd righted myself, Angie was already on the Cloak, who was straddling Johnny; just as they raised their hand up to slug him, she booted them hard to the ribs, and as they grunted and sagged slightly to their left, she brought her nightstick down on them, swinging it so hard that I heard it *thwip* through the air before it smacked down on their back, making them let out a howl of pain.

I heard Johnny bellow for handcuffs as I whirled around to face the stump, wondering what Knight was up to, but the spot was empty, and I had no idea if she'd jumped in to fight with the Cloaks or if she'd done a runner.

I have to say, my money was on the second.

Everywhere I looked, people were fighting. The Cloaks were using dirty tactics, kicking and punching and even biting, and I saw some of them ganging up so that a couple of Bobbies had to take one two or three Cloaks by themselves, and while the cops had started out using very by-the-book tactics, they went out of the window more and more as the Cloaks got dirtier and dirtier; I even saw that most of DSU had ditched their shields, and the ones who hadn't were using them to bash the Cloaks as hard as they could. There were some

Cloaks who'd been overpowered and cuffed getting dragged out of the clearing, literally kicking and screaming, and the cops who'd took them out were reappearing almost immediately, clearly having handed the Cloaks over to some other Bobbies in the trees.

I quickly scanned the clearing for anyone in a white robe, but the crowd was so thick that I couldn't anything, and before I could decide which way to go, a Cloak charged at me, yelling, and I felt my face explode with pain as a solid fist slammed into my cheek. I staggered back a couple of steps, suddenly more furious than anything else, and swung my stick at them as hard as I could; it him them in the side of the head with a loud *thunk*, and as they stood there, seeming slightly dazed, I booted them in the stomach, belting them again with the stick again when they doubled over, this time in the face. They slumped to the ground, their hood coming off enough for me to see that it was a bloke in his mid-forties, but before I could do anything else, Luke appeared out of nowhere and cuffing the Cloak with his arms behind his back.

'Nice work,' he bellowed at me, hauling the Cloak to his feet and keeping a tight grip on him. 'Are you alright?'

'I'm fine!'

'Good,' he yelled, pulling me out of the way of another Cloak, who seemed to be charging at no-one in particular. 'We can take it from here, Armitage, get Angie and get out of here!'

I opened my mouth to tell him that we were fine, that we could handle it and we wanted to help, but he was charging off with the Cloak before I could get the words out, and in the next second, someone was hurtling into me from behind, sending me stumbling forwards. I whipped around and swung as hard as I could, hitting the new Cloak smack in the jaw, but they didn't even seem to feel it; they just kept coming at me, swinging for me, and I had to duck and weave as I backed through the crowd, alternating between going for him with my stick and jabbing at him with my other fist. Their hand fastened around my neck, squeezing it so that I couldn't breathe, couldn't swallow or anything, let alone shout, and when hitting him as hard as I could with the stick over and over again didn't make them let go, I did the only thing I could do and shoved the fingers of my other hand hard into their eyes. They screamed, stumbling back slightly, but I went with them – I had no choice, they still had hold of me – and dug my fingers in even harder, gritting my teeth against the squishy, gooey feeling of it. They let go of my neck to pull my hand away with both hands, and the second they did, I thrust the stick right at them, smashing it into their nose so that it exploded in a fountain of blood.

I didn't wait to see what they did after that; I just took off, racing past *Farley,* of all people, who was going against a Cloak that was half his size, and Luke, who'd thrown himself back into the fray and had a huge, purple lump brewing on his jaw, just in time to see him tackle a Cloak to the ground, flip them over and get another pair of cuffs on them.

I had to find Knight.

I had no doubt that if she wasn't in the clearing, she would've disappeared down her tunnel, and I had at least an idea of where she was going to come out.

I dodged and weaved through the fighting, ducking the odd wayward punch and apparently avoiding anyone's attention. I hurtled past Hadaway, who was wrestling with the biggest Cloak there right on the edge of the crowd; he dealt a swift right hook to the Cloak, making their hood fall down and reveal none other then Pace, and Hadaway seemed to go at him even harder, his face livid.

I took a couple of steps out of the crowd and immediately got slammed into by another fighting couple, sending all three of us sprawling to the ground, and when I whipped my head around to see who it was, I saw Mack pinned to the ground by a Cloak who had both hands tight around his throat, lifting his head up and banging it back down onto the ground. Mack's baton was nowhere in sight and his face was turning purple, with a horrible, gurgling noise coming from his throat, and I don't know how long the Cloak had been strangling him for, but he seemed like he was barely conscious. I hauled myself to my feet and booted the Cloak as hard as I could to their ribs, again and again and again, and when that didn't work, I launched my foot into the side of their head instead; their head jerked to their right and I booted them again, even harder this time, and then I swung my stick down against their shoulders. They collapsed down on top of Mack and I quickly pulled their hands off Mack's neck, rolling him – I could see under his hood enough to see it was another bloke – onto the ground and giving him a swift kick to the chin. I was just about to take off running again when I heard someone bellow my name, and when I whipped around – more on reflex than anything else – I saw another, slimmer Cloak sprinting towards me, only a couple of steps away, holding a knife up in the air and clearly ready to bring it down, straight into me, and I didn't have a chance. I closed my eyes, waiting for impact – but instead, I felt myself getting knocked out the way with enough force to make me stagger a couple of steps to my right. And when I opened my eyes and looked around to see what'd happened, Hadaway was stood there, his right hand exactly where my shoulder had been, with the knife going in through his palm and sticking out of the back of his hand.

Oh my God.

I lurched forward, feeling my stomach drop out and suddenly finding it hard to breathe, and grabbed hold of the Cloak before she could do a runner, accidentally pulling on her cloak hard enough to pull her hood down, revealing the bland-looking lass from Habely Bookshop. She was just stood there, staring at Hadaway like she couldn't believe what she'd just done, and I quickly shoved her at a passing Response officer, who easily took the whole thing in stride, clapping her cuffs on her and pulling her over to the trees. And then I turned to Hadaway, who was staring at his hand like it was something mildly interesting.

'You have to go,' I told him urgently, trying not to look too closely at it; it was in so deep that the top of the handle was pressed against his palm, and blood was running out of him like it was coming out of a tap. 'You can't stay here, Hadaway, you need a hospital.'

He just shook his head, grimacing as he pulled the knife out of his hand by a couple of inches.

'Leave it!' I said in alarm, grabbing hold of both of his wrists, but before I could say anything else or do anything more to stop him, he'd gritted his teeth and given the knife a swift tug out of his hand, with a disgusting squelch and a little spurt of blood.

'I'm fine.'

'You are *not* fine! Look at you!'

'I'm fine,' he said again, in the halting voice that people use when they are not fine. 'I need to get this handed in as evidence. Where's Angie?'

'I don't know,' I told him impatiently, feeling a surge of irritation towards him. Was he really just going to ignore the gaping hole in his hand? 'The last time I saw her, she was fighting over by the stump, Hadaway, Knight –'

'Don't worry about Knight,' he said shortly, already taking off for the trees on the other side of the clearing, towards where the Police vans and cars were parked. 'Get Angie and get yourselves out of here, we'll deal with the rest.'

I watched him go indignantly, and I couldn't tell if I was so worked up because of how blasé he was being about his hand or because he hadn't let me tell him about Knight. How was I supposed to not worry about Knight if I knew she was gone, and there was no sign that anyone else had noticed?

No.

Sod that.

I whirled around on my heel and took off again, diving into the trees and sprinting in the direction that I thought the tunnel must lead, leaving the sounds of fighting somewhere behind me. I have no idea how long I was running for before I burst out into the clearing that Ginger Cloak had found us in the morning before, and for a couple of seconds, I just stood there, catching my breath and wondering if I should go down into the tunnel to look for Knight or if I should look somewhere else.

I hadn't even got close to making a decision before something to my left caught my eye. And when I looked, I saw a flash of white on the other side of the trees, making its way across the felled area, heading for the boulders I'd fell off that Tuesday.

And I didn't think twice.

I charged after her, running as fast as I could and nearly going flying when I hit the logs and branches, which were made even slipperier by the rain. I was having a bit of a nightmare getting across them, but so was Knight, and somehow – probably because I was wearing jeans while she was wearing a robe she had to hold up, or maybe just because I had a good few inches on her – I was gaining on her; I was nowhere near close enough to be able to get hold of her, but she definitely wouldn't be able to lose me any time soon.

'*Knight!*' I bellowed furiously, one of my feet flying out from underneath me as I stepped on a particularly slick log, and I only managed to keep my balance by the skin of my teeth. '*Get back here now, you bitch!*'

She stopped dead a few feet away from the boulders and turned to face me, shooting me a smug smile across the two or three metres between us. 'Why? What are you going to do, Armitage? It's over. I've won.'

'You haven't won,' I bit off, panting slightly as I made my way towards her, tightening my grip on my stick. 'Johnny's still alive. You didn't do your stupid Procedure, and your Cloaks are all getting arrested. How is that a *win* for you?'

'I can get another Johnny,' she shrugged delicately. 'And more followers. I can even get another uncle. Let's face it,' she added viciously, glaring at me. 'Anything is a win for me. It's the beauty of being a witch.'

'Oh, drop the *fucking* act!' I yelled before I could stop myself, a wave of frustration, anger and scorn slamming into me. I'd had *enough.* I'd had *more* than enough. 'You're not a fucking witch! You're not anything! You're Kathie Goldin! You went to Habely Comprehensive Sixth Form, got massively obsessed with anyone who paid you attention, failed all your exams and dropped out halfway through your second year! I *know* who you are, Knight, and you're not anything fucking magical!'

She shot me a hard, furious look at me, and I scowled back at her for a few seconds, wondering if she was going to try and convince me that she *was* a witch, or if she was going to come at me. And then, just as I tightened my grip on the stick even more, she surprised me.

Because she didn't do either of those things.

Instead, she smiled at me.

Not the creepy, benign smile she'd been using all week.

A genuine smile.

'So I'm not a witch,' she said carelessly, shrugging. 'Who gives a shit. What matters is that *they* think I am, and if I can get people to believe in me and follow me, then I've got it made, haven't I?'

I stared at her in shock, hardly able to believe that she was actually – *finally* – admitting it. 'What the hell's wrong with you? Why've you done all this?'

She paused for a couple of seconds, looking thoughtful as she flicked her eyes all around the clearing. 'There always has to be a reason. Doesn't there? Well, what if there isn't one?'

I stared at her in horror, feeling sick to my stomach.

Nothing she could've said would've made my sympathise with her or see her side of it. No chance. But a part of me had wanted her to give me *something,* anything at all that'd make the whole thing make a little bit more sense.

But no.

She was stood there saying that she'd killed those lads because – what? She was bored? It was horrific.

'You're fucking joking.'

'People like to be noticed,' she told me, with another shrug. 'It's nice to have people listening to what you have to say. And it's even nicer to have them do what you tell them to do, no questions asked. Do you have any idea how long I had to wait to get treatment like that? How many *years* it was before it was *my* turn?'

Probably the same amount as every other normal person on the planet, you goddamn lunatic. 'So, four lads had to die because you think the world owes you the Princess treatment? Have I got that right?'

Her face clouded over. 'It's not that simple.'

'It's *exactly* that simple,' I snapped furiously, glowering at her. 'And what happens when they find out that none of it's true, hmm? What d'you think they'll do when they realise it's all been a load of shite?'

'That'll never happen.'

'It bloody will,' I told her, widening my eyes at her, 'when I tell them all about it.'

Her face turned half a shade paler, but she still managed to shake her hair back and give me a self-satisfied smirk. 'They won't believe a word of it. You saw them back there. They're my followers; they worship me. They're *loyal* to me. Do you really think they'd ever turn against me?'

'Your Cloaks are taking a battering while you're out here saving your own neck. I think any loyalty you had has well and truly gone out the window.'

We stared at each other for a few seconds, and this time it was my turn to shrug.

'They're going to find out. They really should've worked it out for themselves, but since they're clearly too dense to do that, I'm going to tell them exactly how you've been playing them as soon as we get to East District. And then we'll see how many people stick by you, won't we?'

Her lip curled back as she pulled something glittery out of her robe sleeve, and I felt my stomach plunge down to my ankles as I took in the situation.

She had a knife.

I had a stick.

Somehow I didn't feel like we were on even footing.

She let out a strangled scream and came running at me, with the hand that was holding the knife right up in the air, but somehow what she was doing didn't register with me until the last second; I swung my arm up in the air so that the knife hit my stick instead of me. The blade landed with a solid thud, and before she could react to it, before she could move to it or anything, I pulled my stick back, pulled it up to my other shoulder and launched it forwards. It smacked into her wrist so hard that a loud crack echoed around the clearing and she dropped the knife with a howl of pain; it landed not too far to my right and I went to kick it away, but before I could take more than a step towards it, she grabbed me by the hair and yanked me back, so hard that I felt more than a few strands snap away from my scalp, and I had to try very hard not to think about how big my bald patch would be. She swung me around and shoved me away, and by the time I got my footing back and span around to face her, she'd already picked the knife back up, and this time I didn't get chance to move out of the way before she came at me; she slammed into me blade-first, and I heard my coat rip as we went over, me landing hard on my back and Knight coming down on top of me. I managed to spin away from her before she could have another go at me, giving her a hard shove off her and scrambling to my feet, and it wasn't until I'd managed to scurry a couple of feet away from her that I grappled with my coat, lifting it up to see the damage. My coat was torn, but instead of the gaping hole in my side that I was expecting to see, I saw a flash of my white stab vest.

It's amazing how quick I'd forgot I was wearing one.

I let my coat drop and we stared at each other for a few seconds, both of us panting heavily, and for the first time, I realised that no-one knew where I was.

I had no idea what was going on in the clearing that Knight had used with the Cloaks; the sounds of fighting had faded away ages ago, and I couldn't even guess whether they were still going at it or if all the Cloaks had been rounded up by now.

There was no way they wouldn't guess that I was with Knight when they realised that we were both missing, but as to where we were?

No.

They'd have no clue.

All I could hope was that Angie would remember where the tunnel led to and put two and two together.

And in the meantime, me and Knight were completely alone.

'You haven't been as clever as you think you have,' I told her as we eyeballed each other warily, thinking that keeping her talking until someone pitched up was worth a shot. 'We know that you have those trees strung up with cable wires. We know about your tunnels. We know that you got into our flat through the bathroom window. There's nothing you've done that we haven't been able to work out.'

'I don't care,' she said breathlessly, letting out a short laugh that was completely empty of any humour or happiness. 'I really don't care anymore. All I need to do is get rid of you, and we can crack on like nothing's happened.'

I shook my head grimly, refusing to take my eyes off her. 'It's not that easy. I'm not the only one who knows.' More anger and frustration bubbled up in inside of me and broke through the wariness, and the next thing I knew, I was throwing my hands out to the sides and demanding harshly, 'For God's sake, why don't you just hand yourself in? Tell them it was temporary insanity or something, it's not like anyone won't believe you!'

Except maybe about the temporary part.

'I have no intention of handing myself in,' she informed me coolly, adjusting and tightening her grip on the knife. 'And I can deal with anyone who knows what you know just as easily as I'll deal with you.'

'Well. You can't,' I pointed out, raising one eyebrow at her as I shifting my weight slightly, making sure I'd be ready to bolt if and when I needed to. 'Two of them are cops, and you know from tonight that they don't go quietly.'

She gave me a cold smile. 'Well, I don't need to worry about that just yet, do I?'

And suddenly she was coming at me again, bringing her knife out in front, but before she could reach me, I darted out of her way, ducking past her and running as fast I could over the fallen trees, slipping and sliding on them as I headed for trees up at the top of the clearing, thinking that I could lead her back to where all the Bobbies were, but I'd only taken a few steps before one of my feet flew out from underneath me, making me slam down hard on a particularly large log, and I'd barely got back on my feet before she was on me. She spun me around, one hand clutching the back of my coat and the other one tightly gripping my hair, and then she gave me a violent shove away from her, and the force of it and the slickness of the trees sent me sprawling forwards, completely unable to stop myself until I smacked into the edge of the boulders, tripping over and landing in the delve between the three of them, my face pressed against the back of the one that jutted out more than the other two.

A sharp pain shot across the cheek that'd collided with the rock, but before I could let myself feel it too much, I forced myself to turn around, but the rocks were so wet from the rain that it was nearly impossible to stand back up, and while my feet were trying to find some kind of grip, I felt one of them slip into a little gap underneath the boulder to my left.

I tried to lift it back out, keeping my eyes glued on Knight as she came towards me, but I couldn't; the stupid thing was stuck fast, and no matter how much I tugged at it, I couldn't get it to move. Not only that, but it felt like it was stuck in a vice, and the more I pulled at it, the longer it was stuck in there, the more it hurt. I felt a swell of panic at how completely wedged in it was, but before I could think about it for too long, Knight had reached the boulders and lunged for me. And this time, I didn't have time to hit her with the stick. She was aiming her knife at my neck and I grabbed her hand before she could stab me, forcing it away from me while my other hand dropped the stick and fastened around her throat, but that left me all out of hands, and when she swung her free hand at me in a fist, there was nothing that I could do to defend myself. Her hand hit my face so hard that it felt like I'd been hit with a brick, and my hand slackened on her neck as tried to catch my breath. She grabbed a handful of hair at the top of my head and pulled my head forward by a couple of inches before shoving it back, hard, into the boulder behind me; a crack like an egg breaking echoed around the clearing and I immediately felt like I was going to throw up, stars exploding in front of my eyes so that I couldn't see anything. She pulled my head forward again, clearly ready to do the same again, and my hand holding her wrist inched forwards, fumbling for the knife; she can't have been paying attention to anything other than my head, because plucking it from her was surprisingly easy, and before she could whack my head back again, I'd pulled my hand away from hers and plunged her knife into her side.

She let go of me and stumbled backwards, making a noise that was somewhere between a gasp and a shriek as she pressed her hand to her side, and I tried to catch my breath against the burning, throbbing feeling on the back of my head as I dragged myself into a crouching position, blinking away enough of the stars that I could eyeball her warily as I used the boulder to my left to pull myself upright. There was a patch of dark red coming out from behind her hand and spreading across her robe, and her shocked face was even paler than it normally was, but instead of coming back at me like I'd thought she would, she just stood there, her gaze glued on my foot until she eventually lifted her head up to look at me, a glint in her eye that told me I was fucked.

Well.

More fucked.

'Is your foot stuck?'

I thought at first that the knock to my head had made me forget how to speak; it seemed to take me a long time to remember how to get my mouth around any words.

'No.'

'It is.' She clucked her tongue, shaking her head slowly. 'How unfortunate for you.'

She pounced forwards and sent me flying backwards again, tumbling into the boulder that jutted out the most, and before I could do anything to get her off me, she had her foot on my forearm, pressing down on it hard – hard enough to make me feel like the bone was going to break, and press it against the rocks underneath us enough to make a low moan get out from between my gritted teeth – as she bent down and plucked the knife from my hand. She scrambled up onto the boulders, straddling the small channel between the boulder behind me and the one to my left with one leg on each, and then she leant down towards me; she grabbed me by the hair again and pulled, this time dragging me up to my feet, and no matter how much I fought against her – no matter how much I twisted from side to side, no matter how much I yanked on her hands to try to make her let go, or slapped and clawed at her wrists, wishing that I hadn't dropped my sodding stick – I couldn't do anything to stop her from pressing the knife to my neck.

I pulled hard on her hand that was holding the knife and I wrapped my other hand around the blade itself, gritting my teeth and squeezing my eyes tight shut against the pain of it slicing into my palm, making it so slippy that it was hard to hang on – but even with me holding on as tight as I could, she pushed the knife into the left side of my throat, and just as I felt panic well up inside me, just as something wet, warm and sticky started trickling down the side of my neck, there was a loud shout from the trees at the top of the clearing.

My eyes popped open and I saw a man in a high-vis vest come bursting out of the trees, a few other people behind him, including someone in a grey, chequered coat, and Knight must've reacted on reflex; she jumped up from her crouch, letting go of my hair and dropping the knife so that it clattered down onto the rocks underneath me as she leapt back by a couple of inches.

Except that she didn't stop.

The boulders must've been even slippier at the top than they were at the bottom, because just as I twisted around to look at her, I saw one of her feet fly up from underneath her; the startled surprised on her face went straight to complete panic as she started to fall, both arms up in the air.

And suddenly everything was going in slow-motion.

I saw her eyes widen just before she disappeared down behind the boulder, and I threw myself into the gap between the two boulders she'd been straddling, dragging myself as far forwards as I could as quickly as I could, holding my hands as far out as they'd go and hoping I could catch her.

But it was no use.

I couldn't reach her.

She missed me and the ground by inches and, sailing past the edge of the moor, and I could see the terror and horror on her face just before she dipped out of view.

I could see the odd flash of white as she tumbled down the side of the moor, and she must've hit something jutting out not too far from the bottom; she flew up and forward for a couple of feet before colliding with a boulder rising out of the heather, just to say in my eyeline.

She landed headfirst with a crack that I could hear all the way up at the top, and I saw her body curl around on itself as it came to rest against the boulder.

I stared down at her for a few seconds, struggling to breathe and feeling nothing but horrified as I tried to take in what I was looking at.

But really... there was nothing more to take in.

I'd already done that, somehow, when I saw her fall off the boulder.

And I'd known she was dead before she even hit the ground.

TWENTY.

'Armitage.'

There were hands on me, on my back, on my head, gently grabbing me by the shoulders and trying to pull me back through the gap. But I couldn't move.

I couldn't take my eyes off the sight of Knight slumped against that rock.

'Armitage, come on.'

I hadn't wanted her to die.

For all she was an evil piece of shit, for all her psychopathic tendencies, at no point had I wanted to see her dead.

I wanted to see her locked up.

I wanted to see her thrown in jail for the rest of life.

I wanted to see the victims' families see justice, and I wanted to see her get beat up every day by people just as sadistic as she was.

Who won if she was dead?

'Tidge?'

And suddenly Angie's face was in front of me. Her face was pale and worried as she crouched on the other side of the boulders, her hair soaked by the rain and messy from all the fighting, with a red welt across one cheek and the start of a bruise on her forehead.

'Tidge, are you alright?'

I couldn't talk.

My throat was too tight from the panic and the horror of the whole thing for me to get any words out, and I couldn't take my eyes off Knight's body in the heather below us.

'We have to get her out of here,' Angie said after a few seconds, glancing up at someone behind me, and the next thing I knew, I was being lifted out of the gap and pulled up to my feet, with someone's hands tight around my shoulders.

Whoever it was murmured my name, and when I dragged my head to look at them, I vaguely recognised Luke, staring at me with more concern on his face than I'd ever seen.

He looked even worse for wear than Angie did. There were three big bruises along the left side of his jaw, all of them already turning black; he had dried blood around his nose, which looked swollen, like it'd taken one hell of a punch; he had a black eye brewing; and one of his earlobes was bloody, with toothmarks in it.

'Can you walk?'

I felt my head shake almost by itself, and without even realising what I was doing, I pointed down to the little gap under the boulder. 'My foot... my foot's stuck.' I looked back at Angie, who was still hovering at the other side of the boulders. 'Knight's dead.'

'I know,' she told me, reaching through the gap to give my hands a tight squeeze. 'I know she is. Don't look, Tidge.'

I felt one of the other officers put their hands on my shoulders, holding me up as Luke let go of me and bent down to get a closer look at my foot. He took hold of my ankle, sometimes tugging on it and sometimes twisting it this way and that, but it wouldn't budge. And suddenly, I felt a little wave of panic hit me. What if they could never get it out? What if I had to live up there, only eating when someone remembered to bring me food or a bird flew into my mouth?

'Listen, Armitage, we need to get you out of here. We've got some Paramedics up where the cars are; they just need to check you over to see if you need to go to hospital. Once they've done that, they're going to take everyone who needs medical attention to go and get some, alright? So we need you to come back with us now, not least because my idiot brother won't get his hand stitched up until he knows you're alright.'

'There are some paramedics back where everyone parked,' Angie told me a tad too casually, as Luke let go of my ankle, unzip his stab-proof vest and dump it next to the rocks.

'They want to check you over before they let you go home. And Hadaway's still there, too. He won't go anywhere until he sees you.'

I looked at her in alarm, remembering how that knife had looked sticking out of his hand. 'Why the hell's he doing that? Why hasn't he gone to get his hand sorted?'

'He wants to make sure you're alright first,' she shrugged, and before I could point out how he was running the risk of getting an infection by being so surprisingly *nice*, Luke's arms were suddenly tight around my waist. I barely had chance to register the fact or realise that Angie had deliberately been distracting me before he gave me a hard yank upwards and backwards, using enough force to not only drag my foot out of the gap, but also to send us both sprawling to the ground, with me landing on top of him as a red-hot pain shot through my whole leg, right from toe to hip.

For a few seconds, I didn't dare look down.

I just laid there, yelling in pain and waiting for someone to interrupt me to break the news that I no longer had a foot.

'Jesus,' Angie said, as she scampered over to where we'd landed, looking almost as concerned as she had when they'd found me. 'Are you two alright?'

Luke grunted as he slid out from underneath me and eased himself to his feet, shooting her a little nod once he was upright. 'I think I've cracked a rib.'

'My foot,' I managed to get out, pressing the heel of my hands into my eyes. 'I don't have a foot.'

For a few seconds, all I could hear was a slightly confused silence.

'Tidge, your foot's fine.'

'It bloody is not.'

'Well, maybe not *fine*. But it's still very much attached.'

I took my hands away from my eyes and blinked at her a couple of times, wondering if she was just saying that to make sure I didn't go hysterical; I have to be honest, it didn't feel like I had anything attached down there. And then, once I was feeling brave enough, I took a deep breath and had the tiniest of peeks at my right leg.

Yep.

There it was. Still holding onto my ankle with not even a drop of blood in sight.

I gingerly twisted it this way and that, just to make sure everything was still in working order, and sure enough, it came with me – first to the right, and then all the way to the left.

It knocked like hell.

But as long as it was still a part of me and doing what I told it to, I wasn't going to complain.

'Right, then,' Luke said, looking fractionally back to his always-amused self as he held both hands out to me, ready to pull me up. 'Come on. Let's get you out of here.'

Five or ten minutes later, the three of us were slowly making our way into the clearing where all the Bobbies had parked, Luke and Angie on either side of me, holding me up as I hopped along on the one foot that I could bear to put any weight on.

The clearing that Knight had used had been completely empty as we went through it, and this one wasn't much busier; other than Farley, Evans and a couple of Inspectors standing around, clearly having a mini-debrief, the place was deserted. All but a couple of Police cars were still there, and there was only one ambulance left, right on the other side of the clearing; Johnny and Hadaway were sat on the floor just inside it with their feet planted on the mud outside, both of them looking considerably worse for wear, Johnny with a blanket around him and Hadaway grimacing slightly as he pressed hard on his bandaged hand. Clearly, all of the

Cloaks had been taken to the hospital or Custody, and the Bobbies had gone with them, either for treatment of their own or to start booking them.

Hadaway was the first one to clock us coming into the clearing; he looked up as soon as our feet hit the mud, and his face flashed from wince to relief to concern as he stood up, coming straight over to us and leaving Johnny to follow a couple of steps behind him.

'Jesus,' he said the second he reached us, and suddenly his non-holey hand was on the side of my face, his fingers in my hair as he stared at me with the same intense look of concern that'd been on his face right before me and Angie had gone into the trees. 'There you are. Are you alright?'

I was not alright.

My right foot was absolutely killing me, feeling like it'd been rubbed raw and crushed. My whole head was throbbing from having been slammed into the boulder, and my back, ribs and arms were aching from having falling onto the felled trees. The cut on my neck was burning, the cheek that'd smacked into the rock was stinging, and we'd had to stop halfway to the clearing so that I could throw up at the memory of Knight landing on that boulder in the heather.

That was the worst part.

I'd never seen anyone die before.

I couldn't get it out of my head.

'Peachy,' I told him, smiling as best I could and fighting the urge to launch myself into arms for a hug. 'How's the hand?'

He shot me a tight smile of his own. 'Still there. What happened to you?' he demanded, frowning slightly. 'What'd she do?'

'She was trying to leg it,' I said, suddenly feeling exhausted as I shifted my weight slightly, trying to stop the leg I was standing on from aching so much. 'And I realised that everyone was too preoccupied to have eyes on her, so I went after her. Anyway, we fought, she tried to kill me, this lot turned up and she fell off the boulder.'

My blood suddenly turned to ice.

I hadn't thought about it before, but what would've happened if they *hadn't* turned up? Knight had had her knife *in* my neck, and it wasn't as if I'd been in the best position to fight her off; there was more than a good chance that if they hadn't found us, if she hadn't been so startled by them, she would've actually killed me.

Hadaway's eyes flicked to Luke. 'Who's got her now?'

'A couple of the lads are with her,' Luke said easily. 'But you don't need to worry about her getting away, mate. She's dead.'

His whole face snapped in shock. *'Dead?'*

'She wasn't quite as lucky as I was when I fell off those boulders,' I explained wearily, hoping that he didn't think I'd killed her. 'She landed on another boulder instead of in the heather.' I glanced at Johnny as Farley and Evans walked over to join us, identical frowns on their faces. 'How are you doing?'

'I'm fine,' he told me, shooting me a smile that made it obvious he *was* fine that I felt relief sweep over me, making me sag slightly against Angie and Luke. 'I managed to make sure she didn't do to me what she wanted to. Here,' he added, holding something out to me. 'We found this back in the clearing.'

I blinked down at his hands.

My cloche.

I hadn't even realised it'd fallen off.

I took it off him with a grateful smile and opened my mouth to ask him exactly what Knight had tried to do and how she'd got to him in the first place, but before I could say anything, he was swapping the smile for a slight frown. 'You're going to have to take us through it.'

It took me about fifteen minutes to tell them everything.

I started with realising that Knight had disappeared and talked them through it all, right up to Luke pulling me out of the boulders.

None of them interrupted me, not to ask questions or bollock me or anything; they just let me talk, and by the time I finished, I barely had enough energy to stand, even with Luke and Angie holding me up.

They were all silent for a few long seconds after I stopped talking, and I could just tell that while every single one of them had plenty more questions for me, they just knew this wasn't the time to ask them.

'You need to go to and get your hand stitched up,' I told Hadaway, mainly just to break the silence, and so tiredly that I was slurring my words. 'You could have an infection in it by now.'

'I'm going,' he grunted, and then he shot me that tight smile again and chucked me under the chin. 'I just wanted to make sure you were alright first.'

Something warm and fuzzy broke through the tiredness and the aching and curled around in my stomach while I blinked at him, suddenly feeling a lump of emotion in the back of my throat and craving that hug more than ever.

But before I could make a tit out of myself by stumbling forwards and snuggling into him, he turned around and walked over to the ambulance, climbing into the back of it and plonking himself down on one of the seats before resuming the grimace as he peeled back his bandage. And even from where I was standing, I could see how bad his hand was shaking, although whether it was from the pain or from whatever damage the knife had done – or both – I couldn't tell you.

'Well done,' Farley said suddenly, making me snap my head around to blink at him. 'You both did a fantastic job tonight. We couldn't have asked anything more from you.'

'I don't know,' I said wearily, feeling myself sag a little bit more so that Johnny and Angie had to readjust their grip on me. 'You probably could've asked that I brought her back alive.'

'That wasn't your fault,' Johnny told me almost immediately, taking a step closer almost on reflex as he frowned at me in out-and-out concern. 'Armitage, you do know that, don't you?'

I didn't know what to say.

I knew there was nothing more I could've done to save her; I'd *tried* to get hold of her, for God's sake, which was a hell of a lot more than she would've done for me.

But at the same time, no-one else had been up there with her. It was on me. I was the one who hadn't got far enough away from the boulders. I was the one who hadn't been able to catch her. I was the one who hadn't done enough to make sure she'd have to face the families of everyone she'd killed.

'Let's get her home,' Angie said gently, as tidal wave of misery filled my stomach and I ducked my head down so that I wouldn't have to look at any of them. 'If you've got questions or anything for her, you can ask them tomorrow, but for now she needs to get some rest. You two go to the hospital with Ade,' she added to Johnny and Luke, 'get yourselves checked over as well.'

'I'm fine,' Johnny said again, an unfamiliarly stubborn look flashing across his face.

'You're going,' she told him firmly, shaking her head. 'For peace of mind, if nothing else. Just make sure you come to ours as soon as they let you go.'

He took a few steps forward and swept her up in his arms – well, as best he could, given that she was still propping me up – and while I was very happy that she had him back, I still tried very hard to ignore the snogging that was going on right in my right ear.

I let my eyes drift back to Hadaway and the ambulance. He'd covered his hand back up with the bandage and was sat with his head resting against the side of the van, his eyes closed – but after a couple of seconds of me watching him, it was like he could feel my eyes on him. He brought his head forward and turned to look at me, and when his eyes hit mine, he grinned at me.

And then he winked at me.

And suddenly there was an explosion of something fluttery inside me, taking up any space it could find and making it slightly harder to breathe than it had been a second earlier, and God knows what my face did; I tried to smile back at him, but I have a feeling that no part of my face did what I was telling it to do.

Oh, well.

I'd just tell him that the tiredness had brought on a stroke.

He'd probably believe that.

By the time we got back to the flat, I was so tired that I could barely put one foot in front of the other.

The paramedics had checked me over and decided that I didn't have any broken bones; just some severe bruising to my back, ribs and face, and sprained ankle that they wanted me to keep elevated. Evans had brought us home straight after they were done with me, and for the first ten minutes after he left, we both just slumped on the settee, staring into space and taking it in turns to absent-mindedly stroke Squidge, who was beyond delighted to have us home.

I hurt everywhere, like I had toothache in my entire body, and it wasn't just the parts that'd taken a beating that night that were aching; my kneekle was throbbing, my right shoulder was pulsing, and the cuts on my forehead that I'd got when Knight slammed me into the window were really starting to sting.

'You do know,' Angie told me eventually, turning to look at me, 'that it's not your fault, don't you? Knight,' she added, when I just looked at her blankly. 'It's not your fault that she died.'

Oh.

I shrugged, watching Squidge mouth his favourite duckie toy as he laid at my feet. 'I don't know.'

'It's *not*,' she insisted, shifting position so that she was sat facing me. 'You didn't make her get up on those boulders, Tidge. You didn't push her off them. You even tried to *catch* her, which is a hell of a lot more than she would've done for you.'

'I just feel like it's too easy,' I said, shrugging again, and I couldn't tell if my voice was thick because I was so tired or because everything that'd happened was catching up with me. 'She doesn't have to face anybody, she doesn't have to answer for what she's done. She just gets away with it.'

'This is the best outcome for someone like Knight,' she said, frowning slightly. 'Jail wouldn't have worked for her the way you think it would. She was manipulative as hell; I'd bet anything that she would've got one of the guards on side and started all over again.'

'She never has to face the families, though.'

'This is probably what the families *want*. I know I would, if she'd killed Anth or Cal. And besides, do you really think she would've apologised to them? D'you think she would've done or said *anything* that would've helped them? Or do you think she would've just been her normal, arrogant self?'

I hadn't thought about it like that.

There was silence again, and I tried to force the image of Knight falling – the image of her terrified, horrified face – out of my head, but it was stuck fast; no matter what I tried to think about instead, I couldn't shake it.

And every time I pictured it, it was like a punch to the gut.

'It's not your fault,' Angie said again, almost like she was reading my mind. '*Do not* start blaming yourself.'

She eyeballed me for a seconds with a hard look on her face, almost like she was trying to make sure I wasn't doing exactly that. And my face must've done something that convinced her that I was not, because after a few seconds, she relaxed and told me,

'We should go to bed. I'm absolutely knackered, and you must be exhausted. You've slept even less than I have this week.'

I didn't wait for her to say it twice.

In fact, she'd barely finished her sentence before I was hauling myself to my feet, mumbling something that was supposed to sound like 'goodnight' and dragging myself into my bedroom.

The very last thing I remember thinking about, just as I climbed into bed, was how Hadaway was getting on at the hospital.

And then my head hit the pillow.

And for what felt like the first time in years, I *finally* slept.

TWENTY-ONE.

I woke up feeling surprisingly refreshed.

Normally, I'm vaguely knackered if I don't get enough sleep and I'm vaguely knackered if I get too much sleep. This time, there was nothing but a few seconds of being mildly disorientated.

I just laid there for a little bit and watched the light coming in through my boarded-up window, wondering what time it was and trying to work out if the whole thing had been some kind of long, seriously intense dream.

I mean, it clearly hadn't been. My Scribbley Wall was right there.

But the whole thing felt like it'd happened days ago, maybe even weeks, not just a few hours earlier. Well, apart from the pain in my head. And my back. And my neck, and my hand, and my right knee and ankle.

That was all still very fresh.

I just laid there and chilled out, reading all the notes and thinking about everything that'd gone on, until my stomach rumbled so loudly that I could've sworn that the board in my window shook, and suddenly I had one hell of a craving for a cheeseburger.

I dragged myself over to my door, wincing every time my right leg had any weight put on it, and stumbled into the living room, straight into a very excited Squidge and a much calmer Angie and Johnny. The two of them were all cuddled up on the settee, Angie still in her pyjamas and Johnny in a pair jogging bottoms and a T-shirt, and both them snapped their heads around to stare at me the second they heard my door open.

'Morning, sleepyhead,' Angie said cheerfully, grinning at me as I fussed over Squidge. 'How are you feeling?'

'Sore,' I told her brightly, flashing her a smile of my own as Squidge flopped down onto his back for a belly rub, a delighted doggy grin on his face and his tail still going like the clappers. 'And insanely awake. How are you two?'

'We're fine,' Johnny said, pulling himself away from Angie and starting to stand up. 'Bit of bruising, and they think I've got some whiplash from the crash, but we got off light. I'm just going to make a cuppa, if you want one?'

I asked him for a can of coke and plonked myself down next to Angie as he headed for the kitchen, Squidge glued to my side, panting happily.

'What time is it?'

'Half ten.'

'Really?' I blinked at her in surprise, wondering why I felt so refreshed when I'd only had about nine hours' sleep. 'Is that all?'

'Mmm,' she said, shooting me an amused look. 'On Sunday.'

I stared at her, feeling a little jolt of shock go through me.

It was *Sunday?*

I'd slept all the way through Saturday?

Jesus.

I had some serious sherry drinking to catch up on.

'I did try to wake you up yesterday afternoon,' she added, grinning. 'But you booted me and shouted something that wasn't English, so I just left you to it. Ade said you probably needed it and I thought so too, so.'

I felt another small jolt as she shrugged to finish her sentence. 'Hadaway's been?'

'Yeah, he came over as soon as he could. He said he'll come back today, see if he can catch you while you're actually awake.'

I saw the satisfied little smirk on her face and raised her one eyeroll. Seriously. Was she never going to give up?

'Don't be getting excited,' I warned her, giving my head a tiny shake. And then wincing, because that did nothing to help with the throbbing at the back of my head. 'He's probably just having withdrawal symptoms from going so long without giving someone a bollocking.'

'No, he wants to see how you are,' she told me, as Johnny came back with our drinks. 'He said so yesterday.'

I blinked at her, hoping she couldn't tell that something warm was making its way through my stomach, along with just a smidge of something close to excitement. For whatever reason, the idea that Hadaway gave a shit about how I was doing was quite a nice one. And for whatever reason – don't ask me what it was, I have no idea – I was actually looking forward to seeing him.

Clearly, all that sleep I'd had had turned my brain to mush.

I didn't bother asking her how Hadaway was; I figured I could hear that straight from the horse's mouth when he came over later. 'So, what's been happening while I've been asleep? What've I missed?'

Half an hour later, I was up to speed.

All of the Cloaks were in East District Custody, and as soon as they'd realised that Knight had not only left them to it but had also been full of shit, they'd spilled everything, falling all over themselves to make sure they incriminated everybody else while insisting that they were a poor, naïve victim who hadn't known what they were getting into. A fair few officers – including Hadaway, who'd apparently gone straight to East District as soon as he'd had some sleep – were doing back-to-back interviews, coming straight out of one room and into another; they'd interviewed twenty-seven Cloaks when Johnny had last spoke to anyone, and they still had another forty-odd to go. Most of the interviews were going on for around the three or four hour mark, starting with how Knight had recruited them all and going right up to what they'd done in the clearing that Friday.

'I've always been really curious about that,' I interrupted, frowning slightly. 'How *did* she recruit them?'

'Infiltration,' he told me, shrugging. 'From what I've been told, this has been *years* in the planning. She started off going to different book clubs and support groups as Kathie, and once she'd got settled in, she started talking about this woman she'd heard of and some of the things she could do. Apparently she started off with maybe ten or twelve people following her, and the longer it went on for, the more they recruited for her. Mind you, I don't think any of them realised that Kathie and Knight were the same person; some of them thought Kathie had moved away, others had never heard of her. They had no clue who she really was until we told them in their interview.'

With Knight not being around anymore, Pace was being looked at as the main ringleader; Hadaway had insisted on being one of the officers to interviewed him, and he'd told Johnny that the guy had alternated between being completely devastated that his niece was dead and trying to pin everything on her. It'd been Knight's idea to rent the house so that they'd have plenty of space to do whatever they needed to do, and he reckoned that he'd only gone along with the whole thing because Knight was his niece and he loved her and he thought it might help her get off her parents' recent deaths, something that Hadaway had apparently said to his face was complete bullshit. According to Johnny, it was no secret that Pace had been looking for a way out of the job that wouldn't cost him his pension; Knight's parents had left her everything, and she was so loaded since they'd died ('and we'll be looking into that to see if that's her work, as well') that she could easily support herself and Pace for the foreseeable. All Pace had to do was help her with her little plan, and it hardly seemed like he'd had any reservations about it. It was win-win for him; he got to quit as quick as he wanted to, and he could say that he was so affected by what Knight had done to him that he had to stay on the sick for the next eighteen months, until he was due to retire.

Lyme was out of the hospital and back with his family, and while he was a long way from being back on his feet, he wasn't in the same state that he had been in Pace's house. Apparently most of what'd happened to him was so hazy that he could only remember bits and pieces of it, which – to be fair – I didn't think was much of a bad thing; if I'd been kidnapped and forced to help a delusional psychopath who enjoys the odd spot of murder, I definitely wouldn't want to remember it.

And there was going to be a Press Conference about the whole thing later that morning; Farley was going to head it up with the Head of Crime, but a few Bobbies from East District were going as well, Evans and Hadaway being a couple of them.

'It's weird that it's all over,' I said lightly, shuffling around and leaning back with my head against the settee arm, stretching my legs over Angie's lap as I closed my eyes. 'I don't know what I'd going to do with myself now.'

'Actually,' she told me, just as lightly, 'I have something for you to do.'

'I am not doing any housework today. I am not doing any housework for the next *week*.'

'That's not what I was going to say,' she said, and I could just tell that she was rolling her eyes. 'I was going to tell you to paint over the Scribbley Wall.'

My eyes popped wide open as I sprang back up, staring at her in horror. *'What?'*

'Well, it's not as if you need it anymore,' she pointed out, shrugging. 'And it violates our tenancy agreement, we're not supposed to redecorate.'

'My windows are broken, and you're worried about a wall that Mrs Miller will never even see?'

'I've already been out and bought all the stuff,' she carried on, like I hadn't said anything, nodding at a little collection of paint cans next to the flat door. 'Except for the wallpaper.

We'll have to try and track that down from somewhere. I'm not kidding,' she added firmly, when I didn't move, just carried on staring at her in horror. I didn't *want* to get rid of my Scribbley Wall. It showed exactly how hard we'd worked, and I was bloody proud of it. 'You're painting over it. And you might as well do it today, before you find some excuse or another to not do it at all.'

I know Angie well enough to know when it's worth arguing with her and when it's not, and this happened to be one of those times that sat very stubbornly in the 'not' category.

Hence the fact that, just over half an hour later, I was stood moodily in front of the Scribbley Wall, paintbrush in hand and a tin of white paint open next to me. I'd already reluctantly painted over the writing nearest the window, going as slowly as I could and lacking any hint of enthusiasm, and I was just moving onto the middle section when I heard a noise from the direction of my bedroom door.

And when I turned around, Hadaway was standing there, leaning one shoulder against the doorframe with his hands in his trouser pockets, grinning at me.

God, he looks good in a suit.

Well. I mean, it's Hadaway, so he looks good in anything. But come on, I can't be the *only* lass who goes a tiny bit weak at the knees at the sight of Hadaway in something more formal than jeans and tops.

'No rest for the wicked, eh?'

'If either of us can be called wicked, it's Angie,' I told him, dumping my paintbrush into the tin and fighting the urge to hug him, which had resurfaced with a vengeance. (That had to stop.) 'She's the one making me do this. How's the hand?'

'Fine,' he said blandly, lifting his stabbed hand out of his pocket and looking at it with disinterest. There was a load of padding and gauze wrapped around it, looping around his thumb and stopping right at the base of his fingers so that his palm looked like it was at least twice the size it really was. 'I got a few stitches and they want me to have physio, but it didn't hit anything vital. It'll be good as gold in a couple of weeks.'

I thought he was being a tad optimistic, but I had a feeling I was best off not saying that to him.

'Good,' I said instead, smiling at him as a wave of relief washed over me, and then I blinked a couple of times in surprise. I hadn't realised I'd been that worried about him. 'What's the physio for?'

'Just to make sure I don't lose any use of it. It's probably more of a precaution than anything else. Anyway,' he added, fixing me with a serious look. 'How are you?'

'I'm alright.'

'Are you?'

'Yeah,' I said lightly, nodding. 'I'm a bit sore and I ache, but it's nothing that sherry and a hot bath won't sort out.'

'Right.' He stared at me for a couple of seconds, looking no less serious; if anything, he looked slightly *more* so. 'And how're you feeling what you had to see?'

I stared back at him, swallowing against a lump that'd suddenly cropped up in my throat as my eyes turned hot and prickly.

I'd been trying not to think about that part.

It'd been there, lurking right at the very back of my mind, but I'd been trying my best to think about anything and everything else to make sure it didn't get in.

'Well, I didn't like it,' I told him, hoping he wouldn't notice that my voice had got slightly thicker. 'But I don't know how else it would've ended. If it hadn't been her, it would've been me, and she was all set to go for it.'

'Yeah,' he said gently, shooting me grim nod as a little glint of something I couldn't put my finger on broke through the seriousness on his face. 'I know. Look, if you think you need some therapy, we can –'

'I'll be fine,' I assured him hastily, waving his words away. I really didn't want to dwell on this. 'And if I'm not, I'll let you know.'

He nodded again, shifting his weight slightly, and suddenly he didn't look quite as sombre. 'So. Are you feeling up to the Press Conference?'

I felt a load of panic start to rise up inside of me as I blinked at him. What did he mean, did I feel up to it? Was he expecting me to *go?*

'I thought you knew,' he said, obviously clocking the look on my face and shooting me a frown that was somewhere between confusion and concern. 'Farley wants you there.'

Nooooooo.

Oh no.

No, no, no.

'What?'

'You helped with the case,' he told me, like it was the most obvious thing in the world. 'And you did some bloody good work. It's only right that you're there.'

I gaped at him, suddenly finding it hard to breathe as my heart started thumping away.

No.

No.

I didn't want to go to the Press Conference.

I didn't want anyone knowing that we'd been involved.

Don't get me wrong, I was insanely proud of what we'd done, but it wasn't something I was planning on telling people about. My family worry about me burning the flat down every time I make *baked beans,* for God's sake; can you imagine how they'd react if they found out I'd been chasing the worst murderer Cattringham County had ever seen all over Habely?

I hadn't quite managed to tell Hadaway that when Angie suddenly appeared next to him, frowning up at him and holding a stick wrapped in loo roll.

'I don't know if you need this, Ade,' she told him, holding the stick out to him. 'I've just found it behind the toilet. I think it could be Knight's.'

'Why d'you think that?' I asked curiously, scurrying over to them as Hadaway took the stick off her, looking just as confused as I felt. 'What is it?'

'I don't know,' she said, shrugging. 'I think – well, obviously I have no idea what it looks like, but I was wondering if it could be that wand she was talking about. She obviously left it here,' she added defensively, when we both stared at her. 'That's what she came back for the other night, wasn't it? I'm guessing she must've dropped it when she came in the first time, and it's just rolled away without her noticing. Look at it,' she ordered, after more staring. 'Doesn't it look like a wand to you?'

To be fair, I could see the resemblance.

It was a few inches long and only a couple of centimetres thick; it was a nice mahogany colour and looked like it was made of metal or some other strong material, but instead of being sleek, it was knobbled and kinked, like it'd been designed to look more rustic than it really was. And at the end – the end that wasn't wrapped in toilet paper – were three tiny prongs, coming together to form a triangular little point.

'It's a fucking taser,' Hadaway said incredulously, taking the stick from Angie for a closer look, and a second later, his face seemed to clear of any confusion. 'Jesus Christ. I wouldn't be surprised if this is what she used to make the lads go with her.'

I whipped my head up to frown at him. 'I thought she'd drugged them?'

'We're still working on it,' he told me, with the smallest shrug I've ever seen. 'We can't tell if they were drugged when she took them or just once she had them. I'll bet owt you like that this was a part of it.'

We all stared at the stick for a couple of seconds more, and I don't know what those two were thinking, but I was thinking about the lads she'd used it on.

I was imagining going off on a night out with my friends that I'd been looking forward to for however long, popping to the toilet and having someone pitch up and shoot fifty thousand volts into me.

I was imagining what they'd gone through once she had them. Had they all been in the same state that Lyme had? Did any of them have a clue what was happening to them?

'I'll put in an evidence bag and take it back with me,' Hadaway told her eventually, shooting her a tight smile. 'Cheers, Angie.' She sidled off and he turned to look at me, the frown back on his face. 'D'you want to get ready?'

'I'm not going,' I blurted out, more abruptly than I meant to, as that tight, panicky knot settled back into place in my stomach. 'I don't need to be there. I don't want anyone to know that I was involved in it.'

His eyebrows came a touch closer together, and the frown definitely shifted more towards irked than anything else. 'What the hell are you talking about? Everyone's expecting you there!'

'Well, people can just change their expectations,' I said sharply, shooting him an irritated look of my own. 'I know what you think, Hadaway, and you're wrong. I didn't do this for the glory. I did it because I wanted to know what was going on, and I've done that, so as far as I'm concerned, I don't need to have anything else to do with it. Except for the interviews,' I added as an afterthought. 'I'd quite like to type up the interviews.'

We just stood there and stared at each other for a few seconds, with Hadaway looking a mixture between incredulous and annoyed, and me keeping my fingers crossed that he didn't just pick me up, chuck me in his car and force me to go.

'And there's nothing I can do?' he tried in the end, raising one eyebrow at me. 'Nothing I can say that'll get you to come?'

'No.'

'Right,' he said harshly, and I stared at him in surprise. I would've thought he'd be *relieved* that I didn't want to go. Happy, even. Why was he pissed off? 'Alright, Armitage. Have it your way, as fucking usual.'

He jerked himself away from my door and strode across the living room, and the last glimpse I had of him was his ramrod-straight back disappearing out of the flat door.

Although, to be honest, I barely registered it.

Something on my doorframe had caught my eye as he walked away, and I couldn't look away from it.

I don't know how I hadn't noticed it before we went up to face Knight, and since I hadn't, I have no idea how long it would've taken me to notice it *after* facing Knight. But right there, at the bottom of the hole that the door latch clicks into, was a *tiny,* thin, flat piece of metal, jutting out at a jaunty angle.

That shouldn't have been there.

Not that I spend a lot of time examining door latch holes, but I knew for definite that that little bronze plate had *not* been there before.

I took a couple of steps closer, holding my breath as I bent down to bear into the little hole. There was dried superglue slathered over the top of the plate and in the rest of the hole, and when I glanced down, flicking my eyes over all the splinters of wood that'd been sent flying over the floor when Hadaway kicked my door in, I spotted an identical plate a couple of inches away, this one with dried superglue on both sides.

Aha.

So that was how she'd managed to lock my door: by making the hole smaller and making sure the latch would get stuck to the two plates once it was wedged in there.

Clever, for sure, but hardly anything you could call *witchy.*

'So,' Angie said lightly, popping her head around my door. 'What'd you do to annoy Hadaway this time?'

I tore my eyes off the metal plate and blinked at her in surprise. I hadn't even heard her coming. 'Oh. Nothing. He wanted me to go and be part of this Press Conference and he obviously didn't like it when I said no. I don't know why,' I added, shrugging as I turned to go back to my Wall. 'He's been bollocking me all week for being involved in the case, it doesn't make sense for him to want me to be there.'

'Johnny said it was Ade's idea to have you take part.'

I stopped dead and shot her a startled look over my shoulder. *'What?'*

'Apparently he thought it'd be a nice thing to do,' she told me, resting against the doorframe. 'He thought you'd worked as hard on it anyone else had, and it wouldn't be right to do the Press Conference without you.'

I stared at her, trying to tally the Hadaway who'd been shouting at me all week for being involved in the case with the Hadaway who wanted me to get some recognition for being involved in the case. 'He said that?'

'Well, I don't know if he said it word-for-word. But that was the gist of it, aye.' There was a little pause while we looked at each other, and then she tilted her head to one side. 'I think you should go.'

'No,' I said stubbornly, crouching down to get my paintbrush. 'I don't want to be involved in it.'

'I wasn't saying you should be *involved* in it. I just think you should go and be there. Think of it as supporting your colleagues, if you like, but I think Hadaway's right and you deserve to be there. And I think he's done a nice thing by wanting you to be there, so you could do a nice thing by turning up. But you do whatever you want to,' she added breezily, pushing herself back off the door frame. 'That's just my two cents.'

I stood back up without touching my paintbrush, blowing out a heavy sigh.

I didn't want to go to that Press Conference.

Not even a little bit.

But she wasn't wrong; it *was* nice of Hadaway to actually recognise that we'd helped, instead of just cracking on like nothing had ever happened.

And if Johnny had it right and me being there *was* Hadaway's way of doing that, then I felt a bit bad that I had – albeit unintentionally – thrown it back in his face.

So.

Yeah.

Looked like I was going to the sodding ball after all.

Police Headquarters was absolutely heaving by the time we got there.

It was about ten minutes before the Press Conference was due to get started, and the Media Briefing Centre was packed to the gills with journalists – some with cameras, some with Dictaphones and notebooks, and the odd one with both – mixed with a much smaller number of cops, most of them in suits and ties. Farley was up at the front with the Head of Crime (who, between you and me, vaguely reminded me of a teddy bear), and a second after I clocked them, I realised that they were talking to Hadaway, all three of them looking considerably more relaxed than they had been a couple of nights earlier.

Jesus, though.

He really did look amazing in that suit.

I noticed Farley looking at us and shot him a little wave, but instead of waving back, he just turned to look at Hadaway and nodded his head in my direction. Hadaway's head swivelled towards me, and in the space of about a second, he'd gone from looking mildly surprised to looking unmistakeably pleased to see me.

And I have to be honest, it actually gave me a really nice feeling.

'Now then,' he said as he reached us, grinning. 'I thought you weren't coming.'

'She changed her mind,' Angie told him chirpily before I could say anything, and I could see the mad matchmaker glint in her eye. 'She thought it'd be fun to come after all.'

He shot me a dry, vaguely amused look before turning towards her. 'What'd you do? Bribe her with sherry?'

'Shit,' I said, suddenly feeling genuinely disappointed as I looked at Angie. 'I didn't even think to wrangle that one. Any chance,' I added hopefully as an afterthought, 'you can bribe me retrospectively?'

'You've still got three bottles of sherry in the cupboard,' she said, rolling her eyes. 'I think you're good. She wanted to come,' she added to Hadaway, as if they hadn't been interrupted. 'I had nothing to do with it.'

Ooooh.

You little liar, Angelica.

I shot him a look that blatantly said that not only did I have no idea why she'd decided that talking for me was her job now, but she was also talking out of her arse, and he shot me a quick wink, looking more amused than ever.

'C'mere,' he said, putting one hand at the small of my back and guiding me towards an alcove at the side of the room, a couple of metres away from Angie and Johnny, and we'd only taken a couple of steps before I shot him a nervous look.

'I'm not going up there.'

'You don't have to. We'll just say we had some outside help and leave it at that.'

I felt a little knot in my stomach unravel itself. 'And what if they ask who the outside help was?'

'We tell them the truth,' he said, shrugging, as we reached the alcove and he pulled me into it, so that we were hidden from the journalists and the officers at the front of the room. 'Say you want to stay anonymous.'

'And you're not mad about it?' I asked, just to check.

I mean, if he wanted to be mad at me, he could go ahead and be mad; God knows it wasn't like I wasn't used to it.

It was just a bit more annoying when I hadn't actually done anything for him to be mad *about*.

'No,' he told me, some of the cheerfulness slipping from his face. 'No. I shouldn't have had that pop at you. I just didn't realise –' He cut himself off as he scratched the left side of his jaw with his bandaged hand, shooting me a genuinely curious look. 'Why'd you do it?'

'Because I'm nosey,' I said, like it was the most obvious thing in the world. Because... well, it *was*. 'And it was the most exciting thing that's ever happened to Habely and I wanted to know how she was doing it.' Not, I added silently, for the sodding glory. 'Speaking of which,' I added, as the thought popped into my head, 'I don't suppose any of the Cloaks have shed any light on this Procedure, have they? They haven't said how it was supposed to give her those powers?'

A look of disgust flashed across his face. 'Yeah. She'd drink the lads' blood.'

'She – *what?*'

'Yeah. There's a few of them who've said she'd catch it in the that knife she had the other night. The lads' used it to cut themselves with, the blood went in the handle, and then she'd drink it all in front of everyone who'd come to watch.'

I felt my stomach lurch. 'That's vile.'

'I know.'

I thought about it for a few seconds, letting it sink in. And when I finally snapped myself out of it, trying not to picture it more than I needed to, he was watching me with a tiny, serious frown on his face and something in his eye that I couldn't quite put my finger on.

'Look,' he said, tucking some of my hair back behind my ear. 'Just do me a favour and don't get yourself involved in something this again, alright?'

'I don't –'

'It's too fucking dangerous,' he interrupted, frowning just a tiny bit more. 'Jesus, look at what –'

'I was going to say I don't want to,' I told him, raising one eyebrow. Nice to know he jumped straight to the (probably fairly founded) assumption that I was going to argue with him. 'I'm not interested in seeing anyone else die, Hadaway. Seeing Knight was bad enough, and she's the only person I've met who you could actually say deserved it.'

He flicked his eyes across my face a couple of times, almost like he was checking that I wasn't having him on, still looking so serious. And I don't know what I did to make him realise I was serious, but before I could say anything to persuade him I wasn't joking, something in his face relaxed and he was grunting,

'Good.'

And then he kissed me.

His hand was still in my hair, buried deep at the back of my head, and as soon as his lips hit mine, my knees just turned into jelly, and I had to cling onto his shoulders just to make sure I didn't topple over. I had ridiculous amounts of surprise and excitement zinging all around my tummy, fluttering so hard that it was almost painful, something that did not ease off when his other hand came 'round to the small of my back and pulled me to him, so tight that I could feel every last inch of him.

I have to say, it was a *very* nice thing to feel.

And then, sadly, the kissing was over, and he was lifting his head up with a look in his eye that made me think that he might just – *maybe* – be feeling as heady as I felt.

'Right,' he said, with definite reluctance. 'I'd better get back up there.' He took half a step back, letting his hands kind of trail off me and looking very much like a man who didn't want to go anywhere. 'Why don't you come and meet us in Sherlock's when this is over?'

'Sure. I can do that.'

I had a feeling that I would've said 'sure, I can do that' if he'd asked me to come and jump into a vat of acid with him.

'Right,' he said again, and I wondered if he knew he was repeating himself.

He shot me a genuinely warm smile that made my heart do a funny little hop, and just for a second, I thought – or hoped, if we're going for full disclosure – that he might kiss me again.

But no.

He didn't.

He just turned and strolled back to the stage that Farley and the teddy bear were sitting on, causing another ripple of head-turning in the crowd and leaving me standing there, staring after him with a small voice in my head wondering if I was drooling.

'So,' a voice in my right ear said, and when I whipped my head around, I saw Angie stood next to me, looking more gleeful than I'd ever seen her and all but trembling with excitement. 'Did you enjoy that?'

'What?' I asked as innocently as I could, something that wasn't too easy to do when I felt slightly dazed and my lips were still tingling.

'Your kiss,' she said gloatingly, as the smile on her face turned considerably more smug. 'Your kiss with your future *husband.*'

Oh, for God's sake.

I cleared my throat, because it was harder to talk than it really should've been. And then I cleared it again. And then I cleared it once more, just good luck. 'I don't know what you're talking about.'

'You know, we were stood right there,' she told me, staring at me like I was insane as she jabbed a thumb over her shoulder to where Johnny was stood with Luke, and I could tell by the identical, slightly too blank looks on their faces as they stared determinedly at the front of the room that they'd been ogling at the alcove a couple of seconds earlier. 'We had a front row seat to the whole thing.'

Mmm.

Yeah.

I could see a slight flaw in that alcove's design.

'It was just a kiss,' I told her, ducking my head down to try and stop her from seeing the smile that was spreading itself across my face. 'It didn't mean anything.'

'Pfft.'

We were both silent for a few seconds, watching Hadaway pass a piece of paper to the teddy bear before hopping off the stage and finding a seat in the second row. I'd just opened my mouth, ready to suggest that we plonk ourselves in the back row, when she said matter-of-factly,

'I think you should have pink for the bridesmaid dresses. Pink looks very good on me.'

OK.

No seats for us.

'Let's go,' I said brusquely, whipping around on my heel and striding towards the door, catching her by the wrist and dragging her with me. 'I'll have to get Squidge out for a walk before we meet them in the pub.'

'He asked you to meet him for a drink?'

Oh my God.

'Us. He asked *us* to meet them for a drink, Angie, it's *not* a date.'

We reached the door to the Media Briefing Centre and stood to one side, waiting for a couple of journalists to come through the door from the other side. I shot one last glance towards Hadaway while we waited, but instead of landing on him, something pulled my eyes to the left-hand side of the room.

The blonde officer who'd been asking all those questions the night that Johnny was kidnapped. She was dressed in her uniform and stood with her back against the wall, level with the row a couple behind Hadaway's, and scowling at me like she was beyond furious with me, like she'd quite happily throw me onto the same boulder that Knight had landed on.

I blinked a couple of times, frowning at her slightly.

What was that about?

Was she one of the notches on Hadaway's bedpost? Had she seen us kissing?

Had *everyone* seen us kissing?

I started turning back towards Angie, ready to point the lass out to her and see what she thought about it, but before I could get any words out, I caught a snippet of the two journalists' conversation as they strutted past us.

'I'm *telling* you, Julia. Something *odd* is going on. There are always strange noises going on in some part of the house, my daughter is acting *so* strangely, and nothing is ever where we leave it. My *car keys* turned up in the *loft* this morning, of all places! And I've *tried* telling David that we're being haunted, but you know he's like, he just doesn't want to hear it...'

We both stood frozen as they walked to one of the rows and dropped out of earshot, and I could already feel something pulling at my stomach, wanting to follow them and find out more.

I think it might've been my nose.

I tilted my chin a smidge towards Angie, only so far that I had to look at her out of the corner of my eye. 'Did you hear that?'

'I didn't hear anything,' she blurted out *too* quickly, like she'd been waiting for me to ask the question and reacted before she could stop herself.

'That lady thinks she's being haunted.'

'No, she doesn't.'

'Maybe we should ask her about it,' I said casually, turning to follow the two of them. 'See what else has been going on.'

I took a couple of steps forward, but before I could get very far, her hand fastened like a vice around my wrist and pulled me back with a vicious tug. I turned around to blink at her in surprise, only to see her standing closer to me than I'd expected her to be, her teeth clenched and her face flushed the dull shade of red that told me Angry Angie was in the room.

'*No,*' she hissed furiously, glaring at me. 'We are *not* going over there. I mean – Jesus, Tidge, are you fucking serious? We've *just* got finished dealing with Knight, and you want to –'

'This isn't going to be anything like Knight!' I insisted, taking a step closer to her and dropping my voice. 'This isn't a delusional psychopath who thinks that murder's an acceptable hobby, it's a *ghost!* And by the sounds of it, it's just being a bit of a wind-up; she didn't say it's *hurting* anybody!' I glanced over my shoulder at the two journalists, who were sat a few rows from the back with the light bouncing off their blonde hair. 'Come on, Angie. Let's just *ask* her. What's the worst that could happen?'

Printed in Poland
by Amazon Fulfillment
Poland Sp. z o.o., Wrocław